HEELS
of STEEL

HEELS
of STEEL

BARBARA KAVOVIT

mira

Recycling programs
for this product may
not exist in your area.

ISBN-13: 978-0-7783-6923-3

Heels of Steel

For questions and comments about the quality of this book, please contact us at
CustomerService@Harlequin.com.

BookClubbish.com

Printed in U.S.A.

This book is dedicated to

My Mom

For giving me the discipline, determination and belief in myself
to never give up and never stop swimming.
You are the true essence of an independent woman, and I love you.

My Dad

My love for you is endless, and I miss you every day. Thank you for
putting a hammer in my hand when I was nine years old and for all the
building projects we did together. Your encouragement and belief that a
young girl from the Bronx could be a successful entrepreneur and own
a construction company was second only to your love and support.

My Sister, Caryn Kavovit

Thank you for your friendship, love and support throughout the years.
You are the best sister anyone can ask for, and I love you.

My Son, Zachary Kavovit

You are my inspiration, my love, my light and life.
Don't forget to just keep swimming! I love you.

PART ONE

CHAPTER 1

Bridget Steele's father taught her two things she never forgot: how to fight and how to build.

The fight lessons started after Bridget was mugged in an elevator by a full-grown man who was either dumb or desperate enough to think a ten-year-old girl would be carrying anything of value.

"Hold the door!" he'd called, and obediently, Bridget held the door, allowing him in.

She would dream about that mistake for years to come; his mouth, slack and wet, his eyes, twin points of bleakness, his breath, hot and foul on her cheek as he turned and almost casually slammed her up against the wall, one hand on her throat, the other crudely groping and squeezing as he methodically rifled through the pockets of her jacket and jeans. He found her two dollars of allowance money, broke the cheap charm bracelet from her wrist and then, when the elevator doors opened, dropped her to the floor and skittered away, leaving Bridget gasping and shaken.

After Bridget managed to make it back to her apartment

and, through chattering teeth, explain what had happened to her increasingly alarmed mother, the police were called, and her father rushed home from work.

"This is the third one this week," the officer said as Bridget sat in her father's lap, resisting the urge to turn and sob into his shoulder. "I mean, this is the first time I've heard of a kid this young being targeted, but—" he flipped his notebook closed with a shake of his head "—it seems like the Bronx just ain't what it used it be, you know?"

Her parents nodded as the officer promised to get in touch if they managed to track the mugger down. They thanked him as he left. When the door shut, Bridget's mother went into the kitchen to make Bridget some warm milk, and Bridget's father knelt to the floor, gently taking her by the shoulders and looking into her eyes.

"You okay, darling?" he said.

She nodded.

"Are you still scared?"

Bridget shrugged, not wanting to let on how her stomach was horribly sour, how a knot in her throat was jerking up and down so that she couldn't speak.

Her father bit his lip. His handsome face was flushed and his warm brown eyes looked suspiciously bright. "Okay," he said, and his voice faltered. He suddenly pulled Bridget toward him and crushed her into his arms, giving her a fierce hug. They stayed that way for a moment, breathing in sync, as Bridget leaned into his familiar warmth. Then he cleared his throat and stood up again. "Okay," he said. "Okay, let me show you how to make a fist."

Every day for weeks, after he came home from work and before they sat down for dinner, Bridget's dad had taken twenty minutes to teach Bridget how to defend herself. First, he made her promise that if she was ever in a situation like that again and she saw a chance to get away, that she would take off as fast as her legs could carry her. Run and scream for help. But if she couldn't run, he wanted her to know some basic self-defense. He taught her how to hold up her hands, how to cover her face, throw a punch, how to find the weak and unprotected spots on her opponent and take merciless advantage of them.

"It's okay to fight dirty if you need to," he said to her as she swung at him and just barely missed. "A good punch to the nose is great, but if you can't land that, use your teeth, use your nails, go for the crotch. For you, honey, it's all fair game. The important thing is that, if you can't escape, you do what you need to do to keep yourself safe. You do what you need to do to win." He chuckled as she moved in closer and swung at him again. "A sweet little girl like you? They'll never see it coming."

But Bridget didn't feel like a sweet little girl any longer. Even before she was attacked in the elevator, Barker Avenue had started to feel like it was changing. Bridget used to move through life safely under the radar, just another kid in a tough, tight-knit Bronx neighborhood teeming with children, but lately, something had shifted. Gone were the days when she could happily skip down the sidewalk, unnoticed by adults except for the occasional fond smile from a shopkeeper or friendly wink from one of the old men who sat on their stoop playing cards in their shirtsleeves. Almost overnight, as if she had been visited by a fairy godmother with a twisted sense of humor, ten-year-old Bridget had opened her eyes and suddenly looked like a woman, with a woman's breasts and a woman's hips and lips and smile. And even more suddenly, adult men were treating her like she was something else—not a child, not a little girl, but a target.

Hey, baby! Look at the way she bounces when she walks! Why don't you move that hot bod right on over here?

Oooeee, Mama! What are you doing later tonight, sweet thing?

The attention confused and embarrassed Bridget, made her feel ashamed of the way her new and unruly body moved and the messages she thought it must be sending. She felt even worse when she would catch her mother's eyes sweeping over her, a disapproving look on her face. Bridget's mother was small and slim and contained, never a thread out of place, and she seemed equally offended and befuddled by the lushness of her young daughter's newly blossoming physique.

Late at night Bridget would lie in bed, replaying the mugging on a loop in her mind. Somehow the unfamiliar curves and softness of her body, the men calling out to her on the street, the way an eighteen-year-old boy had chased her down at the park, insisting on a date, her mother's sudden inexplicable distance and judgment, and the cold, pale eyes of the mugger as his hands yanked at her clothes and his fingers snaked against her skin, all became tangled together into one long, waking nightmare.

Her father saw the dark circles under his daughter's eyes, the way her smile regularly died on her face before it fully bloomed, noticed how her voice got smaller and she hunched over as if trying to shrink herself, and one day, instead of self-defense lessons, he pulled a cardboard box from his briefcase.

Golden summer light poured through the two narrow windows by her bed. Her father handed Bridget the box and she looked at it with a pang of disappointment. She'd been hoping for a new Barbie.

"Daddy?" said Bridget. "Isn't an ERECTOR set a toy for boys?"

Her father just smiled and shook his head. "Open it," he said.

Bridget tore through the wrappings and shook out the pieces onto her bed, then turned back to her father. "What now?"

"Well…" Her father put a warm hand on her shoulder. "Let's look at what we're building first. This is the Flatiron Building, one of my favorite buildings in the world. There's nothing like it anywhere else."

Bridget turned over the box and looked at the strange, narrow building on the cover. It looked like the prow of a ship or a big piece of pie. Her dad was right—she hadn't seen anything like it before.

"It's very famous now. One of the first skyscrapers north of Fourteenth Street. But back when it was built, people hated it. People said it was a big mistake, that it would fall down. But they were wrong."

Bridget traced her finger over the picture. "I like it," she decided. "It's…different."

Her dad laughed. "That's because you are a very smart girl with extremely good taste." He settled onto the floor behind her, picking up the rods and quickly laying them out by size, then carefully smoothing out the written instructions on the bed. "Now, what's first?" he asked, squinting at the papers.

Bridget happily leaned against him and read the sentences out loud, pausing to let him correct or help her when necessary. She loved everything about her father. The way he smelled— like mothballs and freshly cut wood and the ocean. The soft, gentle sound of his voice. The way he always wore a suit and tie and dress shoes—even on the weekends—so he would look proper, no matter what the occasion.

But what Bridget liked best about her father was the way he paid attention. Sometimes Bridget would watch other parents with their kids and she couldn't help but feel that they were only halfway there at best. They were always interrupting their children and turning away and rushing them through. When

Bridget talked to her father, he would stop what he was doing and look her in the eyes and she knew that he was really listening. When he played with her, he would get down at her level and become so absorbed in their games that it almost felt like he was another kid—except better. He made her feel safe and seen.

"You know," he said as they laid out the foundation for the model, "this building reminds me of you." He poked her playfully in the side. "Beautiful. Exceptional. Unique in all the world."

A blossom of warmth unfurled in Bridget's chest. Suddenly, the men on the street, her mother's bewildered glances, even the feel of the mugger's hand on her throat, all paled in comparison to the fact that, when her father looked at her, he didn't see something wrong or twisted or out of control. Instead, he saw something as special as this strange and amazing building.

Bridget and her father had built dozens of models over the years, LEGO and ERECTOR sets, and intricate hobby store creations that they glued together piece by piece. Every one of them meant something to Bridget. She treated each one with pride and care. But it was the model of the Flatiron Building that Bridget kept on her bedside table. Every night for years, it was the last thing she saw before she turned out the lights.

"You taste like candy."

Bridget and her date, Hal, were leaning against a brick wall in the park, taking advantage of a shadowy alcove to kiss and pet while a group of younger kids ran yelling and laughing, playing a game of kickball just feet from where the teens were twined together.

Bridget kissed Hal and giggled. "That's because I just ate a ring pop, remember?" She kissed him again. "You taste like salt."

Hal nodded. "Fritos."

Bridget was fifteen but looked twenty, all pillowy lips, long, thick dark hair and dangerous curves. Hal was fifteen and looked like he was fifteen, with braces and light brown hair that kept falling into his eyes. Sometimes his voice cracked, but Bridget didn't mind. Over the past few years, she had grown into her body and learned to mostly ignore the unwanted attention she got on the streets. Sometimes she even felt a little thrill of power caused by the undeniable impact of her physique. She was Jewish, but people regularly mistook her for one of the flashier Italian or Puerto Rican girls in the neighborhood. She wore tight designer jeans or even tighter miniskirts and artfully ripped sweatshirts. She teased her hair and did her makeup with bold slashes of blues and purples on her brown eyes, spiky mascara, sticky pink frosted lips.

Bridget knew that she regularly disappointed her parents in so many ways. They both had multiple degrees—her mother was the vice principal of a local high school and Bridget's father was an engineer. They expected their only child to follow in their academic footsteps like a good Jewish girl should. But school was torture for Bridget. Sitting still was a chore. She could barely read a chapter of a book without wanting to get up and run around the block screaming, she got so bored.

She didn't fit in socially, either. The boys were all fascinated by Bridget. They followed her around like dumb teenage puppies, and it made the girls in her class suspicious and hostile. Friends Bridget had had since she was little suddenly turned their backs and whispered when she came into the room. Desperate for a connection, Bridget dated early and often, but a movie and a make-out session somehow never made her feel any less misunderstood.

The only respite from Bridget's loneliness came from the place it always did—her father. When Bridget was eleven, her father came home with a stack of two-by-fours and laid them out on the living room floor. He told her they were moving beyond models—they were going to build bunk beds. Her mother said they were crazy—who was Bridget going to share it with? She was an only child. But her father insisted that Bridget would need the space for all the friends he knew she would make. "Think of the slumber parties!" he enthused as he placed the hammer in her hand and carefully directed her to strike the nail. Bridget was filled with pride when she swung the hammer and the first two pieces of wood kissed and stuck.

Bridget didn't harbor high hopes for any slumber parties, but she would never tell her father that. She was just happy to be working side by side with him. They spent weeks working on the project. Bridget was amazed at the way a pile of wood and nails slowly grew into a recognizable piece of furniture. She loved lining up all the materials, nailing things together with the heavy hammer, having her patient and gentle father guide her through the process, until, like magic, they came out on the other end with something new—something that had not existed until they made it together.

Almost every week after that, there was something else to do. Her dad told Bridget that she was going to help him put in crown moldings in the living room and paint the room a soft baby blue. After that they fixed the leak under the kitchen sink. For her birthday that year, Bridget received her own tool belt with her name pressed into the leather. Sometimes, for the bigger jobs, her father's buddy Danny Schwartz, a shy guy who could fix and build almost anything, would come over and help, but mainly it was just Bridget and her father. Bridget liked it best that way.

On the worst days at school, when the girls teased and the

boys leered and the teachers droned on and on, Bridget would sit at her desk and look out the window and longingly wonder what project her father would decide on next.

CHAPTER 2

Bridget made it through high school, but just barely. She was smart, but wildly distracted. She regularly got into trouble, cutting classes to make out with boys under the bleachers, failing tests, mouthing off, picking fights with bullies. She bet her father sometimes wished he'd never taught her to make that fist. Years later Bridget would realize that she probably had an undiagnosed case of ADHD, but at that time she was just told she wasn't trying hard enough.

The neighborhood was beginning to make her feel smothered. She knew everyone and everyone knew her—Bridget Steele, the girl with the big boobs and even bigger mouth. This meant that her every move got reported back to her parents, that she never had the luxury of making a mistake that she didn't immediately have to answer for. She started dreaming of getting out, of hopping the 6 train and heading into Manhattan, where she would be a stranger to everyone she met, where she secretly and desperately started to believe that she really belonged.

But her parents had a plan for her first—Hostos Community

College and then transferring to a four-year CUNY. She went along with it. Good girls went to college, after all, and, despite everything, deep down, Bridget still wanted to be a good girl.

She met Ethan Jackson on her first day of Business Org 101. He was tall and handsome, with dark brown skin and close-cropped hair. He sat directly behind her and poked her in the back with his pencil.

"Ow!" Bridget turned around and glared. "What the hell?"

"I'm Ethan." He smiled. She had to admit that it was a killer smile. "What's your name?"

She rolled her eyes. "Bridget Steele. What do you want?"

He blinked at her innocently. "Pardon me, Bridget Steele, but your hair is too big. I can't see the chalkboard."

Her mouth dropped open, then she turned back around in a huff. He poked her again. She whirled back around.

"What?" she snapped.

"I was just kidding about your hair. Want to get a cup of coffee after class?"

Ethan was from Queens. His black father had died young and he'd been raised by his white mom. He was smart and a little nerdy and spent his childhood lonely and between worlds, just like Bridget had. They went out twice before he kissed her.

They were at the Bronx Zoo—in front of the bear exhibit. The grizzlies were rolling around like fat old men in their wading pool and Bridget and Ethan were laughing hysterically. Bridget turned, giggling, to check if Ethan saw the little brown bear that was trying to sneak into the pool, too—and Ethan leaned toward her, a question in his eyes. Their lips met midlaugh.

The kiss was a disaster. All wrong. Like kissing her own hand or her reflection in the mirror. Bridget pulled back, her nose wrinkled. She could tell from the comical look on Ethan's face that he felt the same way.

"Wow," said Bridget, "that was really, truly terrible."

Ethan laughed. "Truth. You want to try again? Make sure?"

Bridget shook her head. "Nah." She already knew they were never going to be more than friends, and actually, she was more than a little okay with the idea.

Ethan nodded. "Fair enough, Steele. Wanna go see the giraffes? I hear they look frigging hilarious when they run."

Despite making a friend for the first time in years, Bridget continued to live at home and grimly battle her way through college in much the same way she had battled her way through high school, mainly doing it to please her parents—most especially her father. But she was bored, restless and broke, and nothing she was doing seemed to get her any closer to her dreams of getting out of the Bronx.

If she kept following the path set out for her, she knew exactly what would happen: graduation, some sort of half-decent, excruciatingly boring office job until she met the "right" guy, got married and took an apartment, maybe even in the same building where her parents still lived. Kids, bills, temple, Friday night Shabbats split between her parents and her in-laws, an occasional family vacation to somewhere not very far away… It was a fine life; she knew that. One her parents desperately wanted for her. Good, basic, decent and safe. And the thought of it made her want to jump out the nearest window.

One night, close to graduation, struggling through yet another paper she had no interest in writing, Bridget thought about that bunk bed, and she came up with a plan.

She skipped classes the next day to visit Danny Schwartz, the friend of her father's who used to come over occasionally and help them build. Danny was a fixture in the neighborhood. A lifelong bachelor, he worked the night shift as a security guard so he had his days free, and, most important, he could fix almost anything. He was the guy her father called when he'd exhausted his own extensive knowledge of carpentry. Danny had always been more than happy to help, and sweet to Bridget when he visited, bringing her rolls of cherry Life Savers, and teasing her good-naturedly as they worked.

After Bridget visited Danny, she had a stack of business cards printed up: "Don't fuss! Call us! Stand-Ins. Let Bridget Fix It!" and then drove all the way out to Westchester, where she knew people had more money. She stood in shopping center parking lots all over Scarsdale, handing out those cards to rich, harried housewives.

She never forgot her first job. Replacing all the trim around the interior doors for Mrs. King. Bridget still wore the tool belt her father had bought her. It hung neatly just below her slim waist. She hovered by Danny's side as he mitered pieces of three-inch clamshell casing and handed them over to her. She carefully took each piece and nailed it onto the wall jamb around the door. When they were finished, she stood back with a huge grin on her face, and only just barely stopped herself from dancing around the room. It was perfect.

She kept handing out those cards for months, getting more and more projects and combing the local newspaper for tradesmen available to work. She would interview them and try to match the job description of the ladies who called with the trade. She sealed driveways, tightened doorknobs, hung ceiling fans, fixed cracked ceramic bathroom tiles. One satisfied customer referred her to the next, until she had a steady trickle of work.

Bridget made it a policy to never turn anything down. She booked the jobs, bought and delivered the supplies in her brown 1975 Buick LeSabre and made sure the clients were happy. Danny was Bridget's right-hand man and dependably fixed anything beyond Bridget's capabilities. They usually split the profits 60–40 in Bridget's favor.

Time passed, she graduated college by the skin of her teeth and instead of accepting the safe assistant financial analyst job at the local bank that her parents wanted her to take, she invested in power tools, traded up her LeSabre for a Ford Econoline E-250 van, convinced Ethan to come on as her assistant and eventually realized that her little handyman business had grown into something much more than she had expected. They weren't just painting bedrooms and hanging shelves anymore—they were taking down walls, renovating kitchens and then finally, after she delighted a client with a bathroom renovation that came in ahead of schedule and under budget, she was hired to renovate their entire house. It needed a complete gut and rebuild, and they were willing to pay her one hundred and fifty thousand dollars. It was the biggest job she'd ever been awarded.

On the day Bridget got the deposit for the house renovation, she went to the bank, thrilled to see so many zeros below her name. The bank teller was the same woman she always dealt with, probably twenty years older than Bridget, small and sweet-voiced, with brown skin and a neat, shining cap of silver hair. She had a melodious accent that Bridget assumed was Middle Eastern.

"Oh!" exclaimed the woman when she saw the check. "Very good! Very good, indeed! Your business must be doing well, then?"

Bridget laughed. "It really is," she admitted. "Finally."

The older woman hesitated, her hand hovering over her computer keyboard. She looked up and met Bridget's eyes. "You know," she said, her voice dropping to a near-whisper, "pardon me for saying this, miss, but I see you coming in every week and depositing your checks. And I see that you are making excellent progress. And I just want to tell you that you really should have a business account, not just be using your old savings account." Her eyebrows knit as she looked at her screen. "It says here you opened this fifteen years ago with your parents?" She shook her head. "This really won't do for building a successful business. And there are many other options rather than just savings, you know? Ways to invest where your return will be more satisfying than this piddling percentage."

Bridget smiled. Building a successful business. She loved the sound of that. She glanced at the woman's name tag and read, Bibi Hashemi.

"You sound like you know what you're talking about, Ms. Hashemi."

The woman shrugged. "I had my MBA in Iran. I helped run my husband's tea business until we had to leave. It was very successful." She laughed ruefully. "Not that my degree does me any good here. Here, I am just a bank teller."

Bridget bit her lip, thinking. "Maybe I could buy you lunch one day? Pick your brain about investments? About the best way to financially build my business?"

Mrs. Hashemi gave her a shy smile in response. Her cheeks went pink with pleasure. She shot a look at the teller next to her, who was watching them through a suspicious squint. "I would very much like that," she whispered as she hurried to deposit Bridget's check.

Her parents were increasingly alarmed as they saw their daughter getting more and more entrenched in her business. Bridget's mother begged her to stop this nonsense. Whoever heard of a lady contractor, anyway? It was ridiculous and probably dangerous, too. How was Bridget supposed to stay safe in this kind of world, surrounded by nothing but men? What would the neighbors think? She begged her daughter to stop dreaming, get a grip and do exactly as she had done: get a decent, predictable job, find a decent, predictable man, get married and settle down in the neighborhood and be the respectable woman she had been raised to be.

Bridget's father was less worried about what the neighbors thought and more concerned about the lack of a dependable weekly paycheck.

"What if something happens? What will you do for health insurance? How will you put anything away in your retirement savings? We just want you to be safe, darling," he said to her over bagels and coffee at the breakfast table one morning.

They were arguing over whether Bridget should apply for an office job at her mother's school.

"We want to be sure you're taken care of," chimed in her mother.

Bridget took a bite of bagel and shook her head. "Guys, the whole point is that I can take care of myself."

Her mother sighed, her hand to her heart. "But why in the world would you want that? That sounds so terribly lonely."

The house was a mammoth job, bigger than Bridget had initially imagined. Suddenly, she wondered just what she had gotten herself into. What if her parents were right? It was one thing to be running a little side hustle helping housewives hang some wallpaper—but a whole three-story house that needed to be demoed to its studs and then built out again? Who was she to think she could pull this kind of thing off? For weeks she worked all day and worried all night, meeting with the owner and the architect, poring over the blueprints, reviewing the bids of various subcontractors and vendors and finding the extra crew she would need.

Half the men working for her were new. Some had been recommended by Danny, but some of them had simply answered the ad she'd put in the local paper. Bridget almost laughed at the looks on their faces when they came in to interview and found themselves nose to nose with a twenty-three-year-old general contractor wearing a ponytail and red heels. A couple of the men had simply turned and walked out when they saw her; one had immediately suggested that she suck his unmentionable parts, and more than a few had condescendingly sneered through her questions, their eyes bouncing between her lips and her chest like they were watching an X-rated tennis match. But worried about having enough manpower, Bridget hired them, anyway.

The first day of demolition was the worst. Bridget felt the mood change as soon as she walked through the door. She was wearing tight jeans and a fitted black tee, a pair of cute little heeled Timberland work boots that she'd found half off at a fire sale and a custom purple hard hat that Ethan and Danny had presented to her after she signed the contract on this job.

The room was bustling with activity; the men were laughing and teasing each other, setting up their equipment, taping up windows with plastic and protecting the floors. However, as she walked from room to room, pointing out a corner they had missed, a scrap of floor still exposed—this, Bridget would soon discover, was her superpower: noticing the smallest bits and pieces of a job and never letting them go undone—she could see their faces go stony, the darting looks and eye rolls exchanged behind her back. The men needed these jobs, yes, but that didn't mean they had to pretend to like or respect the woman who hired them.

"Hey, Joe," Bridget said to the project manager she had painstakingly vetted and hired, "I heard the architect dropped off some updated sketches for the downstairs powder room. Can I see them, please?"

The older man turned to her, a big, shit-eating smile on his face. "Right there on the table, missy."

Bridget decided to ignore the flutter of anger in her belly at the word *missy* as she bent over the table and unrolled the blueprints. She smelled Joe's cheap cologne as he stepped up next to her, a bit too close for comfort. He reached over, took the papers out of her hands and flipped the pages.

"I think you're reading those upside down, dear," he said with a wink.

The room erupted into hoots of laughter as Bridget rapidly blinked, her face aflame, thinking for a moment that he had been right—that she was the idiot who truly didn't know what she was doing. But then she shook her head. Of course the sketches hadn't been upside down when she was reading them. They were upside down now. He'd done it for a cheap joke. To make her look like a fool. And, judging from the continuing laughter of the men who were supposed to be working for her, it had worked.

Bridget went still, recognizing that her response to this moment was going to be everything. She could laugh it off, pretend that she was in on the joke rather than the butt of it, be the good-natured boss with no grip on her men's respect.

Or she could make a fist like her father taught her to do.

She swallowed, straightened her shoulders and tilted her chin up so that she was looking Joe square in the eye.

"You're fired," she said quietly.

The laughter instantly died. Joe's grin faltered. "Wait, what?" he said.

"You're fired. Pack up your stuff and go."

The man's puffy cheeks flamed red, and a dangerous glitter came into his eyes. "Are you freaking kidding me?" he spat out, taking a step toward her.

Bridget felt, rather than saw, Ethan and Danny walk up be-

hind her, building a wall of support. She made a little sign behind her back, warning them not to step in. "Don't worry,"
she said, smiling sweetly into Joe's irate scowl. "I'll send you
a check for the—" she checked her watch "—twenty minutes
you were on the job."

There was a smothered bark of laughter from one of the
men, and then silence again as they waited to see what would
happen next.

A muscle in Joe's jaw twitched and leaped, his eyes darting
to the men standing behind Bridget, and then back to Bridget
herself. Finally, he turned his back on her.

"I didn't want to work for a bitch like you, anyways," he
muttered as he stepped away.

Danny and Ethan surged forward, but Bridget caught their
sleeves, holding them back. She turned toward the rest of the
room. "Anyone else?" she asked. "Anyone else not want to
work for me? Because I'm not getting any less bitchy, and if
that's going to be a problem, now's your chance to go."

The men shifted uneasily, avoiding her eyes. No one said
anything.

"All right, then," she said. "Get back to work."

It was only after she got home that night, after she'd smiled
and nodded at her parents when they asked how her day went,
calmly ate her dinner and helped her mother clean up, removed
her carefully chosen work clothes, slipped into the shower and
turned it on full blast, that she finally let herself cry.

It wasn't exactly easy after that, but it was better. The men
settled down and got to work, and if they had negative opinions about her, they mostly managed to keep those opinions to
themselves. For the first time Bridget realized that, if she was
going to make it in this business, and be considered equal, she
was going to have to be twice as tough, five times as competent

and ten times as smart as any man. Good enough was never going to cut it for her. There would be no second chances; she didn't have room for even one misstep. But strangely, this kind of pressure brought out the best in Bridget. Every time she caught another mistake before it happened, signed a contract for a larger job, stayed a little later, came in before anyone else showed up—she felt an unfamiliar thrill.

Bridget loved everything about construction. The sweet, sharp smell of freshly cut wood, the whine of a saw cutting through a two-by-four like butter, the way her guys laughed and shouted at each other over the noise of their tools, the power drills screaming as the drill bits were forced into metal, and Guns N' Roses or Metallica blasting at top volume. Bridget couldn't help but admire the contrast between destruction and construction; the sexy controlled chaos of the demo crew as they swung sledgehammers, crashing through walls and making the most spectacular noise and mess, clearing the way, opening up rooms to light and space. She loved to watch the carpenters who followed them in, moving around hundreds of pounds of building material, jaws set, muscles bulging, sweat gleaming on their brows, and then coaxing along the daintiest little detail work, getting the stain on the living room floor just the right shade, laying intricate patterns of pretty pink-and-gold Moroccan tile in the master bath.

Bridget liked the other parts, too. She felt fierce and smart when she ordered building materials, negotiating with supply houses, subcontractors and vendors, making sure her clients weren't being cheated on materials or fees. She loved reading blueprints—her dad's instruction had made her an expert in understanding the details, elevations and sections of the prints. She liked watching the supplies coming off the trucks and being boomed up through the windows. She admired the towers of lumber, the sheets of drywall, the gleaming cans of paint, all arranged and waiting like a promise. She liked meeting with the architect, the way she sometimes got excited about something new and clever he wanted and then often had to fight to hold his budget-busting flights of fancy in check. She was fascinated by the men who could do things she had never mastered herself. The electricians and the plumbers, the engineer who designed the electrical and plumbing and HVAC, coordinating with the architect to make sure everything was safe and up to code. She liked the small feeling of relief and pride she felt every time they passed another inspection and another building permit came through emblazoned with her company name—STEELE CONSTRUCTION—across the page.

Every afternoon, after everyone left, Bridget would walk through and take note of the progress made, make sure everything was neat and put away, that there were no dangerous wires left dangling, that all refuse was safely stored in mini containers, ready for pickup the next morning. She scanned each room, repaired anything that needed to be fixed. And then she walked out the front door feeling like a million bucks.

She had finally found something she loved doing, and, as it turned out, she was truly great at doing it.

"Guys, guys, guys!" she shouted over the building noise as she placed a stack of pizza boxes on the table. "Take a break! We're coming in two days ahead of schedule, so I brought you lunch to celebrate!"

A cheer went up in the room as the men laid down their hard hats, gloves and power tools and crowded around the table, reaching for a slice.

"Pizza's great, but where's the beer, Steele?" said a portly guy in a tight white T-shirt.

"Like you need it, Murkowski. You think I don't know what's really in your water bottle?" teased Bridget.

As the men settled down to eat, Bridget took the time to

do a quick walking tour of all three stories, bottom to top and then back down again. She kept a notepad in her hand and a pencil stuck into the bun in her hair to jot down anything she saw that needed refining or, if she saw something particularly good, a note to herself to praise the trade who did it.

They were nearly done, just doing the finish work on the last few rooms now. As much as Bridget loved walking through the rooms that were complete, there was something even more pleasurable about the rooms that were not quite there, where she could think about the tiny details and little problems that needed to be solved before they could clean it all up and call it done. A sloppy paint line on an electrical outlet, a piece of trim that wasn't mitered correctly, missed caulking around the window, a stretch of ceiling trim that wasn't lying flat—she wrote down each issue as she found it and smiled to herself, imagining what the owners of the house would think when they finally moved back in. She had taken what started as a dated, crowded, dark and gloomy townhouse, and turned it into something modern, light-filled, gracious and welcoming. A place where no detail would be overlooked, where the owners would get so much more than their money's worth.

She sighed, imagining what it would be like to have a place like this all to herself.

Soon, she thought, remembering the long line of zeroes on the last check she had deposited into her new business account—Bibi Hashemi had not been wrong. *Soon, soon, soon!*

She wrinkled her nose, noticing an unswept pile of green dust near the linen closet, took her pencil out of her hair and carefully noted it down.

The afternoon before she handed the keys back to the owners, Bridget took her father for a walk through the house. Normally, he would have checked in repeatedly on any big project she was doing. He loved to come in and look everything over, make suggestions and give her lots of praise, but for some reason Bridget had wanted to make him wait on this one. She had shown him through at the very beginning, and then told him he could come back only when she was ready.

She smiled as they moved through the rooms, near enough to brush shoulders, showing him the wide-board pine floors they'd sanded and stained, the brick wall they had uncovered, the beautiful slate countertops in the kitchen, the antique, stained-glass fan window Bridget had personally dug up in a salvage place and installed above the front door.

She could feel how pleased he was.

"Very, very nice, darling," he said, running his hand admiringly over the pristinely restored mantel around the living room fireplace. "I couldn't have done better myself."

Bridget felt that familiar warmth, that feeling of being completely understood, and took his words, as mild as they were, for the blessing they were meant to be.

Then she took a deep breath and turned to him. "Daddy?" she said softly.

He looked up from where he was inspecting the built-ins around the fireplace and met her eyes.

"You know that I'm moving out, right?"

Her father gave her a slow, sad smile. "I was afraid you were going to say that," he said.

"I mean, I'm twenty-four. It's time, Daddy. And listen, promise me you won't worry, okay? I'm going to be just fine."

He laughed. "You know I can't promise you that, darling. But I'll do my best, all right?"

Bridget felt tears spring to her eyes. She sniffed loudly as he laughed and pulled her into a bear hug.

"Oh, boy," he said as he held her in his arms. "Oh, boy, am I ever going to miss you, kiddo."

★ ★ ★

A couple of weeks later Bridget kissed her parents goodbye, promised to call every night and visit on weekends, took all her savings and moved into a fifth-floor walk-up studio on the Upper West Side. As she stretched out on the convertible futon in her living/dining/bedroom, surrounded by unpacked boxes and a couple of tinfoil containers of half-eaten Thai takeout, she smiled to herself. So what if there were only three windows and a view of the neighbor's bathroom? So what if she could walk from one end of the place to the other in about ten steps? So what if it wasn't a beautiful, spacious, perfectly renovated, three-story townhouse?

It was all hers; and she knew in her bones that it was just the beginning.

CHAPTER 3

Those first few years in Manhattan, Bridget hustled like she had never hustled before.

She hadn't expected it to be easy, exactly. She knew that the Manhattan real estate and construction market was notoriously hard to break in to, that there was an impenetrable wall to keep outsiders out where they belonged. Bridget knew she would struggle. But she'd never realized just how long and hard that struggle would be.

Bridget understood that getting a job in this business was all about connections and how you presented yourself. You didn't get work unless your father, brother and uncle were in the business—or unless you networked like crazy. She had never been afraid to knock on doors, make cold calls, strike up conversations and hand out her card to everyone she met just in case they might be someone who actually knew someone. But even when she managed to find a potential client, a whole host of other unsolvable issues would immediately crop up. Where would she meet with the client? She was still working out of her one-room apartment. She could never let them see that. She could take them out to lunch, of course, but clients at this level were used to going to five-star restaurants—The Regency, Le Bernardin, Freds at Barneys—and ordering anything they liked, and even if Bridget managed to secure a reservation, her savings account was near empty and her credit cards were already maxed to their limits. And what would she wear? She only had one nice designer dress, and chances are they had already seen her in it. She couldn't just show up in department store schmatte and hope they didn't notice. These kinds of people always noticed those kinds of things.

And even if she managed to get around all these issues—figure out the clothes and the hair and the restaurant and the timing—ninety-nine percent of the time the potential "client" wasn't really even looking for a GC. They were looking for a date. And once she made it clear that she was not interested, they would turn the other way with a smirk on their face. End of game. In this business women were limited to being secretaries, girlfriends, wives or whores. Bridget was none of the above. She simply didn't fit in.

It was like being starved and standing with her nose pressed to Balthazar's bakery window. Manhattan was growing ever higher into the sky. Everywhere Bridget looked, huge, beautiful buildings were going up. Men in hard hats were hanging off ladders, setting up scaffolding. Every time she passed a construction site and the workers whistled or catcalled at her, instead of getting mad, she imagined how it would feel when she was the one hiring men like them again. She felt dizzy with the longing to put her purple hard hat and little work boots back on, to have her hands on a set of blueprints, to make something out of nothing. Instead, she was barely scraping by, doing the kind of odd jobs and low-rent work that she had thought she'd left behind in the Bronx. Because no matter what her qualifications were, the only way into the construction industry in Manhattan was through a door marked Men Only.

"You're too beautiful to be a contractor…"

Bridget kept the smile pasted on her face and stuffed down the urge to kick this guy in the crotch and run for her life. Despite her better instincts, she had left a hopping cocktail party chock-full of industry connections and come to this half-built industrial park in Mt. Vernon, in the middle of the night, with a virtual stranger, because he had promised the chance of real work, and she was just desperate enough to believe him.

She'd been invited to the party by a woman named Ava Martinez. Bridget had been at Barry's Bootcamp, sprinting on the treadmill, when she noticed a gorgeous, leggy Latina woman next to her with the perfect ponytail and lime-green running shorts who was doing twelve to her eleven. Bridget gritted her teeth and pushed herself harder and took it to 12.5, and then chuckled to herself when she noticed the woman stepping up her own pace. Later, in the locker room, Bridget overheard Ava mention to someone that she was an architect, and so, despite Bridget's still lingering certainty from high school that, no matter how hard she tried, women were never going to like her, she had forced herself to start a conversation by asking the leggy architect where she got her jog bra.

Ava, who was a shallow B cup on a good day, had raised an eyebrow at Bridget's double Ds and said, "Macy's. But if I had boobs as good as yours, I'd probably want something that showed them off better than this old thing."

They'd chatted a bit more—and Bridget had made a point of telling her that she was a contractor. The next time they saw each other at the gym, Ava had approached Bridget and asked her if she wanted to skip the treadmill and go get pizza with her instead. "There's a place with a wood-fire oven just down the block, and I have crazy bad cramps that the frigging treadmill isn't going to help. I need some serious carbs."

Bridget experienced a rush of giddy pleasure at having another woman confide in her about something as mundane as her period. This was exactly the kind of easy feminine intimacy she'd longed for throughout her girlhood. They'd sneaked out of the gym together, still wearing their workout gear and giggling like they might get caught. They'd split a cheese pie with extra mozzarella and a Caesar salad, then ordered a bottle of rosé and talked until Ava had to rush out for an appointment she'd forgotten about. But not before she'd invited Bridget to this party at her boss's Upper East Side penthouse.

Bridget had dressed carefully for the night. After the brownstone job, she had splurged on a simple, black Stella McCartney sheath dress that hugged her every curve, showed just enough cleavage and what Bridget's mother considered to be too much leg. Bridget loved that dress. She wore it every chance she got. With her five-inch black patent stilettos by Jessica Simpson—she was dying for the day when she could splurge on really expensive shoes, but these would do for now—and a chunky gold statement necklace, she felt so grown-up and professional and sexy that she wasn't at all surprised when a short, dark-haired man in a very nice suit had introduced himself to her within five minutes of coming through the door.

Martin McDonald was the first commercial landlord and real estate developer that Bridget had met in real life, and she was starstruck. Men like him were the key to getting past these little piddling residential jobs she had been subsisting on. All she needed was one big commercial job with a guy like Martin, and she'd have her start.

McDonald looked exactly how Bridget had always imagined a Manhattan real estate developer would: his hair was slicked back, his tan was a deep, lurid orange, his suit and shoes probably cost the same amount as an economy compact car, and his teeth were such an unnatural white that they practically hurt Bridget's eyes when he smiled. Bridget didn't find him particularly attractive.

McDonald, on the other hand, seemed to be absolutely smitten with Bridget. He expressed surprise and delight when he found out she was a contractor, got her a champagne cocktail and then another and another, chatted easily about his many projects and then, as the party started dying down, casually offered to show her a place he was leasing out—two hundred thousand square feet of industrial space right outside NYC that he was planning on converting into a business park, and which, he assured her, he had yet to hire a construction manager for.

Bridget wasn't stupid. She knew what an invitation to inspect an empty work site this late at night really meant. She knew that, when they got there, if it even existed, this guy would be all over her like a cheap coat of paint. But he had monopolized her so thoroughly all night that she had made no other connections, had barely even managed to wave to Ava from across the room, and like hell was she going home empty-handed.

McDonald's driver took them to the site, McDonald doing his best to slide a little closer to Bridget every few blocks. Bridget kept her purse firmly on the seat between them and her face turned halfway toward the window, providing an endless stream of commentary on everything she saw as they drove by. The ride was nearly thirty minutes long, and by the time they got there, her throat was sore from talking so much in her effort to keep him at arm's length.

The night was wet and gloomy, and the site only had hanging temp lights dangling from the open ceiling, but Bridget was relieved to see that it actually did exist. Endless raw space just waiting to be turned into offices and storefronts. Two hundred thousand square feet of work that could be for Bridget and Steele Construction.

Bridget explored the building, leaving Martin in her wake, making a mental list of what needed to be done. She let Martin look at her all he wanted while hitting him with her pitch, rattling off her numbers, square footage costs for each trade, and hoping that she'd impress him enough so that by the time they'd reached the end of the walk-through, he would stop leering at her ass and start talking about drawing up contracts instead.

But when they'd finished, and Bridget finally turned around to meet his gaze, she knew her plan had failed. McDonald's slow, predatory smile proved that he was obviously not thinking about hiring her for any work.

He took a step toward her. Bridget fought the urge to take a step back. "Did you hear what I said about using 5/8 drywall instead of 3/4?" she said desperately.

"Shhh," he said, coming even closer. "Stop talking about construction. You're too beautiful to be a contractor."

One kiss, she thought as he closed the space between them. *I'll give him one kiss just to keep his interest, and then I'll tell him about that electrician I know who will work for half price.*

McDonald kissed exactly like he looked like he would kiss— with way too much tongue. His hands groped and kneaded Bridget's body in a greedy and heedless sort of way.

Bridget broke the kiss and took two huge steps back, plastering a bright smile on her face. "So I know this electrician—"

He made a groaning sound and lurched toward her again like a handsy zombie. In a split second, Bridget had to make a decision. A huge part of her wanted to break this guy's nose just like her dad had taught her, or at least give him a swift, sharp elbow to the ribs. But Bridget knew that if she punched one of Manhattan's biggest real estate developers in the face, there was no coming back. It wasn't even about working with him at this point; that ship had probably sailed, but if he ended up in the ER with a plaster on his nose, not only would he never hire her for anything, he would also surely make certain that she'd never work anywhere ever again.

There was only one thing left to do: play dumb.

As he closed in on her, Bridget sidestepped, her heart pounding, and practically sprinted for the exit. "Oh, wow!" she said in a high-pitched voice. "Oh, gosh! Would you look at the time? My father will be wondering why I'm not home yet!" And then, without waiting for an answer, she hightailed it back through the parking lot and into the car, sliding into the front seat, next to the startled driver.

"Sorry! I get carsick in the back," she trilled, batting her eyelashes and smiling apologetically as McDonald peered at her through the passenger-side window, his face pinched in anger.

For a moment she held her breath, wondering if he was going to reach in and yank her out of the car; wondering if his driver would help her, or just go back to reading his magazine, ignoring her desperate screams.

McDonald paused, darting a look at her, then at the driver, then back to her again. She swallowed, but didn't break eye contact, keeping the desperate smile plastered on her face.

Finally, he shook his head and with a look of annoyed resignation, yanked open the back door and slid in.

The driver started up the car.

For a moment Bridget just breathed. She waited for her hands to stop trembling.

Then she squared her shoulders, turned around, gave him another dose of her best smile and began talking again.

By the time they made it back to the city, she had worn him down. No, he was not going to hire her as his GC, but yes, he would rent her the unfinished loft space at the back of the building for her office, and if she fixed it up herself, she could get it at four hundred dollars a month.

It turned out that Ava Martinez wasn't just a good friend, she was a steady professional contact for Bridget. Whenever she could, she would throw jobs Bridget's way. Unfortunately, she was at the bottom rung at her architecture firm, the only woman, and at least a decade younger than anyone else there, so she was mainly limited to residential renovations. Of course, Bridget was grateful to get any kind of work, and if updating kitchens and refinishing floors was all there was—she wasn't dumb enough to turn her nose up at even the smallest renovation. So when Ava called Bridget one morning while Bridget was working out and left a message to call her back right away, Bridget wasn't expecting anything too exciting.

Another bathroom, whoop-de-do, she thought to herself as she dialed her phone. *Maybe some walk-in closets or a kitchen pantry, if I'm lucky.*

"Oh, my God," squealed Ava as soon as she picked up. "Why did you take so long to call?"

"It's leg and butt day," said Bridget. "Squats take time."

"Shut up about your butt! You know who Kendall MacKenzie is?"

Bridget rolled her eyes. Who didn't know who Kendall MacKenzie was? "Yes, I know who Kendall MacKenzie is. I'm not an idiot," she replied. "Bisexual supermodel. Muse. It Girl. Dated Johnny Depp and Madonna at the same time. They all trashed a hotel room together. Has been to rehab five times in the last three years. Probably needs to go again."

"Yes!" answered Ava. "Yes! Exactly! Well, guess who just bought a five-story Federal-style townhouse on Bank Street in the West Village and wants the whole thing renovated from top to bottom?"

"Gee, let me take a wild guess. Kendall MacKenzie?"

"Kendall MacKenzie!" shouted Ava. "She marched in this morning to meet with our senior partners and she saw me pass by in the hall and she said, 'Wait, are there women architects?' and so they brought me in and then I told her that not only are there women architects, I have a woman contractor she can work with, as well, and she got so excited that she offered to hire us on the spot!"

Bridget's heart sped up. "Seriously? A five-story renovation? Oh, my God."

"See?" crowed Ava. "See! I told you! She wants you to come over to meet her and do a walk-through tomorrow!"

Bridget agonized over what to wear. Her tried and true Stella McCartney suddenly seemed matronly and stiff when she thought about the hip young model. Besides, they were doing a walk-through, not meeting at Le Cirque. She should keep it casual. Good jeans, her work boots, a slouchy purple T-shirt that skimmed her torso in just the right way.

Kendall answered the door in nothing but a black, see-through negligee and a sleepy smile.

"Oh," she said in a mellow Californian drawl. "You're the lady builder, right? I'm sorry. I was asleep. I totally forgot you were coming."

Bridget was startled to realize that although she knew the model's face and body—even the nipples she could clearly see through the sheer nightgown were familiar to her thanks to countless half-naked *Vogue* editorials—she had never actually heard Kendall's voice before.

"I'm Bridget," she said. "Bridget Steele."

Kendall yawned again. "Hi. What time is it, anyway?"

Bridget looked at her watch. "Um. Three p.m."

Kendall nodded. "Wow. No wonder I'm tired. It's so early. Come on in."

As they walked into the house, Bridget couldn't help sneaking a glance at the butt that was rumored to have been insured for ten million dollars before noting the narrow staircase and sloped wide-board pine floors of a typical 1800s-era house. "You could knock out the staircase and make it bigger," she suggested. "Level the floors. It would make the entryway feel much more airy and dramatic."

"Cool," said Kendall as she led her farther down the hall. They passed by the parlor and Bridget glimpsed the topless torso of a very well-built man lounging on a green velvet couch and playing guitar. She couldn't help turning back around to double-check.

"Hey," said the man.

"Hey," croaked Bridget back. Yup. Lenny Kravitz.

Kendall airily waved her hand in unimpressed dismissal. "Don't mind him. He crashed here last night after the party. He is such a frigging lightweight." As they continued down the hall, Kendall grabbed a crumpled pack of American Spirit cigarettes and a lighter and took a deep drag. "Aaaah, yeah. That's better," she said. Her lips were even fuller than Bridget's. Her eyes were huge and slanted and an eerie violet-blue that Bridget had only ever seen on Elizabeth Taylor. Her skin was golden and flawless and looked lit from within. She didn't have a stitch of makeup on and she was easily the most beautiful person Bridget had ever seen in real life.

She offered a cigarette to Bridget, who shook her head. "No, thanks."

"God," said Kendall, "I know you're supposed to see the house now, but I'm totally famished. Like, I don't think I've actually eaten anything in the last forty-eight hours. You mind if we skip down to Nobu and have a bite first?" She yelled down the hall. "Lenny, do you want to get some food with me and this lady builder?"

"Sure! Why not?" Lenny yelled back.

"Okay, cool. I'm just going to go get some shoes or something." Kendall gazed down at what she was wearing with a confused expression on her face. "Oh, wow, there's my boobs." She giggled. "I guess maybe I should change my clothes, too?"

She drifted up the stairs and left Bridget standing in the hall. Bridget swallowed, itching to see the rest of the house, but also super-excited to be having lunch with Kendall and her famous entourage. Maybe they would become best friends. She imagined herself drinking cosmos, dancing at clubs, jet-setting off to LA and Paris at a moment's notice, comforting Kendall after her latest breakup…

"Hey, lady builder," said Lenny Kravitz as he poked his head into the hallway. "I can't find my moccasins."

That Nobu lunch—which somehow Bridget had ended up paying the enormous bill for—was the first and only time Bridget spent any time with Kendall before she got a message from Kendall's assistant, letting her know that the model was going to Marrakesh for six months, but that she had okayed Ava's plans and Bridget should get to work and spare no expense. She expected the whole place to be done by the time she arrived home.

Bridget worked round the clock, seven days a week, taking advantage of the blank check Kendall had essentially left her to hire an enormous crew who would work overtime. Kendall had left a small army of experts who needed to be consulted on every move. Besides Ava, there was her assistant, her manager, two interior designers—who never agreed with each other— her personal chef, who had endless opinions about the kitchen, and Kendall's younger sister, Pam, who reminded Bridget of a gerbil. Apparently, Kendall had helped herself to all the good genes before Pam had a chance.

But despite all the cooks in the proverbial kitchen, Ava and Bridget managed to pull together and make an absolutely stunning space before Kendall, wearing a gem-encrusted caftan, stepped back off her plane.

"She loves it!" breathed Ava to Bridget over the phone. "She wants you to come to a housewarming dinner party tomorrow night. It starts at ten."

"Of course it does. Just me?"

"No, the lady architect was invited, too, but it's my parents' anniversary. I have to lift a glass of wine to thirty-seven years of passive aggression."

Bridget bought a new dress. Then returned it and bought another one. Then changed her mind, returned that and decided to wear jeans instead. She added a gold silk tank top that showed off her shoulders and ample cleavage. She did not return the four-inch-heeled gold Christian Louboutin sandals she bought to match. She paid for a blowout at the salon. She got a Brazilian wax just for the hell of it. Images of the villa she and Kendall would rent for their yearly girlfriend retreat on the Amalfi coast danced in her head as she knocked on the carved mahogany door that she had personally selected and hung.

Younger sister Pam met her at the door. "Hiiii," she breathed. "Like, thank God you're finally here. There's a big problem in one of the downstairs powder rooms and Kendall is not happy."

Bridget blinked. "Um, did anyone call a plumber?"

Pam shook her head impatiently. "Why would we do that when we knew you were coming?"

Knowing that she couldn't afford to alienate a celebrity, Bridget followed Pam down the hall, wishing she was wearing different shoes.

Kendall intercepted them on the way in. She was carrying a lurid green cocktail, wearing a gingham bikini top and cutoff shorts and had a crust of white powder around her nose and a giant zit on her chin. She was still the most beautiful person Bridget had ever seen.

"You suck at building, lady builder," she slurred. There was a dumb, mean look in her pretty eyes. "My new bathroom is all wet and it ruined my babouches that I brought all the way from Morocco and you should give me my money back. I'm probably going to have to sue you."

For a moment Bridget considered telling Kendall where, exactly, she could stick her frigging babouches, but seeing the room full of A-list celebrities behind her—all potential dream clients—sipping their drinks and silently watching this scene play out, she decided it would be best to keep her mouth shut, get to the bathroom as quickly as possible and hope for something simple to fix. After all, although it was unlikely, she supposed the problem could have been her fault.

But it was not Bridget's fault. The toilet was merely clogged, though there was no evidence of what was blocking it. Apparently, Kendall hadn't even been smart enough to turn off the water, so it had overrun all over the Spanish tiles that Bridget's tile guy had so carefully laid. Bridget removed her shoes, and, shaking her head, quickly shut the valve off at the back of the toilet. After a few moments of fishing around with a snake, she dredged up a sparkly pink cell phone, which had apparently been dropped into the toilet bowl and wedged itself halfway down the pipe.

Bridget rolled her eyes and wrapped the phone in a hand towel before marching out into the living room and wordlessly presenting the dripping evidence to Kendall.

"That's not mine," said Kendall like a little kid caught drawing on the walls. "Maybe your plumber dropped his phone down my toilet and then didn't tell anyone. Like I said, you should give me my money back. This place is a total dump."

Bridget gaped at Kendall for a moment, feeling her face go red and her temper surge. The plumber who worked on this job was a sixty-year-old Filipino guy named Fred and imagining him wielding a glitter-covered phone roughly the color of a nine-year-old girl's nail polish was ridiculous. But before she could splutter out an outraged answer, a dignified, red-headed figure detached herself from the crowd and took Kendall's arm.

"Now, Kendall," came the famously Southern and honeyed voice of Scarlett Hawkins, "stop being such a world-class bitch. I know for a fact that is your phone. I was there with you last week in the Fez medina when you bought it. Just because you were probably too drunk to remember dropping it into the crapper, that's hardly a reason to publicly humiliate this poor girl, who, by the way, did a most splendid and professional job with your new home, as you know very well."

Scarlett firmly steered a drunken Kendall toward the dinner table and gave her a long kiss goodbye right on the mouth, then she offered a ride home to Bridget.

"You look like you might still lose your temper and my driver is waiting outside," said Scarlett. "I wasn't going to stay for dinner, anyway. Kendall thinks weed and a small pile of cocaine constitutes a proper second course."

Safely in the Mercedes, Bridget could not help being starstruck by the fact that she was sitting across from a famous billionaire and tastemaker. Scarlett looked even more impressive in person, with her slight, elegant figure clothed in a navy blue cashmere jacket, and her taut, glowing skin that belied the fact that she was at least fifty years old.

Everyone knew Scarlett. She was world famous for her cooking shows, her multibillion-dollar lifestyle brand, her chain of nationwide craft and baking stores, her own personal cable network and her unabashed appetite for young, beautiful women. Hardly a week went by without Page Six splashing her across the headlines, smiling primly, perfectly turned out and escorting some six-foot, half-drunk, blonde model-of-the-moment to a never-ending series of Manhattan's most exclusive events—and, it was whispered, the city's most scandalous S and M clubs. Kendall was just her type.

"Stop gaping, dear. You look like an idiot," said Scarlett as she settled back into her seat. "I have a very good dermatologist, and a backup plastic surgeon, and oodles of money to pay them both whenever I need it. When you are ready and if you are wealthy enough to afford them, I shall give you their names."

Bridget laughed then, the tension broken, and as they drove uptown, Scarlett engaged her in a conversation about the possibility of building a new studio kitchen for filming her show at her private home in the Hamptons.

Bridget was dazzled. Scarlett was funny and down-to-earth, and doing this kind of work for her would take Bridget's business up to an entirely new level. So perhaps that was why she decided to just sit still and see what happened when, at the end of the ride, Scarlett, murmuring, "You are so lovely, dear," leaned over and kissed her full on the mouth.

After a moment Scarlett leaned back, and seeing the look on Bridget's face, slapped her leg and guffawed. "For the devil's sake, girl, why didn't you just say something and save me the effort? Believe you me, I have exactly zero interest in chasing straight women when there is a world of pretty, willing queer ones just out there for the taking."

Bridget thought of Martin McDonald and something must have shown on her face, because Scarlett leaned over and patted her hand in a comforting sort of way.

"Oh, don't you worry, now, darlin'. You haven't spoiled a thing. Let's just see where the road will take us, shall we?"

★ ★ ★

Bridget's father had been laid off and he was not coping well. Every time Bridget called home, she would ask how he was, and if it was her mother on the other end of the line, she would say, "Terrible. You know, he could just retire early. We're fine financially. We've put enough away. But instead, he's still putting on a suit every day and going out looking for work that's just not there. And then he comes home and sits in front of the television watching the stock market on CNN or CNBC, or reads his stock market books on the terrace until it gets dark and he can take his suit off. The poor man doesn't know what to do with himself."

But if Bridget managed to get her father on the line instead and ask him how he was doing, he would just say, "Fine, darling. I'm perfectly fine. But tell me about you."

Bridget had finally moved into the Mt. Vernon office, and she was delighted with it. It was a huge, echoing loft space with soaring ceilings and a wall of enormous metal-framed windows. She had given it a sleek industrial makeover, polishing the concrete floors and leaving the ductwork exposed, making what was already there look purposeful and chosen. It was an impressive, professional space, but she was still lacking many clients to show it to.

"Listen, Daddy," she said after another round of *I'm perfectly fine, what about you?* "Can you come into the office today? I want to build a big conference table and I could use your help."

Her father chuckled. "With all the carpenters you know? Why would you need me?"

"They won't make it like you will. Come on, please? It would be doing me a huge favor."

Her old neighborhood was only twenty minutes from Mt. Vernon, so her father was there by lunch. He brought her a pastrami sandwich he had made himself, and they sat at her desk together, sketching out the table she had in mind.

The table took two weeks to build. Bridget could have had one of her guys knock it off for her in an afternoon, but she loved the chance to look up from her desk and see her father on the other side of the room, his gray head bent, intent upon making the best piece of furniture he possibly could for his little girl. She loved having lunch with him every day. Sometimes he brought her something from home; sometimes she convinced him to go out for a tuna sandwich at the local deli. But he never let her pay.

"You okay for money, darling?" He must have asked three times a day. No matter how she answered, he was always worried about her finances, sticking a twenty-dollar bill into her jacket pocket or the front of her purse whenever he thought she wasn't looking.

Bridget was sad when the table was finished, expecting her father to go back home and take up his job hunt again, but the next day he showed up as usual, a sandwich in one hand and a stack of newspapers in the other. He retrieved a yellow highlighter from Bridget's desk, settled himself at the table he had made, spread out the papers and glanced up at her. "I'll admit that there might be something to this female-led construction company thing, but you need my help," was all he said before he bent his head and began to read.

Every day for weeks, Bridget worked the phones. She called past clients to make sure they were satisfied and see if they needed anything else from her. She called people she had met at parties and luncheons who had shown any interest in what she did. She checked in with the small network of architects, building owners and owners' reps that she had come to know, seeing if they had anything new for her to bid on. But she was still stuck in the small-time renovation ghetto. She couldn't

seem to get anything commercial—everything involved bath-
tubs and new kitchens. She liked working in people's homes.
Small residential jobs kept her afloat. But if you really wanted
to be someone in construction, it had to be bigger—much
bigger. Bridget dreamed of a whole block of condos, an entire
chain of retail stores, ten stories of corporate offices, an entire
building from the ground up. She wanted stadiums and con-
cert halls. She wanted to build a skyscraper. And Bridget knew
she'd never get there if she couldn't find a crack into that side
of the market.

While she worked the phones, her father read every newspaper—from the *New York Times* and *Wall Street Journal* to the
New York Post. He was looking for businesses that were expanding or moving. Every day he would bring her pages and
pages of highlighted names of corporations that he insisted she
should be calling.

"What about this one, darling?"

Her father showed her a news story in the business section
of the *Times* about a chain of bookstores that was expanding
its headquarters.

"Russo Construction already won that bid," she said.

Her father frowned and turned the page. "Well, what about
this place, then?" A celebrity chef who wanted to open up his
own marketplace.

She shook her head. "Russo got that one, too."

Her father knit his brow. "Who is this Russo?"

"One of the biggest and oldest commercial contractors in
the city. If they want something, they get it."

"Hmph," said her dad, pulling out the *Wall Street Journal*.
"Well, have you heard about this development along the waterfront in the financial district? Eagle something—"

"Eagle Point. Yeah. Everyone has heard of it, Daddy. It's
been shut down."

He pursed his lips. "So prime real estate is just sitting there half built? Surely, they'll find the right construction company and start up again?"

She shook her head. "The last construction company tried to get around hiring union workers and hire only nonunion and the delegate shut the project down. Nobody is doing anything there now. Can't get any deliveries and no one will cross the picket line."

Her father looked her in the eye. "So you should call the developer."

She laughed in response. "Daddy, don't be silly. I'm not a union contractor. I don't have experience with that kind of building, and they're not going to want some random woman from the Bronx butting in, anyway."

He *tsk-tsked*. "I know I didn't raise a daughter who quits even before she begins."

"I'm not quitting anything, Daddy. It's just unrealistic and would be a complete waste of my time."

He smiled at her. "But how will you know that's true if you don't even try?"

The next morning Bridget came into the office, hung up her jacket, took one look at her father, who was already sitting there expectantly, highlighter at the ready, and shook her head as she picked up the phone.

"Hello, this is Bridget Steele of Steele Construction. I'd like to speak to Mr. Peter Hannity about the Eagle Point project."

She could see her father's satisfied smile beaming at her from all the way across the room.

"Oh, he's not available? May I leave my number?"

She dictated her number and then hung up the phone and looked at her still-grinning father. "Are you happy now?"

He shook his head. "Not yet."

★ ★ ★

It became a habit. Every morning, for twenty-five days in a row, Bridget walked into her office, hung up her jacket and called Peter Hannity's office. Before she had her coffee, before she started in on her long list of other calls she needed to make, sometimes before she even sat down, she made that call. And every morning, for twenty-five days in a row, she got the same polite refusal from Peter Hannity's secretary to put her through.

She knew it was hopeless. She knew that she had no business going after a job so beyond her experience. She didn't know what the scope of work would be and she'd hardly know where to begin even if she did get it. And every day, after she hung up the phone, she swore to herself that would be the last time she'd call.

But then the next morning she'd walk into her office, see her father's expectant smile and sigh. Then she'd pick up the phone again.

On the twenty-sixth day Bridget's office phone rang. A number she didn't recognize.

"Steele Construction," she said, making her voice both higher and more nasal so it would sound like she was her own secretary.

"May I speak with Miss Bridget Steele?"

"And whom shall I say is calling?"

"Mr. Peter Hannity."

Bridget blinked. Peter Hannity. Peter Hannity!

She was so excited she forgot to put him on hold before she changed back to her normal voice. "Mr. Hannity? This is Bridget Steele."

Hannity paused for a brief moment. "Oh." He chuckled. "Oh, I used to do the same thing when I was starting out. Except I had my wife answer and pretend to be my assistant."

Bridget laughed, embarrassed. "Well, um, I don't have a wife or a husband."

"Indeed, indeed... In any case, Miss Steele, I am calling because every day for this past month I have received a message from you, and every day I have ignored it. But I'm starting to get impressed by your persistence. Plus, my secretary just told me she would quit if I didn't finally call you back."

Bridget's heart felt like it was going to beat out of her chest. Her hands were shaking. She forced herself to sound calm. She looked for her father, who, for once, was not in the room. "Yes, sir. I wanted to speak to you about your Eagle Point development..."

"Daddy!" Bridget was roaring as soon as she got off the phone, running out the door to find her father sitting outside, nursing a cup of Dunkin' Donuts coffee and sitting on a hijacked office chair in the weak sunlight. "Daddy! Oh, my God! He called! He called!"

Her father turned to her, his face placid. "Who, darling?"

"Peter Hannity, Daddy! He wants me to come in and discuss Eagle Point! He wants to speak to me about negotiating with the union!"

Her father's face split into a beaming grin. "Oh, but that's wonderful news!"

Bridget stood there for a moment, suddenly washed in fear. She felt like she couldn't breathe. "But...but what do I know about negotiating with a union? And even if I manage to do that, what do I know about building something this big?"

Her father rolled his eyes. "Good Lord, Bridget. Your entire life has been nothing but negotiations. 'Bridget, take the garbage out.'" He mimicked her voice, "'I will if I can have extra dessert.' 'Bridget, pick up your towel off the floor.' 'I will if I can have the bigger, fluffier towel next time I take a bath.' And as for building something this big, what did I teach you? You can build anything if you take it piece by piece." He beamed at her. "You can do this. You know you can."

Bridget bit her lip, took a deep breath and slowly nodded. "You're right. I can. I can totally do this."

Her father reached for her hand and squeezed. "Now I'm happy."

It was odd, Bridget thought, where life takes you. If she hadn't been mugged, her father might not have brought her a model to build, and if she hadn't built that model, she might not now be standing dockside in the middle of a dead construction site, waiting for the union delegate, Sal Delmonico, from the Local 6, to show up.

Once a site bustling with hundreds of carpenters, electricians and masons all working like ants to build an ultra-exclusive condominium development for the mega-rich, now all that remained were stacks of rotting wood, moldy drywall and crumbling bricks strewn across the ghost town that had been advertised as the new premier private community in downtown Manhattan. Bridget shook her head at the abandoned garbage dump this priceless piece of property had become.

"It's a real shame, eh?" said a voice behind her.

Bridget turned to face a man wearing a blue polyester suit and what she was pretty sure was a fake Hermès tie. He was smoking a cigarette and his mustache put Sam Elliott to shame.

"You Steele?" asked the mustache.

"You must be Delmonico," said Bridget. She put out her hand to shake.

Delmonico waited a beat before he took it. His grip was so tight and clammy that Bridget could swear she heard a squelching noise as their hands parted.

"A girl, huh? What's Hannity's game here?"

Bridget shrugged. "No game. I was asked to negotiate a deal so we can move forward and get this project built."

Delmonico stared at her for a moment and then casually spat off to the side. "Let me paint you a picture," he said, making a sweep of his arm toward the water. "Women who look like a young Cindy Crawford sitting on the decks of their husbands' two-hundred-foot yachts, which are strategically docked smack dead in front of their condos that jet right out over the river. Three-hundred-sixty-degree views, floor-to-ceiling windows, plunge pools and gold-plated faucets. Chefs' kitchens that actually come with their own personal chefs." He paused to inhale from his Marlboro and then blew the smoke out of the corner of his mouth. "It was going to be a candy land sprinkled with diamonds, mink, big dicks, fake tits and cocaine."

"Sounds nice," said Bridget.

"It would've been."

"And you ended it all," said Bridget.

Delmonico smiled a big, satisfied grin. "And I ended it all. Kicked 'em in their balls so hard that they're still down on the floor crying like little girls. They came whining to me about how they couldn't afford to hire union labor. Wanted to make a deal so they could bring in a bunch of scabs. Said the whole job would go down if they couldn't cut costs. So I pulled the plug. One hundred percent union or no deal, I always say."

Bridget nodded thoughtfully. "How about fifty percent union?"

Delmonico's face scrunched up. "Did you not hear what I just said?"

"It sounded to me like you said you killed the chance for a whole lot of your guys to get some solid work. I wonder what they thought about that?"

Something passed over Delmonico's face and Bridget knew

that she'd hit a nerve. "My guys got more work than they can handle."

"Yeah? Because at the very least this is a two-year contract, and if the client likes what your guys and my nonunion guys can do, there'll be plenty of future projects for everyone."

Delmonico sneered. "What makes you think there will be future projects for you? I only brought you here to set you straight. You want to work with me and my local? You gotta know the score. Other guys have messed with me and see that river?" He pointed out to the steel-gray Hudson, still dotted with chunks of late-spring ice. "That's a real strong current. You'd get sucked right under the ice, if you happened to fall in."

Bridget felt her stomach clench, but she forced herself to laugh. "So now you're going to throw me in the river? Listen, Hannity told me to tell you that it's me or no one. He's sick of screwing around. If we can't make a deal, he's donating this property to the city to make a waterfront park and taking the tax write-off. How do you think your boys would feel about that?"

Delmonico looked at her sharply. Bridget kept her face carefully neutral, but her heart pounded. Hannity had said no such thing.

Delmonico threw the stub of his cigarette and ground it under his heel. He looked back at her. "And what do I get out of it?"

She frowned. "What do you mean? How about none of the guys from your local will be sitting on the bench for at least two years? That's what you get."

Delmonico took a step toward her. "Yeah, but say I agree to your terms—fifty percent union, fifty percent whatever dregs you bring in—what are you going to do to sweeten the deal?"

"Are you talking about a kickback? About money?"

He shrugged and grinned. His teeth were yellow and stained.

"Money or—" he let his eyes drop to her breasts "—whatever else you think might make me feel good about things."

She folded her arms over her chest. "Not if you were the last man on earth, Delmonico."

He laughed and reached for her. "Look at them nice big titties."

She grabbed his wrist and twisted just like her dad had taught her.

"Ow! Shit! That hurts!" he yelped.

She twisted harder. "You know what else I've got, Delmonico? A nice big mouth. You think the press would like to hear the story of the union head who molested the sweet, innocent girl contractor?" She glanced at the ring on his finger. "You think your wife wants to hear about that, too?" She threw down his arm.

He sneered at her as he rubbed his wrist. "You're going to be sorry you ever met me, Steele."

She turned to go. "I already am."

Bridget sat in her apartment in the dark, a glass of cheap tequila on the table in front of her. She didn't know whether to drink or cry.

She'd been so close. She'd almost had it in her hands. The kind of project that would have changed everything. The kind of shot that she was pretty sure she'd never see again. Damn Sal Delmonico and his stupid freaking mustache.

She looked at the drink and sighed. She had yet to call Hannity and she knew she couldn't wait any longer. Better to get it over with so she could get drunk in peace.

She reached for the phone, but before she could pick it up, it rang.

"Hello?"

"Well, I guess your persistence paid off again!"

She blinked. "Mr. Hannity?"

"You're a genius, Bridget! I don't know what you said to Delmonico, but he's in. Fifty-fifty just like we planned. We can start work again next week!"

She was stunned. "We can?"

"So I'll see you Monday at my office? We've got a lot to do."

She gulped. Her hands were shaking. "Yes. I mean, yes, sir. Thank you, sir."

"No, Bridget, thank you!" He chuckled. "I had a feeling about you, and honestly, I could not be more delighted that it panned out. Go celebrate! This is a very, very big moment for you and your company."

Bridget hung up the phone, sat for a moment. Her heart was beating so fast, she thought it would explode. She picked up her drink.

"To...to Steele Construction," she whispered as she brandished her drink in the air. She took a gulp and grinned as the tequila burned down her throat.

Then she picked the phone back up to call her father.

CHAPTER 4

After Bridget brought in the Eagle Point job ahead of schedule, within budget and with minimal change orders, her reputation as a premier builder got out, and a flood of requests came rolling in: Bloomingdale's, Carnegie Hall Towers, Yahoo.com, Coty, Inc., work on Scarlett Hawkins's corporate offices and estates that netted Bridget TV and print exposure.

Steele Construction was finally at the top of the NYC construction game. The projects were large—fifty thousand square feet and above—and the brand names she worked for were even bigger.

Bridget found herself walking the halls of Sotheby's painting storage facilities as the curator pointed out Pollocks and Manets and Warhols, Picassos, Cassatts and Kahlos.

"Each piece," said the curator, a tall, angular woman with severely parted silver hair, "is given an individual temperature- and light-controlled compartment before it's brought up for auction. We need to make more room, of course—we're expanding—but we also need to modernize

everything, the HVAC, the lighting, the humidity control."
She slid out a small, brightly colored painting of a chair and
looked knowingly at Bridget. "A lesser-known van Gogh,"
she said, pronouncing the "Gogh" with a hard, guttural *goff*
sound. "Do you like it?"

Bridget nodded, awed. The painting practically gleamed
with otherworldly beauty. She imagined how it would feel to
own such a thing.

"We expect the first bids on this painting to be upwards of
fifteen million dollars. So you see, with these kinds of stakes,
there is no room for error. We are responsible for some of the
finest treasures in the world, and we take that very seriously.
Everything must be perfect. Nothing overlooked. Which is
why we hired you. We have been assured that you never miss
a thing."

Over the next five years, Bridget felt like she was in a
dream. Her life was turning into everything she ever thought
she wanted. She moved out of her dark little studio and into
an airy two-bedroom condo in Tribeca. She gave up her office in Mt. Vernon and rented an entire floor on Forty-Fifth
Street. She built a vacation home in the Hamptons. She had
the clothes, the shoes, the jewelry, the three-hour-long meals
in swanky restaurants and the car and driver. The press got
wind of her and she started showing up on the local news,
the real estate section of the *Times*, then *People* magazine
and *Architectural Digest*: "The Girl in the Hard Hat"; "Female
Contractor Breaking Glass Ceilings!"

Steele Construction was booming. Bridget's head of operations was Ethan Jackson, who had a full staff of project managers, field supervisors—Danny Schwartz was overseeing the
field guys—a chief estimator with five senior and junior estimators under him, CFO, comptroller and a full accounting

department—Mrs. Hashemi kept them all in line—and various support staff at her beck and call. Even though the largest projects were still going to Russo Construction—"Russo!" Her father would shake his fist in the air and say it like a curse every time they lost another top-tier job to the monolith of a company—the requests for proposals and project awards kept rolling in, and Bridget kept accepting them.

It wasn't easy, though. Bridget had come to accept it would never be easy. She still had to scratch and claw to get the projects into her office to bid and get the jobs. Nobody was going to make room for her at the table; she had to force her way in. She was still denied access to the old boys' club and the highest level of the work. No golfing, no fishing, no strip clubs or steam rooms or cigar bars for her. It meant hearing hissing whispers of "Nice ass!" and "Nice tits!" as she walked through the site. It meant that there was always some joker who thought it was hilarious to ask her if she knew the difference between a flat- and Phillips-head screwdriver. It meant letting clients' hands wander when they put an arm around her and finding a way to fend off their passes in a way that didn't hurt their fragile egos. It meant being ogled and leered at, talked down to, grudgingly tolerated, made to feel like an impostor on her own job sites. It meant breaking her back to earn the respect of her workers and clients again and again.

Her father worried about her. "You're working so hard, darling. Why don't you take a day off once in a while?"

But Bridget would just smile, shrug and say, "I'm fine, Daddy. I like working," trying not to notice the ever-present tremor in his hands. A year before, he'd been diagnosed with Parkinson's, though he and Bridget's mother assured her it was hardly progressing at all.

Steele Construction was awarded a contract for a fashion company at one of their new retail stores on Long Island's

South Shore. It was way out of Bridget's territory, but she figured it was a good chance to expand, and she still kept to her longtime habit of taking any reasonable job offered. She didn't have any contacts on Long Island, so when an electrical subcontractor she was working with in Manhattan told her he'd worked with a good carpentry sub out there named Kevin Byrne, after having a lengthy conversation on the phone, she hired him sight unseen. He told her not to worry; he would get things rolling until she could be there in person to meet.

The moment Bridget walked onto the job site, she knew she'd made a mistake. There were clouds of dust everywhere, jagged studs and drywall strewn around like confetti at a New Year's Eve party. The site was a gigantic mess.

"Can I help you?" A deep voice echoed from behind her.

Bridget turned and looked up into the bright blue eyes of one of the most gorgeous men she'd ever seen. Mussed blond hair, golden skin, shoulders and arms that made it very clear he built things for a living, a pair of faded Levi's that hugged all the right places, a slow, sexy smile that only grew wider as she took a step forward and her stiletto caught on a discarded metal two-by-four.

She felt herself begin to fall.

"Whoa, there," the man said as he caught her round the waist just before she hit the floor.

He pulled her upright and Bridget recognized his scent—Tom Ford Oud. *Pretty pricey for a Long Island drywall guy*, she thought. Also, *Damn, his biceps are the size of softballs.*

"It's really not a good idea to wear six-inch heels on a job site," he said, grinning.

She realized his hands were still on her, and took a step away, shaking him off. "They are only three inches," she said stiffly. "And I wouldn't have tripped if you had kept a clean job site. This place is a disgrace. Where are your containers, green dust, temp lights?"

He raised an amused eyebrow. "Bridget, I presume?"

She straightened her spine. "Ms. Steele to you," she said. "And you are Mr. Byrne?"

"Kevin," he said. "And I'm sorry about the mess. You're right. I'll talk to my laborers."

She frowned, only slightly mollified by his apology.

"Anyway," he said, "I was just about to run out to get some lunch. You want to come with or shall we talk when I get back?"

She stared at him for a moment, wondering if he would have invited a male boss out to lunch in such a casual way, but he didn't seem to notice. He took off his hard hat and placed it on a bench, wiping his sweaty brow with his muscular forearm. His T-shirt rode up and exposed three ridges of what Bridget was pretty sure was a rock-hard six-pack. She felt an unwelcome answering tingle in her own belly.

"It'll only be, like, fifteen minutes," he said, heading for the door. "You coming? There's a good sandwich place down the street," he said, pausing to give her a long, slow look over his broad shoulder.

Bridget considered firing him. She knew she should. Certainly no one could possibly blame her if she did. But instead she shook her head. "You go," she said, "I want to inspect the rest of the site."

Kevin shrugged. "Your choice, of course." He turned back toward the door.

"I am not happy with how my job site is being run, Mr. Byrne," called out Bridget. "This all needs to be cleaned up the minute you get back."

He turned back and smiled. "Yes, boss," he said as he headed out the door.

★ ★ ★

He had called her later that night, asking her to meet him for dinner the next day, a Saturday, so he could clarify some questions from the drawings.

"Can't we just discuss this over the phone?" asked Bridget, exasperated.

"No," said Kevin. "We need to go over the plans in person. Seven o'clock? There's a great Italian place next to Town Hall. Francesco's."

"Fine," said Bridget, partially annoyed and partially already planning what she would wear.

He sprang to his feet as she entered the restaurant. His gorgeous blue eyes slowly raked her from head to toe. "You look amazing," he said.

Bridget blushed with pleasure and then inwardly cursed her own weakness. She had dressed carefully, discarding the armor of her usual pinstriped suit for a soft lilac Versace dress that covered up her cleavage but left a mile of leg exposed. It wasn't exactly professional, but she had given in to her desire to look pretty, and now she was paying for it. Because he was not looking at her the way a man should look at his boss.

And she had to admit that some part of her liked that.

"Thank you," she said crisply. She took a seat. "Now, what were your questions?"

Kevin grinned and sat back down. He took a sip of his drink, reached for a briefcase next to his chair.

Gucci, thought Bridget, eyeing the bag with interest. *This guy has got expensive taste.*

The waiter stopped by for her drink order. "The lady will have a scotch on the rocks," said Kevin with a smile.

Bridget frowned. "The lady will have sparkling water," she corrected.

The waiter looked back and forth between them.

"Come on, Ms. Steele," said Kevin. "It's Saturday night. I'm sure you've earned it."

Bridget sighed. "Fine. I will have a glass of Don Julio 1942. Neat." She looked Kevin in the eyes. "I hate scotch."

He smiled to himself as he pulled out a notebook and flipped it open. Bridget craned her neck to see a page-long list. "Those are a lot of questions," she said.

He shrugged. "I like to be thorough." He reached into the bag again and removed a pen. "Okay, so let's start with question number one: What's your favorite flower?"

Bridget knit her brow. "What does that have to do with the job?"

He chuckled. His laugh was deep and warm. Bridget felt it in her gut. "It doesn't."

Bridget paused for a moment. She took the list from his hands and flipped it around. "Favorite flower," she read out loud. "Favorite chocolates, favorite color…" She looked up at him and felt a blush creeping up the back of her neck. "Preferred brand of lingerie?"

He grinned wolfishly. "I told you I like to be thorough."

This was the moment when she needed to either tell him off and leave the table, or simply fire him right then and there. Instead, she shook her head and laughed at his audaciousness.

Their eyes met, and he took that as the invitation it was and reached across the table, placing his hand on her wrist, softly tugging her toward him.

"Mr. Byrne—" she protested weakly.

He shook his head. "God damn it, Bridget, I'm about to kiss you. So I really think you better go ahead and call me Kevin."

Later that night Bridget untangled her limbs from his and stretched out on the bed next to him. She felt like purring.

I've earned this, she thought to herself as she watched him fold his arms behind his head and smile at her with a look of wicked pride. *The way I've been working these past few years, I should be allowed a good-looking distraction.*

"You want anything?" he asked her. "You hungry? Thirsty?"

She shook her head lazily.

He sat up and put his feet on the floor. "Okay, well, I'm going to go fix myself a scotch on the rocks." He winked at her. "Just like you hate."

She felt the breath catch in her throat as he stood and stretched, his powerful naked body on full display. *Holy hell, what a man.* She could still feel the way every part of him had felt against every part of her.

"Peonies," she called out to him as he padded out of the room, not bothering to put his clothes back on.

He turned back toward her. "Huh?"

"My favorite flower." She smiled. "White peonies."

Kevin came through on the Long Island job on time and budget, with very little drama—if you didn't count the fact that the GC was sleeping with her sub—so Bridget decided she wanted to bring him in on something bigger. She was up for a four-floor build-out for the corporate headquarters of iSplash, a mass media company that focused exclusively on female users. It was a much bigger job than the Long Island project had been, but she wanted Kevin to know that she really believed in him.

"I think I have it in the bag," she told him. He had come into town for the weekend and they were having dinner at Nobu. "They loved my presentation. The founders made a point of telling me how great they thought it was. And for once, I think me being a woman is actually going to be a good thing." She laughed. "Suck it, Russo!"

Kevin gave her a crooked grin and swiped a scallop from

her plate as he flagged down the waiter. "Another scotch," he said. He looked at her. "You need anything?"

She shook her head. "Anyway, I'm just waiting for the final call to firm it all up—but I'm pretty sure Steele Construction has it—and I was thinking—" she met his eyes, excited to see how he'd react "—that I'd bring you in as my carpentry subcontractor."

Kevin paused, his fork halfway to his mouth. "Yeah? In Manhattan?"

She laughed. "I think you can do it. In fact, I think you'd be great."

He gulped down the last of his drink. "Why not electrical, too? You know I'm licensed."

Her smile faded a bit. "Yeah, but you're licensed in Suffolk County, not New York City."

He shrugged. "I can have someone cover my license."

"Both? You think you can handle that?"

He shrugged. "Of course I can. I've done bigger jobs."

She frowned. "But it's different in the city. There's greater risk and way more logistics. Maybe you should just start with one trade at a time."

He smiled at her. "Come on. Don't you trust me?"

"Well, sure. That's why I'm offering you the carpentry trade. But—"

He took her hand. "Don't worry. I got it." He looked around. "Now, where's that drink I ordered?"

They were still in bed the next morning when her phone rang.

Bridget slid lazily across Kevin's chest to grab her cell off the bedside table.

"Ms. Steele? It's Bob Jones. From iSplash."

The owner's rep. Bridget smiled happily, anticipating what he was going to say.

"I'm just calling to let you know that Steele Construction is being awarded the iSplash contract."

Her grin got bigger. She poked Kevin on the shoulder and gave him a thumbs-up.

"But I want you to know that your award is against my explicit advice to the client and architect. I am certain they are hiring you simply because you are a woman and not because Steele is the most qualified for this project. They like the optics, but I am more than sure you will be in well over your head. I advised them not to award you this project. And I would advise you to turn this job down before you are embarrassed by getting into something you can't handle."

Bridget felt like she had been punched in the gut. Even with a company founded and created for women, she was getting this bullshit.

"Well, Mr. Jones, luckily you are not the person making the decisions. I will see you nice and early Monday morning." She hung up the phone, her heart beating wildly, trying to hold back the tears. Kevin looked at her expectantly.

"What an asshole!" she burst out.

He cocked his eyebrow. "You didn't get it?"

She shook her head. "I got it. But he said they only hired me because I'm a woman. He actually had the nerve to tell me that I should turn the job down."

Kevin frowned. "Maybe I should talk to him?"

She shot him a confused look. "Why would you talk to him? It's my company."

"Man to man? Let him know there's someone he can communicate with?"

"What the hell are you talking about? Why would I—"

Kevin shrugged his shoulders. "Just want us to get off on the right foot with him, is all." He reached over and kneaded her shoulders and, without thinking, she leaned into him. "But I'm sure you can handle it, babe."

Bridget and Kevin were at a fund-raising party for The Robin Hood Foundation. It had been four months since they started at the iSplash job and things were not going well. Even though their contract was signed, Kevin kept coming to her with extras for things he'd missed on the drawings, claiming that he needed more men to make the schedule.

Bridget was in the corner of the room, talking to Ava and nursing a tequila. Trying not to watch Kevin flirt with half the women at the party.

"So," said Ava, giving Kevin the eye as he placed his hand on a tall redhead's arm. "Your boyfriend seems nice. Real friendly."

Bridget rolled her eyes. "It's harmless. He's a flirt, is all. He can't help himself."

Ava raised her eyebrows but kept quiet, burying her nose in her glass of champagne.

A trio of people entered the room, obviously just arriving. There was a small Asian woman, impossibly chic, wearing a bright red wool cape with an oversize hood, her lips the same crimson as the coat, a dusting of snow still glittering on her shoulders and around the edges of her jacket. She was flanked on either side by two good-looking white men in top coats and suits, one with black hair, one with brown. They both leaned toward her like she was the only woman in the room. The woman smiled as the brown-haired man took her cape, exposing a simple charcoal-colored dress so stylishly cut that Bridget suddenly felt like the Gucci sheath she had on was from Frederick's of Hollywood.

"Who are they?"

Ava followed her gaze. "Ah. The Russos. You've never met them?"

Bridget blinked. "Russo as in Russo Construction? I thought that bastard was, like, eighty million years old."

Ava shook her head. "This is the son, Jason. You're thinking of his father. He died about six months ago."

Bridget bit her lip. "I didn't know."

Ava shrugged. "Jason got everything. Took over the whole company. And from what I hear, he's doing brilliantly."

Bridget laughed. "I'll say. Still taking every other job we're up for."

She squinted, curious about the man who had been her nemesis ever since she had started working in Manhattan. He was tall, with broad shoulders and a tapered waist. Not as big as Kevin, but still well built. His dark, wavy hair was combed back, but one curl kept falling onto his forehead, resisting his attempts to push it away. Unlike most of the men in the room, his suit wasn't a flashy Italian cut, but his clothes were immaculately tailored, the kind of fit that only happened when they were bespoke. She dreamily wondered if they were from Savile Row. Suddenly, he looked up and locked eyes with Bridget, catching her staring. He smiled at her, and she felt her cheeks heat up as she quickly looked away.

"The woman?" she said to Ava to cover up her embarrassment.

"Jason's wife, Hana Takada. She's a painter. Really good. Only moderately successful, but what does that matter when you're married to a billionaire?"

"And who's the other guy?"

Ava looked over again. "Oh, that's his partner and COO, Liam Maguire. Kind of a jerk, actually, but also a brilliant operator."

"No wonder we can't win against them," muttered Bridget.

"Um," said Ava, shifting her attention. "I don't mean to stir up trouble, but is your boyfriend going into the bathroom with that redhead?"

Bridget jerked her head just in time to see Kevin slip into the powder room, shutting the door behind him. She didn't hesitate, just marched across the room and barged right into the bathroom after him.

The redhead was crouched on top of the toilet while Kevin was bent over the sink, about to insert a rolled fifty-dollar bill up his nose.

"Kevin!" She couldn't decide if she was more upset about the woman or the drugs.

He glanced up at her, deadpan. "Oh, hey, babe. You want some?"

"No!" she spluttered. "I want to go home!"

He nodded. "Yeah, this party is dead. Okay. Just give me and—" he looked over at the redhead "—Nadya, right?"

The redhead nodded.

"Just let me finish up with Nadya, here, and then we can go." He bent back over the line of coke and snorted it up, smiling.

Embarrassed and furious, Bridget turned and left, slamming the bathroom door behind her, heading for the exit without even saying goodbye to Ava.

Late that night he materialized at her bedside, waking her from a restless sleep. She regretted giving him a key.

"Hey, babe. You left so fast. I was worried," he said, putting down a shopping bag he was carrying and stroking her hair. "Is something wrong?"

She whipped her head away from his hand. "Are you kidding me?" she choked out. "You were doing coke in the bathroom with some random woman. Of course something is wrong!"

He looked genuinely puzzled. "Oh, geez. I was just having a little fun. I mean, I almost never do the hard stuff, but the party was so boring, and Natalie had some blow and she just asked me if I wanted to share, that's all. Nothing else happened."

"Nadya," Bridget corrected miserably.

He climbed onto the bed next to her, smelling like cigarettes and scotch. "Who?"

"Her name wasn't Natalie. It was Nadya. And that was hours ago. Where have you been?"

He reached for the shopping bag. "I've been shopping. I got you something," he said, placing the bag on her lap and then stroking her arm. "You look so pretty when you first wake up, Bridge. I never met a girl who looks so hot in bed."

She glared at him. "Jesus, Kevin, how dumb do you think I am? You can't just buy me a present and tell me I'm pretty and expect me to forget what an ass you are."

He smiled at her. "You're also the crankiest person I know when you wake up." He nudged the bag. "Come on. Open it."

She looked at the bag for a moment and then sighed, opening it. Inside were five pairs of gorgeous La Perla panties in a rainbow of colors. She shook her head. Bridget knew that each pair cost at least a hundred bucks.

He pushed the bag toward her again. "There's more. I've been waiting to surprise you with these."

She reached past the lingerie and grasped an envelope. Two tickets to Bermuda. For five days. Leaving next week.

"A pair for every day we're there. And I can't wait to rip them off you one by one."

She shook her head. "Kevin. I can't."

"What are you talking about? Of course you can. Ethan can take care of things at work while you're gone."

"Even if he could, I don't want to leave my dad. He's not doing so well lately."

"Babe, he would want you to go! He's always talking about how you need to take a vacation."

She shook her head again. "No, I—"

He moved the bag aside and rolled over on top of her, pressing her down into the mattress and letting her feel the weight of his body on hers. "You can," he said, kissing the tip of her nose. "You can and you will. Do you want to hurt my feelings?" He kissed her cheek and then her neck. "You know how hard it was to get the underwear lady to let me into the shop? She was one of those tough old broads, and they were about to close for the night. I had to tell her that I'd done my girl wrong and needed to make it up to her."

She laughed, imagining Kevin charming his way into the La Perla boutique.

He smiled. "You're laughing. Does that mean you'll come?"

She looked up into his sky-blue eyes, imagined them walking down the white sand beaches together, playing in the warm aqua water, making love in the tropical heat. It was twenty-five degrees outside in Manhattan and snowing...

"Okay," she finally said. "But about Nadya—"

"Shhh," said Kevin as he slowly unbuttoned her pajama top and flicked his tongue down her neck. "We can talk later. Let's not spoil the moment, okay?"

I have to break up with him, Bridget thought as she watched Kevin bodysurf in the turquoise water. It hurt her to admit it, and it especially hurt watching him right now, his tanned and muscular chest and shoulders gleaming in the tropical sun, his smile so bright that Bridget felt her own lips automatically curl up in answer.

She thought about the night before, when they had snuck out after dark to the empty, glimmering, white sand beach. The ocean reflected the starlight in a blanket of tiny sparks as

Kevin dared her to skinny-dip. Never one to back down from a dare, Bridget had instantly stripped off the long, billowing, powder-blue sundress she'd been wearing, and then ran, naked and laughing, toward the surf.

Kevin was two steps behind her, and he scooped her up into his arms as they plunged in together, carrying her out into the sea until Bridget twisted and wrapped her legs around his hips and twined her hands in his hair. He kissed the salt from her lips until she was dizzy with pleasure.

But after, back in the bungalow, he had nonchalantly taken out a small plastic bag and begun chopping a line of coke on the kitchen counter.

"Jesus, Kevin," she said. "What are you doing?"

He laughed. "We're on vacation, babe! Let's have some fun!"

"But where did you even get that?"

He smiled at her. "Smuggled it on the bottom of my stick of deodorant."

She gasped. "You flew with that? Oh, my God, are you freaking nuts? That's a felony!"

He rolled his eyes. "Relax. I've done it a million times. And I didn't get caught, did I? It's no big deal."

But it was a big deal. Bridget was no prude. She'd smoked her share of pot in college—it made her hungry and then paranoid that she was going to double her size from eating so much—and had even tried coke once with an old boyfriend. She liked it so much, she swore to herself she'd never touch it again. But deep down, she knew it was different for Kevin. He'd been staying with her since the iSplash job started and she'd begun to see things that worried her. She thought about the constant glass of scotch in his hand, the way he rolled a joint like it was second nature, the way she sometimes had to beg him to get out of bed in the morning and make it to the work site. Twice now, she'd had people tell her that he'd missed meetings with no explanation, and after all that bluster about being able to do the carpentry and the electrical work, she'd ended up having to sub-contract the electric trade out for nearly twice as much as she had initially estimated.

If it had been any other guy, Bridget would have kicked him to the curb months ago. She told herself it was the sex—which remained phenomenal—or the fact that she was sick of being lonely, and it was so hard to meet a decent guy when she was working all the time. But the truth? The part she could hardly admit, even to herself?

She had fallen in love with him.

Maybe I can fix this, she thought as she watched him play around with a couple of tourist kids who had joined him in the waves. *Maybe if I just talk to him—tell him he needs to cut back...*

But then she thought about the way he'd changed after he'd snorted the cocaine the night before. How pissed he'd been that she wouldn't take any with him. How he started motor-mouthing at her, talking nonsense, going on and on, repeating himself for minutes on end. His eyes had been shining with a crazed light she didn't recognize. It had terrified her.

Tonight, she thought. They were going home tomorrow morning. Better to get it over with tonight and have a fresh start when she got back home.

They had reservations at a restaurant right on the beach, and Bridget dressed carefully in a pristine white, one-shouldered jumpsuit. She pulled her hair back and painted her lips a soft pink, added gold hoops and a shimmer of gold shadow to her eyes to match the slim gold chain belt around her waist. She thought they could enjoy one last nice meal together before she broke her own heart.

"For you, babe," Kevin said as she emerged from the bedroom. He was holding a huge bouquet of white peonies.

She almost cried as she crushed the flowers to her chest and buried her face in the sweet scent. "They're not even in season right now. Where did you get them?"

He smiled. "I have my ways." He pushed a lock of hair from her brow. "This last week has been amazing. Thank you."

The week had been amazing. It had been amazing and beautiful and heartbreaking and now it had to end. If she waited, she'd never be able to do it. It had to be now.

"Kevin, listen—" she began, but suddenly the bungalow phone was ringing. They looked at each other. "Who?" said Bridget as she turned to pick up the phone.

"Bridget?" Her mother's voice sounded so far away.

"Ma?"

"Bridget? It's about your father."

CHAPTER 5

Five years later the phone rang and Bridget opened her eyes with a gasp. She rolled over and groped for the cell on her bedside table, desperate to silence the blast of "Welcome to the Jungle" that had interrupted her dreams.

Kevin groaned and flung himself away from her, yanking the covers and leaving her with just a sheet between her skin and the early spring chill.

She squinted at the phone before putting it to her ear. "Ethan?" She cleared her throat, trying to get rid of the morning thickness. "It's five o'clock in the morning. This better be good."

Ethan didn't bother with a greeting. "Bridget, we've got a problem. I just talked to Manuel and there's a rat over at Scarlett's job."

Bridget rubbed her eyes as she blew out an exasperated breath. "And? Tell him to call the exterminator."

"No, not that kind of rat. Try a thirty-foot-tall, rubber, blow-up rat. I think it's even got a name—Scabby. It's blocking all traffic going in and out of the building."

Bridget sat up, suddenly wide awake. "Wait. A union rat? Why is there a union rat outside our job?"

"The rep, Delmonico? He insists we've got nonunion guys working there."

She groaned. "That's bullshit! My guys are all from the Local 6. It's totally clean!"

"That's what I told him, but he wouldn't back down. And he said that there will be fifty guys over there by eight o'clock with picket signs. Oh, and the press. He said he's contacting the press."

Bridget felt her breath catch in her throat. The press. No. No. Freaking no. This on top of everything else? It was a disaster. Scarlett would murder her.

When Steele Construction landed the job to renovate Scarlett Hawkins's brand-new corporate headquarters, the shock waves were felt from Harlem all the way down to the Wall Street bull. Sure, Steele Construction had always been Scarlett's go-to when she needed her beach house touched up or a gut job on her penthouse on Central Park West, but this was a whole new level. It was the biggest job Steele Construction had ever been given. Every construction company in Manhattan had been trying to get their paws on this contract. The publicity alone—building something this huge for the world's most famous lifestyle queen and tastemaker, the uber-Domestic Goddess herself—was enough to set up a company for life.

"I'm taking a chance on you, darlin'," said Scarlett in her honeyed Georgia accent when she herself called to tell Bridget she was giving her the job. "This isn't just some kitchen in the Hamptons. You know our timetable and the level of quality I expect. I went to bat for you. I'm going to want you to personally inspect every single detail of this project, be there for every meeting, check every god damned bricklayer and errand boy for janky credit scores and canker sores, and I don't want to hear one peep about any other clients your company might be working for. As far as I'm concerned, I own you from the moment we sign the contracts until the day I cut the ribbon with a pair of those delightfully oversize novelty scissors. Are you up for that?"

And there had been a moment—a split second in time—when Bridget had thought *no. No, I am absolutely not up for that.*

Her company had grown too big, too fast in the past few years. Her habit of never saying no had started to backfire. They were already overextended on half a dozen other major jobs. Kevin had branched out and started his own drywall business and it was hemorrhaging cash by the day. They had a four-year-old son who sometimes called the nanny "Mommy," and Bridget's father…good God, she still couldn't think of her father without wanting to lie down on the floor and wail with grief and loss…

But then Bridget took a deep breath and reminded herself that this was the kind of job that she had started Steele Construction for in the first place. She had scratched and clawed for years to make something like this happen. She'd be an idiot if she didn't reach right out and grab this thing by the balls and twist as hard as she could.

So the split second passed, and she gulped down her doubts and told Scarlett yes and thank-you and then hung up the phone and tried to look happy as she asked Kevin to break out their best bottle of champagne.

But maybe, she thought to herself as she sat in her bed, *I should have listened to that little voice inside me.*

Because from that moment on, it had been one disaster after another. The architect Scarlett had hired handed Bridget a set of construction documents that made her eyes pop—five floors and two hundred thousand square feet of exposed two-by-fours. The place would look like the inside of an outhouse. When Bridget raised her concerns, the architect had a fit. "This is cutting-edge and modern," he'd screamed at her. "Something you obviously wouldn't understand." Bridget calmly took his abuse and then turned around and told Scarlett that it would look like crap and that she should fire her architect. But Scarlett shrugged off her concerns, already wed to the design. "I trust you. I'm sure you'll make it look wonderful," she'd said to Bridget, barely taking her eyes off her phone.

Then Kevin's drywall business finally went belly-up and Bridget lost every single cent she had sunk into it, which was a huge financial hit. Not only on cash but also in human resources when she had to replace the drywall subs on all her projects. This in turn necessitated that Bridget put even more attention toward Scarlett's build, so the other jobs Steele Construction had already taken on began to suffer, as well. Practically overnight, her company went from one of the best construction businesses in Manhattan to a heaving, trembling pile of debt and poor planning.

Anything Scarlett Hawkins did was going to attract attention. Not just press, but the kind of attention that brought all sorts of scummy politicians and union reps and two-bit hustlers out of the proverbial woodwork. With one hand in the kitty and the other trying to creep up Bridget's thigh, these men whispered their demands and threats and backroom deals. The Manhattan construction world was small and incestuous and ran by its own set of rules, and Bridget was the ultimate outsider who had muscled her way in. They wanted to test her and test her hard.

The mayor himself called to let Bridget know just what businesses she could and couldn't source her building supplies from. She had to go with a place she'd never worked with before, and when they were delivered, all those thousands of two-by-fours were full of knots and cracks.

"It will look rustic," said the supplier.

"You want your permits to go smooth, don't you?" said the mayor.

"You're already behind," said the architect. "Just get building."

"I trust you to figure this out, darlin'," said Scarlett.

And so, against all her instincts, Bridget started to build.

And the press was all over it. Everyone loved the story of the only woman contractor in Manhattan working with the world's most powerful businesswoman. Poor little Bronx girl clawing her way up the ladder, breaking into the most sexist industry in America. Petite, pretty Bridget Steele—crashing through that glass ceiling, becoming CEO of her own major construction company. A pioneer, they called her. A role model. And Bridget teaming up with the beloved Scarlett Hawkins, to completely redo all two hundred thousand square feet of the Scarlett Hawkins Inc. Flagship Store and Corporate Headquarters? That was the kind of juicy Girl Power story that made and stayed front-page news.

Still, Bridget knew only too well that the same press would be just as thrilled to report on her spectacular fall as they had been to gush about her climb to the top. Nothing sold more copy than a big, fat, public failure.

And that's what this is going to be if I don't fix this, thought Bridget as she closed her eyes and felt a violent headache bloom at her temples. The headline blared in her mind: How Steele Construction Crashed and Burned.

"Has anyone called yet?" she croaked into the phone. "Have you heard from any reporters?"

"Not yet," said Ethan in return.

"Okay, listen, if they do call, don't talk to anyone. No comment from us just yet."

"And what about the rat?" asked Ethan.

She gripped the phone tighter. The freaking rat. "This is insane. Why would anyone think we're not using union—" She stopped suddenly, the pit of her stomach turning to ice. "Oh, my God, hang on a second."

She dropped the phone and shoved her husband's shoulder. "Kevin?" she said. "Kevin, wake up."

Kevin slit his eyes open. "Jesus, Bridget, what time is it?"

"Last week did you deal with replacing those carpenters at Scarlett's job like I asked you to?"

He blinked and scratched his chin. "What are you talking about?"

She tried to stay calm. "The carpenters. Did you do it or not?"

He yawned. The smell of stale scotch on his breath made her wrinkle her nose in disgust. "Oh, right. I told Danny to do it."

Danny.

Danny Schwartz. In his sixties now. He'd always looked out for her. Helped her through. He was like a second dad to her. The only father she had left, really, since her own dad had passed away. But Danny had no relationship with the delegate and had no business hiring carpenters.

She looked at her husband, who pulled a pillow over his head and rolled back over. She picked the phone back up, barely keeping herself together. "It was Danny."

"What?" said Ethan. "But the union knows Danny isn't working with tools any longer and they leave him alone."

She shook her head. "No, Danny brought in ten new guys last week. They must not have cards."

"Oh, no," said Ethan. "Who the hell told him to do that?"

She looked at her husband's naked shoulders. He'd already fallen back asleep. "Kevin," she said flatly.

She felt nauseated. She never used to let things slip like this. She never would have asked Kevin to take care of something she could do herself. Being a woman in this business, she did not have the luxury of ever taking her eye off the ball. For her, there were no second chances. She had to be ten times better to even be considered half as good. She was not allowed mistakes.

But then her father had died.

She flashed back to the day five years earlier when she had rushed straight from Bermuda to his bedside at the hospital in the Bronx. It had all happened so quickly, her mother had said. He'd gone in for testing for the Parkinson's and they had realized he had a UTI and a raging fever, so they'd hospitalized him so he could get IV antibiotics. It was only supposed to be overnight. Her mother had wanted to call Bridget, but her father had insisted she not be bothered when she was finally on vacation.

Overnight had turned into two days, then three and four. The fever kept coming and going. He was in and out of consciousness, sometimes babbling nonsense, but when he was lucid, he still insisted he would be fine. To let Bridget enjoy her time off.

But then he crashed. And he was rushed to ICU. And Bridget's mother panicked. "You need to come home right now," she told Bridget, agony in her voice. "It might already be too late."

Her father was still alive when Bridget arrived, but alone and asleep. Her mother was out of the room, talking to another round of doctors. Bridget had been overwhelmed when she saw how pale and thin he was, the tube in his nose and all the wires and bandages running from his arms and chest.

"Daddy?" she'd whispered. Her voice trembled. And just like

that, an alarm went off—a high-pitched scream and a flat line on one of his screens that hadn't been flat before, and Bridget knew that something was terribly wrong.

She had run out into the hallway, screaming for help, grabbing at anyone she could find, her mouth and throat dry, her heart pounding out of her chest. "Please!" she remembered crying out. "Please!"

And they'd saved him. They'd shocked him and his heart had started pumping again, and then they'd rushed him into surgery, and for two more weeks, Bridget had her father back with her. She was there round the clock, letting Ethan and Danny and Kevin take over things at work, refusing to leave her father's side. Kevin brought her clothes and food, took care of her when she'd let him. Her mother begged her to go home just for a night, to shower and get some real rest. But Bridget's father was not always himself—he'd fade in and out. Sometimes asking her how her trip had been, how work was going, what project was next, sometimes, excited as a little boy, describing the new model he'd bought for them to make together, and sometimes he simply didn't recognize her. Bridget couldn't bring herself to leave, afraid she'd miss those brief moments when he was whole and there and lucid.

Finally, two weeks in, assured that he was stable, knowing that she smelled terrible from not having washed in days, afraid she would collapse if she spent one more night in a hospital chair, she let a kindly nurse talk her into going home—just for one night. She kissed her dad good-night and told him she'd see him in the morning, that she'd be back real soon.

"Darling?" her father had said as she started to walk out of the room. "Are you set for money? Can I give you a little something?"

Tears sprang into her eyes. She rushed back to his bedside. "I'm fine, Daddy. Really."

He grasped her arm. "Are you sure?" His hands scrabbled around, looking for his phantom wallet. "Let me just give you some cab fare, at least."

"Daddy," she said, taking his hand in hers. "I have a car and driver, remember? It's okay."

Suddenly, his eyes sharpened. "Oh, that's right," he said, smiling. "Of course you do. Because my clever, beautiful daughter is also a big success." He squeezed her hand. "But I always knew that would happen."

She waited for him to go back to sleep, kissed the top of his head, whispered good-night one more time and left him there.

They called her that night. They were so sorry, they said, but he had slipped away in his sleep.

Bridget thought she'd never forgive herself for letting him die alone.

And then, two weeks after the funeral, she discovered she was pregnant. And so she married Kevin, because he'd stood by her while her father was sick and she was exhausted and devastated and couldn't stand the thought of being alone. Even though, deep down, she knew she was only bringing more trouble into her life.

And now her marriage was a mess, and work kept coming at her, and by the time she landed this job with Scarlett, she had lost track of so much. When the carpenters quit, she had been dealing with an unexpected asbestos issue at one of her other job sites and she had turned to Kevin, thinking that, just this once, she could trust him to take care of things.

But that, obviously, had been a huge mistake.

Scarlett's job was currently the only thing standing between Steele Construction and bankruptcy. All the money Bridget had poured into Kevin's business; all the money he had spent on the corporate Amex; all the savings he had drained from her bank account... She would be ruined if they lost this contract.

"Ethan," she said urgently, "does Scarlett know? Has she seen the rat?"

He paused. "I haven't heard from her yet so I assume not. But we won't have much time. You better get down here as fast as you can."

"Okay. Okay. Hang tight. I'm on my way."

She put down her phone and felt so dizzy that she had to put her head between her knees. She took a deep, stuttering breath. She felt like she had just run a marathon. Her mouth was dry, her head was spinning, her whole body felt weak. The room was dim and quiet, just the soft breathing of her husband and the quiet tick of the clock on the mantel. The city below was not yet stirring. The light coming in through the long silk curtains was gray and muted. She strained to listen. *Rain*, she thought unhappily.

She moved to get out of bed and Kevin's sky-blue eyes fluttered open. "Aw, come on," he whispered hoarsely. He snaked his arm around her waist and pulled her back toward him. "It can't be that bad. Come back to bed."

Bridget glanced at her husband—despite his bloodshot eyes and stale booze smell, he was still an undeniably gorgeous man. He slept naked, and the blankets only just covered his groin. The muscles across his bare chest rippled as he took a firmer grip on her body.

He had rolled in at three in the morning. She hadn't bothered to ask where he'd been.

"It is that bad," she said, trying to edge out of his grasp. "I can't go back to sleep."

"I'm not talking about sleeping," he growled.

She knew. She knew what he wanted. There had been a time when, no matter what else was going on, she would have laughed, delighted, turned off her alarm and then straddled him. There had been a time when she would have let herself roam over every inch of his glorious body and then lie back and happily let him return the favor. There had been a time when she couldn't resist this man, when it never would have crossed her mind to say no. But that was before. Before her father died, before the baby, before work got so crazy, before he started emptying their bank accounts and running up their credit cards, before he started staying out late every night, coming home speed-talking from the coke, smelling like booze and the sweet, salty scent of other things she forced herself not to think too hard about...before there was a giant frigging rubber rat about to ruin everything she had worked so hard to build over the past fifteen years.

She pulled out of Kevin's arms and stood up, grabbing for her robe at the end of the bed. "Listen. I need your help. There's a problem at Scarlett's job."

She tried to ignore the look of bitter resignation on his face before he shrugged and rolled back over. "Surprise, surprise," he muttered.

She tied the robe firmly around her waist, the green silk sash slipping through her fingers, determined to stay focused, not to take the bait. "I have to get down to the site right now, so I need you to drop off Dylan at school."

He didn't look at her. "What do we pay that nanny for, anyway?" he said sullenly.

She took a deep breath, willing herself not to panic. "I told you, she's not doing mornings anymore. It's ridiculous to keep paying her just to drop him off at school when you're home, anyway. Please, I have to get downtown."

He shrugged. "I'm exhausted. Can't you just drop him off on the way?"

"No. I can't." She was trying desperately not to raise her voice. "I've got to go right now."

As if on cue, the high, sweet voice of her four-year-old

son rang out from the room next to theirs, "Mama? Mama? I gotta go potty!"

"Please, Kevin." She hated the begging note in her voice.

He kept his back turned. "He's calling you. You better get going."

She slowly shook her head. She could feel the rage building in her chest. "You're really doing this?"

He didn't answer.

"Mama? I gotta go!"

"Okay, sweetie!" she called out, trying to hold back the anger in her voice. "One second!"

"Now, Mama!" She could hear the urgency in his call.

"You wouldn't be exhausted if you hadn't been out all night," she said with contempt to her husband.

He turned over and looked at her. His eyes were no longer sky blue; they were glacial. "I wouldn't be out all night if I had anything worth coming home to," he said.

"Mama!" Dylan's voice was a wail. "Oh, no! Oh, no! I peed!"

She raised her chin, forcing down the knot in her throat. She wouldn't give her husband the satisfaction of seeing how his words had slammed her right in the gut. "Great. Thanks for freaking nothing, Kevin."

"Have an awesome day," he said and rolled back over.

"Mama!"

For Dylan's sake, she tried not to slam the door as she left the bedroom.

Half an hour later Bridget could still hear Dylan's tantrum as she ran back out into the rain and slid, panting, into her waiting town car. The nanny had not been amused by the early-morning call, but she'd finally agreed to come get Dylan ready for school.

"Okay, Jean Luc," she said to her driver, "we're going to the Hawkins job, as fast as you can."

"I will try, boss," Jean Luc said in his soft Haitian accent. "But the rain is slowing everything down today."

Bridget fished the phone out of her bag and dialed as they inched out into the stream of Manhattan traffic. "Ethan?" she said. "I'm on my way. You heard anything from Scarlett yet?"

"Not yet."

She took a deep breath, relieved. "Okay. I'm almost there. Maybe we can fix this before she even hears anything. Anyone else call? Any word from the press?"

He cleared his throat. "Yeah. A bunch of reporters called. They want you to get back to them right away. Page Six. The *Times*. And *Good Morning New York*. I'm sorry, Bridget."

Bridget leaned back against the soft leather seat, all the air gone from her lungs. So it was already a story. It was already out. Even if she got in there before Scarlett and fired the guys Danny had hired. Even if she got the union delegates to remove the rat off the street. It was already news.

Bridget knew the score. This story would be everywhere. Everyone would know about the rat and Scarlett would find out and freak. This would be terrible press for Scarlett Hawkins Inc. They were literally branded as "America's Company." They couldn't afford to be seen as anti-union; they couldn't be associated with a rat and a picket line.

Bridget closed her eyes, quickly going over the possibilities. The only way Scarlett could possibly fix it would be to immediately make a big, fat, public deal out of firing Steele Construction. This would be it. It was over. She had bet everything on this job. Bridget had nothing in reserve. There was no coming back from a loss this big.

She felt all the strength drain out of her. It was too much.

Her father. Her husband. And now her business. She couldn't save any of it. It was all being taken away.

"Bridget?" Ethan sounded like he was talking under water. "Bridget, Scarlett just walked in the door. Bridget, she's freaking the hell out."

"I'll—I'll call you back later, okay? Let me just… I'll call you back." She dropped her phone onto the seat and stared blindly at the rain-smeared window, out at the traffic. In the distance, down the block, she suddenly saw the looming, gray, cartoon-like figure of Scabby the Rat.

"Missus Steele?" said Jean Luc. "Everything okay?"

Bridget shook her head. Of course Jean Luc had heard everything. Her driver knew more about her than her god damned therapist.

She stared at the rat as they drew closer. Beady black eyes, long black claws. It jounced softly in the rain and wind, mocking her with its leering yellow grin.

"Just…drive on by, Jean Luc. Take me home."

PART TWO

CHAPTER 6

Jason Russo rolled over with a groan, groping for the glass of water and the bottle of aspirin that he hoped he had been smart enough to leave on his bedside table. He found the aspirin, but instead of the water, there was only half a warm beer.

Good enough, he thought, popping a small handful of pills into his mouth and chasing them down with the flat, bitter brew. He grimaced and rolled back over, surprised to find himself in the center of his bed. He'd finally moved off the right side, spreading out onto the part of the mattress he'd always thought of as hers.

All it took was six beers, two shots of tequila and exactly one freaking year. "Happy anniversary of The Day My Wife Left Me," he muttered to himself. "Ought to be a national holiday."

His head throbbed as he hauled himself into an upright position, leaning back onto the padded headboard and blinking in the dazzling morning light streaming from the floor-to-ceiling windows. The room was beautiful: bright, airy and shockingly large for a Manhattan apartment. He had renovated it himself. But his eyes went unwillingly to all the empty spaces that he had not yet roused himself to fill. The missing carved oak bureau, the place where the antique, silver-framed standing mirror had been, the lost bentwood rocker where Hana had nursed their daughter Alli night after night, crooning that one off-key lullaby about all the pretty little horses…

Now all those familiar things were in SoHo, probably looking ridiculously out of place in his best friend Liam's massive chrome and leather loft; along with the big, pink, overstuffed velvet couch Jason had always complained about being too girly but secretly loved, the set of delicate, intricately painted Imari china they had inherited from Hana's paternal grandmother, and worst of all, the long, chipped farmhouse table where their little family had eaten countless meals. It was the table where they had played family board games, where Alli had done her homework every night, where Hana had sat sketching, her back perfectly straight and her long, shining black hair pinned up and held with a pencil. Jason had never built her that desk he had always promised her.

He shut his eyes against the memories. For a brief moment he fantasized about an electrical short that would start a small but dangerous fire at the loft in the middle of the night—Liam had always tried to cheap out when it came to paying for a decent electrician—and he imagined himself showing up, pulling Alli and Hana safely from the blaze, maybe the table, too, but he'd let Liam burn, damn it. That asshole deserved it.

Or, an unwelcome thought rushed into his brain, *maybe you're the asshole in this scenario.*

He shook his head at his own foolishness and finished the leftover beer in a few swift gulps. The aspirin wasn't working; maybe a shower would. He padded naked into the bathroom.

The tile needed to be regrouted in the master. What was that saying about the cobbler's children not having shoes? You'd think the head of the biggest construction company in Manhattan would have an immaculate home—but his business sucked up practically everything; his time, his attention, his energy… *and a fat lot of good that did for you in the end*, he thought bitterly.

He turned the shower all the way to scalding and stepped under the spray. The pungent scent of day-old alcohol seemed to ooze out of his pores as the hot water hit his skin. He wrinkled his nose in distaste. He'd been known to party back in the day, but it had been years since he'd had a hangover like this. He grabbed the bar of soap—trying to make a mental note that he had to replace it since it was basically down to a sliver. Hana had always taken care of things like this—soap, milk, laundry. Even now, a year later, Jason still regularly encountered a lack of clean underwear, and empty cartons in the fridge.

Jesus, man, grow the hell up.

He managed to work up a lather and ran his hands down his own muscular body, relieved to find that at least this part of himself wasn't slipping yet. He didn't need a gym. Building and running from project to project kept him in shape. He was never afraid to grab a hammer and pitch in on one of his jobs if he needed to. His hand reached his crotch, and he paused for a moment, feeling the involuntary leap under his own soapy fingers. Then the ache in his temples throbbed, and he moved on, thinking that he didn't particularly deserve any pleasure this morning—even if it was a gift to himself, so to speak.

He turned off the shower, ran a towel over his body and wandered back into his bedroom, casting one longing look at the bed before he pulled on some clean jeans and a T-shirt. The hot water had helped a little, but he knew that things weren't going to be set right until he drank at least a pot of coffee.

Of all the rooms in this apartment, the kitchen actually felt the least scarred by his divorce. It had always been his territory. Hana had been an unwilling and indifferent cook, perfectly happy to drink a cup of tea and eat a bowl of cornflakes for every meal if given the choice. Jason, on the other hand, loved to eat, and he realized early on that he would have to take the reins in the kitchen if he wanted more than take-out Chinese and frozen Lean Cuisine.

So when they renovated the kitchen, before work had completely taken over his life, he'd actually designed it for himself—setting the counters and cabinets for his six-foot-two-inch frame, organizing it by his exacting standards, putting in a wood-burning pizza oven. He frigging loved this kitchen. He and Alli, who had inherited his appreciation of the culinary arts, thank God, used to spend hours in here mucking around.

Before you got too busy to spend time with your own daughter, you stupid asshole.

He put the kettle on to boil and ground enough French roast for the pour-over and then sat down, trying to ignore the teetering stack of unopened mail on the kitchen island in front of him. He wrinkled his nose at the pile of dirty dishes in the sink. Maybe he should hire a new housekeeper. He'd fired all the help when Hana left, wanting to be alone in his misery.

He thought about just selling the apartment, leaving it all behind—the mail, the grout, the dishes—starting over fresh. Someplace with no memories. But his wasn't the only history here. Alli had grown up in this apartment; this was her home, and he could only imagine her reaction if he yanked her childhood home out from under her. Things were hard enough between them as it was. He couldn't bear to take one more thing from his daughter.

The only thing he still felt like he had under control was his business. His father's business, really, but now Jason's. Russo Construction had been in his family since Jason's great-grandfather had come over from Genoa and started out as a handyman on Staten Island. His father had made it into a huge success, and just before he died, he'd retired and it had passed down to Jason.

His dad had made a toast at his retirement party, his normally stern voice going rough with emotion.

"I think of the day my own father retired," he'd said, putting his arm around Jason's shoulders. "And how he handed down the business to me. And now here I am, doing the same thing with my own son." He'd looked at Jason, his eyes wet with emotion. "A man couldn't ask for any more than this."

And Jason had pushed away any questions in his head about whether or not he actually wanted the family business and smiled and hugged his father and thanked him and promised to work hard and do him proud.

So far, he'd kept his promise. He was a good contractor—he liked the hands-on part of things just fine, working with the engineers, architects and subcontractors. Building from the ground up or renovating, he didn't really care, it was all the same to him. But what he'd always been especially good at, what he'd been trained in from a young age, was the social aspect of the business. The schmoozing and the drinking and the backroom deals. He'd learned how to seal a deal at his father's knee; he was born and raised to be the best.

He used to really enjoy it. He used to love the chase. There had been no one better at making people want to work with him. But after Hana and Liam left the company, everything had gone sour. He couldn't get it up for any of his old tricks. And now, every time he kissed another old-timer's ass, or forced himself to smoke another rank cigar or down another water and whiskey before noon, when he laughed at another disgusting joke that wasn't funny, he imagined that he could feel a tiny piece of his soul chip off and disappear.

There was the money, of course. Russo Construction had always been successful, but when Jason hired Liam, his old college buddy, to run the operations, they became the best. Between the two of them, they'd built dozens of major buildings from the ground up, doubled the size of their workforce, and tripled the value of the company within ten years. Russo Construction had revenue of more than a billion dollars, and that was a good thing. Jason used to regularly remind himself that he had a wife and a daughter to support, workers who counted on him, his father's legacy to keep intact.

But then Liam had fallen in love with Jason's wife. Or maybe Hana had fallen for Liam first; Jason had never really been entirely clear on that, but in any case, everything changed. Liam left the company and opened his own competing construction business; Hana and Alli moved out. Jason fell to pieces, and yet, Russo Construction just kept growing like the monster it was.

Even when he wanted to lose, he still won. Rather than headhunting a new COO, Jason hired an unqualified but ambitious young woman fresh out of business school named Leela Rajan. She turned out to be brilliant, which was lucky, because Jason knew he wasn't exactly pulling his weight lately. But despite that, and the clients that Liam took with him, they had actually managed to increase profits and expand their territory over this past year. They were still the premier builders in Manhattan, but now they were also building shopping malls upstate, huge estates in the Hamptons. But working with Leela was different than working with an old friend, and Jason, who had once worked and lived exclusively in partnerships, now felt alone both at home and at his office.

The kettle suddenly whistled, a high, shrill scream. Startled, Jason lashed out at the stack of paper, wiping all the envelopes to the floor in one furious move, along with his waiting coffee cup, which shattered with a loud, angry crash.

God damn it, he thought as he closed his eyes to the mess he'd just made. The mess that he'd have to clean up himself.

He couldn't go on this way. He had to pull himself together. He was acting like an entitled child.

He stood up slowly, first turning off the kettle and then fetching the broom to clean up. The problem was, he'd let himself stop and think. He needed to get to work. He needed to be distracted. He emptied the shards of pottery in the trash. He'd get coffee on the way to the office. He didn't want to spend another moment alone in this apartment.

CHAPTER 7

Good God, she was perfect.

Liam Maguire looked across the dining room table at Hana as she absently sipped a cup of tea and read the *Times*. Her long black hair fell in a sweep across her face as she leaned forward, spilling onto the paper. He loved watching her in the morning, when she was still soft and rumpled from bed, before she pinned up her hair and put on her lipstick.

She took a gulp of tea and turned the page of the paper. There was a smudge of newsprint on her cheek. He smiled to himself. He always teased her about reading the newspaper. She must be the last person in America who refused to get her news online.

She reached for the teapot and upset her cup, spilling a few drops of amber liquid on the table. She picked up her napkin but he beat her to it, compelled to reach over and polish the spill away with the cuff of his robe.

She looked at him, amused. "I was going to clean it up."

He shrugged, embarrassed by his protective reaction. He should hate this table. This stupid, shabby-chic farmhouse nonsense had replaced a twenty-thousand-dollar lacquered goatskin Karl Springer extension table. It wasn't his aesthetic, it wasn't of any real value, it clashed with everything else in the apartment, but he still felt a messed up little ache of triumph every time he looked at it sitting here in his kitchen. Hana loved this table, and though he hated to admit it, he knew that Jason had, too.

Hana added tea to her cup and the strap of her nightgown slipped down over her shoulder, exposing the top of her breast. Liam took a sharp breath against the violent thrill in his stomach, the tight rush to his groin. God, he would never stop wanting her. He still couldn't believe she was finally his.

Liam remembered every detail of the first time they'd met. It had been one of those ice-cold February days in New Haven. He'd been sitting outside his dorm, smoking and freezing his balls off. He'd gotten drunk at some sorority party the weekend before, lost his winter coat and he couldn't afford to replace it. Jason, who was his roommate at the time, strolled up with this short, pretty Asian girl casually tucked under his arm. She was wearing a puffy black jacket and a red wool hat, which matched the red of her cheeks, her lips and the tip of her nose. Jason had introduced them and Hana had cracked a smile and then asked for a drag off Liam's cigarette.

"I'm trying to quit, but it's been a long, weird night," she'd said. Her voice was young and sweet, belying the arch look she threw at Jason as she spoke. "I earned a puff."

When she reached for the cigarette, Liam noticed that her fingers were as small as a child's, but looked square and strong. Her nails were painted black and bitten to the quick. She inhaled, her eyes closing in pleasure, and the long, straight sweep of her lashes met the curve of her cheekbones.

She was not Liam's type at all, but as he saw her lean up against Jason, Liam felt himself washed in utter regret over the fact that he hadn't found this girl first.

When Liam had first met his new roommate, he'd immediately sized Jason Russo up as one of those kids who had everything and took it all for granted. The college was teeming with his type—wealthy, pretty golden boys, friendly and dumb as yellow Labs. Never had a hard day or a single damned thing to be worried about in their lives. Liam figured that Jason was just another rich prick in a school of rich pricks.

But it didn't take Liam long to realize that he was wrong. Jay was actually one of the best guys that Liam had ever met. He was generous and funny, loyal and as smart as Liam, but without the bitter chip on his shoulder. They quickly became the kind of friends who stayed up nights, drinking beers and sharing a joint, admitting to things they'd never dared tell anyone else before.

But as close as they were, Liam could never forgive the fact that Jay came from money. It popped up in all sorts of ways. The slick clothes, the Range Rover that Jay drove, the fact that he never had to scramble for beer or weed or cigarette money, the casual way he went to restaurants and concerts, the family trips to Aspen and Capri over winter and spring breaks. Hell, Liam couldn't even afford the airfare back home to Chicago on his breaks. He felt lucky when he could scrape up a campus job working maintenance so he'd have a place to stay. Even their grades—Liam had to work like crazy to keep his scholarship, while Jay, secure that his tuition would always be covered, shrugged off his studies like a B was just fine and a C was no big deal at all.

The only place Liam could compete with Jay was when it came to women. Liam might not have the money for expensive dates, but he knew how to play up his Black Irish good looks and punk rebel attitude. Just a hint of his messed up backstory and girls dropped their panties like they couldn't wait to screw the tragedy right out of him.

Hana and Jay were thick as thieves from the very beginning. She was always in their dorm room, hanging around on Jay's bed, wearing some weird little outfit, her sketchbook in one hand and a novel in the other. Even when Jason wasn't around, she would wait for him there, feet tucked under the blankets—she was always cold—and when she was bored, she would ask Liam questions.

At first, he resisted, refusing to look up from his computer or from the book he was reading, claiming a paper he had to write or a test he had to study for, any excuse not to talk to her. But she persisted, plying him with easy, casual questions at first: What did he like to eat? Anything. He was not picky. What was his favorite color? Purple. He always told people it was blue, but somehow he didn't want to lie to her. If he had to choose between burning to death or freezing, which way would he go? Freezing, of course—an absence of feeling was always better than feeling too much. And then, once he got used to it, and in fact, started to enjoy the attention, she hit him with the more personal stuff: Where did he grow up? Chicago. South Side. What was his family like? Useless, absent. What kind of girl did he like? Blonde. Big tits. Easygoing. At least, that was what he used to like, because the real answer, the one he couldn't say out loud, was: *you, Hana. I like you.*

He became more obsessed by the day, standing quietly by, ridiculously smitten, inwardly writhing in agony as he watched every kiss and touch and secret smile and whispered word pass between Hana and Jay. But never once did he seriously consider the idea of making a move on his best friend's girl.

Besides, he told himself, what would a girl like Hana do with a scholarship hood rat like Liam? Her parents were diplomats, she'd lived all over the world and spoke five languages. She'd had her first solo art show before she turned eighteen.

She was perfectly matched to a golden boy like Jay. Liam was lucky she was even willing to be his friend.

That is, until the day twenty years or so later when Jason stood them both up for dinner. They were supposed to be meeting to celebrate an especially important job Russo Construction had managed to land, and the opening of Hana's newest show in SoHo. But Hana had shown up alone—wearing a red sweater that hit Liam with a sharp memory of the wooly red hat she'd been wearing that day they'd first met—and Jay had never shown up at all. They waited for him almost an hour—something they had grown used to doing over the years—drinking their dinner, before Jay finally called saying that he'd been hung up at the office and they should celebrate without him.

So they had.

And it was everything Liam had ever dreamed it would be and more, somehow. He had been out of his mind with pleasure, overcome with emotion, drunk on her scent, her skin, the way she moved under his hands. She had uncorked twenty years of desperate longing and pent-up need. There was no turning back.

Afterward, Liam had expected her to cry with regret, be sick with guilt, but Hana had been tough as nails, just giving him a little smile and shrug and saying in that same soft, pretty voice that Jason had stopped giving a crap about her and their daughter a long time ago, so why should she give a damn about him?

And just like that, all of Liam's loyalty to his best friend and business partner had slipped away, and his only focus became how he was going to keep this woman in his life now that he finally, finally had her.

Hana put her teacup down and raised an eyebrow at him. "What are you staring at?"

He reached across the table and hooked the strap of her

nightgown with his pinkie, pulling it down farther, fully exposing her breast. "I think I'm going to call into work and tell them I'm taking a personal day," he said.

Hana laughed and shrugged the strap back up again, covering herself. "Stand down, soldier. Alli's going to be in the kitchen any second demanding a cronut, some orange juice and a ride to school."

"Lucy will feed her, and I'll have Roman bring the car around and he can take her. In the meantime, we can go back to bed."

She shook her head, smiling. "Too late. I hear her stomping down the stairs."

On cue, Hana's teen daughter popped her head in from the kitchen. "Mom," she said, annoyed. "We're out of orange juice."

Hana shot a deadpan look at Liam. "Check in the back of the fridge. Second shelf."

Alli rolled her eyes as she ducked back in. "I'll just ask Lucy to squeeze me some."

Hana turned back to him with a smug smile.

He sighed. Romance was severely limited when there was a teen in the house, but he loved Alli like she was his own, and knew that Hana and Alli were a package deal. "Okay, then, we've got that dinner with Mark Harrington tonight at Per Se. Wear something devastating and no underwear," he suggested, "and we can sneak off to the bathroom when it gets boring."

"Oh." She tapped her finger along the edge of her teacup. Her nails were long and perfectly manicured now, the color of dried blood. "I forgot about that dinner. Since Alli is at her dad's tonight, I was actually hoping to maybe hit my studio and pull an all-nighter. Get some real work done. It's been a while, you know."

He frowned. "The whole night? This dinner is really important."

She shook her head as if shooing something irritable away. "You know what? Never mind. Of course I'll be at the dinner." She shot him a comical wink. "Sans *sous-vêtements*."

He reached back over and trailed his hand over her shoulder and down her bare arm, wrapping her delicate wrist in his fingers. "Thank you. You can always paint tomorrow, right?"

She looked at him, and for a second he thought he saw the slightest flash of hesitation in her dark eyes, but then her face cleared and she smiled. "Of course," she said. "There's always tomorrow."

CHAPTER 8

Don't say anything to these Neanderthals, thought Bridget as she stood in her bosses' office. *You know you need this job. You've got a kid to support. You've got alimony to pay. Take deep breaths. Keep smiling.*

She dug her nails into the palms of her hand and kept her face arranged in a friendly expression as she waited for her bosses, brothers Linus and Larry Ludley, to stop talking. Though one was supposedly two years older—Bridget could never remember which one—they were eerily identical down to their fake alligator shoes. It especially creeped her out when she had to deal with them both at the same time.

These days Bridget did a lot to get by. She was always on her feet, had several different side hustles and did whatever it took to pay her bills. But her main money came from working sales for Ludley Construction. It had been a year now and yet every day brought a new humiliation. She earned her pathetic paycheck, there was no doubt about that—she was bringing in the clients and projects—but that didn't mean they treated her with any respect.

"I have to admit," said Linus as he leaned forward in his chair and displayed his yellowed dentures. "I thought Larry was crazy when he hired you. How the hell was a lady contractor going to do sales for us? But," he said, turning to his brother, "then I saw her and I thought, well, what the hell? At the very least we'll have something nice to look at around the office."

Larry chortled in agreement, his already ruddy face turning even redder.

The brothers were almost mirror images. They had the same iron-gray crew cut, the same watery blue eyes, the same droopy paunch that they tried to hide under expensive Italian suits. The only way that Bridget could tell them apart was that Linus had a large mole on his neck—one that she often thought a dermatologist should take a look at.

As the brothers laughed together, Bridget forced herself to smile, fighting down the lump of anger in her throat.

"So anyway," said Linus, "you can imagine how pleased I was this morning when we got a call from Scarlett Hawkins. She asked for you by name, Bridget."

Bridget felt a shock rocket through her gut. "Wait. Scarlett called here?"

Larry grinned. "Surprising, right? Considering what happened the last time you two worked together."

Bridget shook her head, bewildered. "Did she say what she wanted?"

Linus nodded eagerly. "She said she wants to work on a project with you."

Bridget stared at him for a moment. "She wants to work with me," she repeated dully.

Larry patted her arm. "You and Ludley Construction!"

Bridget felt her heart start to race. Maybe Scarlett had forgiven her. She felt a surge of hope. This could be it. Her way back in.

"What work does she need done? Her offices in Manhattan? Oh, wait, her film studio in the Hamptons?" Bridget could hear herself gushing, but she didn't care. "Oh, God, I read that she might be building something from the ground up downtown. Is that what she wants me for?" She felt like doing a jig right there in front of the Ludleys.

Linus and Larry exchanged uncomfortable looks. "Well," said Linus, "that would be very exciting if she chose Ludley for such a prestigious job. And perhaps if we play our cards right, she will! But for now I believe she just wants you to come supervise the renovation of the master suite and bathroom in her apartment on the Upper West Side."

Bridget felt the smile slide off her face. "A bedroom renovation? I haven't done residential work in years."

"It's not a bedroom, it's a master suite. Don't forget the bathroom." Larry squeezed one eye shut in a grotesque approximation of a wink. "And, honey, let's remember that you haven't actually done any kind of building in years. In any case, the Ludleys are delighted to do business with Scarlett Hawkins. So we're going to send you over with Scott to check out the scope of the work."

Bridget bit her lip. The last thing she wanted was to deal with Scott, a younger, even oozier version of the brothers, standing over her shoulder when she saw Scarlett again. "That won't be necessary. She was my client for many years. I don't need Scott to come with me. I can handle her on my own."

Larry shook his head. "No. This is a VIP client. You'll need someone more experienced to review the drawings and walk the site. She wants to start construction right away. We can't have you holding anything up while you learn on the job."

Right, because ten years of owning one of the fastest growing construction businesses in Manhattan was somehow not enough experience.

She took a deep breath, digging for patience. "She asked for me specifically, right? You said she wanted me to supervise the renovation. So you'll have to trust me when I tell you that if she asked for me, she's really not going to be happy if someone else shows up to do my job. I know Scarlett. Remember that I worked for her for years. If you'd like to call her and speak to her directly to confirm that, I have her number in my phone."

She watched the brothers exchange a look, their beady eyes suddenly bright with interest. "You have her personal phone number?" said Larry. "So you're still in touch?"

She nodded. A white lie, though she supposed that Scarlett's old number might still be in service.

"All right, then," cut in Linus. "You can take the lead. But I want you reporting back to us daily. You need to do a good job on this one, Bridget. She could be a very important client to us."

"I understand."

"And if you do a good job on this," said Larry, "who knows what could be next!"

"That would be great," she said automatically. *Oh, goody. Maybe I'll get to do kitchen renovations, too.* She waited a beat. It was past five. "Is there anything else?"

"No, no," said Larry as he bent over his desk. "That's all. Go on home now, honey."

Honey, she thought, inwardly shuddering, *yet another perfectly good term of endearment I'll never be able to use again.*

She darted a glance over to Linus as she gathered up her briefcase. He was staring at her—but not in the face. His gaze had drifted decidedly south, a happy leer twisting his lips. Bridget's fingers itched to fasten another button on her blouse, but instead she quickly made her exit, relieved to be out of their sight.

What was Scarlett up to? After the debacle with her offices, she'd told Bridget she was lucky she wasn't suing her, and then cut off all contact. *Why does she want me back now?* Perhaps she was still nursing a grudge and wanted to humiliate Bridget. Asking her to supervise a bedroom renovation would certainly fit that bill.

Christopher Lee came out of a conference room and waved her down. Lee, a project manager, was one of the only people at the company that Bridget actually liked. He was half Chinese, half Mexican, all gay, and as much of an outsider at Ludley as she was.

Lee smiled at her as they stepped onto the elevator together. "I heard you're working for Scarlett Hawkins. That's major! Nervous?"

Bridget shook her head as the doors closed. "I've worked with her for years. She was my client before she called the Ludleys."

"Oh," said Lee. "Right." He looked doubtful. "But wasn't she the one—"

"Yes," Bridget interrupted. "You know damned well it was Scarlett. Can we change the subject, please?"

Lee arched an eyebrow. "Fine... So which Ludley spent the whole meeting ogling your tits this time?"

She glared at him. "Don't say tits. Just because you're married to a man doesn't mean you can't be sued for sexual harassment." She sighed in frustration. "And it was Linus. I don't know if I can take this much longer. Larry told me that he thinks I'm *scrappy*—you think they'd call a guy *scrappy*?"

Lee shrugged. "Steele, you're gorgeous, barely five foot four, and one of the only female contractors in New York City. *Scrappy* is pretty much your first, last and middle name."

"Former contractor," snapped Bridget.

"What?"

"I'm actually a former contractor."

"Ah, right, you've been demoted to business development. Sucks for you."

The elevator door opened with a little ping. "You're really not helping, Lee," said Bridget as she pushed past him.

"Aw, c'mon!" Lee scrambled to catch up with her. "I was just messing with you! Jeez!"

CHAPTER 9

Jay thought he'd surprise his daughter and pick her up from school instead of waiting for her to Uber home. He used to do surprise pickups when she was at her old school, Chapin, but since Alli and Hana had moved downtown and Hana had insisted that Alli transfer to the closer and more progressive LREI for high school, this was the first time he'd turned up unannounced.

He watched the kids stream out the front gates, heads bent over their phones as they walked. Seeing all the high school–age children with their dyed hair and torn jeans, he felt a pang of longing for the neat little green jumpers and white collared blouses that had been mandatory uniforms at Chapin.

Where Alli would go to school had been a long source of conflict between Jay and Hana. They agreed on private school, but Jay wanted Alli to go to someplace traditional and structured. *What about getting into a good college?* was his rallying cry. And Hana would shake her head like he was suggesting sending their daughter off to a military academy, arguing that an experimental, alternative education was the way to go. *We don't want to kill her creativity!*

Jay won in the beginning. He himself had gone to Fordham Prep, so Chapin's single-sex policy and its long tradition of excellence had felt familiar and safe to him. The best. But Alli struggled academically, and once she was diagnosed with dyslexia, the arguments only got fiercer.

After the divorce, Hana made her move, arguing that Alli was not thriving at her current school and claiming the commute uptown would be too much for the girl. She'd pulled strings with several different people in the Manhattan art community to get a slot in the freshman class at the progressive and in-demand LREI. As for Alli, she had always hated the school uniforms and the unending homework at Chapin, and was particularly delighted to be transferring to a coed class just in time for high school.

Jay didn't have a chance when the two of them teamed up.

He had looked at Alli's course load this semester and wondered what had happened to good old math and English. Alli used to take Latin and biology at Chapin; now she was studying Feminist Literature of the Twentieth Century and making lopsided pinch pots in her ceramics class. It cost the same, too. Jay was paying forty-five thousand dollars a year in tuition—more than some colleges—but he couldn't help feeling that he was getting cheated. They didn't even have grades or test scores—just long-winded reports about how Alli was or was not progressing and challenging herself.

He almost missed her as she walked by. As soon as she started school, she'd cut her waist-length hair to an absurdly short crop—almost shaved—and Jay still hadn't reconciled her vulnerable, shorn head and the rebellious glint in her dark eyes with the dreamy, silly little girl he thought of as his daughter.

"Alli!" he called as she started to turn the corner. "Wait, honey!"

She glanced back and frowned, turning to the crowd of kids she'd been walking with and quickly waving them on.

He hurried over to her as she stood waiting, exasperation written on every line of her fierce little face. He tried not to remember how, when she was small, she used to launch herself into his arms with a delighted yelp whenever he surprised her.

"What are you doing here?" She sounded accusatory.

He looked at her and realized she was wearing a silver hoop through her nose. It made her look like an adorable, tiny bull.

"What is that?" He tried not to sound panicked. "Does your mother know you did that?"

She rolled her eyes. "Calm down. It's a clip-on." She yanked it out and held it up, and then clipped it back on again. "What's up?"

He smiled, trying to change the mood. "Surprise! I thought we could go to the Milk Bar. Do cereal milkshakes and compost cookies?"

She snorted. "Gluten, Dad. And besides, I already have plans with my friends. We're going to Free People. I need a new raincoat."

"But I took the afternoon off." Even to himself, he sounded pathetic. "Maybe we could stop at Free People or whatever it is on the way to the restaurant? Coat shopping could be fun."

She glowered at him, pointedly ignoring his invitation. "You can't just show up and expect me to drop everything. My friends are probably already halfway there by now. I have to go." She turned in the direction her friends had disappeared. Her narrow shoulders were set in a stubborn little plank as she started to march away.

"Do you have money for the coat?"

She held up a dismissive hand. "Mom gave me her credit card."

"Will you be home for dinner?" He raised his voice as she got farther away.

She didn't look back. "Don't worry about it. We're going to get a pizza."

"But what about the gluten?" he yelled after her.

No answer as she turned the corner out of his sight.

He sighed, feeling foolish. What had he been thinking? She stayed with him every other weekend and twice during the school week, but he couldn't remember the last time she'd greeted him with anything more positive than a look of blank boredom on her face. The idea that he could just show up at school and charm her with sweets was beyond stupid.

Except that, of course, sweets used to work. Sweets, or a split pastrami on rye at the corner deli, an afternoon matinee, or a frozen hot chocolate at Serendipity—the promise of his uninterrupted time—had been a virtual guarantee that a delighted Alli would drop nearly anything else she had going on and suck up his attention like a love-starved puppy.

They used to have semiregular daddy-daughter dates, giving the nanny a surprise afternoon off, before Jay's business had become so overwhelming that he had pushed everything else aside for work. Then suddenly, the nanny was working overtime and Hana was picking up the rest of the slack, and Jay hardly saw his daughter.

And now she's making me pay for it.

He tried to tell himself it was only natural. That no sane teen girl in the world would choose a milkshake with her father over an afternoon with her friends. But he imagined all those other teen girls rejecting their fathers weren't quite so brutal. There was an anger to his daughter's dismissals that he felt was particular to their relationship, that he had to admit he had justly earned.

He had crushed his marriage the same way. Hana told him that he'd simply stopped showing up. That even when he was physically with her, she never had his full attention. And she had warned him, as she left, that it wasn't just her he had hurt. His daughter had been scarred by his lack of attention, as well. He had taken them both for granted.

He balled his hands into fists. He knew that there was no getting Hana back, of course, but he was determined to fix things with Alli. He had four years before college. Surely that was enough time. He would just keep trying.

That is, if I can get her to hang around long enough to let me try.

He looked over at the empty corner. *What now?* he thought. He'd taken the whole afternoon off, planning on spending it with her. Instead, he'd ended up with a disastrous amount of unwanted time on his hands.

As if in answer, his phone buzzed with a text. He checked it. Right. Work. He could go back to work. He squared his shoulders. At least it gave him something to do.

CHAPTER 10

They were halfway through the nine-course meal at Per Se when Liam got sick of trying to pretend this was just another friendly dinner and decided to steer the conversation around to business.

"So the skyscraper project," he said, cutting to the chase. "What kind of competition am I up against?"

Mark Harrington, the silver-haired real estate magnate they were dining with, smiled and took a sip of wine. "Who says you're even up for it?"

Out of the corner of his eye, Liam could see Hana shake her head. Up until that moment they had all been pretending to be two couples enjoying a very expensive dinner together, but now Liam had spoiled it by rushing in.

Liam knew that there was an art to this. It was like a seduction—no matter how much you wanted it, you didn't just reach over and grab a woman's tit. You complimented her hair. You asked about her day. You made her a sandwich and held her hand first, told her that she smelled good. You waited for her to come to you. Jay had coached him, time and time again, that, at the beginning of negotiations, he should at least wait for dessert, and multiple glasses of wine, before ever bringing up a job. But Liam never bothered listening. Jay had always done all the foreplay and then Liam crunched the numbers with the estimators and sealed the project in the field.

And this crazy restaurant? This was Jay's world, not Liam's. Jay had grown up at ease in private clubs and fancy hotels; he'd been born to hang out on two-hundred-foot yachts and winter in St. Bart's. Liam had been born in a three-story walk-up, to an alcoholic mother and a father who left before he turned two.

Actually, he mused, most of the men in this industry didn't hold this against him. His South Side backstory played almost as well with titans of industry as it had with college girls. They liked Jay because Jay was one of them, born into the business just like the rest of them were, but they liked Liam because he actually was as tough and street-smart as they all imagined themselves to be. Plenty of clients had followed him out the door when he had split from Jason and opened his own place. Maybe not as many as he would have liked, but he was going to change all that tonight.

He swiped the heavy linen napkin across his mouth. "Okay, so if not me, then who is?"

Harrington looked at him, amused. "You mean Russo?"

Inwardly, Liam cursed, annoyed that he was so transparent. But outwardly, he shrugged and kept his cool. "Sure. Them and anyone else. I just want to know who my competition is."

Harrington twirled some pasta onto his fork and then chewed slowly. "This is a huge and important project," he said, after he swallowed. "The anchor tenant insists that we consider as diverse a cross section as possible. I'm bringing in all sorts of qualified construction managers to see what they have to offer."

No use in pretending now. "But one of them is Russo, right?"

Next to him, Liam felt Hana press her arm to his; a warning to ease off. He forced himself to take a sip of his wine and tried to look relaxed.

Per Se was the kind of restaurant that many people would only go to once in a lifetime. And, let's face it, most people would never dine in at all. The chef and owner were world-renowned. They brought ballerinas in to train their waitstaff to be more graceful as they served. They only offered two nine-course tasting menus, and a lesser, five-course menu at the bar. The menu changed every night—chef's choice—either vegetarian or not.

Harrington's date, a Latvian model named Iveta, who looked like Gigi Hadid with Anna Nicole Smith boobs, frowned as she pushed her pasta around with her fork. It was hand-cut tagliatelle showered in a generous pile of shaved black truffles. It cost one hundred and twenty-five dollars extra per portion, on top of the already astronomical price tag for the prix fixe meal. So far, Iveta had ordered all the extras, but hadn't eaten more than a bite of anything that had been put in front of her.

"Is this a date or business meeting?" she pouted in her thick accent. "I thought we were having nice double date."

"Agreed," said Hana firmly. She shot Liam a stern look and then turned to Iveta. *"Iveta, no kurienes tu esi Latvija?"*

Iveta smiled, delighted. "But you speak Latvian! How wonderful!"

Hana held up her hands. "Just a little. My family spent a year or so there when I was a teen. It's a beautiful country."

Thank God for Hana, Liam thought as the two women chattered on about the small village Iveta had grown up in. *She can smooth anything over.* Hana was perfectly at ease in this rarified environment, wearing a sleeveless black leather Balmain sheath, her hair pulled back and gathered at the base of her neck in a thick knot, highlighting the enormous ruby earrings that he had given her for Christmas. This restaurant was full of the most powerful men in Manhattan, all of whom had ridiculously beautiful women sitting at their sides. Liam thought that Hana outshone them all.

Liam saw Harrington brush her with a frank look of admiration and he quelled a jealous surge in his chest. He reached over and took her hand. Hana's ring finger was empty, but there was still the faintest light mark where her wedding ring used to be. Liam hated that mark.

I'm going to marry her, he thought, imagining a stone the size of a sugar cube covering up that spot, something that would leave no doubt that this extraordinary woman was his.

It wasn't the first time he'd thought this. In fact, he'd asked her to marry him the moment her divorce was final, and five times, in more and more extravagant ways, since then. The top of the Empire State Building, in a floating cottage in Bali, on the cliffs of Lake Como under a full moon, waist-deep in the ocean on the Cayman Islands, on a rooftop of a private riad overlooking Marrakesh… And every time she had shaken off his grand gestures with a tender kiss and a small smile of regret. "Too soon," she always said. "I'm happy the way things are." And he had backed down, secretly planning something bigger and better for the next time, wondering what he could do to change her mind.

A phalanx of waiters silently slid their pasta dishes away and replaced them with a playing card–size slice of Miyazaki Wagyu beef dotted with honeycombed morel mushrooms and tiny wild onions. Another hundred dollars extra, each. Liam did a quick calculation in his mind. With cocktails and wine, the bill would be nearly four thousand dollars.

Liam felt a rush of frustration as he looked at Mark Har-

rington cutting into his steak. He needed this project. It was a
skyscraper. The kind of building that he'd done a dozen times
over with Russo Construction, but that South Side Construction hadn't landed yet. One skyscraper was all it would take.
Then they could eat in this stupid restaurant every night if
Hana wanted to. He could buy her the moon, and maybe she
would finally see just how serious he really was.

He was startled when Hana gently slid her hand out from
under his so she could eat. He'd forgotten he was holding on
to her.

"Try a bite," she whispered to him. "It's delicious."

He smiled at her and dutifully picked up his fork and knife,
certain she was right.

CHAPTER 11

Bridget checked her reflection in the mirrored doors of the elevator as she rode up to Scarlett's penthouse. Hair, good. Lipstick, good. Violet silk crepe de chine Stella McCartney blouse, good. Black suede Versace miniskirt with a matching black suede trench, better. And of course, her signature Louboutin work boots. All her clothes were at least three years out of date, relics of another time when she thought nothing of spending an afternoon at Barneys and coming out with five new outfits with shoes and lingerie to match. She had sold some pieces here and there to make ends meet over the past few years, but she had always been careful to keep enough of her old wardrobe so that she could go anywhere in Manhattan and blend in.

For Scarlett Hawkins, Bridget had pulled out some of her best. Knowing that the mega-star never missed a detail.

Scarlett, citing her unusual private life, had always needed a certain level of trust and discretion from the people who worked in her many homes, and for years she had depended on Bridget and Steele Construction for her most sensitive requests. So even after Steele Construction had outgrown most residential work, and up until the rat incident, Bridget always personally oversaw anything Scarlett needed done on her New York properties.

The doomed corporate renovation of Scarlett's offices had felt like not just a natural next step in their professional relationship, but a personal thank-you gift from Scarlett for all the discretion and loyalty Bridget had shown her over the years.

But, thought Bridget, as the old feelings of shame and anger started welling up just as the lights on the elevator ticked ever upward, floor by floor, *best not to think about all that just now.*

She took a deep breath as the elevator stopped at the private hallway of Scarlett's penthouse. The doors opened, revealing the grand dame herself.

"Bridget, darlin'," sang out Scarlett as she stepped forward and engulfed her in a warm, sweetly scented embrace. "It's been much, much too long."

"Scarlett," murmured Bridget politely as they broke the hug. "It's good to see you."

Exactly the same, thought Bridget. The woman must drink the blood of virgin club kids. Scarlett's face had none of the tight, shiny, pillowy look most Manhattan women of a certain age and class sported. If there had been nips and tucks— and, of course, Bridget knew that there had been more than a few—they were done so cleverly that Scarlett could always just claim healthy living, good genes and a vat of La Mer, and you could almost—almost—believe her.

"Well," said Scarlett, stepping back, "you look as sexy as ever, Miss Steele. Come on back to my kitchen where we can chat. I just baked up a strawberry crisp. First of the season. I hope you're hungry."

She followed Scarlett into her bright and airy kitchen— easily as big as Bridget's entire current apartment in the

East Village, and, like all the rooms in Scarlett's penthouse, adorned with a breathtaking view of Central Park from every window. Bridget sat down at the enormous marble-topped island and tried to calm her fluttering stomach. The room smelled heavenly, of course. People made fun of Scarlett's extensive staff and ridiculous wealth, claiming that they all could have perfect homes and perfect lives just like Scarlett if they also had all her cash and help, but Bridget knew that Scarlett was no fake. If she said she baked a crisp, then she herself had been in that kitchen all morning, stewing up fruit and toasting those almonds. And Bridget knew from experience that whatever Scarlett put in front of her was going to taste better than any other version of the dish she'd tried before. But still, she didn't feel much like eating at the moment.

"Tea or coffee, darlin'?" asked Scarlett as she bustled around, setting out bowls and cutlery and dishing out the dessert. She was wearing an acid-green Chanel cashmere twinset, a tweed Burberry skirt and a long strand of black Tahitian pearls. Bridget amused herself for a quick second, imagining the extremely risqué underwear the multibillionaire was undoubtedly wearing underneath her preppy drag.

"Tea," Bridget answered, watching Scarlett put out cream and sugar in what she was sure was a sedate little multi-thousand-dollar tea service. That was probably Queen Victoria's favorite teapot, she thought as Scarlett carefully poured hot water from the kettle into the homely white pot.

"You just go ahead and try that crisp and tell me what you think," said Scarlett.

Bridget reluctantly tasted a bite of the warm dessert and, despite her nerves, held back a groan of pleasure.

"Good?" asked a smiling Scarlett. She always liked to watch a woman eat.

Bridget nodded and took a second mouthful. "Amazing."

"Good." Scarlett poured out the tea for both of them and sat down across from Bridget. "Because now that I've made you comfortable, we should probably clear the air."

Bridget gulped, the sweet dessert suddenly turning to ashes in her mouth. "Oh?"

Scarlett rolled her eyes. "Don't play coy with me, Bridget. You know there's venom between us that needs to be sucked right out of the wound."

It felt like a trap, so Bridget tried to swerve. "Well, I heard you wanted to renovate your bedroom suite," she said.

"Yes," said Scarlett. "I do. And it says something about how highly I think of your work that I went through those toad-licking Ludley brothers to hire you."

"They're not that bad," she said, unwilling to let Scarlett see how far she had sunk.

Scarlett shook her head mournfully. "Well, now you're just lying to me, darlin'."

Bridget pushed the dish of dessert away, not willing to play cat and mouse. "What do you want, Scarlett? What am I doing here?"

Scarlett took a sip of her tea, pinky straight up in the air. "Fine. Cards on the table. I'm taking Scarlett Hawkins Inc. public this year."

Bridget's eyes widened. Scarlett had resisted going public for over a decade, insisting she would know when the time was right.

"Doing something like this is a big god damned deal with many tiny and moving parts. Nothing can go wrong. Not a hint of scandal nor a sniff of gossip."

Bridget nodded, wondering where this was going.

"Of course, my fans have long accepted my Sapphic predilections. Lesbian chic is part of my brand. It makes America feel warm and openhearted to embrace my sexuality. But as you know, I also like to indulge in other, less wholesome pro-clivities that might not be so readily accepted."

Bridget nodded, keeping her face carefully neutral. Scarlett was so deep into S and M that she made Christian Grey look like Pope Francis.

Scarlett took another sip of tea and then looked at Bridget's untouched cup, one eyebrow raised. "Do you not care for Lap-sang souchong? I'm so sorry, I should have asked."

"It's fine," said Bridget. She took a hasty swallow. "It's de-licious."

"In any case, I have been informed that I might need to, shall we say, tone down my more public forays a bit for the sake of Joe and Josephine Q. Public. But I have absolutely no intention of giving them up altogether. After all—" she took a large bite of her crisp "—what's the point of life without a little bit of fun?"

"So you need me to fix up your sex dungeon and keep my mouth zipped."

Scarlett looked startled, but then, after a second, she laughed. "Well. I'd rather we called it my pleasure palace. And I'm hop-ing for a rather substantial upgrade, not just a fix-up. I'll be unable to go to some of my favorite clubs, but if I must go un-derground, I shall do it in the utmost style."

Bridget shook her head. It wasn't that she really minded doing this kind of work for Scarlett. She had done it for years. But this was definitely not the foot back in the door she had hoped for. "Does your master suite even need any work?"

Scarlett waved a hand in the air. "Oh, yes. The bathroom, too. Oodles of work."

She looked at Scarlett. "Why me? After all this time?"

Scarlett calmly met her eyes. "Because I can trust you, dar-lin'. After all the bad blood that passed between us, I expected you to go running straight to Page Six. Sell my story. Tell them all my dirty secrets. Maybe even get a book deal out of it. But you didn't even peep. And I know you needed the money. I've kept tabs on you, sugar."

Bridget felt tears of anger well up and threaten to spill over. "Then why didn't you call?" she blurted out.

Scarlett widened her catty gray eyes. "I think mistakes were made on both sides, darlin'."

Bridget felt almost compelled to spit out her anger and hurt, like she'd been holding it in a knot in her throat for years. "I know I screwed up, but I can't believe you just dropped me like that, Scarlett. Did you know that I lost everything? That Dylan and I had to move back in with my mother and live with her for an entire year while I looked for work? It was the lowest point of my life and you just abandoned me. I thought we were friends."

Whoa. Definitely hadn't meant to go there.

Scarlett nodded. "We were. That's why I want to hire you now."

Bridget pulled her dish back over and stuffed another bite into her mouth, trying to muffle her anger. The dessert had gone cold and gummy.

Scarlett sighed. "You made huge mistakes, Bridget. You know that's true."

"I made mistakes, Scarlett. But I never meant to hurt you or your company in any way."

Scarlett re-poured herself a cup of the golden tea, and used a pair of silver tongs to add two lumps of sugar. "And yet, you did. I nearly had a boycott on my hands after the mess you pulled, Bridget. Not to mention that I had to hire a new contractor, and we ended up a year behind schedule."

Bridget held down a bitter laugh. "I can't believe you brought in Russo to finish my work."

Scarlett shook her head. "Well. I had to bring in somebody. And they were the best."

Bridget stirred her tea. "And how did those exposed two-by-fours come out?"

Scarlett rolled her eyes. "Oh, you know they were hideous. I had Russo pull them all down and had to hire a new architect for a redesign, which added another four months to the job. You were absolutely right about that. I can admit it."

Bridget picked up her cup and took a sip, hiding a small smile of satisfaction.

Scarlett reached over and placed her hand on top of Bridget's. "In any case, I should like this all to be water under the bridge. I forgive you and you forgive me and then you come and do your work in that lovely way you always did before."

"And keep my mouth shut."

Scarlett nodded, a complacent look on her face. "I will tell your horrible bosses that you are totally in charge. I only want people working here that you absolutely trust. You will have full say over who comes in and out. Oh, and there will be some structural work, so hire that architect you used to work with. That pretty Ava girl."

"Ava Martinez?"

"Yes. Another woman who knows how to keep her mouth shut."

Bridget nodded. It wasn't like she really had a choice. It was this or keep working in sales forever. And who knows, maybe it would lead to more than it seemed. "Okay. I'll set it all up. It might take a minute to figure out what subs to hire. But I'll find them."

Scarlett clapped her hands together. "Excellent. We're back in business." She swung off the stool and headed to her gleaming Sub-Zero, hauling out a bottle of Cristal. "I think this calls for something a little more celebratory than tea, don't you?"

She popped the bottle open before Bridget could answer, pouring the fizzing drink into a pair of sleek stemless glass cylinders. The handblown glass was so thin that Bridget felt she could break through it with the slightest pressure of her fingers.

"To our reunion, to this project, to letting bygones be bygones," said Scarlett, tipping her glass against Bridget's with a pretty, bell-like chime. She raised the drink, but then paused for a moment, holding it a few inches from her mouth and catching Bridget's eyes. "Don't screw it up," she added, and then, just barely, smiled.

CHAPTER 12

Jay was standing at the cheese counter in Eataly, the five-thousand-square-foot, all-things-Italian food hall in the Flatiron District. He was pressed shoulder to shoulder with a crowd of well-heeled, hungry Manhattanites on their lunch breaks, and thinking about what his Italian-American grandmother would have made of the fact that he was seriously considering buying some cheese for fifty dollars a pound.

It wasn't even that extravagant compared to other things he could buy in this place: twenty-five dollars for a sixteen-ounce package of pasta, a nugget of black truffle for three hundred and fifty dollars, five hundred dollars for a bottle of balsamic vinegar that came in its own velvet-lined box.

She would have been horrified, he thought. But then, his nonna had hand-made her own mozzarella and ricotta. She also spent every Sunday slow-cooking her sauce made with tomatoes she had grown and canned herself and patting together dozens of meatballs so that the whole family could gather around the table and enjoy the fruits of her labor. She always joked that she held the family together with marinara sauce.

I should do that, he thought. *I should make Sunday sauce for Alli and insist that we have dinner together at least once a week.*

He bent closer to the case, considering a large, pear-shaped blob of Caciocavallo Podolico. "I'll take a half pound of that," he said to the pretty redheaded cheese monger, "and another half pound of the Rogue River Blue," he added.

"Brilliant choices," the redhead said as she reached into the case. She shot him a wink before she turned away to weigh out his order. "I can tell you're a man of good taste."

For a brief moment Jay idly thought about asking her out. She was pretty and young, she knew about cheese and he was fairly certain she'd say yes. It all seemed so uncomplicated and easy. The opposite of his marriage. But he'd dated a few women like this since Hana had left—in fact, these were really the only kind of women he'd dated—and he knew he had to break the habit. Things with young women never ended well. They got attached, and he got bored, and feelings were inevitably hurt. Plus, he felt like he would be ashamed to introduce Alli to a woman who was probably only ten years older than she was.

"The blue is especially nice with pears," said the redhead as she rang him up.

He nodded, and she waited a beat as if to see if he would engage more before she passed over his paper-wrapped cheese parcels with a wistful smile.

Bullet dodged, he thought as he imagined that sad little smile as they inevitably broke up a couple months from now.

Jay threaded his way through the food hall, stopping at the seafood counter to ogle the ahi tuna, bending to smell a fragrant pile of lush and glowing strawberries brought down from upstate, and then taking a detour to the café and ordering a cappuccino and a pound of Leela's favorite chocolate hazelnut cookies to bring back to work with him. After all, she had been keeping his business running practically single-handedly this past year; the least he could do was keep her in cookies.

He walked out onto the street, bags, packages and coffee cup in hand. For a moment he thought about calling for his driver, but then decided it would be faster to hail a cab. Or take the train, he thought, eyeing the subway entrance right across the street. He hadn't taken the subway in years, preferring to walk or use his own car and driver, but he knew it was a straight shot from here to his office on the 6.

Why not? he thought, and he gulped down his coffee and descended underground.

He ran for the train, sliding in just as the door closed, and grabbed hold of a pole as the car lurched forward. The train was exactly the same as always. The bright orange plastic seats, the *bing bong* chime as the doors slid shut, the cold and greasy feel of the pole under his hands.

Suddenly, he remembered being sixteen, skipping school and heading down to the East Village with three of his buddies, crowded onto the subway together, all determined to convince some tattoo artist that they were actually eighteen and could legally get some ink. He'd ended up with a Celtic tribal band on his left biceps that he hated and which he'd hidden from his parents for two years, wearing T-shirts even on their tropical vacations. Hana had laughed the first time she saw it and, later on, as an anniversary gift, she'd designed an intricate fill of flowering and fruited vines for him and carefully researched the best tattoo artist in Manhattan to cover up his youthful mistake. These days he often looked at that tattoo, as beautiful as it was, and wished he still had the tacky Celtic tribal band.

The train screeched to a stop and more people got on. It was crowded now, but Jay didn't mind. He liked to people-watch, and New York City had the greatest people-watching in the world. He smiled at a heavy man with a blue cap who sat down across from him. The man looked back, stony-faced, then his eyes narrowed. "What are you looking at, ya freak?" he sneered.

"Nothing," said Jay, looking away and trying not to laugh. Man, he was out of practice. What was he doing smiling and making eye contact on the subway? You'd think he was some tourist. The smile slid off his face. It seemed he was out of touch with everything these days, his daughter, his own city… Work had erased everything he really cared about.

He shook his head and accidentally locked eyes with the man in the blue cap again. The man's face went red and he looked like he was going to stand up and punch Jay, but luckily the train stopped and it was Jay's station.

CHAPTER 13

Dylan was asleep when Kevin showed up at her door to drop him off.

"Damn it," Bridget whispered as she took her little boy from her ex's brawny arms. "You know he can't nap after four. Now he'll be up for half the night."

Kevin shrugged and gave her an innocent smile. "He fell asleep on the subway. What could I do?"

Bridget shook her head. She couldn't believe she used to fall for that fake grin. Sometimes she wondered what she'd ever seen in the man. Then she saw his biceps bulge as he handed her Dylan's backpack and remembered.

"Sweet boy," she whispered, stroking his pink cheek. "Dyl. Dylan. Time to wake up."

Her son murmured and flopped against her, nuzzling into her shoulder. She smelled the soft warmth of his hair.

"You better help with this if you want to say goodbye to him," she said to her ex.

"Hey, little man!" boomed Kevin. "If you wake up now, I will give you some candy!"

Dylan's head popped up, his blue eyes suddenly wide open. "What candy?" he piped.

A shadow of guilt crossed Kevin's perfectly sculpted face.

Bridget rolled her eyes in exasperation. "Do you even have any candy? Because I don't have any candy."

Kevin held out his hands. "You said you wanted him to wake up."

"I want candy!" wailed Dylan.

Bridget bit her lip. Great, now there would be a temper tantrum, too. "Dylan, how about we go for soup dumplings, instead?"

He blinked, considering. "At the Bao?" he said. "Because they taste the best, Mommy."

She smiled. Only in New York would a seven-year-old have an opinion on where to get the best Chinese food. "Sure. Run and get your warm coat. It's cold outside."

She put him down and he turned back toward her. "Can Daddy come with us?"

"Oh," said Kevin. "Not tonight, Dyl. I have a date."

Bridget grimaced. Of course he did. And she was sure he'd be using the alimony money she paid him to take this girl out. And of course he mentioned it in front of their son. Not that she'd wanted him to come to dinner, anyway.

"Okay," said Dylan as Kevin reached down to kiss him goodbye. "Maybe next time. Bye, Daddy. Have a nice time. Say please and thank-you and don't forget to wash your hands before dinner."

Bridget laughed. For a moment she caught Kevin's eyes and gave him a half smile. Her ex had been a major mistake, but she would always be grateful for her son. What a nice kid they had made.

It was past eleven before Dylan finally fell asleep again. Bridget had put him to bed at nine, but when she'd checked on him later, he was up quietly drawing in bed. She let it go; she couldn't force him to sleep, and at least he wasn't running around the apartment or begging for screen time.

After she pulled the blankets up over his little shoulders and kissed him one last time, she fished a half-empty bottle of Domaines Ott out of her refrigerator, poured herself a generous glass of the pale pink liquid, grabbed her phone out of her purse and headed into the bathroom to turn on the water. *Hot baths and expensive rosé*, she thought to herself. *My last remaining luxuries.*

She put the lid down on the toilet and then sat down to pry off her Louboutin work boots. Leftovers from a previous life. She remembered how Kevin used to laugh at her insistence on wearing the extravagantly priced heels—even when they were on a job site—but she loved the extra inches they gave her. She spent all her time around men who were twice her size; she needed every prop she could get. She sighed with relief as the boots came off, letting her fingers linger over her sore instep, and then stood back up and stripped off her jacket and skirt, standing at the sink in bra and panties, wiping off the makeup from her dark brown eyes, scrubbing the lipstick from her full mouth and then looking in the mirror at her bare face and scrunching up her nose.

She was thirty-six but without the makeup and the heels and suit, she could still pass as seventeen. She looked like a sweet little Jewish girl from the Bronx—not the glam, smart, ballbusting boss she had grown up to be.

But, she reminded herself as she peeled off her underwear and stepped into the hot, fragrant bath, *it's not like I'm that boss anymore, either.*

She thought about Scarlett and her ridiculous sex dungeon again. What would Bridget's father say if he knew what his baby girl was building these days? After she left Scarlett's apartment, it had taken every ounce of self-restraint to not pick up the phone and tell her to forget the whole damned thing. After all, she reminded herself for the hundredth time, this might be her big chance.

Yeah. Your big chance to be humiliated.

She sank deeper into the warm water, trying to shake off the doubt. This would have to work. She wanted back in. She wanted her crew back. She wanted to build. And she was ready. She had relentlessly run over the mistakes she'd made, with a cold and unforgiving eye. When she finally got her chance again, she had mapped her every move; what she'd do and not do, what path she'd follow. All she needed was a decent break.

A woman in construction was a freak on her best day, and an outright aberration the other 364 days a year. And a female general contractor working in the commercial sector? That was like a one-legged, fire-eating, bearded-lady lion tamer performing on the trapeze. It was hard enough climbing up the first time, but getting another shot at it? It was a frigging miracle.

She sighed as she trailed her hand through the water, playing the same loop of her glory days that she always played in her head; the work, the money, the taste of fame, the glorious feeling that she was doing the one thing that she had been put on this earth to do…the memories still stung. At least her father hadn't lived to see her fail. That was the one blessing in all this mess.

She took a drink of the wine, savoring the warmth that spread, tingling, all the way out into her fingers and toes. She dipped her head back under the water, letting her long, dark hair drift around her like seaweed. She would have to get up early in the morning to give herself enough time to blow out her natural curls, but at the moment she didn't care. She needed the hot, steamy water, the supersize glass of wine to chase down her anxiety over Scarlett. And after she got out of the bath and dried herself off, instead of going to bed like she should, she was going to put on her most comfortable flannel pajamas and eat a giant bowl of popcorn while she binge-watched *Californication*—again. Because she needed that, too.

Her phone chimed from the sink where she'd left it. Bridget, realizing that she hadn't checked messages in hours, dried off her hand and groped for it, and then swiped and squinted at her day's mail.

An unbelievable rush of excitement passed through her small frame as all thoughts of Scarlett Hawkins and her stupid renovations flew out of Bridget's head.

"Oh, my God," she said out loud and laughed. "Oh, my God!" And she dropped the phone on the floor and immersed herself completely back into the bath for a moment, trying to contain her glee. It didn't work. She burst back up, the water running down her face and body in glimmering rivulets, not even caring that she had just swamped the floor with her enthusiastic splash.

"This is it!" she whispered, hugging herself. "The hell with Scarlett. I'm back!"

CHAPTER 14

"We need this one, Jay," said Leela as she charged into his office, waving a set of papers over her head. "We haven't had a shot at Harrington since before your father passed away. It will be extremely good for the business."

Jay looked up and laughed. Leela was twenty-seven but she looked young enough to be one of Alli's friends. And in her pegged jeans, baggy red dress shirt and skater-boy haircut, she kind of dressed like them, too. "You think we need every building that comes our way. It's just another skyscraper."

Leela shook her artfully disheveled, bleached-blond hair. "Just another skyscraper," she said in a mocking imitation of his voice. "Oh, Leela, just another skyscraper, no big deal." She returned to her own voice. "No, this one is different. Lots of publicity, a prestige project. And a client Russo Construction hasn't worked for in years."

Jay rolled his eyes. "Why do we need more publicity? We're pretty much building half of Manhattan and three quarters of Westchester these days."

Leela plunked down on the giant leather couch and then

immediately sprang back up again as if she couldn't stand to sit still. She started pacing the room. "We are. And the reason we have all that work is because I have worked all of your projects. Responded to all your RFPs and have been very careful to run the kind of jobs that will then bring in more jobs to pursue. And trust me when I tell you, this is one of them."

Jay laughed. "Give me the papers. I'll look. But no promises."

She slapped them onto his desk. "Mark Harrington is the developer. HealthTec is the anchor tenant."

He ruffled through the papers. "Harrington, huh? I know him. Not my favorite."

She glared at him. "Who cares? You think I like any of these guys? They all treat me like something they scraped off the bottom of their shoe. But if they pay, we build."

He blinked and looked up at her. "My dad used to say the exact same thing. I mean, not the shoe part—but the pay and build thing."

She threw up her hands. "Well, he was right! Why wouldn't we go after a half a billion dollar project? Why wouldn't we want to build another skyscraper? Isn't that literally what we're supposed to be doing?"

Jay sighed. He knew she was right. Of course she was right. "I'll think about it," he said, shoving the papers aside.

"Listen, Jay, can I say something?" Leela sat back down on the couch. This time she stayed sitting.

"Go for it."

"Please don't take this the wrong way, but I am pretty hot stuff. Top of my class. I could have worked anywhere, you know."

He laughed. "You're very good at what you do, Leela. No doubt at all."

"When I was looking for a job, I did my homework and I

decided that I wanted to work at Russo. I tracked the history of your company. Your dad did a lot for it, for sure, but it was only after you got your hands on it that it turned into a real powerhouse. You climbed the ladder faster than I've ever seen anyone climb."

He shrugged. "So?"

"So, I want to know what happened to that guy. Because I took this job thinking I was going to have a mentor, that I would get a master class in business. And you know, I was willing to take any job here. I figured I'd have to start at the bottom and really work my way up, but imagine my surprise when I was hired as COO. That was a shock, but I decided I could do it. I thought if I tried hard enough I could pull it off."

"Well, you've proven that you more than deserved it."

She nodded. "Thank you. But COO is a big job." She stood back up and began pacing again. "And can I speak honestly, sir?"

"Please do."

She took a deep breath. "I can't be the kind of COO this company deserves when I have to babysit you. I end up spending more time making sure that you are on top of your work than I do on my own responsibilities."

Jay blinked. *"Babysit?"*

She whirled on him. "Yes! Babysit! Do you realize that this place should be in pieces by now? I am twenty-seven years old! You hired someone with almost no experience to be your COO, and then you basically checked out on your own job, as well! I'm sorry, sir, but those are some idiotic moves!"

He smiled. "We seem to be doing fine."

Her eyes bugged out a little. "That is pure luck! We are getting by on your previous reputation. By all rights, you should be filing for bankruptcy by now!"

He shook his head. "I don't understand what you want. Do you feel that your compensation isn't fair? Do you want a raise?"

"Do I want a—" she muttered. She ran her fingers through her hair in frustration, making it stand up in short, sharp spikes. "No, I do not want a raise. My salary is more than generous. What I want is for you to do your job and let me do mine before this entire house of cards falls apart and we go belly-up!" She pointed a finger at the looming portrait of his father that hung over his desk. "What do you think he would say if he knew you were so dependent on some rando Indian chick who wandered in here straight out of grad school?"

Jay laughed. "Well, luckily, he's not here."

"Jay!" Leela sounded like she was on the verge of tears. "Are you hearing anything I'm saying? Listen, I can see that you're probably going through some personal stuff lately, and I'm very sorry for that. I like you. You're a very nice man. I appreciate that you bring me cookies, but I need you to take an interest in your own damned business!" She met his eyes. "I mean, even if you don't care, what about your dad? I know he cared. And what about your daughter? Isn't this a family business? Don't you want to do well for her?"

He raised his eyebrows. "You're getting a little personal, Leela."

She didn't flinch. "Because I have to."

"A lot of people would say you're going over the line."

"Fine! Fire me, then! Maybe it will wake you up!"

He shook his head. "Of course I won't fire you. I know you mean well."

She glared at him. Her eyes were practically shooting sparks. "You know I mean well, and you also know that I'm right. Because I am right."

He looked at her for a long moment and then dropped his gaze. "Fine. What do you want me to do?"

She exhaled and collapsed back onto the couch in a bone-less heap. "I just want you to get this job. Build this skyscraper. Get back in the game. Don't make me do all the work. Let me stick to the numbers like you hired me to do, and you do all the rest, okay? Take your business back. I am good, and we have been very lucky, but I can't keep worrying about whether or not you'll show up."

He nodded.

"And Jay?"

"Yes, Leela?"

"Please try to get excited about this skyscraper. I think it will help a lot if you're excited."

He nodded again. "I will try." He took a deep breath. "Thank you, Leela."

CHAPTER 15

"Do you think she'll want to keep the swing?" asked Ava as she handed Bridget her latte.

The two of them were taking a coffee break up the block from Scarlett's penthouse. There were more than a few delicate matters to discuss away from the prying ears of the workers, and even Scarlett herself.

Bridget sipped her coffee. "Of course she'll keep the swing. In fact, she told me that she wants it reinforced so that it can hold up to five hundred pounds. We might need to put in a steel beam."

Ava's eyes widened with surprise. "What? Five hundred? That's like five and a half of Scarlett's girlfriends! The woman is coming up on sixty. How can this be good for her health?"

Bridget laughed. "We should all be so healthy. But listen, can we come back to Scarlett in a minute? I actually want to talk about the Harrington job."

Ava's pretty mouth twisted into a frown.

"What?" said Bridget. "Why are you looking at me like that?"

Ava took a drink of her tea and then primly patted her lips

with a napkin. "I just haven't heard nice things about Mark Harrington."

Bridget shook her head. "Who the heck cares about nice? Nobody's nice in this business. I'm not nice. I don't think you're really understanding how big this is, Ava. This isn't some kitchen renovation. It's ground up, new construction. Mark Harrington is talking about building a skyscraper. A skyscraper! This is exactly what I need to get back in and get back in with a splash. It's fate."

Ava shook her head. "I don't understand why he even contacted you. This is way over your head. No one in their right mind would ever hire you to build a skyscraper at this point in your career! And everyone knows you're working for the Ludleys now."

"Maybe he just heard I can build. Maybe he's impressed with my history and the projects my company built."

Ava laughed. "Confidence much, girl? But even if you get the opportunity, I don't understand how you think you're actually going to build it. You don't have a business. You don't have an infrastructure. You don't have the money or the staff or the office."

"I can pull everything back together. I can rebuild."

"And what about your relationship with the union?"

Bridget frowned. "You know that was bull. Ten guys out of the hundreds I employed. It was a setup."

"Wasn't it Danny who hired those nonunion workers? You going to bring him back in?"

Bridget sighed. "I wish I could. It won't feel right working without him. He's been there from the very beginning of everything. He was always someone I could count on."

Ava laughed. "Until he wasn't."

Bridget shook her head. "It doesn't matter, anyway. He hasn't talked to me since it happened. I lost my temper with him.

Said some things I wish I could take back. I've tried to apologize, but he won't see me."

She cringed, remembering the way she had laid into him on that awful day with the rat. He and the guys he had hired were the only men on the job when she had finally arrived. Scarlett had already come and gone and all the union workers had seen Scabby and turned right around and gone home. Bridget, still reeling from her fight with Kevin that morning, the disappointment of losing yet another project and the absolute dread of what was going to happen next, had come after Danny with her claws out. Asking him how he could be so stupid to hire guys without union cards, yelling at him that if the business went belly-up, it was his fault. She'd been completely out of control.

And he'd just stood there and taken it. He'd stood there while she yelled and screamed, his face going paler and paler, his lips getting tighter and tighter, and then, when she'd shouted herself out, when she was just standing there, trying to catch her breath, trying not to sob, he picked up his tools and walked out.

As Bridget watched him disappear through the door, she felt a great tearing in her chest, a sharp, burning pain, something she hadn't felt since the day the hospital called to say her father was gone. Ava's eyes widened. "Seriously? He won't talk to you?"

"Yeah. I tried. But listen, even if I have to do it without him, I'll figure it out. This is not something I'm going to let slip through my fingers. I can't keep working for the Ludleys forever."

Ava sighed. "Look, I get it. I just want you to be careful. You need to walk again before you run. What about something smaller? Something in retail? It was hard enough for you to get hired with the Ludleys after everything happened.

What if they hear you're taking meetings behind their back? If this goes bad…"

Bridget leaned forward and put her hand on Ava's arm. "Enough. I know what I'm doing."

Ava sighed. "Okay. I hear you. Just…take it slow, okay? Don't get in over your head."

Bridget stood up. "Ava, I've been in the deep end of the pool since I was nine years old. Come on, we better get back to Scarlett. Her pleasure palace needs a new dildo closet."

CHAPTER 16

All that afternoon Jason tried to ignore the banging sounds above his head. It wasn't like he was doing much. It was supposed to be his day with Alli, so he'd cleared his schedule and stocked up the fridge, determined to start his new plan to make red sauce together after she got home from school. But Alli had texted at the last second, asking if she could stay at her friend's house for the night so they could work on a history project together.

Daddy-daughter dinner at Shake Shack on Saturday instead? he texted as an afterthought, feeling like he hadn't seen his kid for ages.

Dad. Don't call yourself daddy. That's gross.

He stared at the text.
Should he take that as a yes?
Bang!
His coffee cup rattled against the saucer.
Bang! Bang!

This time the table shook, too.

He groaned. He knew where the noise was coming from. Scarlett Hawkins had bought the entire floor above his apartment two years ago and she was perpetually renovating. She had twice sent down gift baskets full of homemade baked goods after particularly loud days—which was canny on her part. A warm chocolate walnut scone went a long way with Jason. But today was getting to him like it never had before. He wasn't sure if it was the noise that was bothering him more or the fact that she was using a construction firm that wasn't Russo to make that noise. After all, Russo Construction had swooped in to rescue her and finish her building after that debacle with Steele Construction. It's not like they didn't have a history.

Bang Bang Bang!

A cloud of plaster drifted down from his ceiling. White flecks floated in his coffee. Okay, that was enough. If she was going to fail to protect his space, he wasn't going to stay quiet about it.

Scarlett had a private elevator so the only way up to her place was the stairs, which he took two at a time. Inside her hallway, the banging continued, even louder, and he could hear the whine of a Sawzall. He knocked on her door and waited.

"Peters, I told you, just let yourself in. I don't have the time to— Oh. You're not Peters."

A petite, dark-haired woman with huge brown eyes blinked up at him, her nose scrunched in puzzlement. He quickly took in her black jacket and jeans, skintight over an incredible figure. One of Scarlett's many girlfriends, undoubtedly. Or at least, she was pretty enough to be.

"Hi, I live downstairs," he began.

"Jason?" came a voice from behind the brunette. Ava Martinez, an architect he had worked with on more than a few projects, stepped into view. "What are you doing here?"

Jay looked at the tall, willowy woman. He liked Ava; he had even contemplated asking her out once or twice before he realized that something about the way she held herself and the slope of her high cheekbones reminded him a little too much of Hana. But to be fair, there wasn't much that didn't remind him of Hana these days.

"Actually, as I was saying, I live downstairs—" he began.

"Oh, no," said the petite woman. She had a slight Bronx accent and her voice was husky and full of laughter. "Don't tell me. A piece of your ceiling just fell down." She turned back toward Ava. "I told you we'd be hearing from the neighbors today."

"Jay's a contractor, too," said Ava. "I'm sure he understands. Jason Russo, this is Bridget Steele."

Jay stared, fascinated, as he watched Bridget's face register who he was. She did not look happy.

He'd heard of her, of course. Everyone knew the story of her spectacular fall from grace. But he'd always imagined she would be...different, somehow. Harder. Taller, at least. This woman was all curves and lips and sultry bedroom eyes. She looked like a pocket-size pinup model.

"Nice to meet you," he said and offered her his hand.

She paused a moment, frowning, before she took his hand. Her grip was firm, as he knew it would it be. No one in this business had a weak handshake. Shaking hands among construction workers was basically a game of who could crush whose hand first. But even though she wasn't particularly squeezing his fingers, he had to admit that he felt a little unmoored.

She released her grip. "So did you come up to poach this job, too?"

He blinked. "Actually, I didn't even know you were still in the business."

She stuck out her chin. "Well. I am. So what do you want?"

He laughed nervously. "Um, as a matter of fact, you ruined my coffee," he said. "I mean, my cup is full of plaster and dust from the vibration of the walls from your tools."

Bridget didn't give an inch. "Well, it's a prewar. Of course you're going to get plaster dust. What do you want me to do, drywall the whole building?"

Before he could answer, Ava stepped forward, a sly look on her face. "Bridget, Bridget," she said in a conciliatory way, "you should buy Jay a new cup of coffee to make up for it. You guys have a lot in common."

Bridget cast a quick, stormy look at the architect before turning back toward him and smiling. But the smile didn't reach her eyes.

"I'm sure Mr. Russo doesn't want to talk shop with me," said Bridget tightly.

Jason suddenly felt a perverse desire to win over this woman. "I don't mind," he said, giving her his sweetest smile, "I'm always happy to talk business. And please, call me Jay."

"Bridget works for the Ludley brothers now," offered Ava. "She's always looking for a new opportunity. She's a great salesperson, but an even better builder."

Bridget's eyes narrowed briefly and a spot of pink appeared on each of her cheeks. She looked like she wanted to strangle her friend. "Actually, I'm perfectly fine at the Ludleys' for now."

Jay laughed. This woman was sexy when she was pissed. "You know what?" he said, "I would love to take you up on that cup of coffee, Ms. Steele."

Bridget's smile grew wider, but her eyes were still hard. "I didn't offer you coffee. Ava did. And besides that, we're in the middle of work."

"Oh, go ahead," said Ava. Obviously, her friend didn't intimidate her in the least. "We were just going to call it a day, anyway. And Jay doesn't want any coffee from me. I remind him of his ex-wife."

He jerked his head up, meeting Ava's smirk.

"I heard you talking to the project manager on that last job we did on Mercer," she said. "Great acoustics in that place."

"Sorry," he muttered, embarrassed.

She shrugged ruefully. "At least you weren't talking about my butt like the other guy was."

He squeezed his eyes shut for a moment. It was one of the reasons he'd always avoided bringing Alli around his building sites. Deep down, most men were pigs, and in a 98 percent male environment, very few of them bothered hiding it.

"Seriously, sorry," he said again. "If it makes you feel any better, my ex-wife is a perfectly nice person."

Ava waved her hand. "Believe me, my heart was not broken. And listen, I'm sure that Bridget isn't anything like your ex-wife. In fact," she said, grinning, "she was just telling me that she's not nice at all."

"Ava, shut the hell up," said Bridget. She wasn't even trying to hide her annoyance anymore.

Ava looked at her friend. "Just saying. I'd rather work for Jay than the Ludleys."

"I'm not looking for a new job," gritted out Bridget.

Jason was enjoying this. "Well, we're always looking for new blood," he said, arranging his face in what he hoped to be a winning look.

Bridget rolled her eyes. She knew she was being teased. "Fine," she said at last. "I do not need a job, but I'm hungry. You can buy me dinner. A nice dinner."

Jay raised his eyebrows. "Wait, I thought you were buying me coffee."

She met his eyes. "Take it or leave it."

"He'll take it!" said Ava. She looked at him. "I'm doing you a huge favor, Russo."

"Well, in that case," Jay said, hiding his smile, "I know a place. Just down the street."

Bridget bit her lip and the sight made a sudden rush of heat flood through Jay's body.

Wow, he thought, *I can't remember the last time that happened.*

"All right. I'm up for trying something new," said Bridget. And she smiled. A genuine smile this time. She was softening up.

"Good," said Jay, grinning in response.

"Good!" piped in Ava.

Bridget rolled her eyes and looked at Jay. "Come on, let's go before I end up socking this girl in the nose."

CHAPTER 17

Bridget couldn't wait until she could call Ava and ream her out. Her friend was so pushy. Bridget did not need to be set up—not for a job or a date. Especially with some entitled golden boy who had been messing with her business for years.

"You look pissed," said Jay in a mild voice. She blinked her eyes and looked at him from across the table. She had been fuming so hard, she had honestly forgotten he was there.

"I'm sorry," she said. She took a sip of her wine, trying to calm herself down. "I was just thinking about something else."

She looked around. The place was not what she expected. Dim lighting, red velvet booths, candles in old Chianti bottles, corny Italian accordion music wafting through the air.

"Sexy place," she said. "Looks like a red-sauce tourist trap."

He grinned at her. "It is a red-sauce tourist trap. But I know the chef, Omar. He's from Morocco. His Italian food is crap, but if you order off-menu, chef's choice, he's a genius."

He pushed forward one of the many little dishes of vegetables that the waiter had laid out on the table. "Try this eggplant. It's amazing."

She broke off a piece of warm flatbread and dipped it into the spread. He was right; it was amazing—smoky and velvety smooth with a nice little bite of heat at the end.

"It's great, right? This is just temporary. Omar will get his own place where he can cook his own kind of stuff, and then we can say we knew him when."

She laughed and looked at him with more attention. When Bridget dated, which wasn't often these days, she usually went for rich, powerful, hypermasculine older men, or, God help her, muscle heads likes Kevin, but this guy was different. He was less showy, for one. No big gold Rolex watch, no tailored suit, no wafts of expensive Tom Ford cologne. Lean and built, but not overly developed. He looked a bit rumpled in his T-shirt and Rag & Bone jeans—boyish. Bridget guessed he was close to her age, maybe a little older. The same thick, unruly dark hair, wide shoulders and easy smile she had noticed at the party so long ago. There was something quiet and watchful about his heavy-lidded green eyes that made her feel...seen.

"Wait. Don't you have a wife?" she blurted out, remembering the stylish woman in the red cape.

He raised an eyebrow. "I did. We've been divorced for a year now."

"Oh," said Bridget, chastened. "Right. The ex-wife Ava reminds you of. Sorry. Me, too. For a little longer than that." She took another hasty gulp of wine before changing the subject. "So you've been in the business for a long time?"

He nodded. "Born and raised in it. Russo Construction was started by my great-granddad."

She wasn't surprised. Most of the construction bosses in Manhattan had the same story. Nepotism. Five of the largest companies were at least third generation. The industry was almost impossible to break into if you were an outsider.

He helped himself to some carrot and mint salad. "And I think I already know most of your story."

She snorted. "I doubt it."

He raised an eyebrow. "Well, you're a bit of a legend."

She shook her head. "Let's see, so I'm guessing what you heard is that I'm a Bronx girl who bit off way more than I could chew, and I got what I deserved."

He sipped his wine. "Pretty much."

She shook her head. "Well, screw you."

He laughed. "You fit right in, don't you? Are you really looking to leave Ludley Construction?"

"No," she said, lifting her chin. "I'm not."

"I wouldn't blame you if you were. Linus and Larry are a couple of assholes."

"Yeah, well, they hired me when no one else would. And I bring in a lot of business for them."

"Let me ask you something," he said. "Are they up for the Harrington job?"

Her heart raced. She didn't break eye contact as she lied. "What job is that?"

He smiled, dabbed at his face with his napkin. "Nothing. Just a little reno."

"Oh? I didn't think your company did such small jobs."

He shrugged. "I didn't say we were up for it."

So he was a good liar, too. She understood. She hadn't told him anything, either. But if, once more, he was her direct competition, that ended the chance of anything serious between them. Which was fine. What the hell, right? Maybe he'd be fun for a fling and a couple of trips to the Hamptons in his Ferrari before they squared off over the job.

"Do you know Harrington?" she asked in what she hoped was a casual way.

"Yes, but I haven't actually worked for him before. Why do you ask?"

She turned up her hand. "Well, he's a pretty big developer. He'd be a good guy for me to know."

"Oh?"

"Sure. Connections aren't always the easiest thing for me to make."

"No? Why not?"

She had more wine, a longer drink this time. "I wasn't exactly born into the business like some people."

He laughed. "Point taken."

"Lots of places I'm not invited in due to my lack of a penis. Dinners, athletic clubs, strip clubs, golf courses…"

He nodded thoughtfully. "I never thought of that. I make a lot of deals playing racquetball."

"Exactly. No one ever asks me for a game. And I'm damned good."

"Maybe we should play together sometime."

She looked him in the eye. "I'm pretty sure I'd kick your ass."

He didn't look away. "Oh, yeah? I think I might enjoy seeing you try."

She felt a warm shimmer in the pit of her stomach. She groped for her glass and hastily gulped down most of her drink.

Damn, he was hot.

The moment was broken when a slim young man with shaggy dark hair under his chef's toque arrived at the table bearing an enormous conical serving dish.

"Omar!" said Jason, beaming. "Is that a lamb tagine? You didn't!"

The chef smiled modestly as he placed the dish on the table, lifted the lid and revealed the glistening lamb and vegetables inside. "No soggy spaghetti for you, my friend."

Jason laughed. "Hey, spaghetti is fine when it's done right. Omar, this is Bridget. She now knows to never order your lasagna."

"Hello," said Omar, giving her a curious look. "Jay must like you very much if he brought you to me."

Bridget laughed. "We just met, actually."

Omar smiled and gave a little nod as he turned away. "I must return to my kitchen and make chicken parm for those who don't know better. Enjoy the meal."

"Oh, my God," said Bridget, leaning over the tagine and helping herself to the steaming meat and vegetables. "This smells amazing."

Jason smiled at her. "A woman who likes to eat," he said.

She shot him a look, her fork midway to her mouth. "Contrary to popular belief, we don't live on air."

He held up his hands in defense. "I just meant, my ex was not into food. She was definitely more 'eat to live' than 'live to eat.' It always made me kind of sad—that we couldn't share that interest."

Bridget relaxed and brought the forkful of lamb to her mouth. It was delicious. "I'm Jewish," she said after she chewed and swallowed. "Food is important."

He laughed. "And I'm Italian, so I understand." He helped himself to more bread. "My daughter likes to eat, too, which I've always been grateful for."

She looked up at him. For some reason she hadn't expected him to have kids. "You have a daughter? How old?"

"Fifteen. Her name is Alli. Want to see a picture?" He already had his phone out and was scrolling.

"Really? You don't look old enough to have a teenager."

"I'm forty-two. Got married young." He turned the screen

toward her and Bridget looked at the picture of a pretty girl with short black hair. Bridget could see that she had her father's broad smile.

"She's beautiful," she said.

He took the phone back and smiled fondly at the screen. "She is, right?" He looked back up at her. "How about you? Kids?"

She smiled. "I have a son, Dylan. He's seven."

"Picture?"

She took out her phone and scrolled until she found a picture of him just after he lost his first tooth.

Jason looked at it. "He looks like an adorable little jack-o'-lantern."

She smiled. "He's the best."

He handed the phone back to her and their fingers touched. She could feel the heat rushing through her body.

He smiled at her. "So you going to tell me the truth about Harrington now?"

She blinked. He'd surprised her. "I told you the truth. The Ludley brothers aren't being considered."

He cocked his head and narrowed his eyes. "But...you are."

She choked on the bread in her mouth. Reached for her wine.

He watched her gulp her wine. "You okay?"

She nodded.

He took a sip of his own. "To be honest? I have a hard time seeing Harrington hiring a woman builder."

Bridget felt a cold lump of anger swell in her chest.

Every god damn time.

"Huh. Well, pretty strange that he would reach out to me then, huh?"

Jason raised an eyebrow. "So he did."

She glared at him. "You know he did. Just like I know that you're up for it, too."

He shrugged. "It's a little weird. I mean, why you? You don't even have a construction company anymore."

Bridget felt the anger grow. "Gosh. Right? Why ever would anyone want to hire little old me? I was only the CEO of one of the best construction companies in New York, with over a dozen years of experience. I've only built millions of square feet of space, countless projects for major corporations—"

He held up his hands, interrupting her. "Listen, I'm not questioning your credentials. I've never heard anything but good things about your company. I mean, before it all went to hell, of course. But it's what you were saying before—this is a boys' club, and Harrington is pretty much the president. I'm not saying this is fair or right, but he's got his people. He's old-school. He only works with a select group of companies from his network. People who've been around forever. I mean, this is actually the first time he's even put me up for a job, and I'm pretty sure the only reason he's doing it is because he knew my dad."

"Lucky you," Bridget said drily.

"I just don't get why he's reaching outside his usual people. It's not like him."

"Well, maybe this project is going to be different. Maybe he needs to build a team that's outside his typical network. Maybe he wants a different approach."

He laughed. "Maybe. And you think you can handle it?"

She stuck out her chin. "I don't see why not."

He didn't believe her. She could see it on his face. And she knew she shouldn't give a damn whether he believed in her or not, but for some reason, she did. She really did.

She checked the time on her phone. "Hey, this has been fun, but I have to get back home to my son. The babysitter isn't expecting me to be late. But—" she hesitated for a moment and then decided to go for it "—what are you doing tomorrow?"

"What have you got in mind?" he answered.

CHAPTER 18

Numbers were Liam's toys. Ever since he was a little kid, when his mother brought home a pocket calculator, and he realized that he could do simple sums in his head faster than she could punch the numbers in, he'd felt like math was his language. He could have gone in all sorts of directions with it—programming, robotics, physics…but even more important to him than the joy of working with numbers was the need for him to convert that math into cold, hard cash. He always knew it was an MBA or nothing. He knew he would run a business, he didn't really care what kind, just as long as he made a ton of money doing it.

It wouldn't have surprised anyone who knew him to find him at a party on a two-hundred-foot yacht, hiding in the guest cabin, smoking a joint and running numbers for Harrington's skyscraper job.

The Per Se dinner had paid off; the official request for proposal, RFP, had come in earlier in the day, and his chief estimator was already starting to put together the budget. Liam had hired an excellent chief estimator but he knew he wouldn't rest easy until he double- and triple-checked every digit himself. In the end, he'd only trust his own numbers. They hadn't failed him yet.

He took off his jacket and sprawled out on the bed, smoking and scrolling through charts on his iPhone, almost forgetting where he was, except for the mild bobbing sensation of being on the water. They were berthed in the Chelsea Pier. The developer who owned the boat never took it anywhere, just kept it docked, his own private tax break, and threw blowout parties every month so that he could write off the yacht as a business expense. They were always the same: Katz's Deli and Jean-Georges would cater, pastrami sandwiches and half-sour pickles at one table and caramelized foie gras brûlée and egg caviar at the other, the open bar was all top-shelf and the champagne would be flowing. Little silver candy dishes of rolled joints, edibles, pills and coke were left out like so much potpourri, just there for the taking. Some B-list pop star would be performing on deck, and everyone who was anyone in the industry, plus a bevy of scantily clad models, actresses and socialites, would be there.

Liam had enjoyed these parties a lot more when he and Jay used to go together. In the beginning of their partnership, when Liam was still learning the ropes of the business, Jay used to force him to go to every party, lunch, golf game and strip joint that they were invited to. "It's all about networking," Jay had told him. "It won't matter if you're a financial wizard if these guys don't like you. And they're not going to like you unless they know you. You've got to show up and play the game, my friend."

And Liam did. He showed up and, with Jay's help, he pressed flesh and laughed at jokes and kept his secret derision for most of these guys buried. And if he ever got too quiet, or tried to retreat to some dark corner, Jay was always there to drag him back into the light again, make him rejoin the party and engage with the sweaty masses, as he jokingly called them.

Liam knew he should be doing the same thing right now. He should be up on the deck, getting coked up and dancing with a stripper/actress. He should be telling dirty jokes and bragging about his cars and beach house and his last trip to St. Bart's. But he'd put in a good couple of hours already; he'd made the rounds, he'd shown his face, and without Jay there to tell him otherwise, he'd decided he'd earned a little bit of a break to do something he really enjoyed.

He took another hit off his joint, closing his eyes for a moment, and felt the sway of the boat, heard the *thump thump thump* of the bass playing on the deck and the sound of people laughing and yelling just outside the cabin in drug- and alcohol-induced glee. He wished Hana was here. She absolutely refused to go to these parties anymore after she had her ass grabbed by a local politician and Liam had tried to break the guy's nose. But she understood that he needed to go.

Liam smiled to himself, imagining her sitting up in bed, wearing that long white nightie that he liked, thumbing through the stack of back issues of *The New Yorker* she kept on her bedside table. She wore her glasses in bed. They were big and clunky and constantly slid down her nose. Her feet were probably cold. She always complained that she couldn't get them warm if he wasn't in the bed with her so she could tuck them under his thigh. He kept quirks like this about her cataloged in his head and enjoyed pulling them out to examine every now and then.

He opened his eyes and sighed. It was near midnight, but really the party was just getting started. He should get out of this room and join in some more if he wanted to stay on the radar. After all, he still had the money he'd made with Jay, which was a fortune by most standards, but that didn't mean he could sit back and relax while he was launching this new business. *Never rest, stay on your feet, keep your eye on the ball*, Jay had repeated it like a mantra. And Liam was sure his old friend was doing just that—maybe he wasn't here tonight, but he was definitely somewhere, working the crowd, remembering everyone's name, making sure everyone liked him. And Liam couldn't fall behind.

He took one last toke and then stubbed out his joint and pocketed his cell phone. The cabin opened up into a huge room, complete with bar and lounge and a great view of the water. Everywhere he looked, overly tanned men with slicked-back hair and expensive suits sat with scantily clad women, drinking and laughing and groping. One guy was doing blow straight out of a woman's cleavage. Liam would bet there wasn't an actual wife or even a girlfriend in the place.

He grabbed a glass of champagne as he made his way through the room to the upper deck. Tonight's pop star, someone he didn't recognize, a young, pretty woman with a huge pink Afro of a wig, writhed on stage and shout-sang all about her broken heart as a dozen guys stripped down to their shirtsleeves and undershirts sweated and danced with a bunch of women who Liam was pretty sure were hired strippers.

"Hey, Maguire, what's going on, my man?"

It was Sal Delmonico, the union head, smoking a fat cigar and wearing the ugliest tie Liam had ever seen. Liam bit back the urge to turn his back on the guy and walk away.

"Hey, Delmonico," he answered instead, finishing his drink.

"So I heard you got the official request for proposal on the Harrington job?"

Liam shook his head. How did this guy always know everything as soon as it happened?

Delmonico grinned, guessing what Liam was thinking. "Just got my ear to the ground, my friend."

"Apparently so," said Liam. "You know so much—who else got invited to the table?"

Delmonico took a drag on his cigar and then let the smoke trickle out of his mouth. "The usual crowd." He shrugged. "The only one I can't figure is that Steele chick. Remember her? For some reason Harrington's bringing her in."

Liam lifted his eyebrows. He did remember Bridget Steele. They used to bid against each other before the whole Scarlett Hawkins thing hit the fan. He didn't know her personally, but she was an outsider like him, and if the stories were true, she was funny and tough and a real boss lady, not afraid to mix it up with all the assholes in this industry. But if she was up for the Harrington job, she was just one more person he needed to get rid of. "She's good," he said. "Why shouldn't she come in?"

Delmonico sneered. "She's a bitch. Someone ought to tell Harrington that she's poison to work with."

Liam raised an eyebrow. "Huh. Don't tell me. You must have had something to do with shutting down her work on Scarlett Hawkins's project."

Sal smiled and it was just about as ugly as his tie. "Maybe," he said slyly. "But whatever happened, trust me when I tell you that the bitch brought it on herself."

Liam once again held back an urge to walk away. He knew guys like this. He'd grown up with them. The kind of guys who simply didn't believe that a woman, no matter how smart or accomplished, could ever be as good as a man at anything that really mattered. Women were bitches, whores or wives, and that was it.

Delmonico disgusted him, but he might be useful.

He flagged down a passing waiter and handed Delmonico a fresh glass of champagne. "Tell me more."

CHAPTER 19

Before his appointment the next afternoon, Jason sat down with the RFP on the Harrington job. He'd already gone over it once after Leela had confronted him in his office, and his team had combed every angle and given him a dozen different ways to approach this project and presentation. But since his conversation with Bridget the night before, he was suddenly more interested.

He assumed Russo Construction would get this job. They were the number one construction management company in Manhattan, and when they went out for a project of this magnitude, they generally got it. But now he wondered...how much did he actually want it?

He pushed the paperwork away and walked through his living room out onto the terrace that overlooked the park. His mind was whirling. The anchor tenant for the building, Health-Tec, had risen out of nowhere in the past five years as an online site to address the public's health-care needs. You could search your symptoms, be linked to a doctor who was standing by, ready to Skype at a fraction of the cost of a face-to-face visit, and then either have a next-day appointment scheduled at one of their nationwide clinics to follow up, or, if your symptoms were declared mild enough, have your prescriptions emailed to your pharmacy. They were a huge, immediate success and had changed the face of the health-care industry in America. Jay didn't use their services, and he'd certainly never let Alli get diagnosed for anything over the internet, but he knew that, for some people, it was their best, and sometimes only, option. Still, he wasn't particularly excited about building for them.

Financially, he didn't really need it. His company was worth more than it had ever been before. But, as Leela had pointed out, at two million square feet and nearly fifty stories, it was easily a half a billion dollar job and he'd be a fool to ignore it. It would only make the business stronger and that much more of a powerhouse.

And then someday Alli could inherit the company just like he had.

The thought made him pause. He knew he'd been lucky, but he also knew that, for him, there had never been another choice. Did he want to put the same burden on his daughter? Did he want to make her eat, sleep and breathe this business?

And what about Bridget? He hadn't met a woman like that in…well, maybe ever, now that he thought about it. She was smart and funny and brash and sexy as hell. And mercurial— that woman changed from cold to hot in a split second, and god damn if it didn't turn him on. He hadn't felt that attracted to anyone for years. Since Hana left he had sometimes wondered if that part of him had been swept away with all the rest of the things she took: the good towels, the Cuisinart and his ability to really want a woman. He worried that he had become broken beyond repair. Not that he hadn't had a few flings over the past year, some one-night stands, dated here and there—but all that had felt like work more than anything.

Work to pay attention, work to fake real interest, work not to compare them to Hana. But last night he had felt like a high school student again—almost everything Bridget said and did had made him rock-hard.

Well, you can forget about all that if you steal her job, buddy.

Maybe it wasn't worth it. Maybe he should just bow out and give her one less real contender to worry about. She obviously needed it; working for those god damned Ludley brothers had to be a nightmare. And sure, there would be other companies up for the job, but Russo Construction stepping out of the way would certainly increase her chances...

He thought about what Leela would say if he told her he didn't want Russo Construction to respond to the RFP. She would murder him. He wondered what his father would do. Actually, he knew what his father would do—he'd get the job, come hell or high water. The company always came first. He'd taught him that from day one.

"Dad?" He heard the front door slam and his daughter's voice echoed from the front hallway. "Dad? You here?"

He turned, alarmed. "Alli? What are you doing home? Why aren't you at school?"

She looked at him, her eyes half-closed. There was a definite tinge of green to her skin. "Daddy, I don't feel so great. Lulu's mom made this chicken thing last night and it wasn't really cooked all the way and—" Suddenly, her eyes flew open and she clamped her hands over her mouth, desperately pushing past him and into the bathroom.

CHAPTER 20

There is nothing to be nervous about, Bridget reminded herself for the fifth time in a row. *Harrington said you didn't need to have anything prepared. This is just him showing you the rendering. Feeling you out. Letting you know the scope of the project. You just have to smile and nod and sound like you know what you're talking about—which you do. You can do this with your hands tied behind your back, sister. Pull it together.*

"Ms. Steele?" The pretty young assistant behind the massive glass desk looked up at her. "Mr. Harrington is ready for you now. Just through there."

Bridget stood up, her heart beating double time, and smoothed her cream-colored YSL suit down over her hips. She'd chosen a fitted jacket with wide-legged pants, three-inch Manolos and had her hair blown out into sleek waves. Yes, there was a touch of lipstick and an inch or so of cleavage just to hedge her bets, but Harrington had called her, after all. She didn't have to show it all. She already had his attention.

The door to his office slid open at her touch. Mark Harrington was already up from behind his desk, ready with a firm handshake and a gentle palm on her shoulder to steer her to-ward a comfortable sitting area facing a sixty-inch flat screen.

"Ms. Steele—" his voice was warm and deep "—thank you so much for making the time to see me."

"My pleasure," said Bridget. "Thank you for giving us this opportunity."

There was no "us" yet, of course, thought Bridget, but if she pulled off this meeting, she'd make damned sure there would be.

She had been expecting someone chubby and schlumpy with the five-thousand-dollar suit, de rigueur hair plugs and overly tanned hide of most of the Manhattan developer set, but this guy was a silver fox. Tall and powerfully built, with a strong jaw, ice-blue eyes that crinkled when he smiled and a thick head of white hair. When he leaned in toward her, she smelled leather, musk and a hint of dark chocolate.

"Nice office," she forced herself to say, looking around at the silver leaf columns and the polished concrete floor.

"Thank you. I paid an arm and a leg for Gensler to send in some guy with much better taste than me to come and cre-ate this. If I'd been left on my own, there would probably be nothing but fishing trophies and La-Z-Boys."

He laughed loudly at his own joke and suddenly Bridget felt better. He might be good-looking, he might hold the keys to her future in his hand, but no one who laughed at their own lame joke could be too intimidating.

He sat down on the Eames recliner next to her and flipped on the television screen. "So," he said, "I hear you're very good at what you do."

Bridget nodded. "Yes, I am."

He raised an eyebrow. "So confidence isn't a problem, huh? Listen, I did my homework. This project is too important to waste time with any lightweights. I know your story. And I know how much you've accomplished. And from what I've heard, you got the short end of the stick when your company went down."

She nodded, hoping she wouldn't have to explain more.

"I also know that you're working for the Ludley brothers now, but if you got this contract, I'm wondering just how you think you'd pull together this size of a project. I want to be clear—I am not interested in working with Linus and Larry. I need someone who can really think outside the box. I am interested in only you."

She didn't even hesitate. "It won't be a problem. I haven't signed anything with them. I'm a consultant on retainer. And as for the infrastructure, I built it once, I can do it again."

He cocked his head. "Well, that's saying a lot."

She nodded. "I'm proud of the team that I had."

"So—" his eyes met hers "—tell me why you should be considered for this project."

"Building is all about taking a plan, understanding every single component and obstacle that will go into making it happen and knowing how to put them together. And I can do that faster and smarter than anyone."

He leaned back in his chair. "Yeah?"

"Yeah. I am all about the details. I notice things no one else does. I foresee problems and solve them before they interfere with schedule or budget. My communication with the men is crystal-clear. I make sure they know exactly what I want and how to give it to the project. My jobs always come in on time, and I can anticipate possible cost overruns and design flaws before they occur, which will save you time and money. I know every page of the construction documents backward and forward. We pass every inspection and my clients are always happy."

He looked at her, considering. "That all sounds good but how I can be sure it's true?"

She nodded. "Because honestly, I would not still be in this business in any capacity if it wasn't true. I need to be five times better than the average company run by a man to be considered an equal, so that means I have to be ten times better to win the projects. I can't afford to make a mistake. I don't have room to mess around." She held up her hand. "Now, I know I had some bumps in the road, but as you said, I got the short end of the stick. I want back in, and this project would make it possible. You know the renovation for L'Oréal's corporate headquarters?"

He raised an eyebrow. "That was excellent work."

"I built that. How about Simon and Schuster?"

He pursed his lips, impressed. "Yours?"

"Mine."

"Also, the entire five floors of law offices for Murphy and Jacowitz on Park Avenue, the reno on the Museum of Math and Science in SoHo, the Colicchio chain of bakeries. Mine. Mine. Mine. Shall I go on?"

He locked eyes with her and she felt a little shiver run down her back. It was not an entirely unpleasant feeling. "Not necessary," he said. "I told you, I already did my homework. I know what you're capable of, Ms. Steele."

She nodded again. "Anyway, I'm very excited to see the rendering."

He smiled and picked up a remote control. "Yes, ma'am."

As he fiddled with the remote control, Bridget sat back against the couch and took a deep breath. This was a huge moment for her—it was the chance to get back everything she'd lost. And for a split second she thought, *I wish I could call Dad and tell him about this.*

"These are just a few of the preliminary renderings." Harrington's voice cut through her thoughts. "Obviously, we're still very early in the process."

She examined the renderings, feeling a pang of disappointment. The images he was showing her were nondescript. A basic, tubular gray high-rise with the expected amount of steel and glass thrown in. It looked like a dozen other buildings in Manhattan.

But the point is, this is the one you would build, she reminded herself.

Harrington used the mouse on his computer to point out different things. "Fifty stories, West Chelsea. We'll be taking down two previously existing buildings to make space. We're hoping to do it in two and a half years, from demo to ribbon cutting."

Bridget gave a low whistle. "That's fast."

He turned toward her, his ice-blue eyes meeting hers. "I thought you said you were better and faster than anyone?"

She laughed. "I'm not saying it's impossible. I'm just saying it's fast, even for me. But go ahead, tell me more."

Harrington took her through each floor, describing what HealthTec envisioned. "This will be more than just their campus. This building will be the concrete symbol of their entire business. They've done research—people like HealthTec's availability and responsiveness and price points, but everyone says the same thing—HealthTec is faceless. Given the choice, they would never go to them for their day-to-day health needs. HeathTec can put as many friendly doctors willing to Skype with you online as they want—but people still feel like they're dealing with an uncaring corporation."

"They miss the human touch," said Bridget.

"Exactly."

Bridget raised her eyebrows. "And this building is somehow supposed to solve all that?"

"It's going to be more than a building. It's going to be a place where miracles will happen. Where sick children come to get well. Where dedicated scientists work on new, futuristic ways to cure deadly diseases."

"Where the shareholders in HealthTec rake in billions of dollars while they enjoy a really nice view of the Hudson."

Harrington laughed. "Yeah. That, too."

Bridget held up her hands. "No judgment. If they can do both, more power to them. But if they're hanging so much on this one building—don't you think they'd somehow want to make it more…distinctive?"

Harrington turned his eyes toward her. "What do you mean?"

Bridget shifted in her seat, wondering if she was about to say too much. "I just mean…you'd think they'd want it to stand out a little more, be something that really makes you stop and look? Maybe something with curves and angles, twisting planes that create figure eights like DNA strands? Something that telegraphs the amazing medical-related phenomena that are supposed to be going on inside. Skyscrapers were originally designed to connect earth to sky, you know? They were meant to create awe and wonder. This building doesn't look like a place where miracles happen. It just looks kind of like old-school, old design. Apartments or ad agencies, insurance offices—"

Harrington frowned. "Insurance offices? I thought you were a contractor, not an architect."

She shook her head. "I know. It's outside my purview, but I just thought maybe you'd like some honest criticism. I told you that I notice details, right? This design is generic—it simply doesn't stand out."

Harrington aimed the remote control at the screen and the image disappeared with a faint little snip sound. "Well, thank you, Ms. Steele. We will definitely take your thoughts into consideration."

For a moment Bridget couldn't speak. She felt like she'd been punched in the gut. "Wait, listen, I'm sorry if I somehow stepped over the line, I only meant—"

He cut her off. His face was a mask. "Not at all. I just have another appointment I need to move on to."

"But I still have some questions. I mean, we didn't really finish discussing—"

He held out his hand for her to shake. "It's been a pleasure meeting you. We'll be in touch."

Bridget swallowed hard, stood up and took his hand, willing herself not to dig herself in any deeper. "It was a great pleasure meeting you, Mr. Harrington. I hope that we talk again soon."

"I'm sure we will, Ms. Steele." He didn't meet her eyes.

Bridget felt numb as she let herself out of his office. She couldn't believe what had just happened. She'd had the opportunity of a lifetime and she had completely screwed herself.

CHAPTER 21

Jay's heart skipped when the office door slid open and Bridget Steele stepped out. He had been hoping against hope that he wouldn't run into her here. He knew that Harrington had appointments all day—what were the chances that he'd overlap with Bridget?

Obviously, better than he had anticipated.

For a moment she didn't seem to see him, and he had a split second to look at her unobserved. She looked sophisticated and professional and god damned gorgeous. Her tailored suit jacket couldn't hide her curves, and her hair was pulled back and her face nearly bare of makeup—except for the dark red lipstick that made her full lips look so tempting that he found himself imagining the way the color might smear when he kissed her, the marks she might leave over his body...

But then her eyes met his and she looked...furious. Like, underneath that hard-as-nails veneer, there was something bleeding and raw—an animal in a trap, chewing off its own tail.

At first, he thought the fury was directed at him—for stepping into the competition. And for a moment he thought, *I shouldn't have come. This was her big chance; it was unprecedented she was even invited back to the table; I shouldn't stand in her way...*

But then out of nowhere, he remembered the last time he was at the office with his father. Retirement was just around the corner and even though he had worked at Russo Construction for years, his dad seemed frantic, as if there was so much left to learn. "Mondays we go over the books," his father had said.

"Yes, Dad, I know."

"And listen, Lane Percy will sometimes take more sick days than he's allotted if you let him—but there's nothing wrong with the guy except that he's lazy. You gotta call him out. Remember that."

"Yeah, Dad, I know Lane."

His dad opened his mouth to tell him something else, but Jason cut him off. "Dad, listen, really. I've got this. You don't have to worry."

For a moment his dad stared at him, and Jason inwardly shuddered, seeing how old and lost he looked. "This company is everything," his father finally said. "My father spent his whole life building it up, and his father before him, and now me. Tell me that you know that, Jay. Tell me that you understand that the company always comes first, no matter what."

And Jason had nodded, taken his dad's hand and promised. He would make the company everything.

And he had. He'd lost his marriage, alienated his daughter, but the company always came first. And that rule couldn't just crumble for some woman he'd just met, no matter how attractive he found her to be.

He looked back into Bridget's face, steeling himself for her reaction. And that was the moment that he realized she wasn't even looking at him with any recognition. She was staring right through him.

"Bridget?" He spoke before he thought. "You okay?"

She blinked and her eyes focused for a moment. She looked confused. "Jason? Why? What are you—" And then understanding seemed to dawn. Spots of color mounted in her cheeks as her mouth hardened.

"Right," she gritted out. "Right. Well, go ahead. It's all yours now." Then she swept out the exit.

Harrington's receptionist stared as the door slammed behind Bridget. Then she looked at Jason. "What in the world did you do to her?" she asked, wide-eyed.

Jason sighed and shook his head. "It's a long story."

Hana was still at the apartment when Jason got back, which was the last thing he wanted to deal with. Despite the fact that the meeting with Mark had gone well—in fact, Mark had asked him to submit a preliminary budget for the existing design—all he could think about was Bridget. The look on her face when she realized he was there, the way she had walked past him. Obviously, things must have gone badly between her and Harrington.

"Hey," said Hana as he came into the kitchen. She was sitting at the island, doodling on a piece of scratch paper, her hair pulled back into a long braid. For a moment Jason could almost pretend that the past year hadn't happened. Here was his wife—ex-wife, his brain immediately corrected—in their home, their daughter in her room, a little sick, but basically safe and sound.

The illusion was quickly shattered when Hana hopped off the stool and grabbed her purse. "She's fine. Slept all day, but I didn't want her to be alone while you were gone. I've got to go. I'm meeting Liam at a gallery in SoHo."

Jason tried to keep his face neutral at the mention of his wife-stealing ex-business partner and former best friend. "New show?" he said.

She squeezed her eyes shut for a moment and shook her head, her long eyelashes brushing against the curve of her high, polished cheekbones. She always made that face when she didn't want to talk about something. "No, not mine."

"You got something coming up, though, right? It's been a while."

She avoided his eyes. "Yeah, I guess it's been a while. And no, nothing coming up."

He looked at her carefully. This was new. The Hana Takada he knew was an incredibly driven artist—someone who had at least two shows a year since he'd first met her.

She shook her head again. "Stop looking at me like that."

"Like what?"

"Like—like you feel sorry for me or something. I'll do a show when I want to do a show. I've just been…busy, you know? Liam has so many social commitments, so much networking for the business, and he likes me to come along with him to everything."

He held his hands up. "I was definitely not feeling sorry for you. And that's good, right? I mean, I thought our problem was that we didn't see each other enough? That I left you on your own all the time? Sounds like Liam's got it covered."

She looked at him and sighed. "I'm not going to fight with you right now, Jay."

"Hey, I don't want to fight, either."

She hauled her purse strap up over her shoulder. "Then I'm just going to go, okay? Have Alli text me when she's feeling better, and I'll come back to pick her up." She started to leave.

"Hana?"

She turned and looked at him, suspicion and exhaustion equally written across her face.

"All I meant to say was that you're an amazing artist, and I hope you do more soon."

She looked at him for a long moment. The ghost of a smile brushed over her mouth. "Okay." Thanks."

And then she was gone. And it was funny, but for the first time in a long time, Jason didn't feel sadness or anger in her absence. In fact, he stopped thinking about her almost as soon as she was out the door.

CHAPTER 22

Liam wished he was almost anywhere but at a gallery opening. He frigging hated art openings. The cheap wine, the precut cubes of cheese and rapidly dehydrating plates of crudités, the same crowd wandering around wearing the same clothes, saying the same things. And 99 percent of the time, the art was crap. Certainly not one of these artists tonight could touch Hana's work.

The name of tonight's show was Tragique. Piece after piece depicting trauma and tragedy.

"This one makes me want to cry," intoned a woman in a shapeless brown dress and cape standing in front of an equally shapeless gray blob on canvas.

Yeah, of freaking boredom, thought Liam.

"Hey." Hana appeared at his elbow and he suddenly felt his night get 50 percent better. "Sorry I'm late."

He kissed her hello. "That's okay. I haven't been here long. How's Alli?"

"Better. She said she will never eat chicken again. Then she threw up all over my shoes."

He laughed. "I guess that's why you're late."

She nodded. "Pit stop at home to wash my feet and burn my boots."

"Sounds like you could use a drink?"

She grabbed his arm. "Yes, but not here. Boxed wine gives me a headache."

He grinned. "Are you saying what I think you're saying?"

She smiled back. "I did my face time with the gallery owner on the way in. Let's sneak out."

It was still early evening when they slipped out back onto the street. The weather was finally warming up a little, feeling, if not like summer exactly, then at least like spring had some intention of ending. Hana tucked her hand around the crook of Liam's arm and they steered their way into the crowded SoHo sidewalk.

"Where do you want to go?" he asked. "Hungry? Or just drinks?"

Hana shrugged and Liam felt that her mood had suddenly shifted. "You okay?" he asked.

She looked up at him. "Yeah. I was just thinking of something Jay said to me today."

Liam felt his jaw clench. He couldn't help it. Anytime Hana spent time with Jay, it went two ways—they fought or they didn't. When they fought, Liam was pretty much convinced that it was proof that they still cared about each other. When they didn't, he started to think that they must be getting along, so Hana would obviously come to her senses and end up back with Jay.

He tried to keep his voice light. "Yeah? What did he say?"

She shook her head. "He just thought that this was my show we were seeing."

Liam cocked his head. That wasn't so bad. "So?"

"So. It's not."

"And?"

"And…it's not. That's why I wanted to leave. You know I can drink boxed wine until I'm blotto and it doesn't matter. I didn't want to be there because I haven't had a show in almost two years, Liam."

"So have one. You need me to rent a space?"

She rolled her eyes. "And just what would you suggest I put on the walls?"

"Something new, I guess. How about a series of portraits of me? I'll even pose in the nude if you want."

She didn't laugh like he'd hoped she would. Instead, she dropped her hand from his arm. "You know. I have money of my own. I've sold plenty of paintings. I have the divorce settlement and money from my parents. I don't need you to buy everything for me."

He felt a small wave of panic at her words. "I never said that I wanted to buy you everything."

"You didn't have to say it. You just do it." She sped up, marching ahead of him as he hurried to catch up.

"Hana, wait—"

She looked back over her shoulder. "Let's just go home, okay? I've had a really long day."

He caught up with her. "Are you sure? I thought you wanted a drink?"

She shook her head. "We have plenty to drink at home. I just want a night in." She slipped her hand back under his arm. "I'm sorry. I'm not mad at you. I'm mad at myself. I just need to really buckle down and work more."

"Of course. And I want to help you," he said, inwardly cringing at just how relieved her words left him. *You're like a frigging dog,* he thought to himself, *she beats you and you come back ready to lick her face.*

They threaded through the crowd. Suddenly, she stopped

and turned her face up to his, reaching for a kiss. Her mouth was soft and warm and sweet, and her hands crept up and locked behind his neck while his went to her waist and pulled her closer. He wished he could travel back in time and show this moment to the teenage version of himself. Here he was, with more money than he could have ever dreamed of, kissing this beautiful, sophisticated woman, on the streets of Manhattan, on a soft spring night.

"I really am sorry," she whispered. "I love you. I'm sorry I'm being such a jerk. All I meant was that I want to paint more often."

He nodded, pulling her back in. "Whatever you need," he said breathlessly before kissing her again. "Anything you want."

CHAPTER 23

There was a moment, just after she walked out of Harrington's office and was still standing in the waiting room, when Bridget felt so sorry for herself that she decided to go home, get really damned drunk and not emerge until she had succeeded in forgetting everything that just happened. She quickly plotted it all out—go downtown instead of up, stop at her favorite liquor store for a bottle of Gran Patrón Platinum tequila—wine was definitely not going to get the job done—lock her door, take off her shoes and then drink until she forgot what a gigantic, awful mistake she had made, and what a huge, probably once in a lifetime, opportunity she had just blown.

But then she saw Jason Russo sitting there, and for an unreasonable, disoriented second she thought that, for some reason, he was there for her. And for another second she suddenly didn't feel quite so bad, and in fact, she was actually happy to see him. And then her mind cleared and she realized why he was really there, like some frigging jackal—ready to go feast on her kill just like he had with Scarlett's job—and she was so filled with rage that she actually had to hold herself back from launching at him from across the room.

It wasn't fair, of course. He had as much right to be there as she did. More, really, since he actually had a real company. But somehow, in her mind, her failure had become bound up in his success.

Her phone went off. Larry Ludley, wondering where she was. So much for drinking her pain away.

All that afternoon she resolutely went from one job site to the next. She spent the day checking in with project managers about how her clients' projects were being handled. She had to stop herself from doing too much. Back when it was her business, she would have been bringing in the jobs, overseeing the estimating, submitting the RFP response, making sure the subcontractors were doing what her field supers and PMs told them to do. Now she did merely what she had to do, and then stood in the wide, echoing spaces, taking in the walls and ceilings demoed to the studs, the ground strewn with green dust, the sounds of reggae being blasted in the back, the screech of wet saws running in the front, the smell of sweaty men, metal and paint.

It should have made her feel better. It usually made her feel better. On her worst days back when she was still CEO, she would select a couple of sites to live on, overseeing everything, calling on manufacturers to expedite the schedule on lighting fixtures, pushing the subcontractors to ensure that each trade was meeting their deadlines so the schedule didn't fall behind, ticking every little box and detail off her list—and it would leave her feeling safe, in control and powerful.

But today the building sites just reminded her of everything she'd lost. Today she could only think about walking out Mark Harrington's door and knowing that she had lost her one chance to build something that would have put her on the map again. She'd been offered redemption and she'd thrown it away. This was the kind of project that would have left her without financial worries permanently. She would've never had to fret about not having enough for Dylan again. They could've moved out of that tiny apartment and back into their condo, picked up where they had left off before the bankruptcy. Everything could have come roaring back. The money, the travel, the clothes, the house in the Hamptons… and most important, the chance to work in the place where she really belonged. And it had all slipped right through her clumsy fingers.

She tortured herself, replaying the scene, making her mistakes over and over in her head. And then seeing Jason Russo—it was salt in her newly bleeding wound. He had been a witness to her failure.

At last, it was sunset, and she was nearly done. The crew was working on taking down an old cooling tower to make way for a rooftop restaurant. They were pushing a deadline and had an overtime permit and variance for night work. Larry had told her to check in with them—make sure everything was going as planned. The night before, while she was still being stupid, Bridget had invited Jason to meet her there. She'd said they could watch the water tower be taken out and then go out for dinner again. Demoing and removing large pieces of steel was always sexy to watch, even if you were already in the business.

She glanced at her phone—wondering if she should actually cancel. But surely he wouldn't show after she'd blown him off like that at Harrington's office? She'd made herself pretty clear. She scrolled through the screen absently. There were multiple texts and missed calls from Ethan—which she ignored. She had told him about the Harrington project, promised to bring him onto her crew if she got that far. She didn't have the heart to tell him how badly she had screwed up just yet. She hesitated again, looking for Jason's contact, but then put the phone back in her pocket. What was the point? No way would Russo show up and she certainly had no stomach for talking to him right now.

She climbed up the stairs to the rooftop, already hearing the crash and hum of the men at work. She opened the door and her heart lifted a bit. There was something almost festive about the way the sun was starting to set, and then the balloon lights and plant towers got switched on, the way the air cooled and the workers' spirits perked up. The metallic sparks flying off the torches and grinders, the men calling to each other across the site, the smell of smoke and melted metal.

"Hey, Bridget! You come for the show?" Charlie called out. He was a short, broad man with a friendly smile that belied just how tough and cutthroat he could be when he wanted. He was one of her favorite field supers, not least of all because he genuinely seemed to like and respect her.

There were very few men in this business who could get over working for a woman. Oh, they said they could, of course, when they wanted the work. Back when she was a CEO, Bridget had always been astounded by the way men she had personally interviewed, who knew from day one that she was the top dog, could get a little comfortable in their jobs and slip into talking to her like she was a secretary there to bring them coffee. Once they did that it was either start yelling at the top of her lungs and scare the hell out of them until they remembered just who she was, or, if she didn't feel like putting in the effort, simply telling them to get their stuff and get out. A guy like Charlie, who honestly seemed to have zero issues with his coworker not having a dick, was a rare gem, indeed.

"You're here just in time to see the first cuts," he said as Bridget put on her purple hard hat. They walked over to the massive structure. Lean, muscular men in hard hats and thick leather gloves, work boots, tight, faded jeans and white T-shirts, their faces partially obscured by masks designed to filter out the dust in the air, hung off ladders on all sides of the water tower, preparing their saws and torches to start taking it down piece by piece.

"I saved you a seat," said Charlie, indicating a cleared off piece of brick wall safely away from the fall zone.

Bridget smiled and perched on the wall, trying to take the advice of every therapist and yoga teacher she'd ever had.

Be in the now. Stop worrying about things you have no control over. Take deep breaths and—

"Hey!" She was up and striding over to the tower. "Jenowski! What the hell do you think you're doing? Are those tennis shoes on your feet? Where are your work boots?"

God, half these guys were like a bunch of children. They wouldn't survive a day if she wasn't around to keep them in line.

Jenowski, a skinny kid with blond hair cut so close to his head that he practically looked bald, sheepishly climbed back down his ladder and went to change into his boots. "I was hot," was his ridiculous excuse.

"You should have caught that," Bridget shot at Charlie as she went back to her seat. "He could have lost a foot." Charlie held his hands up in a gesture of surrender. She caught him glancing at her own stiletto-clad feet.

"They've got steel toes, Charlie," she said. "And it's not me up on that ladder. I'm in sales, not demo."

The first cut was loud and shrill. Sparks flew and Bridget was squinting through the cloud of black smoke that had been released into the air when the door to the roof opened and Jason Russo emerged.

Bridget stared at him, not quite believing what she was seeing. He'd showed. And god damn it, why did he have to look so good while he was doing it?

Russo was wearing a lightweight, tailored dress shirt, rolled up to show his tan, muscular forearms, and open at the neck. Jeans—faded to perfection and clinging to all the right places, and a well-worn pair of Timberland work boots. This guy wasn't dumb enough to wear sneakers on a work site. His dark, wavy hair was mussed, and he had a brushing of stubble across his jaw—something new that had shown up since she'd seen him that morning.

He spotted her right away—giving her a wide smile and casual wave that seemed to deny everything that had happened between them earlier in the day. Bridget felt an ache in her stomach—and she honestly couldn't say whether it was anger or lust.

She jumped down off the wall and cut him off before he could get any farther onto the roof. The last thing she needed was for the crew to see her having it out with some guy like a hysterical teen girl.

"Hey—" began Russo, still smiling. "You look good in a hard hat."

She cut him off. "What are you doing here?"

"Um," he said, cocking his head to the side. "Didn't you invite me?"

She stared at him for a moment, and then grabbed his shirtsleeve and roughly yanked him forward.

"Everything okay, Bridget?" called Charlie.

She forced herself to smile and waved her hand. "Yeah, we're fine. Go ahead. Don't wait for me. I'll let the Ludleys know everything is good. I just need to talk to my associate here." She continued yanking Russo's shirt, pulling him around the other side of the roof where they couldn't be seen. The whine and screech of saws and smell of torches filled the air as the crew started back up again.

Bridget looked around to make sure they were alone and then leaned close. "I didn't think you'd show. Not after this afternoon."

"About that," said Jason. "I'm guessing it didn't go well?"

She looked away, upset. "No," she admitted grudgingly. "I completely blew it in our meeting."

"What did you do?"

"I basically told him that I thought the design was a common, hard-edged, boring corporate tower. He didn't appreciate the input."

He laughed in disbelief. "Oh, Jesus. Why would you say that? That would have pushed every button Mark has. He's such a snob about architecture. He thinks any design he likes is top-grade shit."

"You could have told me that last night!" she wailed, covering her face with her hands.

His voice changed from amusement to concern. "Hey, so you lost your chance. Another one will come along."

She could feel her face go hot. "You really don't get it, do you?" She laughed. "I mean, of course you don't. You inherited your business from your daddy, who inherited from his daddy and on and on!"

"Just three generations back," Jason put in mildly.

She ignored him. "Do you know how hard it was to build what I built? Do you have any idea?"

He shook his head. "I'm sure it was hard to lose your business. I can't imagine. But I'm also sure you can build it back up somehow. Learn from your mistakes. Make it bigger and stronger this time. Maybe not with this project—but something else. Something much smaller that doesn't have as much risk and that won't take as much capital to get started."

She laughed bitterly and then took a deep, ragged breath. He had no idea. She had been so close. She could feel the tears swelling in her throat. She didn't want to cry in front of this guy.

He opened his mouth to say something more and suddenly it was like slow motion. She saw his full lips, the five o'clock shadow around them, the way his green eyes met hers filled with pity and concern. And she couldn't take it anymore. She didn't want to hear anything more from him. She didn't want him to look at her that way. So before he could make her feel even worse, she thought, *the hell with it*, snatched off her hard hat, tilted her face up and covered his mouth with hers.

He didn't even take a second before he was kissing her back. It was as if he'd been expecting it. He grabbed her by the shoulders and crushed her to his chest and she could feel that he was already iron-hard. She dropped her hard hat on the ground with a loud *thunk*.

This is a mistake. This is a mistake. This is a mistake.

She didn't need this right now. She didn't need the complications. She didn't need to get involved with the competition. She hardly knew this guy...

He moved his mouth over hers, teasing her lips apart with an insistent tongue. He slid his leg between her knees and urged her thighs open. She could feel herself melt.

God, he feels so good.

He swept his tongue into her mouth, bit down lightly on her lower lip. She heard herself groan.

He's the competition.

His hands moved up from her shoulders and settled in her hair. He gripped her head and positioned her face under his, tilting up her chin so he could get deeper access to her mouth.

But you didn't get the job. There's no conflict. He's not the competition anymore.

He left one hand in her hair and moved the other over her cheek, trailing down her neck, slowly heading for her cleavage. Her breath caught and her chest swelled, urging him on, offering herself.

This could be trouble. But I don't care. I want it.

She pulled back with a gasp, looked up into his eyes, which had gone almost black with desire, kept her hands gripped on his shoulders. "My place is closer than yours."

CHAPTER 24

Bridget's place was like her—small, but beautiful, sexy, earthy, generous. Seeing it, finding all the cozy little pockets of comfort, the layers of color and texture, made Jason realize just how much his own home was lacking these things. His place felt piecemeal and thoughtless compared to hers. A perch, not a nest.

Her apartment felt lived-in in the best kind of way. Worn braided rugs scattered over pine floors, a deep, comfortable couch covered with brightly colored pillows and throws, a few toys thrown around here and there. No view to speak of—just the street down below, framed by pretty, bright green curtains. Only her tiny kitchen felt less than loved. He raised his eyebrows when he saw how empty it was.

"I don't cook," she said defensively.

"I do," he answered, sweeping his hand over the single butcher-block counter and wondering how she lived with only one cabinet.

She showed him Dylan's room. His window looked out onto a brick storefront, but the walls and ceiling were painted sky blue with white fluffy clouds floating through; his toys were cunningly arranged, and when Jason looked at the tiny bed he felt a pang. It didn't seem that long ago that Alli would have fit into something that small.

"He's with his dad tonight," she said, and he nodded, knowing that she never would have brought him here otherwise.

He'd peeked into her bathroom on the way into her bedroom and seen the claw-foot tub, the original subway tile. It all looked newly refurbished.

"Did it look like this when you moved in?" he asked.

She laughed. "The last time it had been updated was probably 1987. Think popcorn glitter ceilings, entire walls of mirrors and every room painted either fuchsia or aqua. I cut a deal with my landlord to trade work for rent."

Her bed was small by today's standards, only a full-size, stacked with purple pillows and made up with a lofty, shimmery down comforter hidden under an apple-green cotton quilt. Once he was in it, he was surprised to realize that he actually liked the lack of space. There was a way you could lose each other in a California king. He and Hana used to make love and then roll over to sleep on opposite sides of the mattress, sprawled out but never touching. In this bed, all flesh pressed to flesh and if one person moved, the other always felt it. It was erotic and satisfying, creating an instant intimacy. Her small body curled into him, her smooth, supple limbs tangled with his, her sweet breath warm on his cheek, her long, dark hair tossed over his chest and shoulders like a silky mantle of cloth.

Jason had slept with his share of women and he'd had some good and even great times. He thought he had understood everything sex could be, but there was something different in making love to a woman as powerful and strong-willed as Bridget. Not only because she didn't hesitate to take control when she felt like it—there was an incredible pleasure in being led down her particular roads and paths—but because when he flipped the script and she surrendered, he felt like he had won some hard-fought battle, and that it was absolutely necessary that he be the most gracious kind of champion.

She was beautiful, of course. Her body was as breathtaking as he had guessed it would be, all firm curves and silky skin. When she bared her breasts, he had stopped in his tracks and just stared, feeling like a giddy adolescent boy drunk on wonder and excitement. And she was generous. Generous with her body, generous with her touch and his pleasure. And she was surprising; after he had kissed off her lipstick like he had been waiting to do all day, her face was revealed to be young and sweet, but that feeling of innocence was contradicted by the darkly intense look in her eyes. He wasn't sure what to believe.

It all felt...new, which Jason had never guessed this particular thing would feel again. And after she shuddered underneath him, soft and delicious and wildly exciting, and then he followed with an almost violently pleasurable ending of his own, he lay there with her, full of wonder, chuckling softly to himself that, at forty-two, he had somehow started all over again.

CHAPTER 25

Bridget felt like she was made of butter. No, not butter; there was nothing greasy or oozy about what she was feeling. Maybe whipped cream—soft, formless, but airy and light.

"Or maybe I'm just hungry," she said out loud.

Jason turned toward her, stroking the length of her neck. She shivered in pleasure. He had hard, rough hands—a builder's hands—but he had shown her he could use them in surprisingly gentle ways. "I'm starving," he announced. "Let me cook for you."

Bridget looked at him out of the corner of her eye, still not quite able to comprehend what had just happened between them. There was no doubt in her mind—this had been the best sex of her life so far. Maybe the best she would ever have. She couldn't explain it, but they had come together in a whirl of chemistry and passion and unslakable need so complicated and shocking that she felt like her brain had simply shut down from the pleasure. She had been out of her head with lust, completely immersed in his body, in the way her body responded to his body, in the weird and wonderful feeling that they somehow already just seemed to know each other. There had been no self-consciousness, no awkward bumps or mismatched moments, just fluid grace and uncontainable excitement.

He peeled back the lilac-colored sheet she had pulled up over her chest, baring her breasts and making her nipples pucker in the cool evening air.

"God, you're gorgeous," he said.

She smiled and sat up, pulling the sheets back up over her. "So you never told me. How did it go for you and Harrington today?"

He groaned. "Do we really want to talk about that?"

She nodded. "Just tell me. It's going to bother me all night if you don't."

He rolled toward her. "I'm going to be here all night?"

She scooted away from him. "That's not what I said."

He sighed. "It was fine. The usual. He asked me to submit a budget. The end."

Her mouth turned down. "The usual for you, maybe."

"Bridget," he said. "Is this really how you want to spend our time? Didn't you say you were hungry?"

She thought about it for a moment. He was right. "Didn't you say you were going to cook for me?" she said in return.

CHAPTER 26

Jason was looking at the fish counter in Whole Foods. He wanted to make something special for Bridget, something delicious and comforting, but he knew that he couldn't do anything too fancy or she'd spook. In fact, he was probably taking a risk by even going out to shop. He was pretty sure that there was a fifty-fifty chance she would bolt the door and refuse to let him in when he returned, but there had only been some withered lemons, a bottle of wine and something green and unidentifiable in a take-out container in her refrigerator. Even he couldn't do anything with that list of ingredients.

He looked at the careful piles and neat stacks of fish and crustaceans all spread out in front of him, glistening on the ice. Salmon? Sure. That was safe. Everyone liked salmon, right? He'd get some of the sockeye and slow-cook it in that way that left it juicy and tender. It wouldn't take long, even slow cooked; salmon was a quick dish.

He ordered a pound and a half—the woman needed some leftovers to fill that sad refrigerator, for God's sake—picked up a loaf of sourdough bread, a wedge of triple crème cheese, a container of arugula, a bulb of garlic, some butter, olive oil, a small bottle of good balsamic vinegar and then, making a wild guess, two chocolate-covered Rice Krispies treats from the bakery.

He carried his bag of groceries out of the store and walked down Greenwich. It was pleasantly warm tonight. Spring was ending and summer was really starting to kick in. The streets were full of couples—women in bright little dresses and miniskirts and sandals, men at their sides in lightweight suits, their jackets tossed over their shoulders and shirts open at the collar, women with women, men with men, too. Everyone seemed to have big grins on their faces, and Jay found himself grinning right back. Was there a better city on earth? He freaking loved Manhattan.

Jesus, he couldn't remember the last time he felt this good. His body ached in that satisfying, tired way that only happened after great sex. He could still smell Bridget on his skin—sweet and musky like sandalwood or lilacs, but also something more primal and earthy—her deeper, sexy, natural scent underneath the perfume, like salt and sugar. Just smelling it turned him on all over again.

What a day! He had dealt with his ex-wife in a way that didn't make him cringe in regret or want to punch a hole in the wall afterward; Alli had given him a kiss and thanked him for taking care of her while she was sick before she had gone back to her mom's place; and then, to top it all off, he'd just had the kind of sex that he was certain he was going to remember for the rest of his life.

Also, he heard a voice in his head that sounded like his father, *you pinned down a pretty big job opportunity for the business. Don't forget that.*

He shifted the bag of groceries to his other arm and steered around an elderly couple shuffling down Broadway together, hand in hand.

He wished Bridget had come out with him, but she had shooed him off, saying something about taking a hot bath while he was gone. He imagined her walking with him through the summer streets of Tribeca, her arm looped in his, him slowing down to make up for those crazy heels she seemed to like. He imagined them arguing good-naturedly about where they'd go for dinner. He knew that if he was with Bridget, there would be a lot of discussion. She was a woman who wanted her way. But he didn't think he'd mind so much.

Hell, just thinking about it made him grin like a fool.

CHAPTER 27

Bridget stepped out of the bath and wrapped herself in a big, thirsty towel. She checked herself in the mirror; not too bad. Her hair had gone to curls—it was a humid day and the bath hadn't helped, but she'd pinned it up and off her face, and she figured it looked good enough. She reached for some lip gloss but stopped. Her cheeks were pink, her eyes were bright—she had that natural flush that couldn't be replicated with anything but hot sex. Why mess with it?

She wandered back into her bedroom, dreamily searching through her closet for something to wear. Something comfortable but not too sloppy. Something sexy, but not over-the-top... Finally, she settled on a short, Marc Jacobs tunic dress made of pine-green jersey that would leave her legs bare and show just a little bit of cleavage.

A pretty navy-and-net La Perla bra underneath, a matching pair of boy shorts, a spritz of Escentric Molecule 01 perfume in all the obvious places and a few more subtle ones. She slid on the green dress and looked at herself in the mirror one more time. Okay, maybe just a touch of lip gloss and a little

mascara. Sex flush or not, it never hurt to improve from good
to sexy best.

She sighed happily as she went to the kitchen for some wine.
She couldn't believe she was in a good mood. Six hours before, she'd basically had her dreams shattered, lost the chance
to compete for the biggest job of her life, and here she was
humming in the kitchen while she poured the rosé.

Maybe it wasn't the worst thing ever that the job fell through.

After all, she wouldn't have let things go any further with
Jay if they had truly been in competition. And maybe he and
Ava were right. Maybe she should start small. Maybe the whole
thing was crazy. An image of him holding himself up over her,
his biceps bulging, his eyes shut in pleasure… She felt a bolt of
heat dash through her.

Maybe there really could be some winning in losing, she
thought.

She tried to remember the last time she'd had sex before
tonight. It had been a while. Months, actually—a brief fling
with a landscape architect in the Hamptons. He'd had great abs,
a nice smile and was boring as shit. It had taken her a couple
of months before she realized his conversational skills weren't
getting any better and the sex probably wasn't, either.

She was starving. She wondered what Jay was going to cook
for her. Then she rolled her eyes, thinking how she best not
get her hopes up. Knowing her history with men, chances
were he'd probably show up with some frozen pizzas and call
it nouvelle cuisine.

Her phone chimed from inside her purse where she'd thrown
it when she and Jay had first come into the apartment. Probably Ethan again, but what if it was Jay with a question about
dinner?

She sipped her wine as she dug through her purse and unearthed her cell. Squinting at the screen, she saw that she had missed a call from—her heart sped up—Harrington & Kim.

She held her breath as she hit Play on the voice mail and lifted the phone to her ear.

"Hi, Ms. Steele!" the voice of Mark Harrington's assistant chirped over the line. "It's Liza from Harrington & Kim. Mr. Harrington asked me to call and invite you to submit a preliminary budget for the HealthTec project. He said to tell you, and I quote, 'I thought about it, and you just might be right about the design.' End quote. Anyway, please call back if you're interested so we can make sure you have all the information you need. I hope to hear back from you soon, and have a great afternoon!"

Bridget's hand trembled as she slowly lowered the phone to the counter. Everything had changed all over again. She wasn't out, after all. They wanted a budget. She was still up for the biggest job of her life. A skyscraper. Half a billion frigging dollars. Her eyes darted wildly around the room. Who should she call first? Ethan? Ava? Her mother?

Jay.

Damn. Jay. Jay, who had also been asked to submit a budget. Jay, who was now her direct competition.

Her doorbell chimed.

Jay, who was freaking standing outside her building waiting to be buzzed in.

For a moment she hesitated, then she hit the button. "Jay?"

His voice crackled over the speaker. "Hey. Yeah, it's me. Do you like salmon? What am I saying, everyone likes salmon, right?"

"Hang on." She hit the button again, letting him in.

What should she do? Should she even tell him?

A rap on her door. She slowly walked out of the kitchen to answer. There he was. Tall. Gorgeous. Smiling at her. A heavy bag of groceries on one arm. He leaned forward to kiss her as he came in, but she stepped out of reach.

"I have to ask you something," she said.

He scowled. "I knew I shouldn't have left," he muttered. "What?"

"Nothing. Never mind. What do you want to ask?"

"Have you ever slept with another contractor before?"

He raised an eyebrow and laughed. "Well, since you're the first woman contractor I've ever met, that would be a no."

"But you've dated other people in the industry, right? Architects? Assistants? You know how complicated it can be."

He shook his head. "I told you I married young. My ex is an artist. What are you getting at?"

She shrugged. "My ex was my drywall subcontractor. Until he talked me into hiring him as head of sales. At first, he thought it was sexy that I was a CEO. He liked my money and he liked my power. But then things fell apart in a spectacularly horrible way."

He stared at her, confused. "Are you worried that I'm going to resent that you work?"

She shook her head. "No. But I am wondering if you can manage to date someone who is your direct competition."

He blinked. "So you're back in?"

She nodded, watching his face carefully.

He smiled. "That's great. I'm happy for you."

She searched his eyes. He honestly seemed happy.

"But—"

He raised his hand. "Hey, the budget's just a tiny part of things. You and I both know that it's the presentation and the project team that's going to win or lose it. And there's an awful lot between now and then." He moved past her into the kitchen where he began unpacking the groceries. "So may the best construction manager win, right?"

"Russo—"

He paused and looked at her. "Oh. I see. I'm Russo again?"

She shook her head. "No, I mean, Jay—"

"Listen, this doesn't have to change anything. I want to build that building. You want to build that building. Only one of us can get it—and hell, maybe neither of us will. I'm sure we're not the only ones up for it."

She shook her head. She didn't even like to think about the rest of the competition.

"But Bridget, what happened between us tonight? You and I know both know that was no one-night stand."

She nodded slowly.

"Look. I'm just going to say it. I don't mean to freak you out, and I won't speak for you, of course, but for me, that was something special, and I'd hate to see it end before it had a chance to begin."

His green eyes met hers and she watched them slowly go dark. She shivered, her body answering his gaze, but then she forced herself to look away. "So is this job."

He blinked, confused. "So is this job what?"

"Something special."

She saw the faintest trace of hurt pass over his face, then it cleared. "That's true. But like I said before, one doesn't have to change the other."

She shook her head. "You're my direct competition, Jason."

"We won't talk about it. We can leave work at the door when we see each other."

"I can't do that. It's who I am. I'm ninety-nine percent my work."

"So, I'll take the one percent of you that's left."

"That's ridiculous."

"There was no work in that bedroom tonight, Bridget," he shot back. "You and I, we were somewhere else. Am I right about that?"

She shrugged, not wanting to admit to what he was saying, but knowing it was true.

"And believe me when I tell you—it's not always like that. In fact, as far as I'm concerned, it's never been like that."

She was quiet for a moment. He waited.

"For me, either," she finally admitted.

"So I'm pretty damned interested in seeing where this could go. Aren't you?"

She blew out a long breath. "Maybe," she said.

He strode across the kitchen, crushed his mouth to hers. For a moment her eyes flew shut and she was lost again, feeling nothing but his lips, his arms, the hungry, knowing way his hands moved all over her. Her mind was hazed over. Her body was roaring. Her heart was pounding out of her chest.

He broke the kiss and stepped away, short of breath, glaring at her. "That doesn't feel like *maybe* to me."

Her hands fell open. She hated how helpless she felt, how out of control.

But he was right.

"Fine," she said.

He looked at her. "Fine what?"

"Fine. I'm going for this building, and we can keep seeing each other. And the only rule is, we never talk about work. Other than that—I will do anything and everything to get this job. I will not stand down. I won't let anyone get in my way. And you need to hear me clearly when I say this, Jason. I will play dirty if necessary. Can you accept that?"

He smiled. "Fine. I like the sound of playing dirty."

"I'm not joking."

He looked at her and clenched his jaw. She watched the muscle leap in his cheek. "How hungry are you?" he said softly.

She walked toward him, held out her hand. "Dinner can wait," she said.

CHAPTER 28

Hana turned toward Liam when he slipped into bed that night, and whatever bad blood might have lingered from earlier seemed to have passed. She was warm and naked, burrowed under a cloud of silk and down comforter, sandwiched between crisp white sheets, her eyes glowing in the blinking city lights that cast through the windows, her hair tumbled around her shoulders in streams.

He gathered her to him, fitting her small body against his much larger one, sliding his arm under her neck and then round her shoulders, so he could pull her even closer. She smelled like lime and jasmine, the same scent she'd worn since the day he'd met her. She still mail-ordered it from a woman in India who had mixed it for her since she was a teen living in Chennai. Her hair brushed against his neck and he reached to twine a lock in his hand. He loved how heavy it was, how substantial and alive it felt to him. He gently tugged on it, and she tilted her face up toward his, and he felt the warmth of her breath on his cheek.

She slid her leg between his, pulling her hips tight against him, making his cock leap as she trailed her hands down over his shoulders and back. She kissed his neck, once and then twice and then again. He rolled over on top of her, wanting to feel every part of her pressed up against him.

"I'm sorry about today," she whispered.

He shook his head. "Why do you keep apologizing? I get it. Honestly."

She looked up at him, her eyes wide. "Do you, though?"

"What do you mean?"

"I just think that maybe I need to explain."

He sighed and rolled off her. "And I guess we're going to have this conversation right now?"

She wiggled closer and put her head on his shoulder. "Have I ever told you about the year that my family lived in Saudi Arabia?"

He shook his head helplessly. "No."

"We moved there when I was eleven. Up until then, my mother was the perfect ambassador's wife. She was well educated and witty, beautiful and cultured, kind and stylish. She loved everything about our life. She loved the travel, picking up new languages and cultural traditions, the parties and the dinners and the socializing. She was a jewel on my father's arm. I heard more than one person say that my father never would have made it as far as he did without my mother by his side."

Liam nodded. Hana's parents were in their midforties when she was born—a miracle baby, they had called her—and had both passed on before he had a chance to meet them.

"But then we got assigned to Saudi Arabia. It was a challenging job for my dad—things were messy in the Gulf. And there wasn't room for my mother's usual role. The limits on women were so strict, the separation between the sexes so enforced, that my mom was told she would basically need to stay at home all day with the servants. She couldn't drive. She was trapped in our compound. That's what women did there at that time—at least women who didn't want to stir up any problems."

Hana sat up in bed, pulling the sheet up over her chest. "My father was completely wrapped up in his job. He worked crazy hours and was hardly ever home. We never saw him. We were living in the utmost luxury. Our compound was like a palace, but my mother was so depressed. She barely made it out of bed, and when she did, it was like she was sleepwalking. I'd never seen her like that before, and once my father's time there was over and we moved on to India, I never saw it again. But it was terrifying. Like all the light had just disappeared."

Liam nodded, stroking her hair.

"After that I promised myself I would never be like her. I would never lose sight of my work, never depend on a man like that. I would never allow myself to get sick over how much I loved someone. A woman has to have a purpose, something outside of men, outside of her marriage, so that if something happens, she won't collapse."

He stiffened. "I don't have any problem with you working, Hana."

"I'm not saying you do."

He held up his hands, confused. "So what are you saying?"

"I think," she whispered, "I think I'm in too deep. I've gone too far. I gave you everything I have to offer. And I don't even know if you—you feel the same way."

"What are you talking about? Of course I feel the same way," he said dismissively.

He could feel the warm tears on her face slide down onto his neck. "I'm not sure that's true."

He shook her off, angry. "I gave up everything to be with you, Hana. You know that."

She laughed—a bitter sound. "Did you?"

He sat up in bed and violently pushed the covers back. "I'm going to get a drink."

"Liam?" She reached for his arm but he shook her off.

"Don't." And he left the room.

CHAPTER 29

Bridget called in sick to work the next day. Then she hopped on the 2 train and headed for the Bronx. Back when Steele Construction still existed, she would have gathered everyone into her oversize conference room, around the gleaming twelve-foot oak table built big enough to seat all of her estimators, her VP of construction, PMs and field supers. Then they would have spent the day reviewing the budget, rehearsing their presentation and figuring out the best approach to building this monstrosity. But now? She only had one person she wanted to talk to: Danny Schwartz.

She had to go to him. He'd been there through everything and she knew it just wouldn't feel right unless he was part of this job. He wouldn't take her calls, didn't respond to email. It had been so long since she'd even seen his face. She had tried to keep tabs on him through her mother—making sure he was okay—but her mom said he would hardly see her, either. That he wasn't around the neighborhood like he used to be.

Bridget knew she was going to have to show up on his doorstep in person if she wanted to hash this out.

As she stepped out of the subway station into the bright mid-day sun, Bridget took a moment to orient herself. She could never get over how different things were when she came back to the old neighborhood. Her mother had moved to Florida after Bridget and Dylan had moved back out, so it had been nearly two years since she'd been back in the hood. Every-thing looked worn out and smaller than her memories. The park was strewn with litter and graffiti and not as green as she remembered; the brick wall that she used to lean against while making out with her first boyfriend had been turned into a car wash with flickering neon lights. Here was the street where she was knocked off her brand-new bike, a gang of neighbor-hood kids demanding that she give them a dollar or the bike itself. She refused either, standing her ground, tears and snot running down her face, until one of the shopkeepers came out and chased them all off. Sal's Pizza place, Luigi's deli, The Tasty Bake, with its handmade cannoli and home to the four bald men who never left the front stoop, wearing sleeveless tees, gray trousers and black belts...all gone. Transformed into bodegas, check-cashing places and nail salons.

The public pool that used to open every Memorial Day and close on Labor Day was now filled with dirt and covered in pavement. For a minute Bridget stopped and stood there, watching her child-self do laps down the long, murky blue pool.

This neighborhood had been dangerous and smothering and unpredictable, as sticky and binding as tar, and she'd spent most of her childhood wondering if she'd ever make it out. But, she mused as she turned the corner onto Danny's block, it had made her. This is where she learned to fight like hell and work until she dropped and to never take shit from any-one. Without the Bronx in her blood, she never would have climbed as high, and she certainly wouldn't have survived these past few terrible years.

Danny's place, what used to be an immaculate Victorian row house that he'd always taken great pride in, looked run-down and shabby. The solid little porch needed a coat of paint; there was a crack in one of the windows. Bridget felt a little shiver of apprehension. The Danny Schwartz she knew would have never let things go like this.

She knocked.

No answer.

She knocked again.

She stood on the porch, waiting, certain that he was inside—his old yellow Ford pickup was in the driveway—but not sure at all how she would get to him.

Finally, she remembered something—slid her fingers under a windowsill, and found the little plastic box and the key inside.

"Danny?" she called as she slowly opened his door. "Danny? It's me, Bridget. I'm coming in."

"Girl, what the hell do you think you're doing?"

He was just standing there in his living room, watching her come through the door. She felt immediate relief when she saw him. He looked tired, maybe a little worn down, definitely pissed off, but it was still Danny Schwartz. Short, shaped like a fireplug, his wispy gray hair waving in the breeze.

"This is breaking and entering! I could have you arrested!"

She smiled at him. She couldn't help it. "Aw, Danny. I missed you so much."

He glared at her. "Well, I didn't miss you at all, ya little jerk. Now get out of my house."

She looked around. As usual, his place was clean as a whistle, everything perfectly ordered. She felt something slide off her shoulders. He was doing okay. She hadn't realized how worried she'd been about him until that moment. She looked at the little man.

"Danny, listen. I'm sorry. I came here to apologize. I never should have talked to you that way. I was crazy that day, out of control. I hardly knew what I was doing."

He glanced away from her, the color rising in his gray stubbled cheeks.

"I should have come sooner—I should have fixed this—but everything got so bad after that. I found out that Kevin was cheating on me, and we got a divorce, the company went bankrupt, I lost my condo, I was scrambling for work, trying to support Dylan. It was a nightmare."

He shook his head, still wouldn't meet her eyes.

"But now I need your help, Danny. Something's come up. Something huge. A skyscraper. And I want to bring back Steele Construction, but I can't do it without you."

He finally looked at her, rapidly blinking. "You'd—you'd want me to come back?" He sounded bewildered. "After what I did?"

She took a step toward him. "Oh, Danny, of course I do. You've been with me from the beginning."

His mouth dropped open. "But I—I ruined you. I took down one of your most important projects, ended your whole company. I—I knew Kevin wasn't coming through for you, and you needed workers fast, and I heard about some guys from the neighborhood who needed work. I figured there were so many men on the job, no one was going to notice a few guys without cards. I just wanted to help. And then—" his voice shook "—and then it all fell apart. After all that work you did, after everything you accomplished. Ruined. I thought you'd never want to see me again."

She felt all the air leave her lungs, realizing that he hadn't been angry with her at all—just regretful and ashamed. That he had done the best he could after Kevin had dumped the problem into his lap, and that he believed every cruel and furious word that she'd spit out at him on that day. God, what an asshole she'd been. She swallowed and blinked back her tears. "Come on. Are you kidding? How could I do this without you? You didn't take down my company. Of course not. I made huge mistakes. Kevin screwed us both. I know you were just trying to help."

A tear ran down his face. His jowls trembled. He held out his arms. "Come here, kid. Gimme a hug before I make an even bigger fool of myself."

She stepped into his surprisingly strong embrace, a giant grin on her face, letting the tears flow. For a moment she leaned into him, just enjoying the feeling of fatherly arms around her once more.

Then he stepped back, wiping his eyes on his shirtsleeves. "Now. Tell me about this skyscraper."

Two hours later Danny, Ethan and Mrs. Hashemi were all huddled around Danny's kitchen table.

Ethan flashed an electric smile at Bridget. She could see that her tall, handsome friend was excited and ready to get to work. He had shown up without a question, telling the boss at his workplace that he thought he was coming down with the flu. They had stayed close, even after Steele Construction folded and Ethan had moved on to another company.

Mrs. Hashemi hadn't seemed to age at all over the years, still sporting the same neat cropped head of iron-gray curls, wearing the jewel-colored cashmere sweater sets that Bridget remembered first admiring at the bank.

Bridget knew that Mrs. Hashemi had found another job after her business had fallen apart—mostly because she had made sure it had happened. Bridget hadn't been able to guarantee everyone who worked for her would fall onto a soft place, but she'd made it her priority to see that Mrs. Hashemi was okay.

Maybe that was why the older woman had come all the way up to the Bronx to help Bridget this morning.

Harrington & Kim had emailed a set of the preliminary plans to Bridget that morning, and she printed them out and now had them spread all over Danny's kitchen table.

Developing a comprehensive budget was always complicated, but this was even more so because of the magnitude of this project. But Bridget also knew that this was the first step. Doing the budget properly would help them get invited to present to the development and investor team—which was the golden apple, the real way in.

Even with smaller projects, it could take a couple weeks to put accurate numbers together. Done right, it could cost a company thousands of dollars in estimating time. Every trade and material cost, from the largest to the smallest, had to be checked and rechecked. All direct costs paid by the construction manager had to be accurately estimated as part of their general conditions. In the end, there would be hundreds of line items that Bridget herself would go over before they brought it back to Harrington, and no guarantee that their team would be called in to present. They would necessarily do it on a shoe-string, but it was still a risk. It could be nothing but money down the drain.

"Okay," said Bridget, accepting the hot mug of coffee that Danny offered her and making room for Mrs. Hashemi to stand next to her. "I need to get this budget in fast, and it's got to be perfect, no box left unchecked. What do you guys think?"

Mrs. Hashemi adjusted her glasses and bent to look at the thick sheaf of papers. She was silent as she meticulously worked her way through the stack, only occasionally letting out a little whistle or hiss when she came upon something particularly interesting.

At last, she straightened up and looked at Bridget and Danny, worry in her deep brown eyes. "I don't mean to question your judgment, my dear, but do you really think that you are capable of taking on such an extensive project?"

"Mrs. Hashemi," said Bridget, "this is exactly where I left off when I lost everything. This is my dream. It will bring Steele Construction back."

Mrs. Hashemi considered this for a moment. "And do you have the resources for this project? The infrastructure? The office space?"

"Not yet," said Bridget. "But if we can get this project I'll pull the rest together."

The older lady hesitated.

"Listen," said Bridget, "I know this may seem absolutely crazy. I know everyone thinks I should be starting small and building my company back up. This is obviously an enormous long shot. And I know that you all have other jobs and responsibilities, and it's not even remotely fair for me to be asking for this help. It's a ton of work and time and, honestly, I can't pay you guys anything yet—"

"Wow. You're making this sound better and better," muttered Ethan.

"And I absolutely get it if you can't help. You can just say no to me and I will understand, no hard feelings at all. But you guys were the core of my team. You were the people I trusted more than anyone, so I wanted to come to you first."

"And you need our help," said Danny. "You can't do it on your own."

Bridget nodded, humbled. "I do. I need you guys. I don't know what Steele Construction would look like without you." She choked back tears.

"And you won't have to, dear," said Mrs. Hashemi. "Of course we will help. You took a chance on each of us once upon a time, and now we will take a chance on you. It's an investment opportunity for us. With the prospect of excellent returns."

"If we get the job, guys. There's no guarantee."

Ethan laughed. "Oh. You'll get the job, Bridget. I've got a gut feeling about this."

"He's right," said Danny. "You'll get it."

"I'm definitely in," said Ethan. "I hate my boss. Not nearly as fun as you were."

"And I am also in," said Mrs. Hashemi. "I regard this as an excellent business opportunity, and frankly, I am a little bored at my new job. I could use the challenge."

"And you know I'm with you, kid," said Danny hoarsely. "I always am." He reached over and ruffled Bridget's hair.

Bridget nodded. "Thank you, guys," she said softly.

Mrs. Hashemi took off her glasses, removed a handkerchief out of her pocketbook and slowly polished first one lens and then the other before putting them back on. "Then this is what we will do," she said at last. "We will bring back Steele Construction."

Bridget swallowed. She could feel a small ping of hope in her chest. "How long do you think it will take to come up with the bid?"

"Well..." Mrs. Hashemi smiled a slightly pained smile. "The good news is that my current job is very slow. There is little to do. So I have plenty of time to work on this." She looked at the plans again. "I think we can do it in three weeks."

Bridget blinked. It was way more than she'd hoped for. "Seriously?"

Mrs. Hashemi nodded, looked at Danny and Ethan.

"We'll get it done," Danny said.

Bridget looked at them all for a moment, choked with emotion. She reached out and grabbed their hands. "You guys. Thank you so much."

The three of them smiled back at her.

"Now, let's have some lunch," said Danny.

Bridget took the train back to Manhattan with Ethan. "So," he said as they gently swayed back and forth, "I heard you're sleeping with the enemy."

"God damn it. When did you see Ava?"

Bridget had called up Ava on her way to the train that morning in a fit of anxiety and spilled the whole story before she'd even had her first cup of coffee.

"She came in this morning to drop off some plans," said Ethan, laughing. "Anyway, you were going to tell me eventually."

"Just not yet," muttered Bridget.

"Well, I think it's brilliant. Like some high-level Mata Hari shit. You'll have total access to all his secrets. You'll know what makes him weak. You'll keep him distracted with your magical—"

"I do not have a magical anything," she interjected.

"You're missing my point. My point is, you've got an in on the competition. You can get him to talk and then exploit his weaknesses, knock him out."

She shook her head. "Work is off the table with this guy. We're trying something else."

Ethan laughed. "Work is never off the table for you, Bridget. And don't even try to pretend it can be."

She rolled her eyes. "Anyway…"

"Anyway, steal a copy of his budget. We can undercut his fee."

She threw up her hands. "I'm not going to steal anything, Ethan. Calm the hell down."

The woman across from her on the train glared at her and covered her young daughter's ears.

"Sorry," Bridget mouthed.

Ethan sighed again. "The Bridget Steele I know would use this to her own advantage, putting her work before anything else like the good Lord intended her to do."

She shook her head. "This is why I didn't want to tell you. Listen, I'm not going to do anything to endanger this project."

Ethan raised an eyebrow. "I'm sorry, but how is sleeping with the competition not endangering this project?"

"We're keeping things separate. Surely, you can understand what that means?"

"I only understand the fact that there is a god damned skyscraper dangling in front of our faces, which could mean you could finally stop selling for Gross and Grosser and get back to what you were meant to do, but you won't steal anything or do anything fun to make this any easier for you to win."

"We don't need to cheat or steal anything. We just need to put together our team and be the best."

She could practically hear him rolling his eyes. "Well, I hope you're right, boss. And if not—at least you'll have a way to get behind enemy lines."

CHAPTER 30

"Dad... Dad... Dad!"

Jason blinked and looked at Alli. She was on her bike, riding next to him as they made their way through Central Park. It was their weekly afternoon together after school—a miracle that he'd convinced her to take a bike ride with him—and he had been thinking about...well, he had been thinking about Bridget's legs. Again.

Jesus, his daughter was right there. He had to get a hold of himself.

"I'm sorry, honey. A lot going on at work right now. What did you say?"

She rolled her eyes under her helmet. "I said I think I like Shake Shack better than In-N-Out burgers."

"When did you have In-N-Out?"

Her voice rose. "I already told you. Liam had a big meeting so he took me and Mom to LA last month. We stayed at the Beverly Hills Hotel. I had my own room. And you can order anything on room service. I mean, anything. It was so cool. One night I had In-N-Out."

He stared at her for a moment, desperately trying to bite his tongue. He had things he would've liked to say. He very much wanted to say that it was a waste of good room service to order fast food. Even if it was very good fast food. He wanted to say that a fifteen-year-old had absolutely no business having her own suite at the Beverly Hills Hotel—and that Liam was obviously trying to buy her affection. And that maybe it was working, judging from the way she was talking about him. But mostly he wanted to say that he was furious with Hana for taking Alli out of the state and not even bothering to tell him. He'd had no idea that his daughter had even been gone.

But he didn't say any of that. He just kept pedaling.

"Dad, stop being so extra. Chill." Alli always knew when he was upset, even when he tried to hide it. "Liam surprised us at the last moment. I mean, we didn't even know we were going anywhere until we all got to the airport."

Jason shook his head. That used to be one of the things he liked best about his former friend; he was spontaneous and wild and filled with crazy plans. A week before Jason and Hana got married, Liam had literally put a pillowcase over Jason's head, chartered a jet and taken him to Saint-Tropez for the weekend.

But it was harder to appreciate these qualities when they were being applied to win the affections of his daughter and ex-wife.

Maybe if I had been more like him. Surprised them more…

He shook it off. Second-guessing had become a torturous habit for him and he didn't want to do it anymore. Instead, he turned to his daughter. "Hey, we still on for the Hamptons house next weekend?"

She wrinkled her nose. "Do we have to? I made plans with some friends."

"Bring 'em," he shot back. "We've got plenty of room."

Her face lit up. "Really?"

"Sure," he said. *See, I can be cool, too! Suck it, Maguire.*

"Awesome! Hey, can we pull over for a second? I need to text everyone."

They pulled over and he felt a little twinge of apprehension as he watched her speed-text. *I wonder how many kids she's actually inviting...* She looked up at him and flashed him the rarest of things—a happy smile. *Don't ask. Don't screw it up.*

CHAPTER 31

Liam was playing tennis with Mark Harrington's business partner, Henry Kim, at the Manhattan Plaza Racquet Club. Men who actually knew how to play tennis liked to play against Liam—he was just good enough to make them work a little, but almost never good enough to win. Like golf and racquetball, Liam had learned tennis as an adult, after he moved to New York. Jay had insisted he take lessons. Along with strip clubs, cigar bars and overpriced restaurants, they were the cornerstone of business world socializing in Manhattan and absolutely necessary in order to break in to the inner circle. Liam suspected that, with a little practice and effort, he could be much better at all of these games, but why mess with a good thing? Passable was fine. He didn't mind losing if it meant cultivating clients, and he got a workout either way.

But today, distracted by his problems with Hana, he was playing like it was his first time. He could see the frustration in Kim's eyes as he missed shot after shot and botched serve after serve.

"Love—game point!" called a clearly annoyed Kim as he

lofted the ball into the air and sent it spinning directly at Liam. Liam managed to hit it back, right into the net.

"Jesus, Maguire!" yelled Kim. "Where is your game today?"

Liam shook his head as he approached the net to shake hands. "Sorry. Just a little distracted. Let me buy you a drink and make up for it."

In the locker room, after showers, the men toweled off side by side. As always, Liam noticed how fit Kim was. He had to be in his late fifties, but with his broad shoulders and taut, muscled belly, the man looked like a professional athlete with his shirt off.

"Sorry about the shitty game today," said Liam as he packed up his gym bag. "At least you won."

Kim shot him a comical look. "No joy in winning that game, Maguire. My ten-year-old daughter could have beat your ass. What's your problem, anyway? Or do you need a beer before you can spit it out?"

"No beer," said Liam. "Whiskey."

They took Kim's car to Bemelmans, a piano bar in the Carlyle Hotel. It always made Liam feel slightly uncomfortable with its fashionably worn and exclusive atmosphere. He liked the food just fine, but he would never feel okay about having another man squirt the soap into his hands, as the bathroom attendant was solely there to do.

He and Kim took a seat in a booth, ordering drinks, shrimp cocktail, smoked salmon and a cheese plate. But just before their orders arrived, Kim's phone buzzed and he looked at it, annoyed.

"Ah damn, sorry," he said. "Apparently, Harrington pissed off an investor again. I gotta go do clean-up duty. You want me to cancel the order?"

Liam lifted a hand. "It's okay. I'll stay."

"All right. Rain check. And next time you better hit that ball like you actually know what you're doing, all right?"

The waiter cleared Kim's place settings and offered to return his drink to the bar, but Liam told him it was okay, he'd double-fist it. Suddenly, spending the afternoon sitting in a cushy leather booth slowly getting drunk seemed like a better option than going home to a woman he didn't know how to please.

The place was only half full, but the guy at the piano was softly playing "My Funny Valentine," and the lights were warm and low. Liam knew that if he looked hard enough he'd find the usual old-school New York celebrities, safe and unbothered in their exclusive little clubhouse.

Liam sipped his Macallan 12 scotch and casually glanced at the blonde at the table next to his, who, judging by the outraged look on her face, had been stood up. She frowned at him, but then did a double take and sent a hopeful smile in his direction, which he answered with a practiced look of blank boredom. Beautiful, rich women hitting on him had been a dizzy novelty when he first came to town, but once he paired up with Hana, he gave up all his extracurriculars. Screwing around wasn't classy.

The waiter hovered over the table. "How is everything, sir?"

"Fine. Great." Suddenly, Liam desperately wished he was back in the corner dive in South Side where the bartender always made him pay up front and it smelled like stale beer, pickled eggs and mouse piss.

"Very good, sir." The guy all but bowed as he backed away from the table.

He took a gulp of the scotch, giving up the pretense of sipping. How was he going to fix things with Hana?

He wished he knew even one woman he was friendly enough with to get a female opinion on all this. Hell, these days, he wished he even knew a guy that he could really call a friend. He had been ready to spill his guts to Kim, of all people. A decent enough dude, but not exactly his bosom buddy.

It's not like he'd ever had lots of friends. Even back in the hood, he was on good enough terms with everyone, he could always find a pick-up game of basketball or someone to shoot the shit with, but when he really thought about it? His first, and maybe only, real friendship had been with Jay. And then he'd blown that by running off with Jay's wife. And now here he was—having chased them both off, apparently. Jesus Christ, he'd even be happy to talk to Alli right now. He shoved aside his empty glass and started in on the other as he shook his head. What a pathetic asshole he was.

You could call your mother. The idea made him chuckle bitterly. Aside from his monthly call to make sure she got the check he sent that kept her in booze and, he hoped at least, kept her lights on and fridge stocked, it wasn't like he and his mom had much to say to each other.

But the hell with it. He had to talk to someone. He downed the rest of the scotch in one gulp, threw a couple of hundred-dollar bills on the table next to the untouched plates of food, and wound his way out of the bar, pulling out his phone and dialing Chicago as he walked outside.

"Li?" said his mom. She sounded out of breath, but a two-pack-a-day habit would do that to you. "Everything okay? Why are you calling?"

"Hey, Ma. Everything's fine. Just checking in."

"What? Why?"

He laughed. Fair enough. She wasn't even going to pretend like this was normal. "No reason."

"Bull. What's wrong?"

He paused. She always could see right through him. "Ma,

if you were a woman—" He heard the little huff of protest. "Sorry, I mean, how do you…what does a woman need to stay in a relationship?"

"You and that Chinese girl having trouble, huh?"

"Don't be an asshole, Ma. She's Japanese-American and you know it."

"Same difference. She dump you?"

He shook his head and sighed. Why had he called her again? "No. She didn't dump me. But she's not happy, okay? I'm not sure I can make her happy."

"You messing around on her?"

"No, Ma, no."

"You rough with her? You throwing her around?"

"Jesus, no! Come on."

"Oh." Something softened in his mother's voice then. "Well, some people, you can't do anything to make them happy. It might not be your fault."

"I don't think—I don't think that's the problem. I think maybe—she's the real thing, Ma. Like she grew up rich and educated, she's traveled all over the world. Maybe I'm just—not enough?"

There was a long pause. "She sounds like a frigging snob." Her voice shook with contempt. "I don't know why you don't come home and find a nice girl from the neighborhood. Stick with your own kind, Li."

He swore in his head. What else had he expected? "Okay, yeah, thanks for the advice. I'm good. I'm fine."

"You sure?" She sounded doubtful. "You don't sound fine."

"I'm good," he repeated. "Listen, Ma, I gotta go, but you need anything? You okay for money?"

Another long pause. "Well. I mean, I could always use—"

He cut her off. "I'll wire some into your account tonight,

okay? Talk soon. Bye." He hung up without waiting for her to answer.

He looked around, trying to get his bearings. He had just walked as he talked, without thinking about where he was going, and now he was turned around. One of Liam's most carefully hidden secrets was how, after all these years, he still got lost in Manhattan.

CHAPTER 32

"Well," said Ava as she reached over and snagged a chip from Bridget's bag, "this is so not what I thought was going to happen."

"What do you mean?" yelped Bridget. "This is all your fault! You made this happen! You freaking threw us together!"

The friends were lunching together on the High Line, enjoying the early summer sunshine and pulled pork sandwiches from the Chelsea Market while they watched Dylan run up and down the path.

Ava widened her eyes. "Yeah, but I just thought you guys would have dinner, and Jay would offer you a job. End of story." She leaned back against the bench and stretched her long legs out in front of her. "I mean, I guess I should have figured that you'd end up sleeping together, but then either you'd get all squirrely and controlling like you always do and push him away for no reason, or he'd start moping about his ex-wife again and get all gross and weepy. I certainly didn't think you were going to end up having soul mate sex and then squaring off over a billion dollars."

"It wasn't soul mate sex. And I do not get squirrely and controlling."

"Uh, when you say it was the best sex of your life, that certainly sounds like soul mate stuff. And you do so get squirrely. You can't even order a meal without being totally, ridiculously controlling about it. Don't even try to deny it."

"Dylan!" Bridget called at the rapidly retreating back of her son. "Not so far, honey, okay? Stay where I can see you!" Ava reached for another chip and Bridget pushed the bag toward her. "Here, just take it. Don't you get paid enough to buy your own chips?"

Ava raised an eyebrow as she took the chips. "Case in point."

Bridget glared at her. "You're not helping."

Ava laughed. "I don't know what you want me to say here. Congratulations on the amazing not-soul-mate sex? I hope you become a billionaire? Lean in, sister, you can have it all? What?"

"I want you to say that I'm not crazy! I want you to tell me that I'm not putting this job in jeopardy by seeing this guy! I want you to tell me to cut it the hell out!"

"Oh, you're definitely crazy. But that's nothing new." She popped a chip into her mouth. "But I don't know, I mean, why end something so good before it even really begins? Don't you want to see how it turns out?"

"Because I hardly know the guy. Why not just cut my losses now?"

Ava shook her head. "This is why you haven't stuck it out with anyone since Kevin."

"What are you talking about?"

"You find something wrong with everyone. Remember Chris Helborg?"

"Jesus, Ava, this is a little bigger than chewing with your mouth open."

"Exactly. That was literally the only thing wrong with

Chris—he had bad table manners. Other than that? Hot, rich, funny, he was crazy about you…"

"I once watched him eat an entire salad with his hands."

Dylan came running back. "Can I have a popsicle, please, Mommy?"

"Of course you can, honey," interjected Ava. She loved to spoil her friend's kid.

Bridget snorted in protest as Ava reached for her purse and started to stand, but Dylan shook his head. "I can do it. Just give me the money. It's two dollars and seventy-five cents. I asked."

Ava raised her eyebrows. "So independent." She handed him a ten-dollar bill. "Bring one for me and your mommy, too, and tell him to keep the change."

"He doesn't need more sugar right now," muttered Bridget as Dylan ran toward the ice-cream stand. "He had a cookie with his lunch."

Ava put her finger in the air and turned back to Bridget. "Please hold for a moment. I want to back up to the part where you told Harrington his architect's renderings were boring and he threw you out of his office, but then for some mysterious reason, he agreed with you, after all—do you think that means he needs a new architect?"

Bridget laughed in disbelief. "What happened to Harrington being an asshole? Now you want to work with him, too?"

Ava shrugged. "Well, I can't spend the rest of my life designing Scarlett's rumpus rooms."

"Well, actually, you probably could…"

Ava waved her hands. "Look at this beautiful, beautiful park we're in. It's original, it's useful, it's iconic. It changed New York City permanently and for the better. And it was created in our lifetime. And look over there." She pointed to the way the Empire State Building rose up out of the skyline, seem-

ingly cradled at its base by the twisting spires of the General
Theological Seminary. "Look how timeless those buildings
are. They're art. They're poetry, Bridget. That's what I want. I
want to design something even a fraction as amazing as those.
I want to change the landscape. Make something so important
that it will be here making people's lives better for years after
I'm gone. And I don't want to do it anonymously. I'm sick of
men claiming my work for their own. I'm in it for the glory.
I want my name on the buildings. Architect, Ava Martinez—
in big, bold gold letters."

Bridget took a bite of her sandwich and chewed slowly, taking in the view of the historic buildings, the wildflowers dipping in the breeze around them, the sense of being tucked up
away from the busy streets. People were lolling on the benches
or walking dreamily hand in hand down the never-ending
bridge. "Next time, we're gonna sit where we can look at the
IAC Building," she said, referring to the famously modern
Frank Gehry–designed office.

Ava snorted derisively. "Gehry. He watched too many monster movies. His stuff looks like the Blob Who Ate Manhattan."

Bridget rolled her eyes. "The Empire State is the past. This
park, the IAC, that's the future."

Ava widened her eyes. "And that's why I want to work for
someone like Harrington. I want a chance to design a building that will stand up to the test of time."

Bridget shook her head. "Okay, can we be done talking
about your need to be immortal and get back to my problem,
please? Before Dylan gets back?" She could see him struggling
to decide on a flavor a few yards away. "I just need to know if
I'm making a huge freaking mistake here, A."

Ava took a sip of water. "Look, I didn't want to give him
the satisfaction of knowing this, but it actually kind of disappointed me when I heard Jason say that I reminded him of his

ex. He's hot, he's smart, he's funny, he's mega-rich. And if you managed to have crazy, mind-blowing, totally awesome sex with him? What is there to discuss? Go elope with him for goodness' sake. Or at least go on a second date."

"But the job——"

Ava held up her hand. "You're going to get it, Bridget."

"But what if——"

"I have never known you to go after something you really wanted and not eventually get it. You are absolutely terrifying that way. And when you get it, because Jay is a decent guy and already worth like twenty bajillion dollars, he will be happy for you. And then you can get married and have tiny miniature super-rich contractor babies together."

"So you think this all can actually work?"

She shrugged. "I don't see why not."

Bridget sighed. "No. I've got to end it."

"So glad you asked my advice."

Bridget reached over and grabbed the chips. "Give those back to me."

CHAPTER 33

Jay went to her apartment late that night. He knew that the smart thing would be to give her space, let her come to him, but he couldn't resist. He'd lain in bed for an hour, fruitlessly trying to sleep, his mind and body on fire, before finally deciding to pull on a pair of jeans and take the train downtown.

"It's me," he said into her intercom, and she buzzed him up.

She'd obviously come from her bed, as well. Her hair was down, and her face was bare. She was wearing nothing but a thin, oversize men's T-shirt, the neck big enough so that it slipped carelessly off her tanned shoulder.

The rules were followed. In fact, not only did they not talk about work, they didn't talk at all.

Jason reached over and slowly pulled the shirt off her, dropping it in a pool at her feet. He sucked in his breath. He was so hard it was almost painful. She made him ache with need. He took a step forward and then swept her up into his arms, carrying her into the bedroom.

There was something almost hallucinogenic about making love to her. They lay together in her darkened room and he shut his eyes and trailed his hands over her skin, and imagined tracers, swirling colors, shooting stars radiating off her body. She gasped, grabbing his hand and insistently guiding it to where she wanted to be touched. When his fingers found their warm, wet mark, he felt a jolt of absolute, pure joy run through him.

They bathed after, tangled together in the warm glow of the candles lit around her tub, her back spooned to his chest, the ends of her long, wet hair drifting around his waist. He scooped a handful of warm water and poured it down her front, over her shoulder, watching it cascade in a silver rush down her breasts and back into the bath. Then he brushed aside her hair and kissed the nape of her neck, cradling her breasts in his hands as she arched back against him with a sigh.

He would have given almost anything to have climbed back into her bed with her that night. He wanted to hold her as she slept, smell her hair and feel her skin against his, wake with her the next morning. But he knew better than to ask. He knew he was already pushing the bounds of what he could take from her.

It rained as he walked back uptown, misty and warm, soaking his hair and his shirt, turning the streets a gleaming black that reflected the streetlights and headlights in wavering golden pools and streaks. He savored the strange sight of the Manhattan streets almost empty of people. It was late and wet and the few brave souls who were out dashed quickly from cover to cover, trying to keep dry.

He arrived back at his apartment wet and chilled, didn't even bother turning on the lights, just found his way to his bedroom, peeled off his damp clothes and collapsed, naked, into his own bed. He should have been sated and exhausted, but instead, images of Bridget played through his head, and he had to control the urge to get right back up and return to her again.

CHAPTER 34

Liam turned in the budget and proposal to Harrington & Kim in record time. He'd been using the job as an excuse, spending all his time at his office, crunching numbers and collating pages, avoiding going home until after Alli and Hana were asleep.

After his conversation with his mother, he became convinced that the answer to his problems lay in his getting this job. Hana was used to the best things in life, she always had been, and obviously, he was not supporting her in the way that Jay had been able to. If he got this Harrison job, South Side Construction would be launched into a whole other sphere.

He'd spent the night at his desk, poring over the numbers on the HealthTec budget, double- and triple-checking, before sending it off to Harrington & Kim via email. After, instead of going home, he'd stretched out on the couch in the office lounge and fallen asleep.

His field manager, Alexander Redetzke, was the first to stumble upon him the next morning. He stood over Liam, clearing his throat until Liam said, without opening his eyes,

"Redetzke, if you don't freaking shut up I'm going to kick you in the nuts so hard, they'll ooze out your nose."

"Well," the man had squeaked indignantly, "excuse me for trying to get you up before all your employees see you drunk on the couch."

Liam opened his eyes. "I'm not drunk, you moron. I pulled an all-nighter reviewing the numbers on the Harrington and Kim budget. And what the hell do I care what my employees see? They're my employees. I'm the boss, remember?"

"You finished the—" Redetzke looked astonished.

"Yeah, well." Yawning, Liam sat up and ran his hands through his hair. "I finished it. Sent it to them last night."

Redetzke blinked. "Shouldn't you have had the chief estimator give it one more look?"

"Don't worry about it. The numbers were right." He sniffed the air. "Did you make coffee?"

Redetzke frowned, offended. "That is not my job."

Liam rolled his eyes. "Your job is whatever I tell you to do. Either make some coffee or do a Starbucks run. In fact, definitely do that. I need a flat white, extra hot."

Redetzke's mustache quivered. "You know I have a degree in engineering."

"Yeah, from SUNY frigging Binghamton. My degrees are from Yale, so you go get the coffee."

The man's face went red, but he turned and left the room as instructed.

Liam fell back onto the couch with a groan.

He knew he shouldn't be messing with his employees like that. Redetzke was a top-notch field super, OSHA and LEED certified with a mechanical engineering degree, and Liam was lucky to have him; he'd be nearly impossible to replace. But he was exhausted and worried over Hana, raw and anxious, and the idea of making nice with his whiny, humorless employee seemed pretty much impossible.

He made a mental note to apologize later, after he got more sleep and was back in Hana's good graces. But for now he dragged himself back into his office, to get started on the day's work.

CHAPTER 35

Scarlett was showing Bridget where she wanted to put in a hidden door in her bedroom. Normally, Bridget would be racing off to the bathroom to relay this information via text to Ava—they had a running bet on who had to do the weirdest stuff for this job—but today she could hardly focus enough to hear what Scarlett was telling her.

"Bridget," said Scarlett. Her tone was sharp. "I just asked you three times if we can put the door behind these bookshelves. Where the hell are you?"

Bridget ran her hands over her hair. "Sorry. I'm exhausted. Um. Yes, sure we could, sure."

Scarlett looked at her. Her shrewd gray eyes gleamed with sudden understanding. "Oh! Why, Bridget, did you get laid last night?"

Bridget groaned and covered her face with her hands. Why couldn't she hide this from anyone? First Ava, then Ethan and now Scarlett. Next thing she knew her ma would be calling to say that she'd read all about it in Page Six.

"Why, you did! You little minx! I didn't even know you were seeing anyone!" Scarlett sounded inordinately pleased.

"I'm not," said Bridget from behind her hands. She uncovered her face. "I'm just…sleeping with him. In fact, last night I don't think we said more than ten words to each other."

"Oh, my," said Scarlett. She sat down on her enormous, perfectly made bed and patted the spot next to her. "Come sit by me, said the spider to the fly."

Bridget threw herself down next to Scarlett, lying across the bed and closing her eyes. "I don't know what the hell I'm doing, Scar," she said. Then she popped her eyes open again. "Oh, my God, what is this comforter made out of? It's so soft!"

"Nothing you can afford," said Scarlett smugly. "Less than a dozen goats in the Himalayas can make this fabric."

Bridget rolled her eyes. Leave it to Scarlett to find the rarest wool in the world.

Scarlett primly crossed her legs. "So, tell me about this silent young man. I assume it is a man," she said as she rolled her eyes. "Such a waste of your talents."

Bridget didn't sit up. "Yup. Sorry."

"Well, what's he like?"

Bridget pondered this for a moment, staring up at the mirror on Scarlett's ceiling.

"He's amazing in bed. Like, I-can't-stop-thinking-about-it kind of amazing. Like, if I could just climb into bed with this guy and screw him until we both starved to death, I would call that a pretty good way to go."

"Well, I approve of that. What else?"

Bridget wrinkled her nose. "He's a good guy, I think. Except, he's the competition."

"Oh?"

"Well, I mean, he wasn't when we started sleeping together. But then he was."

"Hmm."

"He's got these eyes. They're like crazy intense green and all sleepy-looking, and these super-cut arms and shoulders... I think I have to break up with him."

Scarlett laughed. "That is not where I thought this conversation was heading."

She sat up. "I mean, we're not even really together, so how can I break up, right? But I suppose I could stop letting him into my apartment."

Scarlett patted her hand. "You could. Lord knows that has been a final solution to many of my own peccadilloes."

"Yeah? You just ice them out? Pretend they never existed? That doesn't sound very polite, Miss Manners."

Scarlett smiled. "I only do it when they just can't take the hint."

"Anyway, I know I should get rid of him. No doubt at all. There are, like, five million complications already. And actually, yesterday I had decided to do just that. I was going to text him that we needed to pack it in, but before I could, he showed up at my place and all of a sudden we were doing it on the kitchen floor."

"The kitchen, eh?"

"The kitchen, my bed, the bathtub, the couch, the dining room table..."

"Oh, if you're doing all that—don't break up with him yet, Bridget. Why miss all the fun?"

Bridget sighed. "Why does nobody want me to do the right thing? You're all a bunch of enablers."

Her phone buzzed in her jacket pocket and she fished it out and looked at it. "Harrington and Kim. Oh, I've got to take this."

Scarlett waved her off. "Be my guest."

"Hello? This is Bridget Steele." Bridget stepped out into Scarlett's hallway and shut the door behind her.

"Hello, Bridget Steele, it's Mark Harrington."

Bridget swallowed. "Oh. Hello, Mr. Harrington. Is there something I can do for you?"

"I think I owe you a lunch."

She blinked. "You do?"

"Yes, at a very nice place, because this morning I met with the HealthTec executives and we were looking at the rendering, and I could see that they weren't happy. And because of you, I was able to let them know that we were already looking to redesign the generic nature of their building—that we envisioned something much more worthy of their name—and so, in a roundabout way, you might have had something to do with saving this project."

"So I was right."

He laughed. "Yes. You were right."

"Well, I love being right."

"Don't we all? So are you free now? Hungry?"

"I'm at a client's, actually, but—"

"Oh, honey, just go," whispered Scarlett as she breezed by her. "You're all screwed out and useless at the moment, and I have an appointment, anyway."

Bridget coughed loudly, hoping he hadn't heard Scarlett's comments. "Actually, looks like my schedule just cleared. Where would you like to meet?"

"How about the Union Square Café? I want to see their new space."

"Yeah, me, too," Bridget agreed. "I heard it's huge. Okay, I can get there in twenty."

"Excellent. I'll grab us a table and see you there."

CHAPTER 36

Jason was shopping on his lunch break. After he had used one of Bridget's nice, big, soft towels the night before, he'd realized that his own linens were severely lacking. He wanted some of those—what had she called them?—bath sheets. She had said they were nothing special—he could get them anywhere, but all he knew was that when he'd looked at what was hanging in his own bathroom that morning, they had been flimsy little pieces of rags compared to what he had wrapped around his waist and then she had torn off him again later that night.

He stared at the massive wall of folded towels in front of him. So many frigging towels. And apparently, Bridget had been right—because half of what he was looking at were labeled "bath sheets." He touched one. Not as soft as Bridget's had been. He touched another. Better, but he didn't like the color. Who the hell had black towels? He grabbed another towel and shook it out—what color should he pick? Was he supposed to do all the same color or pick a bunch of different ones?

He put the towel back and took out his phone, texting Bridget before he thought too much about it.

Is it weird to have more than one color of towel?

He stared at the phone for a moment, willing her to answer, then put his phone back into his pocket in frustration and pulled another towel down from the shelf. Soft. A nice bright blue. He wrapped it around his waist, tucking it into the waistband of his jeans.

"Jay?"

He'd recognize that voice anywhere. The hackles on his neck went up and he turned around to face Liam Maguire.

"Liam."

His former best friend hadn't changed a bit. Dark-eyed, compact, pale and intense. His black hair flopped over his brow like it always had—making every woman he met want to reach up and push it back for him. And he wore his usual uniform of jeans, T-shirt and hoodie—still dressing like a college student even though he was worth millions.

"Nice towel."

Jason snatched it off. "Need to replace my old ones."

Liam eyed the wall of towels next to them. "Well, looks like you came to the right place."

Jason remembered the last time he had seen Liam. It had been at least six months before. He'd stopped by Jay's apartment to pick up the last of Hana's stuff. Some records, a sweater that had turned up in Jay's wash on one particularly painful day, and, nonsensically, a framed picture of the two of them and their extended families on their wedding day. They had fought about it over the phone the night before—which is why Liam had shown up to claim the things, not Hana. She had insisted that she should have the picture because it was one of the last ones taken of her grandmother before she died. She didn't care if it was their wedding photo—for her, it was a family photo, no matter if Jay was in it or not.

Her saying that had hit Jay like a kick in the balls and he wasn't in any kind of better mood when Liam showed up to take it the next morning. Jay cringed to remember; he had tried to pick a fight—like a fistfight—with Liam. He had actually swung at the guy. He was bigger, but Liam was fast and he had guessed what was coming—so he ducked, grabbed Jason's wrist, twisted him to the ground, picked up the bag with all of Hana's stuff and made a quick retreat to the door.

"Look, Jay," he had said from the safety of the hallway, "I'm sorry. I know none of this is easy. You gotta believe me when I tell you that I never meant for any of this to happen. I miss you, man."

"Fuck off," Jay had spat. And that had been the end of that.

"I like the bright green ones," offered Liam, still looking at the towels.

Jay frowned. He liked them, too. But he sure as hell wasn't going to buy them now.

Liam turned and looked him in the eye. "How you been?" he said. "Everything okay?"

For a moment Jay had the impulse to tell him. Like, really talk to him about what was going on—with Alli, with work, with the Harrington job, with Bridget. For a minute it just felt like he was standing in front of Liam—his old friend. The guy he used to share almost everything with. And he missed him.

And then he remembered. Work, Hana, Alli—if he was having issues with any those things, it was literally because of Liam. This guy, this old friend—had ruined Jason's life.

"I'm fine," he said, grabbing some plain white towels—not nearly as soft as Bridget's had been—and turning away. "Actually, I'm better than fine. Work is great. Everything is great."

"Jay!"

He stopped, but kept his back turned.

"So is Russo Construction going up for the Harrington and Kim job?"

Interesting.

He turned around. "Of course we are."

Liam nodded. "Us, too."

Their eyes met. Jay smiled as he smelled the faint scent of revenge. He knew that Liam's business was still new, that getting something like the Harrington skyscraper would propel him into another league. And man, was he going to enjoy making sure that didn't happen. "Big job," he said. "A lot to take on for a new company."

Liam smirked. "So may the best man win, then, right?"

Jason thought about this for a moment, and then laughed. "Or woman."

Liam looked at him oddly. "What?"

Jay shook his head and then put the white towels back and grabbed a stack of the green ones. "I'll see you around, Liam."

CHAPTER 37

Idiot! thought Liam as he walked away from Bed Bath & Beyond and headed back downtown toward his office. He'd heard rumors that the owners of the building were thinking of doing a renovation and had wanted to see if it was worth his time to pursue, but seeing Jay had chased that errand right out of his head. Huge mistake. Why had he opened his big, fat mouth and mentioned the Harrington job? There had been basically no doubt that Jay would be up for it. Russo Construction had worked for Harrington back when Jay's father was still alive. But Liam couldn't help himself. He just had to make sure, and the minute he'd said the words, he'd regretted them, because he'd seen the killer light turn on in Jay's eyes. That look he used to get whenever they were up for anything that wasn't an absolute done deal; the look that meant he loved a challenge, and that he was going balls to the wall to get what he wanted.

Liam used to be delighted by that take-no-prisoners look. It meant work, money, security, success.

Now it was trouble.

He had been shocked when he turned the corner to find his ex-partner hovering in front of a wall of Turkish linens. Liam had stood there, just watching him for a moment, as Jay foolishly wrapped himself in a towel like there weren't fifty other people in the store to see him do it. Liam wanted to laugh but he felt a tinge of envy, as well. It was exactly like Jay not to give a damn what people thought. That was what happened when you grow up rich and good-looking.

He must be seeing someone new, he mused as he made his way downtown. A man doesn't just go buy new towels without a woman being involved somehow. Hana had replaced every towel in Liam's loft when she moved in. The sheets, too. And Liam had nice linens.

Well, good. If he knew Jay had moved on to someone else, maybe he could shake the queasiness he always felt when he thought of his old friend. The ping of guilt, the knowledge, deep down, that he had stepped on the back of someone he cared about to get something he cared about more. But if Jay found someone else to love, then maybe, once Liam had worked all this stuff out with Hana, of course, they could all be friends again—merrily laughing about how unhappy they'd all been in their previous lives, yukking it up over how Liam had actually done Jay a favor by stealing his wife…

Liam stopped at a corner and waited for the light to change. Yeah. No. New woman or not, Liam had seen the look on Jay's face. He would do everything he could to screw Liam's chances with Harrington. He would win the job just to spite Liam. And Liam only had himself to blame.

He remembered when Jay's father died. After the funeral they had stood in a little huddle, Liam and Jay and Hana, in Jay's parents' huge Upper East Side penthouse. Servers floated around them, silently offering food and drink. Titans of the industry, dressed in sober suits with their wives clutching their arms and making little moues of sadness with their Restylane-filled lips, took turns offering Jay their condolences. Jay's mother had died two years earlier, and the apartment was now Jay's to do with as he wished. Liam remembered looking around in silent awe and wondering what it would be like to know that everything, the apartment, the house in Aspen, the place in the Hamptons, the stocks, the bonds, the savings and most of all, the actual business, would be passed down to you like a father handing his son his grandfather's watch on graduation day.

"So on the bright side," Jay had said in a moment between elderly developers wringing his hand and clapping his back, "you'll come work for me, now, right, Liam?"

Liam looked at him, confused. "As what?"

"My COO, of course."

Liam had been working at an entry-level job at Goldman Sachs, surrounded by guys with half his brains, taking the ferry in from Staten Island every morning so he could fetch coffee and answer phones and wait for his chance to climb another rung on the ladder. What Jay was offering made his breath catch in his throat.

Liam remembered Hana smiling at him. She had known that Jay was going to bring this up.

"Your COO?" he choked out.

Jay nodded. "I hate the operations guy my dad left me. He's a sexist, racist dinosaur and he still thinks he can treat me like I'm the boss's son. But firing him while my dad was still alive would have been more trouble than it was worth."

"Wait, you've been waiting for your dad to die so you could offer me a job?" Liam could hear that his voice was two octaves too high. And loud. Inappropriately loud.

"Of course not." Jay looked around uneasily and then put his hand on Liam's arm. "But when it comes to running the field and numbers, you're the smartest person I know, man. We'd be lucky to have you."

Another gray-faced, white-haired man started to approach. "We can talk about it later," whispered Jay.

And just like that, Liam's life had changed. The money came flowing in. He moved out of his one-room efficiency on Staten Island and into a two-bedroom in Midtown. Then a year later he bought his loft in SoHo. A year after that the house in the Hamptons. He bought his mom a two-bedroom condo in Chicago and sent her money every month to live on. He picked out an Audi R8 and then a driver to go with it. He hired a staff to keep his properties in order. He slipped into this lifestyle just like Jay had actually handed him that heirloom watch.

Sometimes he woke up and still expected to be back in his stuffy childhood bedroom in Chicago, either too cold or too hot, and wondering if his mom had made it home the night before and whether there was anything in the kitchen for breakfast. But then he would look around at whatever beautiful room he happened to be in, Manhattan or the Hamptons, and he would see Hana curled up next to him, and smell the good, clean air, and silently catalog the luxuries he was surrounded by now, and slowly remind himself that he had done it. He had actually made it out.

He owed Jay everything. He knew he did. Everything good that had come to him in this life, including Hana, had been given to him by, or taken from, Jay.

But that wasn't going to stop him from doing his very best to get this Harrington job. Maybe he'd woken up a sleeping tiger. Maybe Jay was going to go for it, balls-out, just to punish him. He couldn't blame him if he tried. But Liam had learned from the best. And lately he had a pretty good track record of getting what he really wanted.

CHAPTER 38

Despite its new location, the Union Square Café still felt like itself. The venerable restaurant had recently opened in a new, much bigger space, and a certain part of Manhattan had let out a sigh of relief when they had been able to ascertain that their favorite eatery still had its original soul.

It was the service, of course, thought Bridget as she was led down to the lower bar. The food was delicious, the wine list was great, but it was the way the staff famously made you feel—like a guest in their home—that kept the customers coming back. It was a business lesson to learn. The aesthetic and space were replaceable, but the people were not.

Harrington stood up and smiled as she approached. Bridget felt torn about his frankly admiring gaze. She had worn a black Fendi sheath dress, perfectly professional, but suddenly she wished it covered up a little more. She wanted to look good, of course. But she wasn't able to change before meeting him so she had to make it work. She knew that, like it or not, looking good could help her cause, but it was a fine line. She needed him to take her seriously as a CEO—not as a potential date.

"Bridget," said Harrington, briefly touching her hand and giving her a light kiss on each cheek. "May I call you Bridget?"

That scent again—leather, chocolate and musk. Bridget swallowed. "Of course, but only if I can call you Mark."

"Perfect," said Harrington as he waited for her to sit and then sank back into his own chair. "Glad to be on a first-name basis."

She unrolled her napkin and took a sip of water, giving him an inconspicuous once-over. He was older, but still a handsome man. Those bright blue eyes, the perfectly cut suit, strong, manicured hands, not a hair out of place. He smiled at her and she noticed a deep dimple appear on one side of his full mouth.

"I hope you don't mind," he said, "but I took the liberty of ordering for us both before you arrived."

Bridget felt a streak of defiance. "Oh, did you?"

He laughed. "Uh-oh. I see I've annoyed you."

She shrugged, toying with her empty wineglass. "I just find it interesting when a man thinks he knows exactly what a woman wants."

Harrington grinned. "I usually hit the mark."

The waiter approached with a basket of warm bread and a bottle of champagne. Bridget frowned as he popped the cork. "I thought this was a business lunch."

"It is," Harrington said as he lifted his glass. "If you hadn't spoken your mind to me, I wouldn't have been open to changing the design, I'd have lost HealthTec and instead of this champagne, I'd probably be drinking cheap whiskey alone in my apartment right now."

She paused a moment and then clinked her glass against his. "Cheers, then," she said. She didn't want to seem ungracious.

The champagne was delicious, as was the first course of beef tartare followed by ricotta gnocchi so light and airy that they melted in her mouth, but as they chatted, Bridget couldn't help but feel uneasy. Despite his assurances, this did not exactly feel like a business lunch, and as Harrington smoothly questioned her about her family and growing up in the Bronx, she felt her unease grow. Harrington was exactly the kind of man Bridget usually went for: smart, handsome, urbane and powerful. And in other circumstances, she might have enjoyed his attention. But this felt all wrong. Bridget made a point of wining and dining as many potential clients as she could. It was part of the job. She was all business, all day, and she did her best to be professional, but the nature of the job meant things could get blurry, and opportunities had been lost when men decided they'd rather date her than hire her.

"So tell me about college," he said, leaning in a little. "I bet you were the kind of girl who was always in trouble." His hand almost touched hers as he refilled her glass of champagne for the third time without asking.

She subtly pushed it away. If she were a man, he wouldn't be chatting her up about her sorority days. She decided she had to change the dynamic before it was too late.

"I think we'll have our preliminary budget on your original design ready for you soon," she said, ignoring his question. "We're making great progress."

Harrington raised his eyebrows, "Oh? How soon?"

"Soon. Maybe even next week." This was not true. Mrs. Hashemi told her that they were still at least two weeks away, but she was feeling a little desperate.

He nodded. "Really?"

"I've got my top people working on it. We're giving it all we've got."

Harrington smiled. "No beating around the bush, huh?"

"I know Steele Construction is a long shot. But no one will work harder on this project than I will."

He looked at her for a moment. "You know, I might actually believe that." He looked at her empty plate. "Digestif?"

She shook her head. "I can't. My work day's only half done."

He nodded and sighed. "Mine, too. Too bad, really. This has been very pleasant. Thank you for coming out last minute like this. I really did want to thank you."

"Oh," she said, remembering Ava, "I wanted to ask. Are you considering another architect for your design change?"

He shook his head. "I want to give my original guy a chance to do a redesign."

Bridget nodded, but inwardly she was rolling her eyes. She knew his architectural firm—they didn't much believe in redesigning.

The waiter brought the check, along with a small dish of chocolate truffles and carefully arranged cookies. Harrington walked with Bridget out into the surprisingly bright sunshine, and Bridget hid a yawn, wishing she hadn't had such a heavy lunch and that second glass of champagne. She was going to fall asleep at her desk.

She smiled to herself; maybe she'd call in sick again, then call up Jason, get him to play hooky with her.

"Can I take you somewhere? My car is on its way," said Harrington.

She shook her head, leaning in for the double kiss goodbye that had become de rigueur in Manhattan society in the past few years. "Thanks, but I need to walk off the champagne."

"So I'll hear from you next week, then?"

She paused. "Next week?"

"The budget? You'd said you'd have it done?"

She blinked. Damn. "Right, of course. Yes. Next week. Thank you again for lunch."

He smiled at her. "Thank you. It was an excellent distraction."

She turned away, and inwardly, she sighed. Those did not

sound like the words of someone who was taking her particularly seriously. Forget calling Jay, she had to get back on the phone and find out if Mrs. Hashemi could speed things up.

She took out her phone as she rounded the corner, checking for messages.

She wrinkled her nose in puzzlement. Why the hell was Jay asking her about towels?

CHAPTER 39

Jay stretched his arms out over his head and then pulled Bridget closer. She lay her cheek on his chest, and the press of her naked skin felt like silk against him.

"Why don't you come with me to the Hamptons this weekend?" Jay said. He was imagining her in a bikini and the words just popped out of his mouth before he thought about it.

She lifted her head and looked at him. "With your daughter?"

Damn, right, Alli. "Well, she's bringing some friends, so I don't see why I shouldn't, too, right? There's plenty of room. We can be sneaky about things."

She laughed and pushed herself up onto her elbow. "Yeah, I'm sure she wouldn't notice anything."

He grinned down into her face, reaching out to push a stray lock of hair out of her eyes. "Alli's going to think you're so cool."

She knit her brow. "Um. A little early for introductions, I think."

He laughed. He knew he should slow down, he knew that

he was making her skittish, but he couldn't help himself when he was around her. He tugged at her arm, and she rolled over and straddled him. "I know, right?" he said. "Way too early. It's all your fault. You make me want to do all these crazy things. Break the rules." He reached up and caught her nipple in his mouth, flicking it with his tongue and relishing the sweet little groan that he coaxed from her lips.

She arched her back, straining against him.

"I was actually heading out there, anyway," she said breathily. "Scarlett is having this charity gala for Habitat for Humanity, and I promised to go." She gasped as he continued to work his tongue at her breast. Her words came between little pants, "You can be my date, if you like."

He released her nipple. "Is it the bachelor auction?" he said, grinning up at her. "She actually asked me to be part of that a few weeks ago."

She laughed. "You're getting auctioned off?" She slid her body down, flattening herself against him. "So how much do you think I'll have to pay to have you to myself?"

He exhaled, loving the way her skin felt against his. "I'm pretty sure I can arrange something pro bono."

She groaned at his bad joke and shook her head, laughing, but then grew quiet as he kissed her neck, nibbling down to her collarbone, and moved his hands down the curve of her waist, grasping her firm rear.

"Hey…" She lifted her head and looked at him. "How close are you to getting the budget done?"

His hands froze. "What?"

She looked slightly abashed, but plowed on. "I just wondered, you know. I mean, my guys are getting pretty close and—"

"Bridget," he said, staring up at her, "this is not the kind of rule I was talking about breaking."

She sighed—a different kind of sigh—one of frustration—and rolled off him, facing the ceiling. "It's really hard not to talk about work," she said.

He snorted. "Actually, considering what we were just doing, I think it was very easy not to talk about work," he said. He turned on his side and faced her. "We should probably drop the subject, right?"

She bit her lip and nodded, but kept staring at the ceiling. He trailed a finger across her shoulder, working his way toward the hollow at the base of her throat.

"I had lunch with Mark Harrington last week," she blurted out.

He laughed in disbelief. Removed his hand. "Okay," he said. "Like, a business lunch?"

She finally looked at him. Her cheeks were red now—no longer pink with desire, but spotted and blotchy with embarrassment. "I don't know why I didn't want to tell you," she said.

"Because we said we weren't talking about work stuff, remember?"

She squeezed her eyes shut for a moment. "I'm not so sure he thought it was just work."

He was quiet for a moment. Wondering over the fact that he felt a gut punch of absolute jealousy at her words. On one hand, he'd been numb for so long that it was almost pleasurable to feel this violently about anything again. But on the other hand, the sick, angry feeling that engulfed him was all too familiar, jealousy and grief being the mainstay of the last six months or so of his marriage. "And what did you think?" he said softly.

"I thought it was a chance to keep my name in the mix," she said swiftly. "That's all."

He closed his eyes, almost laughing over the instant relief

he felt. Frigging hell, this woman was going to make him insane. "Then why are you even telling me this?"

"I don't know!" she wailed. "I just wanted to know how close you were to done on your budget!"

"Jesus, Bridget. If I tell you, will you drop the work talk?" She nodded.

"We're nearly done. I'm just doing a review on it now."

The corner of her mouth twitched. She didn't look happy.

"We've built three other skyscrapers in the past few years. This isn't new to us. We've got drop boxes filled with previous budgets and estimates right there in the office that we can compare them to, along with a department of estimators." She nodded.

"Okay?" he said. "Anything else you need to know?"

She shook her head. He could practically see the gears grinding in her brain. He sighed and sat up. He wanted to pull her back on top of him, but he could see that the moment had passed.

"Are you hungry?" he asked. "You want to go get dinner somewhere?"

She looked at him. He could read relief in her eyes. "Yeah, sure," she said.

"Actually," he said, "would you mind if we stopped off at my office? I've got some people working overtime and I feel like I should at least make an appearance out of solidarity."

"Sure," she said, getting out of bed. "Not a problem."

CHAPTER 40

"Oh, good, you're home! I was just trying to decide what we wanted to do for dinner."

Liam had been dreading the inevitable confrontation with Hana. He'd ghosted her for days on end, ignoring her calls, answering her messages with perfunctory texts about how busy he was, sliding in after everyone was asleep and leaving before anyone woke up. He figured she'd be angry once they finally crossed paths, but soon he'd have the Harrington job and they'd have something to celebrate. At least, that was what he hoped, but he had mistimed his arrival home that night, thinking she'd be working in her studio.

She looked up at him from her perch on the couch with a big smile on her face. The smile somehow made him feel even worse.

"Hi." He shuffled his shoes off and stood, uncomfortable.

"It's Lucy's night off. You'll either have to suffer through my cooking or we can get some takeout."

"I can cook," Liam offered. As he said it, he realized how

ridiculous that sounded. He was an even worse cook than Hana was.

Her eyebrows shot up but she kept the smile plastered onto her face. "That would be great!"

This was when he realized she was actually pissed at him. The old Hana would never have missed a moment like this to tease him mercilessly. She would have told him he couldn't boil water and then bossily insist he go out to get the good Thai— at the place that didn't deliver. But relentlessly cheerful Hana? That was a danger sign flashing full-stop.

"Hana—" he began but she plowed over him. She was beginning to sound a little manic.

"Oh, and this weekend is that bachelor auction for Habitat for Humanity in the Hamptons. I promised Scarlett Hawkins you'd be available."

He blinked in disbelief. "Wait, as one of the guys who gets auctioned off?"

"Yes, won't that be fun?"

"Jesus, Hana. You could have asked me first."

"It's for charity. I told her you'd be happy to help."

"What if I end up being bought by some Botox-faced debutante?"

She rolled her eyes. "Nice, Liam."

"But I'm not even a bachelor!"

"Well, technically, you are. I mean, it's not like we're married or anything."

It was a low blow. A kick in the balls. He turned toward the kitchen. "I'm going to see what I can make for dinner," he said stiffly.

"Great!" she called after him. The slight edge that her voice had taken on disappeared. She was all fake sweetness and light again.

In the kitchen he sat down at the island, leaning his elbows against the cold marble and putting his head in his hands.

Growing up, he never knew if his mother was going to be drunk or sober. Up to a certain point, she was good at hiding it. She could drink about a bottle and a half of cheap wine, or four shots of rotgut gin, or a six-pack of beer, and you'd never know the difference. But one more drink after that, and she would reach, as he always thought of it, her Good Mommy stage. Suddenly, her focus, which had previously been somewhere between distracted and oblivious when it came to her son, would be on him like a beam of light. "Oh, Liam! You need a haircut! I just realized I never saw your grades this semester! Are you cold, honey? Hungry? Let me make you a sandwich!"

He hated Good Mommy. Because it felt so good in that brief moment when she was present, but it was always over as soon as she took her next drink. Halfway through making the sandwich or getting him a sweater or reading his report card, she'd bring that glass to her lips and the light would just switch off, and he'd be invisible again.

Good Mommy had also taught him not to trust the sincerity of women. He wasn't oblivious to this fault. He took Psych 101 in college and could connect A to B. He was smart enough to know where his damage came from and that it wasn't fair to apply it willy-nilly to anyone and everyone. But he also understood that was not how these childhood traumas worked, no matter how self-aware you were. His mother's indifference had been a cut that had been slashed open over and over and never really allowed to heal, and even all these years later, it was easy enough to pick the scab. Almost every woman he dated had eventually dealt with that particular wound.

But he'd never felt that way about Hana. Until now.

He got up and left the kitchen.

"Fine," he said. "I'll be auctioned off. But I'm not cook-ing. I'm going to go get Thai." He whirled around and faced her before going out the door. "And you sure as hell better bid on me."

CHAPTER 41

The skies opened up in an early-summer thunderstorm on their way over to the building site. The usual New York crowd of men with cheap umbrellas to sell were nowhere to be found, so Jason grabbed Bridget's hand and they ducked from awning to awning, getting a few seconds out of the pouring rain before they ran back into it again. Soon they were soaked through, so they just put their heads down and ran, laughing, through the city streets.

They arrived at his office dripping and out of breath, and as they rode up in the elevator, Bridget tried hard not to think too much about how she must look. Like a drowned rat, she imagined.

Jay, on the other hand, looked incredible. His hair was wet and dark and slicked back, the rain had molded his shirt to every gorgeous muscle in his arms and chest and there was a little trickle of water slowly running down his neck that Bridget had to muster every amount of willpower she had not to lean over and lick right off him.

Before they went in, Bridget did what repairs she could in

the hall bathroom, making liberal use of the hand dryer and a stack of paper towels until her hair and makeup were somewhat under control again. But there was nothing much she could do about the way her blouse had turned translucent and showed the outline of her black bra underneath, except fold her arms in front of herself and pretend that she didn't care.

He met her in the hallway, his eyes going straight to her shirt. "Jesus, Bridget," he said hoarsely. "Do you have any idea what you look like?"

She blushed, wrapping her arms tighter. "I'm sorry. I tried to dry out in the bathroom but—"

He took a step closer. "No, I mean, do you have any idea how sexy you look, all soaking wet from the rain? You're driving me crazy."

She darted a look around. They were alone, so she turned toward him and let her hands creep up the back of his neck and tangle in his hair. She felt him throb against her as he pulled her hips to his.

She took a long, shuddering breath. "We could go back to the apartment."

He ran a finger down her arm. "My office is closer."

"Oh, yeah?" She trailed her hand down his neck and flattened it against his chest. "But what about the guys working overtime?"

He smiled. "I checked. They've all gone home for the day. Guess they're not as dedicated as I thought." He bent to kiss her. A long, lingering kiss. Jesus Christ, but the man had a talented mouth. When he went down on her, she saw stars. "The cleaning guys are still here, but they'll be gone soon. We can sneak in," he said.

"What if they hear us?"

He moved his hands down her back. "I have a lock on my office door."

"Let's go," she whispered.

They broke apart and Bridget followed him in, dropping back a little to create a decorous amount of space between them.

Ten seconds after he had shut and locked his office door he had her blouse open and she was sitting on his desk, her skirt around her waist, her legs twined around his hips, her hands in his hair.

He kissed her temple, his breath hot on her skin as she buttoned her blouse back up. "I'm just going to go out for a second and make some phone calls," he said. "Catch up on a few things. Won't take more than fifteen minutes and then we can go get dinner, okay?"

She nodded, still breathless and shuddering from the way he had moved inside her. She'd had plenty of boyfriends, mostly powerful, older men who knew their way around a woman's body, and once upon a time, things had been special with Kevin...but it had never been like this.

Whatever this was between them—and she hardly knew how to name it—it was outside her experience in almost every way. She couldn't even think about it for too long—it scared her a little, the intensity of the way he made her feel.

She was out of control when it came to this man.

She leaned back in his office chair, bumping his computer mouse with her knee. The screen on his computer lit up. She squinted at the document.

Harrington Skyscraper—Budget.

Damn.

It was all there in black and white. All the work done. He'd probably have it to Harrington within days. Meanwhile, despite Bridget's pleas, Mrs. Hashemi said they were at least two weeks away.

She thought of the way Harrington was already expecting her numbers...

She stared at the screen, sick to her stomach. It was like someone had handed her the key to a test. Everything she needed was right there in front of her.

Steal a copy of his budget. We can undercut his fee. Ethan's words echoed in her head.

She remembered what she had told Jason. *I'll play dirty if I have to.* She had warned him. He had agreed to her terms.

She reached over, her hand shaking, and clicked onto his email. She pulled up a new message, attached the budget and then sent it to herself. Then she clicked into "Sent Mail" and erased the copy of the email she'd just sent. Then she emptied out his trash, clicked back to the document and leaned back in the chair.

Her heart was pounding.

"All right," he said, walking back in. "That's all done. Let's go have an amazing dinner somewhere."

She blinked up at him, her breath caught in her throat. She could still feel his hands on her body, his lips on her lips; she was still weak from all the delicious things he had done to her.

God, she thought, *I think I'm actually falling for this guy. What the hell did I just do?*

She took a deep breath. She hadn't done anything she couldn't take back yet. She could simply go home and throw the budget out. Erase that email without even opening it. No harm, no foul.

She stood up, smiled at him and took his arm. "Great, I'm starving."

He smiled back, oblivious.

But if you did use it—he'd never know...

She hushed her inner monologue. She'd figure it out later.

CHAPTER 42

Jay knew he only had himself to blame when Alli showed up at the apartment with six girls and one androgynous-looking boy, all ready to weekend in the Hamptons with him. She had asked if some friends could come, and he had been dumb enough not to specify just how many people she could bring. This was exactly what he deserved.

"Um, honey?" he said, eyeing the giggling group of teenagers milling around his living room. "I'm not sure how we're going to get all these people out to the house. My car isn't big enough."

Alli rolled her eyes. "Duh, Dad. Max's mom sent her Escalade and a driver to take everyone up. We'll just meet you there."

He blinked. "Oh. Which one is Max?"

"Daaad." Her voice was a drawn-out whine. "I already introduced everyone." She pointed to the crowd. "The one with purple streaks in her hair is River F. River M is wearing the red Margielas—"

"Margi what now?"

"Sneakers, Dad. Don't be dense. Cho Li is in the leather shorts, Minerva has the glasses, Hetty is wearing the Free Meek Mill T-shirt, Brooklyn is the short one, and the one in the kilt is Max."

He squinted. "Max is the one with the car?"

"Yes, Dad. God."

"And I'm driving up alone."

"They're my guests, Dad. I can't just abandon them."

"And how will everyone get back?"

"We have the car and driver for the weekend."

"And the driver will stay...?"

"Oh, my God, why are you asking all these questions? This is all worked out. Max's mom has a place in Sag Harbor. The driver will stay there and be on call when we need him."

He scratched his head. "Okay, then. I guess you do have it all worked out."

"I told you, Dad. Stop stressing."

As the teens grabbed their bags and left, Jay saw a sudden bright side. He picked up his phone and dialed.

Bridget answered right away.

"Hey," she said. "An actual phone call? Not a text? This must be big."

He smiled. "I just didn't want to miss you. How are you getting up to the Hamptons this weekend?"

"Jitney. I don't have a car."

"You want to ride with me instead? Alli and her friends have left me behind like the old man I guess I am now."

There was a pause. "I dunno. What kind of car do you have?"

He laughed. "Well, now that the teens have provided their own transportation, we have a choice. Land Rover or Mercedes."

"What model is the Mercedes?"

"Hard to please, huh? It's an S-Class. Convertible."

"What color?"

"Is there any other color but red?"

"And the seats?"

"Black quilted leather." He was getting a little turned on by her line of questions.

"Mmmm. Do the seats recline all the way back?"

Okay, now he was definitely turned on. "You know they do."

Long pause. He listened to her breathe.

"Okay. I guess I can skip the jitney."

"I'm relieved. Can you be ready in an hour? I'm afraid if I wait much longer, the teens will have burned down the place by the time I get there."

"Sure. Oh, and Jay?"

"Yes?"

"Thanks. I freaking hate the jitney."

CHAPTER 43

After being dropped off at Scarlett's place, Bridget stood facing the mammoth mansion and almost regretted not taking Jay up on his earlier offer to stay with him. In return for helping her with the fund-raiser, Scarlett had given Bridget the guesthouse for the weekend, a two-bedroom cottage tucked behind the main residence, with views of the pool and the beach. Like all of Scarlett's homes, Bridget knew it would be as luxurious as any five-star hotel, but the last time she'd been there had been pre-everything—pre-divorce, pre-bankruptcy, pre-ruin—and she suddenly felt exhausted.

East Hampton had once been Bridget's favorite place. Even at the height of her success, when she and Kevin could afford to vacation anywhere—Capri, St. Bart's, Ibiza—there was nowhere that Bridget would rather be than their house on Georgica Road.

My house, she thought bitterly. She had bought the land before she met Kevin, after Steele Construction was not just in the black, but making money hand over fist. She remembered the day she'd found it. Her Realtor had woken her up with an excited call. Two acres had come up for sale on the famed road, and Bridget could be the first to see them if she came out right now.

"I'll take it," she'd said as soon as she got there. "Full price. Cash. If there are other bidders, up my bid until I get it. This is mine."

She'd been stone-cold and determined. Two acres with pond views was more than she thought she'd ever get her hands on in this part of the village. She wasn't going to let it slip through her fingers.

"Don't you have any questions?" the Realtor had asked.

"Nope."

"Do you want to discuss it with your husband?" he added tentatively.

She shot him a deadly glare. "No husband. And I don't have to ask my daddy, either. I want contracts by Monday morning. Get it done."

At first it had been all about the location. South of the highway was key. That was where the true jet set lived. How many times had she heard, "Is the party north or south of the highway?" which was code for, "Are they just rich or crazy rich?" Bridget was determined to be on the right side of everything, including the god damned road.

But then, once she started planning the actual house, the real magic happened. She hired Ava as her architect, counting on her friend's immaculate taste to help realize her vision. She didn't want the usual twenty-thousand-square-foot monstrosity that would practically fill her lot. She didn't need gold-plated faucets or a four-car garage or an indoor pool. She wanted a classic, shingle-clad "cottage." On Georgica Road you would be expected to hue to the original architecture of the closed-off community. She wanted it to be open and airy on the inside, and streaming with the gorgeous Hampton light. She wanted walls of windows and a view of the water from every room. A sprawling, comfortable house big enough to fill with children and family and friends. She wanted to have cozy parties and long, lazy weekends, and celebrate all the holidays in this house. She wanted it to be a home.

After Ava gave her the first set of blueprints, Bridget went back to the Bronx for the weekend and spread the plans out on the kitchen table and pored over them with her dad. It was just like building the bunk beds all over again. Her mom coming in and out, bringing them sandwiches and coffee and cake, and wondering out loud why Bridget would ever need such a huge house. "You're a single girl," she'd said. "What are you going to do with all that space?"

But her dad understood. "So what if she's single? So what if she doesn't have the husband or the kids or even that many friends out there yet? She's going to build this house so she's ready for them when they do come. She's going to build this house first, and then she's going to build her family."

She could have hugged him, he understood her so perfectly.

He was there the day she broke ground, squeezing her hand in excitement as backhoes and bulldozers scooped up the dirt as if it was as light as cake batter. And he was there for every step after, too, helping her pick the finishes and inspect the progress, and swinging a hammer whenever he got a chance. She remembered nervously watching him up on her roof, hammering nails into shingles. He didn't need to help, of course. She could afford the best carpenters money could buy, but he simply loved building. And he especially loved building things with his little girl.

When it was nearly finished, she showed him the suite of rooms that she had specially designed for him and her mom on the first floor. The big bedroom with the amazing view of the pond, the en suite bathroom with separate tub and shower kitted out with metal grab bars and skid-proof surfaces so it would be safe for them as they grew older. The snug little corner with twin bookshelves where he could sit and read. The walk-in closet and built-in dressing table in front of the window so her mother could sit and do her makeup in natural light as she preferred. "It's yours anytime you guys want it, Daddy," Bridget had told him. She imagined how they would spend summers here with their future grandchildren. How he would teach her kids to build, just like he taught her.

She and her parents had only two summers in that house before her father was gone.

He never met his grandson.

"Bridget? What in the world are you doing standing out here on my roundabout looking like you're a little lost lamb?" Suddenly, Scarlett was standing at her front door and waving Bridget in.

Bridget blinked. She'd been so lost in memories that she had forgotten where she was.

"Pick up your bag and get in here, girl. I'm running around like a chicken with her head cut off trying to get my ballroom ready for this gala tomorrow. I could use any hands I can get."

Shaking off the haze, Bridget grabbed her bag and went in to help Scarlett.

CHAPTER 44

Every time they came to the Hamptons, Liam wondered if he should have bought something bigger. The house was huge—twelve thousand square feet—but plenty of people out here had much bigger places. Jay's place was bigger. Liam had been sharply disappointed when Hana hadn't even tried to get it in the divorce settlement.

"Do you want me to ask Jack to open up the pool?" he asked Hana. She was lingering at the window, watching the surf crash against the shore.

"No." She shook her head. "It's too cold to swim. I think I'm going to go for a walk on the beach, though."

She didn't invite him to come along, so he bit back the urge to offer his company. Instead, he watched her out the window as she slowly grew smaller and smaller in the distance. It made him feel sick to see her disappear.

Shake it off, he commanded himself. He was determined to use this weekend to do whatever it would take to fix things between them. She'd hardly said a word to him on the drive up, and had obviously been more than eager to get away from him once they were here.

What does she want?

This question used to give him pure pleasure to figure out. In bed, in life...what did Hana want and how quickly could he give it to her? A string of emeralds? A trip to France? For him to go down on her until she couldn't stop coming? Figuring out her needs and desires had been the happy focus of his life over the past year. But now it was all spoiled. Now she wanted something intangible, something he couldn't help thinking he didn't have the capacity to buy.

She was nothing but a pinprick on the beach now, still purposefully striding away. He turned from the window and wandered into the kitchen. *I should eat*, he thought. But he wasn't hungry.

I could work. But hiding in his work wasn't the answer, either.

Maybe I'll inventory the house.

He did this sometimes. Walked from room to room and made himself take note of every stick of furniture, every piece of art on the walls, every crystal vase and gilded candy dish.

Poltrona Frau Kennedee sofa. Nakashima Milk House coffee table. Chuck Close portrait. Yayoi Kusama pumpkin sculpture. Beni Ourain Berber rug...

There was something soothing about the way his possessions made a nice, neat list in his brain. He used to do the same thing when he was a kid sitting in his room. He'd list all his comic books. *Uncanny X-Men*, #136, *The Amazing Spider-Man*, #300... Then he'd list the items on his desk. Swingline Optima Stapler. X-ACTO KS manual pencil sharpener. Three Pee-Chee folders... The clothes in his closet, the books on his shelf, the posters on his wall... But when he was a kid, there was always a separate, but concurrent list of the things he needed or wanted, as well. Winter jacket. Converse without a hole in the toe. New backpack...

Now he could buy whatever he wanted, most things a hundred times over if he cared to. He opened the huge pantry off their kitchen. Brawny paper towels, twenty-four rolls. Jasmine rice, five bags. San Marzano canned tomatoes, an even dozen... It was even better when there were multiple numbers involved.

He loved the feeling of excess. The presence of all these perfect things that made him feel protected and prepared for whatever would come.

But today even the list felt interrupted and jagged in his mind. The neat, ordered calm that he usually achieved eluded him.

Maybe he'd just open a bottle of wine instead, drink until Hana decided to come back home.

CHAPTER 45

If you counted the servants' quarters, there were nine bedrooms and fifteen bathrooms in Jay's house, but apparently the teens all wanted to sleep piled up together like a bunch of puppies on the floor of the media room in the basement. They were streaming *Bob's Burgers* on the wall-sized flat screen, eating platters of take-out sushi from Zok-Kon, extravagantly large bowls of popcorn, whole trays of brownies and cookies from Levain Bakery, downing dozens of cans of LaCroix, and laughing like sugar-drunk hyenas. Alli had raided every bedroom but Jay's for the bedding, and made a teenage version of a blanket fort—comforters and pillows all twisted together in a tangle on the floor. Jay sniffed the air. No smoke, tobacco or marijuana or otherwise, seemed to be lingering. This was actually all pretty damned adorable, he thought. He felt relieved that it was still just junk food and cartoons and sleepovers.

He did, however, wonder about the presence of Max, the single boy in the puppy pile of teen girls. He suspected that he was gay. How many straight fifteen-year-old boys had the balls to wear a kilt, after all? But he supposed he should make sure of this fact before granting permission for these sleeping arrangements to continue.

"Psst, Alli," he whispered, trying to be inconspicuous, "can I talk to you in the kitchen for a moment?"

His daughter scowled but stuffed a brownie into her mouth and followed him out the door.

"What?" Her mouth was still full of chocolate, but Jay decided not to reprimand her.

"Um, that Max guy, am I right in assuming that he's gay?"

Alli's eyes went wide. "Dad! Why would you even ask that? Oh, my God."

"Well, because if he's not, I don't know that I feel comfortable letting him sleep in the same room as all you girls."

Alli swallowed. "I can't believe you would even say that! What do you think is going to happen? Nothing is going to happen! This is so stupid!"

He shrugged his shoulders. "Sorry. Look, I just want to know if I need to set up a guest bedroom for him?"

She shook her head. "Definitely not. I'm not banishing him to a room by himself just because he's not a girl. Don't you just trust me?"

That softened him up a little. "Of course I trust you."

"Good. Then I'm going back in." She wandered to the refrigerator instead and peered in forlornly. "I'm starving. Can we order pizza?"

He laughed. "Knock yourself out. I'm going to bed soon. Big day tomorrow. Your dad's gonna be auctioned off at Scarlett Hawkins's house!"

She wrinkled her nose as she scrolled her phone. "Gross. TMI, Dad."

After she wandered back out, her phone to her ear, instructing Fierro's to bring her four large pies, Jay got a pilsner out of the fridge and headed up to his bedroom, swigging from the bottle.

Now that he had done his fatherly duty, he could forget the eight teens in his house and think about something much more pleasurable. Namely, the way that he had pulled off the road behind an abandoned auto garage on the way up, and he and Bridget had pushed the seats all the way back and taken advantage of each other.

He still felt her thighs on top of his, the skirt of her little sundress hiked up as she straddled him, her fingers tangled up in his hair, as he spanned her waist with his hands. God, she was fun and fearless and sexy as all hell.

He picked up his phone and dialed. "Hey. Where are you? What are you doing?"

CHAPTER 46

"In bed. Scarlett's guesthouse," said Bridget, smiling at the sound of his voice, "thinking about how sore I'm going to be tomorrow."

"Oh, yeah?" Jay purred. "Did I do that?"

She snorted. "No, helping Scarlett's party planner inspect one hundred and fifty different centerpieces and then playing tennis against Scarlett for two hours after did that. God, that old woman is in good shape."

He laughed. "You want to sneak out and meet me somewhere? I think the teens are distracted."

She yawned and stretched. "What have you got in mind? Because right now, I kind of just want to sink into these fifteen hundred–count sheets and call it a night."

"Fifteen hundred? Seriously? I've never heard of that," he said.

"Um. I'm staying on Scarlett Hawkins's estate, remember? You probably haven't heard of half the stuff she uses on a daily basis."

"A walk on the beach," he said. "It's warm out. And there's a big, fat moon."

"Romantic," she admitted.

"I'll bring a bottle of champagne," he wheedled.

"Tempting," she said.

"How about some chocolate walnut cookies from Levain? I think I can snag a couple from the teens."

"And sold," she said. "Where were you thinking this carb fest was going to happen, exactly?"

"I have a private beach behind my house. Should I come and pick you up?"

She shook her head. "Naw. Too hard to get onto the estate this time of night. And Scarlett gave me the keys to her Fiat, anyway. Text me your address, and then just give me a chance to put my clothes back on and I'll be over in a bit. I'll text you when I get there so we can avoid the teen hordes."

"As far as I'm concerned, there is absolutely no need to put your clothes back on."

"Well, I think Scarlett's night watchman might have a heart attack if he saw me in what I'm currently wearing."

He laughed. "Okay. Let's not kill anyone. See you soon."

She lay in the bed for a moment after she hung up the phone, smiling to herself. She knew she was being foolish; she knew she shouldn't get attached; but when was the last time she'd received a late-night call inviting her for a romantic, moonlit stroll on the beach?

Actually, never, she admitted to herself.

She rolled out of bed and slipped on a pair of Chloé leggings, a formfitting light pink James Perse T-shirt and long, royal blue Burberry hoodie. She went into the marble-encased bathroom adjacent to her bedroom, where she brushed her teeth and pulled her hair back into a loose ponytail. A little mascara, a smear of lip balm, and she was ready to go.

At the door, she pocketed her keys, slipped on a pair of flip-flops and checked her phone for the address. Her eyes bugged a little when she realized where she was headed. She knew the estate from afar. It was not quite as grand as Scarlett's, but then again, whose was? But it was pretty dang close.

The little Fiat Spider convertible was parked out front of the house and Bridget thrilled to the feeling of getting behind the wheel of a car again. She'd always loved driving. She still missed the Porsche 911 convertible Carrera she'd given up after her divorce.

She stopped at the gatehouse on the way out. "I'll be back late tonight, Ed," she called to the guard as he nodded and pressed the button to open the fifteen-foot iron gate.

As she hit the road, Bridget pushed a toggle and the convertible top slowly rolled back, allowing the warm night air to rush in and the moonlit sky to open up above her. Bridget felt her ponytail whipping behind her as she drove. Maybe she was taking the roads a little faster than she should, but she couldn't help her lead foot, the car was so zippy and fun.

Jay's house had a long driveway lined with towering lilac hedges on either side, and then an elaborate metal gate with an intercom. Before Bridget could call in, the gate buzzed and opened. *He must have been waiting for me*, she thought. She blew a kiss to the camera on top of the fence as she drove into the circular driveway and pulled up in front of the house.

It was shingle style, a perfect Queen Anne with four stories, a giant wraparound porch, multiple balconies, ocean views from every room and two matching turrets on either end of the house. Bridget ran an expert eye across it and judged it to be about twenty thousand square feet, and worth a solid fifty million in today's real estate market. She put the top back up, quickly checked her hair in the mirror and then hopped out, waiting for Jay to meet her out front. The air smelled salty and sharp and she could hear the hiss of the tide dragging in and out somewhere very nearby.

"Psst!"

She looked around for the source of the sound.

"Psssst! Bridget! Up here!"

She looked up to see Jay hanging over a small balcony fronted with a window box packed full of red begonias.

She waved.

"Meet me around the back!" he said and then ducked back into the room he'd come out of.

She shook her phone and turned on the flashlight app so she could pick her way through the densely planted garden beds, through a side gate and around to the back porch.

Jay was waiting for her at the bottom of the stairs. Bare feet, rolled-up jeans, a fitted black T-shirt, his hair a little mussed. He looked ridiculously handsome as he gave her a wide, warm, goofy smile.

For a moment Bridget flashed on to the stolen budget still sitting in her inbox and felt a wave of guilt, but she pushed it down when he kissed her hello and then turned her out toward the view.

"What do you think?" he asked.

Low hedges of hydrangeas flanking a narrow path down to the water did nothing to block the wide-open vista of an endless ocean dressed in moonlight. The sky was huge and the moon so bright that the stars were barely visible. The moon doubled itself, reflected in the sea, as the tide softly hushed in and out.

"Amazing," whispered Bridget.

Jay put his arm around her. "I know. I've seen this my whole life and it still blows me away. My mother used to call it proof of God."

Bridget nodded. "I love that. Exactly right."

He grasped her hand in his and tugged her forward. "Come on, before the kids get the idea to come out, too."

She shook off her flip-flops and they walked down to the beach together, hand in hand. Bridget marveled at the soft white sand glittering in the moonlight, the empty, wild beach without any signs of a human presence besides the two of them. "This is all yours?" she said.

He nodded. "It's been in the family for three generations. We spent almost every summer here. My parents kept an open house. I could invite any of my friends, and my parents' friends and my cousins and aunts and uncles would come out and stay for weeks on end. The house was big enough for them to just pile in and everyone was still comfortable. We'd light bonfires and bring a huge table right down to the water's edge for big, elaborate family dinners. We'd eat and eat and then after, the kids would run around chasing the tide, playing in the water, while the adults sat back and drank wine and laughed and talked." He smiled, his eyes on the horizon. "It was perfect."

Bridget felt a deep pang of regret. "That's exactly what I wanted for my house out here," she said.

He looked at her. "You have a house?"

She felt her face twist into a bitter smile. "I used to. Not anymore. Had to sell it after my divorce." She shook her head. "I don't think I'll ever forgive Kevin for that. It was my house. I designed it and then built it with my dad before I ever even met Kevin, but of course, he demanded half of everything, and I couldn't afford to buy the bastard out…" She drew her toe through the wet sand, watching the little trench she made refill with water and then disappear. "It was supposed to be for Dylan. I wanted him to have exactly what you just described. Summers here, parties and sweet memories and someday he could bring his own kids and relive it all through their eyes." Her voice shook. "Now some country record producer and his D-list actress wife own it. No kids. I hear they come out maybe for a week a year. Otherwise, it just sits empty."

He squeezed her hand. "I'm sorry. That's a lot to lose."

She nodded. "My dad passed away, my business fell apart, my marriage ended..." She laughed. "I don't know how I survived, honestly. It's amazing that I'm still standing."

"You're strong," he said simply. "I mean, all I had to deal with was a divorce and I barely made it out of bed for about six months. I don't know what I would have done if I'd been hit as hard as you. I'd probably be living in a box somewhere, ranting about the end of the world."

She felt tears spring to her eyes. "It pretty much felt like the end of the world," she said softly. Then quickly wiped her eyes and shook her head. "Sorry, sorry. Damn, I haven't gotten choked up about all this for years." She sank to the ground, sitting in the soft sand and drawing her knees up to her chest. "It's being here. I guess it's harder than I thought it would be."

He sat down beside her, shoulder to shoulder. "Here," he said, popping the bottle of champagne he'd been carrying. It made a little hiss as a thin plume of blue mist curled out. "I didn't bring any glasses. Have a swig."

She brought the cold bottle to her lips and took a long draw of the dry, bubbly wine and then passed it back to him. He tipped it and gulped.

"And here," he said, fishing a fat cookie out of the little paper bag he'd been holding. "I had to fight eight hungry teenagers for this. It better be worth it."

She smiled and took a big bite, then offered half to him. "Definitely worth it."

He laughed and put his arm around her. She took another swig of champagne, then scooted even closer and laid her head on his shoulder.

They sat like that for a long time, eating the sweet dessert, passing the bottle back and forth until it was empty, watching the moon on the water, listening to the hiss of the sea.

"This is nice," she finally whispered.

He nodded. "It's the nicest time I've had in years, truly."

"Me, too."

He kissed the top of her head. "You want to sneak up to my room and fool around? I'd say let's do it here, but I'm sure that you and I both know that sex on the beach is never as good as you think it's going to be."

She laughed. "Sand all up in everything."

"We'd be picking it out of our crevices for weeks."

"Okay," she said, jumping up. "Let's sneak in!" She started toward the house at a little trot.

"Shhh," Bridget whispered as they tiptoed through the darkened house. She bumped into the corner of a sofa. Or at least, she thought it was a sofa. "Ow! Damn! That hurt!" She rubbed her leg. "I think I'm a little tipsy," she admitted.

"Oh, you think?" he said. Jay put his arm around her shoulders and steered her away from the offending furniture.

She giggled. "Aren't you?"

He smiled. "Maybe a tiny bit buzzed. Nothing to worry about. Listen, before we go upstairs, do you mind if I go down and check on the kids? I'm sure they've got to be asleep by now, but I'd feel like an ass if I didn't at least look in on them."

She nodded. "Sure. Go ahead." She felt around for the sofa again and then sank down into its cushions. "I'll be right here."

He kissed her once—and then again, slower this time. "Don't move," he whispered.

"I won't move," she solemnly promised as he backed out through a wide doorway and into a hall.

She squinted, trying to make out the room around her. It was huge. It looked like a formal living room—a parlor, actually. She could see the dull gleam from a slate mantel around a fireplace she could practically stand up in. A little desk and chair over there, a grouping of love seats and what looked like ottomans and poufs over here. Long, heavy drapes at the massive windows that overlooked the ocean view...

Suddenly, she heard a shout, then a short, unhappy scream, then the sounds of multiple voices all yelling at once.

"What the hell?" She bolted up, following the sounds out the door, through a huge farmhouse kitchen and down the stairs to what she assumed was the basement entertainment room.

There she found Jay looming over a crowd of freaked-out-looking teen girls, all dressed in skimpy and skimpier versions of nightclothes, and one teen boy in the unmistakable posture of an adolescent caught in the act, standing awkwardly, his cheeks red and his hands crossed over the crotch of his kilt, undoubtedly covering up an unwieldy boner.

"You said I could trust you!" Jay seemed to be venting his fury on one particular teen. Bridget recognized the dark-haired, pretty girl from the picture he'd shown her in the restaurant that first day they met.

"This is none of your business, Dad!" the girl screamed back. "I don't know what you think you saw, but oh, my God, we were hardly even doing anything!"

"Are you kidding?" he yelped. "He—" he pointed a finger at the boy "—was making out with her!" He changed direction and jabbed his finger at a short, pretty, dark-haired girl who was wearing an ultra-short satin jumper.

Well, at least it wasn't Alli, thought Bridget.

"And you—" he turned back to his daughter "—were kissing her!"

A slender girl with crooked glasses, like they had rather hastily been put back on, cringed as he looked at her.

"Oh, wow," said Bridget out loud. "Did not see that one coming." And everyone turned and stared at her. "Oops."

"Wait, who is that?" Alli had a look of horror on her face.

"Oh. That's…" said Jay, suddenly at a loss for words. "That's…"

Bridget stepped forward and stuck out her hand. "Hi, I'm Bridget. And you must be Alli. I've heard a lot about you."

Alli stared at her hand for a moment, and then, eyes bulging, turned back to her father. "Are you frigging kidding me?" she screamed. "You are such a hypocrite!"

"Hey!" he yelped. "You do not talk to me that way!"

Alli rolled her eyes so hard that Bridget wondered if they'd get stuck in that position. "Dad," she said. Her voice had gone soft and seething. "Dad, listen. We are going to sleep now. So why don't you and whoever—" she threw a look of loathing at Bridget "—that is go upstairs and carry on doing whatever it was you were going to do, okay?"

"Actually," said Jay, and mirroring his daughter, his voice also dropped to a dangerous whisper, "you, you, you and you—" he pointed at his daughter and the other three offenders "—are going to bed in your own separate rooms. In fact—" he looked down at the other three girls, who were sitting cross-legged in a pile of blankets on the floor and observing the whole spectacle like it was the latest binge-watch on Netflix "—I think you can all sleep in separate bedrooms. Luckily, there are plenty in this house. Get your stuff and let's go."

He looked at Bridget for a moment as the kids grabbed their bags and blankets. "I'm really sorry about this," he said under his breath. "This is killing me that you're seeing me like this."

She smiled and shook her head. "Hey, I'm a parent, too, remember? By all means, carry on. You're doing great."

He gave her a weak smile in return and then turned back to the teens. "Okay, everyone, you all got your stuff? Let's go. Upstairs, everybody."

"I'll be right back," he said to her as he marched the kids up the stairs.

Bridget cheerfully waved at him but then quickly dropped her hand as Alli turned around to give her one last poisonous glare. *Sorry*, she wanted to say as the girl's dark eyes drilled into her own. *Sorry to have been witness to your humiliation. Sorry to have met this way.*

Not exactly a great start with the boyfriend's kid.

Boyfriend, huh? rang a voice in her head. *When did that happen?*

Suddenly, she was bone-deep tired. She made her way over to one of the massive leather couches and lay back and closed her eyes…

"You okay?" said a deep voice. She startled.

"Oh, God, shit. I'm sorry," she said. "I must have dozed off for a moment."

Jay scrubbed his hand through his hair as he sank down beside her. "Well, that was fun," he said.

She blew a little puff of air out of her nose. "That's one way of seeing it."

"God damn, god damn," he said. "I really screwed the pooch on this one, didn't I?"

She looked at him, his face twisted in regret. "How so?"

"Well, um, I'm pretty sure my kid was just forced out of the closet to me, and my reaction was pretty terrible."

She blinked. "Oh, wait. You didn't know she's gay?"

"I had no idea." He groaned. "Some father I am. I mean, how could I have not known? Who misses something like that?"

"And are you okay with her being—"

"Of course I am," he said. "Whatever makes her happy. I just feel like an ass for not knowing."

She shook her head. "It might not have anything to do with you, really. Maybe she just wasn't ready to tell you yet."

"I bet her mother knows. Jesus, Liam probably frigging knows, too."

"Liam?"

"My best friend. The guy my wife left me for."

"Oh." She blinked. "Oh. You hadn't mentioned that part."

He threw out his arms. "How could I? Oh, by the way, Bridget, I was such a lousy husband that my wife ran off with my best friend. Did I mention that he was my COO, too?"

She laughed. She couldn't help it. "Jesus, Jay."

He laughed, too, a little more bitterly than she did. "I know. I mean, if I had told you, you probably would have run the other way screaming, right? And hell—" he banged his head against the back of the couch "—after the performance I just put on, you're probably going to run screaming, anyway."

She was quiet for a minute. "My ex-husband is an alcoholic, coke-addicted narcissist who cheated on me pretty much constantly."

He looked over at her, his eyes wide. "Okay, that actually makes me feel a little better."

"He tried to screw my cousin at our wedding, and everyone in my family knew about it but no one told me until after I divorced him."

"Keep it coming," said Jay with a smile. "This is making me look great in comparison."

"He convinced me to invest a ton of money into his drywall business and then he took almost all of it and gambled it away on online poker."

Jay's smile slid away. "Is that why you went bankrupt?"

She shrugged. "Part of the reason. I mean, there were mistakes on my end, too."

"Your ex sounds like an amazing asshole," he said.

She bugged her eyes. "You think? Your ex doesn't exactly sound like peaches and cream, either, though."

He frowned. "Actually, she's all right. I mean, yeah, not the nicest move screwing my best friend and business partner, for sure, but I have to admit, I wasn't the greatest husband."

Bridget bit her lip. "Did you screw around?" she asked.

He shook his head. "No, no. Nothing like that. I was... not there much, I guess. My business came first, always. She just got tired of waiting around for me, I think, and Liam had wanted her for years. I should have known better. I basically drove her into his arms."

"Really? You knew that all along?"

"That my best friend wanted my wife? Yeah. Hard to miss. I knew him really well. He wasn't good at hiding anything from me. I mean, I'll give the guy credit, he kept it tamped down for years. But I guess when the opportunity finally came his way, it was too good to miss."

"Wow," said Bridget. "So obviously, we are both really bad at relationships and we both have terrible luck in love and we both really, really suck at picking out people to be with. Great to know we're doomed from the start."

He laughed and brought her hand to his mouth and kissed it. "I don't know. Should I feel doomed? I really don't feel doomed at all."

She smiled and leaned her forehead against his. "I guess I don't, either," she whispered.

Later that night, after she had sobered up enough to drive herself back to Scarlett's, Bridget went straight to her laptop, and before she could stop and let herself think, she clicked on her copy of Jay's budget and dragged it into her trash. *There,* she thought, *it's gone.* Completely out of her hands.

She sat down with a little *whomp* as all the air left her lungs. *Well. That's that. I guess I'm playing fair now.*

She laughed to herself, wondering how tough, nasty Bridget Steele, the Bronx girl who was never afraid to fight dirty if she had to, had suddenly turned so damned soft.

CHAPTER 47

Try as he might, Liam never felt comfortable in a tuxedo.

He was wearing the best, a bespoke suit from Gieves & Hawkes on Savile Row. It was the same place that had once made Winston Churchill's famous three-piece suits, and now dressed half the royal family, for God's sake. Hana had insisted he have one made last time they were in London, and it fit him like a proverbial glove, but he always felt foolish when he put it on, like a kid clomping around in his daddy's oversize shoes. Except his daddy hadn't stuck around long enough for Liam to even experience that particular pleasure, so what the hell did he know about that?

But a gala at Scarlett Hawkins's East Hampton estate called for a tux. And a gala where he was being auctioned for charity? Well, he could hardly expect to show up in his favorite hoodie and bring in the dough.

"You look good," said Hana when he emerged from the bedroom. For the first time he could remember, it had taken him longer to get dressed than it had her.

He searched her face, trying to see if she was being polite

or if she really meant it. For a moment he thought maybe he detected a real glimmer of attraction in her eyes, but then the moment passed and her face became unreadable to him again.

"You look beautiful," he said fervently. And she did. Of course she did. She was wearing a white silk Chanel jumpsuit with a halter top that fastened at the back of her neck and then swooped down daringly low, leaving her back completely bare. Her hair was unbound and hanging to her waist in a heavy curtain, moving this way and that and giving him excruciating little peeks of the soft, glowing skin of her shoulders, the elegant twist of her spine. She wore no jewelry except for Lorraine Schwartz gold and diamond bangles on her left arm, stacked all the way to her elbow, no makeup but a slash of vermilion red on her generous mouth and matching red nails—fingers and toes. Flat gold Christian Louboutin sandals completed her outfit. Looking at her made his mouth go dry. He felt the way he used to feel when she'd show up in his dorm room looking for Jay and then stick around waiting, giving Liam the brilliant shine of her attention without one speck of hope behind it.

"Thank you," she said, not looking at him as she placed her phone in her clutch and checked her reflection in the hallway mirror one last time before they went out the door.

He put the radio on for the ride over so it wasn't so obvious that they didn't have anything to say to each other. He hummed along tunelessly to the music, not even caring what came on, relieved when they pulled into the private drive leading to Scarlett's house. Ahead of them was a long line of cars waiting for valet parking, but even the driveway was dressed for the party. On either side of Lily Pond Road were dozens of perfectly spaced old oak trees, each one hung with large, cream-colored paper lanterns. The glowing orbs looked like they were just floating amidst the crooked branches, magical and strange and perfectly matched to the full moon that hovered over them.

"It's like she bought the moon," said Hana, her voice dreamy in that way it got whenever she saw something she found particularly beautiful. "It's like she just picked up her phone and ordered that tonight's moon would be exactly right for this very moment and, of course, it worked."

He laughed but it came out dry and brittle. "What Scarlett Hawkins wants…"

He was startled when someone knocked on his window. Outside, standing on the grass, were two men in evening suits, carrying silver trays filled with sparkling crystal glasses.

Liam rolled down his window.

"Ms. Hawkins regrets that you must endure this wait for the valet," said the man. Both men looked like models, but this one was slightly better-looking than the other. "She wanted to offer refreshments and thank you for your patience." He bent at the waist, swooping his tray full of drinks closer to Liam's window. "We have a choice of Pimm's, a sour cherry gin sling, a dry martini with a twist and a nonalcoholic sparkling punch."

Liam looked at Hana. "I'll take the Pimm's," she said, and the waiter walked around to her side of the car and waited for her to roll down her window before he handed it over.

"I'll have the martini, I guess," said Liam, waiting for the server to make his journey back around.

"She thinks of everything, doesn't she?" said Hana as she sipped her drink and gazed up at the paper lanterns. "Sometimes I actually quite miss living below her."

Liam shot her a look and resisted pointing out that living below Scarlett Hawkins would also mean that she still lived with Jay.

He drained his martini. "Hey," he said, "you're going to

bid on me tonight, right? You're not going to leave me just
hanging there?"

Hana's mouth thinned impatiently. "We already talked about
this," she said.

He shook his head. "I mean, we did, but I don't think you
ever said whether you would or wouldn't."

"This is just for fun, Liam. You don't have to worry."

"Yes, but I just want to know if—"

She cut him off. "I'm not going to let you be embarrassed,
okay?" Her voice was sharp.

He blinked. "Jesus, Hana—"

But before he could finish the valet was, at last, knocking
on his window, ready to take his keys.

CHAPTER 48

Jay was late getting dressed. In fact, he had vacillated all night, not sure that he felt okay about leaving the teens alone in the house for the evening. He considered calling in their housekeeper, asking if she wouldn't mind doing a night shift and just keeping an eye on things for him, but then he figured that the woman probably wouldn't appreciate being asked to perform something so far outside her regular job requirements.

Maybe he should stay home. He slowly fastened his cuff links and slipped on his Ferragamo loafers, but then he thought of Bridget. There was no way he was leaving her without a date at the last moment.

At last, he decided to take the bull by the horns and walked out onto the back porch to find his daughter.

Alli had avoided speaking to him all day, loudly instructing her friends to go to the basement or the beach or call the driver and head into town so they could get some lunch at Serafina whenever he came within spitting distance. And now she was lounging out on the sand, wearing a bikini so small that it made

Jay wince to look at her. Lying next to her, so close that they were practically sharing the same towel, was the girl with the glasses, Minerva. *Alli's girlfriend?* he thought to himself. *Is that what I should call her?*

"Alli," he called down to the beach, not wanting to take off his shoes and socks nor fill them with sand. "Alli, can you come up here for a moment?"

He could see the look on her face from where he was standing, and he knew that she had decided to pretend not to hear him.

"Alli!" he yelled. This time he let his voice go where it wanted. "Get up here."

Sighing deeply, his daughter reluctantly stood up and then made an elaborate show of wrapping the towel around her waist before slowly making her way up the path. She got to the porch but refused to come up the steps. "What?" she snapped. He couldn't see her eyes behind the gigantic bug-eyed sunglasses she was wearing.

He picked his battle and walked down to meet her instead of insisting that she come up. "Listen, honey, I have to go out to this auction thing—"

"I know, Dad," she interrupted. "You already told me about it, remember?"

He bit the inside of his cheek, trying not to let her draw him into a lecture about manners and respect, trying to remember what was really important.

"I just wanted to say, before I go, that—" he took a deep breath "—I'm sorry for how I reacted last night. I was surprised, and honestly, I was a little uncomfortable when I stumbled in on you guys."

"Oh, you think?" sneered Alli.

He charged on. "But mainly, I felt bad that I didn't know that you…like girls, I guess, right? I mean, I just felt like I was kind of a bad father not to know something so important about you. I didn't realize you're gay."

The look she gave him was almost comic in its exasperation. "Dad. We really don't have to talk about this, okay? You're late for your party."

"Don't worry about the party. This is important."

"Daaad." She cut her eyes to her friends all lying on the sand. "I am asking you nicely. Can we please just talk about this some other time?"

He sighed, frustrated. "Fine. But we are going to talk about it, okay?"

"Okay. Whatever."

"And can I trust that tonight, while I'm gone, you guys will stay here and try to keep things to a dull roar?"

She shook her head. "You're so corny, Dad."

"Fine. I'm corny. Can I trust you?"

"Yes. We will stay here. We won't raid the liquor cabinet. No one's going to get pregnant."

He held up his hand. "Yup. Don't need to get the details of what you won't do. I trust you. Have a good time. There's a lasagna in the fridge that I made for you guys. You can warm it up at three-fifty for about forty-five minutes, okay?"

She was already walking back to the beach. She waved her hand behind her, dismissing him. "We're just going to order delivery. Thanks, anyway."

He frowned. Her rejecting his lasagna almost stung worse than her refusing to talk about her personal life. If he couldn't count on her affection for red sauce, pasta and cheese, he wasn't sure where to find any more common ground.

CHAPTER 49

"Oh, is that what you're wearing tonight?" said Scarlett when Bridget slipped in through the back door to help prepare for the onslaught of guests. "Would you like to borrow something from me? I'm so sorry, I should have offered sooner."

Bridget gave Scarlett an annoyed look. "Yes. I am wearing this tonight, and no, I do not want anything of yours, thanks."

Despite Scarlett's negative opinion, Bridget knew she looked good. Perhaps her dress wasn't this season's offering, but it was still Versace. And it was dark, dramatic violet. And it fit her like someone had poured it over her from a pitcher full of sexy.

Scarlett paused a moment and looked at her. "I'm sorry, darlin'. You actually look perfectly ravishing. I'm just being an old bitch. You know I get like this before I have to pull off anything big."

Bridget smiled. "Thank you. Now, what can I do to help?"

Scarlett shook her head. "Well, absolutely nothing, honestly. My staff has everything in place. It's just a matter of opening up the doors and making everyone feel like I give a damn. So maybe a little liquid courage is what I need. Let's go sit by the pool for a moment and do a couple of tequila shots."

Bridget laughed. She hadn't wanted to admit it before, but God, she had missed this woman.

"Marty!" called Scarlett. "Bring a bottle of the Dos Lunas and two shot glasses out to the pool, will you?"

They sat at the table under an arbor twined with wisteria in bloom. The sweet smell was so strong that Bridget felt like it was turning the air around her purple.

"Well," said Scarlett, pouring them both out a glass of what Bridget knew to be a three-thousand-dollar bottle of tequila and lifting her cup to meet Bridget's, "here's to the party. Let's hope it's a smashing success."

Bridget clinked her glass against Scarlett's, tipped back her drink and gulped it down. She felt a little bad, knowing that it was supposed to be a sipping tequila, but if Scarlett Hawkins wanted to shoot it, then who was she to say no?

"One more?" Scarlett didn't wait for Bridget's answer. She just poured out another shot for each of them and raised her glass again. "And here's to whatever you've been hiding up your sleeve lately, too, darlin'. Don't think I haven't noticed."

Bridget paused with her drink still in the air. "What do you mean?"

Scarlett gulped her tequila and slammed the empty glass on the table, then reached over and took Bridget's out of her hand. "If you're not going to drink that, I will." She finished it in one swig.

"I'm not hiding anything up my sleeve, Scarlett. You know I have other work to do besides your job."

Scarlett smiled a soft, muzzy smile. "Oh. I feel so much more ready for this party now. God bless the blue agave and the little worm that loves me. I know you have other work, darlin', but I also know it's not for those repugnant clowns you call your bosses. You're up to something, Miss Bridget. Can't hide it from a canny old bitch like me."

Bridget gave an exasperated laugh. "Yes. Fine. What the hell ever. I'm sure you're going to find out, anyway. I'm up for a big project, building a skyscraper."

Scarlett raised her eyebrows. "Now, how in the world do you think you're going to pull that off?"

"I can do it." Bridget raised her chin defiantly. "I have the core of my old team working for me already."

Scarlett giggled. "Oh, let me guess. You mean Ethan and that ancient woman who used to cook your books?"

"Mrs. Hashemi is younger than you, Scarlett. And yes, them. Plus Danny Schwartz."

Scarlett let out a laugh in a hysterical hoot. "Oh, well, then. I guess you've got it all under control." She laughed harder, her creamy cheeks turning a bright red. "Do you have any pros behind you yet? Seasoned engineers, project managers, field supers who can help you sell this project? Someone with an actual degree who you did not just Pied Piper out from the bowels of the Bronx?"

"All I need to do now is get my budget in play," said Bridget defensively. "One step at a time."

"You are deluding yourself if you think you can manage this step by step. Where is that smart girl I knew so long ago? You know very well that you have to be ten steps ahead of everyone else in this industry, darlin'. Because you're already nine steps behind when you walk into a room sporting a pussy."

Bridget sighed. "I know. It's just that I can't get access to those guys yet. They won't take me seriously. I'm hoping after I submit the budget and we're invited to present—"

"Steal 'em," said Scarlett. "There will be some of those types here tonight. A bunch of gray-faced nerds who hate their bosses and feel vastly misunderstood. Hike up those magnificent tits, turn your tongue to molten sugar and poach 'em wherever you can find them."

Bridget laughed. "If only it was that easy."

Scarlett looked her in the eye. "Darlin', it is that easy. And the old you would have known that and planned accordingly." She stood up from the table. "Well. It is time to let the screaming hordes through my gates. Thank you for having this libation with me, missy. I must begin the festivities." And then she executed a perfect little curtsy like an oversize Shirley Temple and walked away with a tiny wobble in her step that only someone who knew her very well would ever notice.

CHAPTER 50

Liam should not have been drinking. He almost never drank to excess in public, preferring to do his occasional binge solo, behind well-locked doors. But that martini in the car and the fact that Hana had left him in the hands of the auction organizer the moment they walked into Scarlett Hawkins's ballroom had unleashed a desperate need for several more strong drinks delivered as fast as possible into his bloodstream.

"So in about thirty minutes, the band will take a break and we'll line you all up on the stage," said Robin, a moonfaced man with a British accent, to the assembled men who were to be auctioned off. He had something green in his teeth, which Liam could not help but fixate on as the man yammered on about how they all needed to smile and look as appealing as possible. It was for charity, after all.

"Hey." Liam's hand shot out and caught a passing waiter with a promising silver tray. "What have you got?"

"We have a choice of a raspberry Sgroppino, a champagne mojito and a sipping whiskey from the outskirts of—"

"I'll take the whiskey," interrupted Liam. "I don't need to

know about the tiny Scottish children who mashed the barley with their bare feet."

The waiter looked unhappy about losing his chance to wax rhapsodic as he had so obviously been prepped to do, but he handed Liam a half-filled tumbler of golden, fragrant liquid.

"And so," concluded Robin, "once you have been sold, we will make contact with your buyer and ask her, or him, a series of questions so that we can arrange an evening or event that will be an exceptional pleasure for you both."

"Does that mean we have to screw 'em?" said an orange-faced goon. He was one of an army of men here tonight, all obviously modeled after the same pattern: spray tan, patent leather hair and overly bleached, moronic grin.

"That," said Robin with a wink, "will be left entirely up to you and your dates, gentlemen. Of course there is no obligation to be anything but a pleasant companion. But please, if things progress to an intimate juncture, do be sure of consent. It would not do to have Habitat for Humanity sued for an unfortunate misunderstanding."

The men guffawed.

Jesus, thought Liam. *What am I doing here?* He looked around for Hana. Maybe he could talk her into leaving early. They didn't need him. They had a dozen assholes in monkey suits to auction off. But she had apparently disappeared.

"Scarlett got ya, too, huh?" came a familiar voice behind him. Liam turned to see Jay standing behind him with, if not exactly a friendly look on his face, somewhere close to neutral. As always, his ex-best friend looked like he had been born in his tuxedo.

"Who can say no to charity?" Liam answered back, trying to pretend that it was perfectly normal that the two of them were chatting. "I mean, what am I, some kind of monster?"

Jay raised an eyebrow as if considering his answer.

"Never mind. Don't answer that."

"Nice suit," Jay said.

Liam's hand flew to his bow tie, defensively tugging at his collar. "It cost enough. I ought to get buried in it."

Liam noticed the way Jay slightly winced when he mentioned the price of his suit. Ah yes, the very rich can't stand to actually acknowledge that money exists.

"Where's Alli tonight?" asked Liam.

Jay frowned and shook his head. "She's supposed to be back at my house with her friends, but I suppose there is no guarantee."

"Which friends?"

Jay closed his eyes for a moment. "Max. And two Rivers?"

Liam nodded. "F and M."

Jay looked annoyed. "Yeah. And Joleen?"

"Cho Li, I think you mean."

"Damn. Yeah. And Hatty, no wait, Hetty. And Brooklyn. That one I can remember. And Minerva."

"Wow. You got the whole crew there."

Jay widened his eyes and nodded. "I guess I do. You obviously know them all, eh?"

"Well, they come around a lot. You know, the loft is near the school. They like to hang out and do their homework together. That kind of thing."

Jay frowned. "And what do you think about Minerva?"

"Oh." Liam smiled. "Did something finally happen?"

Jay's frown deepened. "You knew?"

"That Alli likes Minnie? Sure. She's been mooning over her for months."

"Months?"

"What, she didn't tell you about her?"

Jay looked away. A muscle in his jaw twitched.

Liam suddenly got it. "Wait. You mean you didn't know—"

Jay looked at him. "How long have you known?"

"Since—since before you and Hana got a divorce even. She told me she thought she might be like three years ago."

Jay's face flushed red. "And you never thought to tell me?"

Liam held up his hands. "She asked me not to. Said she wanted to tell you in her own way. I had no idea you didn't know. I figured she'd done it years ago."

"What about Hana?"

"She knew before me. But she just guessed it."

Jay swore under his breath.

"Look, Jay, I'm sure she was just worried about how you'd take it."

"Why? I know plenty of gay people."

Liam laughed. "Yeah, the fact that you once had a threesome with two bisexual women in college doesn't really count, man."

Jay balled his fist like he was going to punch Liam. Liam stepped back. He didn't want to have to unman him again. Luckily at that moment, a small, dark-haired woman in a purple dress stepped between them, smiling up at Jay. "Hey, there you are."

Jay's face instantly relaxed.

Ah, Bridget Steele. Interesting, thought Liam.

"Hey," said Jay. He reached out and touched her hand. "You look amazing."

Wow. He's got it bad.

Bridget's smile widened. "You don't look so bad yourself."

And she's into him, too.

The band, a full swing orchestra, struck up a rendition of "I Only Have Eyes for You." Liam snorted. How on the nose could they get? They both looked at him, suddenly remembering he was there.

"Bridget, this is Liam Maguire."

Bridget wrinkled her nose as she shook his hand. "Right," she said. "We've actually met before, I think?"

"Here or there," said Liam.

Jay's eyes narrowed.

Suddenly, a hand was on Liam's shoulder. "Hey, boss," came a voice in his ear. "Fancy meeting you here."

Liam turned and found Alexander Redetzke, his project manager from the office, grinning at him.

"Redetzke. What are you doing here?"

Redetzke was wearing a polyester tuxedo, complete with tails. "Isn't this wild? Actually, my sister-in-law has done some legal work for Ms. Hawkins, and I was out visiting them in the Hamps this weekend so they invited me to tag along."

"Redetzke," said Liam. "Nobody calls it the Hamps."

Redetzke shrugged happily. "Well, maybe they should! We can start a trend!"

He looked meaningfully at Jay and Bridget.

"Yeah. Okay. Alexander Redetzke, this is Jason Russo and Bridget Steele. Jason and Bridget, Redetzke is my project manager and also has his mechanical engineering degree."

"Structural," corrected Redetzke, putting out his hand toward Jay. "So great to meet you."

Jay started to return his handshake, but Bridget cut in and took Redetzke's hand instead. "I think you were on a few of my past projects. I'm familiar with your work," she said, looking up at him through her eyelashes.

Redetzke flushed red. "You are?"

She took his arm. "Yes. I'd love to talk with you about it. Would you mind coming over to the bar with me? I can't seem to wave down any of the waiters for a drink." She looked back at Jay and winked. "Save me the next dance. I'll be back."

As they walked away, Jay looked at Liam and shrugged, mystified. "Beats me. Maybe she likes talking about erosion?"

He looked around. "I'm going to go find the waiter with those little serrano ham tartlets."

Liam shook his head ruefully and snagged another drink.

CHAPTER 51

It only took about twenty minutes of undivided attention for Bridget to have Alexander Redetzke eating out of the palm of her hand. While standing in a glittering ballroom, surrounded by the rich, famous and beautiful, she laughed uproariously at a "mathematician, statistician and an engineer walk into a bar" joke. She made herself appear completely mesmerized as he breathlessly recounted how he once saved an entire parking garage from collapse by reconsidering the position of a very important rebar, and she listened sympathetically as he described a particularly mysterious and persistent rash he had in the crook of his elbow.

He was actually talking to her about something interesting—a new exterior paint made from titanium dioxide that absorbed fumes generated by traffic—when Liam Maguire walked over, drink in hand, and interrupted them. Bridget was more than a little annoyed.

"Hey, Redetzke," he said. His speech was just slightly slurred. "I had an idea. Why don't we cut out early and go work on the Harrington presentation? I have everything we need back at my place. We can get a pizza and some beers—none of this finger food bullshit. Guys' night in. What do you say?"

Redetzke looked horrified, but judging from the fifteen minutes she had just spent with him, Bridget knew he wouldn't have the guts to say no.

"Hey!" She waved frantically as Scarlett rolled by, dressed in a pale green gown shot with gold thread, flanked on either side by two Victoria's Secret models. "Scarlett!"

Scarlett looked a bit irked to be interrupted but separated herself from the models and walked over.

Bridget grasped her arm and said, "I just wanted you to meet my new friends. Oh, but I think you already know Liam Maguire, right?"

Scarlett smiled at Liam as she gave him a double kiss on his cheeks. "Indeed. Liam is one of my prime bachelors tonight. I can't wait to see how much he goes for."

"And this is Alexander Redetzke. Alexander is a project manager and structural engineer for Liam's company."

Scarlett raised a very subtle eyebrow. "Oh, is that so? What a fascinating line of work."

"So, Redetzke, you in or what?" Liam sounded more insistent.

Bridget leaned in toward Scarlett and dropped her voice. "I just need you to get Liam off his back. Can you keep him busy?"

Scarlett put her hand on Liam's arm. "Liam, darlin', the auction should be starting very soon. I have already heard numerous women speculating on just how much money they will have to pony up for the privilege of your company."

Liam scowled. "You know I'm not actually a bachelor, right? I live with Hana Takada. We'll be married pretty soon."

Bridget worked to keep a blank face. Married? She wondered if Jay had any idea. She shot a look at Liam. He was good-looking enough, she supposed. He reminded her of some of the boys back in the Bronx, handsome in an almost pretty way, but rough around the edges, and full of attitude. But compared to Jay? She couldn't understand why any woman would ever choose someone like Liam over someone like Jay.

"Well, I don't see any ring on your finger yet," said Scarlett, steering him toward the stage and allowing Bridget to resume her conversation with Alexander.

Bridget handed Alexander another drink and placed her hand on his arm. "Now, what were you saying about that paint?"

CHAPTER 52

They lined up the men behind the stage, a dozen in all, smirking in their tuxes, drinks in hand, and acting like a bunch of high school football players waiting to see who would be crowned homecoming king. There was a fairly well-known actor who was a regular, but not the star, on a Shonda Rhimes show, a rotund chef known for his creative use of offal and his chain of high-end restaurants, a morning host on NBC who was rumored to be gay, an over-the-hill rock star whose last hit was fifteen years old, several different high-powered lawyers with varying amounts of hair, a former congressman, a very famous film director, a not-so-famous but very handsome author, and then, rounding it out, Liam and Jay.

For Jay, it was almost a relief to have something else to think about. Bridget was still chatting up the engineer, which somehow Jay instinctively knew not to be jealous about, though he wasn't exactly happy to have lost her attention for so long. But what he was really smarting over was his conversation with Liam. He kept thinking about how close he and Alli had been when she was little. How she always ran to him first when she got hurt. How he used to give her a bath and read to her every night, and she would take a pinch of his shirt and rub it between her fingers as she drifted off to sleep. And then inch by inch, year by year, he'd put less and less time in with her and more and more time at his office. He'd let Hana take over on bath and story duty. He'd stopped spending his Sundays in the kitchen with Alli at his side, cooking and fooling around while Hana painted in her studio, the three of them sitting down for a meal of whatever he and Alli had come up with that day.

He'd lost Hana the same way, of course. Benign neglect that turned malignant. But there was a part of him that believed that no matter what he had done, that loss had been inevitable. He and Hana were probably never really meant to be forever. But how had it become so bad with Alli, his little girl, that Liam, of all people, had been the one she had confided in, not her own father?

"And sold for five thousand dollars to Mrs. Horowitz!" called Jimmy Hilton, the late-night TV host and comedian that Scarlett had talked into being the emcee and auctioneer for the night. "I hope you like pig intestines, Mrs. Horowitz, because you know Chef Simon will be cooking some up for you on your date! Next, we have ex-Congressman George Novano! Now, ladies, I want you to remember that the congressman voluntarily resigned, he was absolutely not forced out and nobody ever proved that was actually his penis in those texts!"

The crowd, already well into their fourth or fifth drink, roared with laughter as the politician headed for the stage with an angry flush on his face.

Jay looked over the audience, first searching for Bridget, who was sitting at a table up front with Alexander Redetzke and Scarlett, laughing along with the crowd. She was radiant in her purple dress, her dark hair pulled up in an artfully arranged bun that Jay thought looked like she had just rolled out of bed in the best of possible ways, a thin gold chain glimmering at her throat. He loved the way she laughed, with her full body, as if she had too much joy to contain.

His eyes scanned the crowd and he picked out Hana sitting in the back, alone at a table. She was as austere and beautiful as always, but Jay recognized something sad in her expression. He shot a glance at Liam, who was waiting to be called up next, and saw that his face mirrored Hana's—strained and unhappy—and wondered what was happening between the two of them.

For a moment he almost felt as he had back in college—when Hana and Liam were the closest people on earth to him. When he'd felt like the luckiest guy alive to have such a great girlfriend and such an awesome best friend. It had been a double blow to lose them both at the same time. And honestly, he sometimes wondered who he was angrier with—and who he missed more—his wife or his best friend.

The room was full of the beautiful, the rich and the famous, all in their haute couture, eating and drinking unimaginably rare and delicious things that they simply took for granted, jockeying for seats at the right table, making sure they talked to the right people, constantly comparing their jewelry and jobs and press clippings and trophy wives… Jay had grown up around this crowd, or at least many who were exactly like it, and yet, he'd never felt like they were his people. Hana and Liam had been his people.

And now Bridget…he was starting to think that she might be his person, full-stop.

"And next on the docket is Mr. Liam Maguire, the CEO of South Side Construction! Liam is young, handsome, rich beyond your wildest dreams, ladies, and a little birdie told me that he's dynamite in bed! Oh, wait, that little birdie once told me that Ted Cruz was a master of cunnilingus, so maybe that little birdie is full of shit. Anyway, come on up, Liam! The bidding starts at one thousand dollars!"

Liam looked like hell, thought Jay, watching his friend's face as he stood on the stage. There was nothing appealing about him at the moment. He looked nervous and sweaty, like he wanted to do nothing so much as claw off his jacket and tie and dive from the stage. He just stood there staring past the crowd at Hana with a look of forlorn hope on his face.

"One thousand!" said Jimmy Hilton. "Do I hear one thousand? Come on, ladies! You all were willing to bid on the guy who posted his balls on Twitter—okay, yes, allegedly, Congressman Novano—but you can't pony up for this handsome devil?... Nothing?... Okay, I'm going to slash the price and see what happens. Cut-rate bachelor on the loose! An incredible bargain! Let's go to five hundred dollars! Five hundred dollars for a night with this hunk of a man! He might even build something for you! How about that, ladies! He's a contractor, after all! Don't you want your kitchen redesigned? A little bathroom remodel?"

Liam was still looking at Hana, but the forlorn hope had now changed to something more like horrified betrayal. Jay turned to see her, staring dully at the table, refusing to even glance toward the stage.

"Have you ladies lost your minds? Five hundred dollars and I can't get one bid? Do you all know something I don't? Because I see a virile, handsome man with a full head of hair before me. I mean, hell, maybe I'll bid on him myself! Okay, I hate to do it but I'm going to cut his price again because—"

"Oh, for heaven's sake!" came a voice from the audience. Scarlett Hawkins stood up at her table, sloshing her martini as she waved her hands in the air. "Y'all are a bunch of god damn fools! Fifty thousand dollars! I bid fifty thousand on that nice boy. And he is a bargain at the price!"

The crowd gasped and laughed.

"Now, that is more like it!" crowed the emcee. "Our illustrious hostess with impeccable taste has done it again. Sooo I am just going to assume that no one else is going to top that bid and say, sold to the lovely lady in the green dress who could buy and sell us all ten times over if she felt like it!"

The crowd applauded wildly, and Jay watched as Liam slowly left the stage, looking like he didn't know his way home.

CHAPTER 53

Bridget had been worried all night. She wanted to bid on Jay. Really, she felt that she must bid on him, all things considered, but she no longer had the kind of money to throw around on something like this. And she was sure she would not be the only one bidding. Jay would be in demand. Everyone knew who he was, the scion of a family known for its wealth and power, the CEO of a multibillion-dollar company. Everyone knew that he was recently divorced. Nobody knew that he was seeing Bridget, and since she had spent the evening talking to Alexander Redetzke about the role of 3-D printing in building design instead of being on Jay's arm, she only had herself to blame for that particular issue. She was certain there would be a line of women all ready and willing to whip out their checkbooks and buy themselves a shot at being the next Mrs. Russo.

How much could she spend? Nothing really, especially since, if she made it as far as making a presentation for Harrington, she would need every cent to put on the kind of dog and pony show that he expected. Still, she knew that she would bid. Even if she didn't win, she wanted Jay to know that she thought he was worth bidding for. She set a mental limit of two thousand dollars.

"And next, ladies and gentlemen," intoned Jimmy Hilton, "we have yet another CEO of his own construction company, but this time you've probably actually heard of him. I bring you Jason Russo of Russo Construction! Jay was born and raised in Manhattan, has almost as much money as God—and by God, I actually mean Scarlett Hawkins—and, well, just look at him in that tuxedo, I mean, hellooo George Clooney before he hurt his back playing basketball, am I right? The bidding starts at one thousand dol—"

"One thousand!" yelled a fifty-something blonde in a bright yellow catsuit. Bridget scowled at her and mentally promised herself that she'd body block that woman herself if necessary.

"Well, okay! That's more like it! I've got one thousand dollars. Do I hear twelve hundred? Twelve hundred dollars?"

"Twelve hundred!" yelled Bridget, waving her paddle and rising from her seat.

She was rewarded with a dazzling smile and a wink from Jay, and a measured look from Scarlett. "Now, wait a minute," said Scarlett, sotto voce. "Jason Russo is the man that you were screwing on your kitchen floor?"

"Yes," replied Bridget. "And I really don't want him to be bought by anyone else!"

"Do I hear fifteen hundred? Fifteen hundred for this prime cut of man meat—"

"Fifteen hundred!" shouted a woman who looked so much like a Disney princess that Bridget suddenly had a flash of Jay and the girl running down the steps of the palace, church bells ringing, while the girl lost her shoe.

"Seventeen hundred!" yelled Bridget before the emcee could even speak.

"Two thousand!" screeched the blonde in the yellow jumpsuit.

"Three thousand!" yelled Bridget, losing all reason.

"Twenty-five thousand dollars," came a cool, steady voice from the back, and everyone turned to see Hana Takada, artist and recent ex-wife of the bachelor in question, calmly holding up her paddle.

"Twenty-five thousand dollars going once! Twenty-five going twice! Sold to the elegant lady in the back who probably could have got this guy for a lot less money if she had tried!"

Bridget looked up on the stage and saw Jay, standing stock-still, a look of complete shock on his face, as he locked eyes with his ex-wife. Moments passed and he didn't break his gaze with Hana, and he didn't look down at Bridget, and she was pretty sure that, as far as he was concerned, she might as well have disappeared off the face of the earth.

CHAPTER 54

Liam bent over the toilet, violently puking.

A moment ago he'd been standing outside the ballroom, watching Hana make a twenty-five-thousand-dollar bid for Jay, wondering if it could be real, and then suddenly he was running for the bathroom, his stomach in his throat.

He stood up and leaned against the wall, wiping his lips. What the hell had just happened? Surely, there must be some logical explanation about why Hana would have betrayed him so thoroughly. Okay, yes, maybe he could understand her letting him hang up there on stage like a fool, forcing Scarlett Hawkins to pity-bid on him. They were not in a good place and she obviously wanted to see him suffer, but then publicly offering up a small fortune for a date with her ex-husband? The man who had taken her for granted for years, who had driven her away? Was she drunk? Drugged? Time traveling? There had to be a reason.

His stomach churned and he bent over the toilet again, heaving until there was nothing more he could bring up. He sank to the floor, pressing his forehead against the cold tile, his stomach still in a spasm. He had to get back out there. He had to find Hana and figure out what the hell was going on.

He pulled himself back up and staggered to the bathroom sink, glancing at himself in the mirror and then stopping to stare in disdain. He looked like he felt. Pale and miserable and weak. There was a spot of puke on his collar; his hair was plastered down with flop sweat; the dark circles under his eyes looked like bruises.

He bent to rinse his mouth with water, and then rooted through the medicine cabinet, knowing that of course Scarlett kept a brand-new, pristine bottle of mouthwash in her guest bathrooms for those who might need it. He rinsed again, gargling this time, and then closed his eyes, gathering his strength, before he lurched back through the door and out to find Hana.

CHAPTER 55

"Well. That was quite the turn of events. You okay, darlin'?" said Scarlett under her breath as Bridget watched Jay stumble off the stage and head straight for his ex-wife.

Bridget quickly knocked back her drink, plastered on a smile and stood up. "You know what? I just need—I think I'm going to—" She didn't bother finishing as she headed out the door and away from the ballroom, grabbing a full bottle of champagne from a surprised waiter as she left.

What had she been thinking? Why had she trusted this guy? She hardly knew him, really. A few decent rolls in the hay and she'd been dickmatized, willfully, stupidly blind to the fact that all men were the same—assholes.

As she wandered down the hall, chugging the wine as she walked, she passed Liam Maguire on his way back into the ballroom. He looked like hell—desperate and broken. She considered stopping him, warning him, telling him to keep away from the shit show that she had just managed to extricate herself from, but instead, she let him pass. Let him figure it out on his own. *Not my problem.*

The night air felt almost mockingly good as she slipped out the kitchen door. The moon hung fat and shining. The tide continued to sweep quietly in and out like nothing had happened. Halfway to the guesthouse, Bridget changed her mind, slipped off her high heels and headed for the beach instead, bottle in tow. She couldn't sit still right now. She didn't want to think. She needed to keep moving.

CHAPTER 56

"What the hell was that, Hana?" Jay stood over her table, trying to keep his voice down below a shout. He knew that everyone in the ballroom was watching them—they weren't even pretending to continue the auction—but he didn't care.

Hana stood up, biting her lip. "Come outside with me," she said quietly.

She reached to take his arm, but he violently shrugged it away. "Outside," she insisted.

He tailed her out. "Well, god damn!" Jimmy Hilton's amplified voice followed after them as they left the ballroom. "I just feel like maybe we should shut down this whole night right now because, really, how are we going to top all that drama, folks? No? You want more? Well, I guess I can bring out the next guy but I don't know that he's going to be nearly as fun…"

The doors swung shut behind them and the emcee's voice faded into the background as Hana stopped and turned toward him. "Jay—" she said.

"I don't know if I even want to hear this," he said. "I should go talk to Bridget."

Hana crinkled her nose. "Bridget? Who's that?" He opened his mouth to answer, but she grasped his hand instead. "Never mind. Don't tell me. I don't care. Jay…" Her words came out in a rush. "I think we should get back together."

He laughed. He couldn't help it. It was an involuntary reflex. There was nothing to do but laugh.

She laughed, too, weakly. "I know," she said. "I sound insane. I know I do. But hear me out." She looked up at him, her eyes searching for his. "I made a mistake. I had been angry with you for so long. I felt like you didn't care about me or Alli."

"Of course I did," he spat out.

She held up her hand. "I know that now. Like I said, it was a mistake. I thought I needed…something else. But I don't. I mean, it was working fine. I had my work, you had yours, we had Alli, we were friends. It was so easy. It was good. Why did I think I needed more than that?"

Jay felt like his head was about to explode. He'd waited days, weeks, months, for her to say this to him—and now that she had—he felt like running as fast as he could in the other direction.

"We're ruining Alli," said Hana, hitting him squarely where it hurt most. "She hates us both now. She's going through so much, and she doesn't have anyone to confide in."

"Liam," he said. "She talks to Liam."

For a moment Hana's face spasmed; just a hint of pain flashed in her eyes. "Liam isn't her parent," she said. "Liam isn't her father."

That's right, thought Jay. He wanted to roar it out. *Damn right he's not.*

"She needs us, Jay. She needs us together. She needs us to be a family again." She tightened her grip on his hand and he realized with a start that she was still holding on to him. "We can go slow," she whispered. "Nobody needs to know."

"Um…" His voice sounded strange to him, hollow. "I think you kind of blew our cover back there with that twenty-five-k bid."

She blinked. "It doesn't matter. They're all going to forget about this by tomorrow. We'll take it from the beginning all over again. We can, you know, date, like we used to. Remember how good it all was back then?"

This was madness. Like some kind of crazy fever dream.

"We won't tell Alli at first," she continued on. "Not until we see how it feels. We can just figure it out as we go. But Jay, we owe it to her to at least try. I mean, what if it's possible to just…go back to the way things used to be?"

"What about Liam? I mean, Jesus, Hana, I thought you guys were in love? Isn't that why you left me?"

She shrugged. Her lower lip trembled. "I don't know. I don't know why I left you. I can't explain. It was stupid. I was wrong. I thought there was something between Liam and me, but—" She grasped at his sleeve and then bent her head against his shoulder. "I'm sorry. I'm so sorry, Jay. I just want things to be like they used to be. I want to be a family. I want it to be easy."

He stepped away from her. "Hana—"

"Shhh," she said, and put her hand to his cheek. "Shhh."

And then she reached up and kissed him.

CHAPTER 57

Liam felt the wind go out of his lungs as he watched Hana kiss Jay. He felt like sinking to his knees. He felt like rushing out and pulling them apart, dragging her away screaming "Mine!" He'd stood in the doorway, frozen, listening to everything they said. Every word out of Hana's mouth hitting with a blow to his chest until he couldn't speak, he couldn't breathe, and now he couldn't move.

Jay was kissing her back. For a split second they were entangled in each other's arms and it was like back in college; of course they were meant to be together and Liam was watching them from afar and eating his heart out, but this time, it was so much worse. Because Liam knew how Hana's lips felt. He knew what she tasted like. He knew her scent and the little murmur of contentment in her throat she made when he kissed her the right way, what her hands felt like when they reached up and twined themselves in his hair.

She'd been his. And now she wasn't.

Jay broke the kiss and stepped back. "What are we doing?" Liam heard him say. "This isn't right."

"You're wrong," said Hana. She reached up and kissed him again. Liam felt his stomach lurch. "This is exactly right."

Jay gently pushed her away, holding her at arm's length. "Listen, I'm not going to lie and say I never wanted this. Because you know I did. And maybe I even still do. I don't know. And maybe you're right about Alli. Maybe she needs us to be together. I don't know about that, either. But you can't just kiss me, Hana. I didn't ask for that. I'm not ready for that."

"I'm sorry," she said swiftly. "I won't. I won't kiss you again until you say you're ready. But shouldn't we just try? For Alli's sake?"

Jay shook his head, looking blindly past her. Suddenly, his eyes widened. "Liam?"

Liam stepped out of the doorway. Hana swung around and locked eyes with him. "Liam?" she echoed.

He couldn't speak. He couldn't move. They all just stood, staring at one another. Like the worst kind of hell.

I deserve this, thought Liam. *This is exactly what Jay must have felt when he lost her.*

"So that's it?" he finally said. He sounded eerily calm compared to the writhing, screaming emotion inside him. "Hana?"

She stared. She stared and stared. And then she nodded. The tiniest nod. Her eyes full of pain.

He blinked. "Okay, then. Okay." And he stumbled back into the ballroom, looking for another drink.

CHAPTER 58

Bridget hadn't slept at all the night before, wandering down the beach in the dark until she was afraid that she would be too drunk to find her way back if she didn't turn around. Once she made it back to the guesthouse, she checked her phone, hoping maybe there would be a message from Jay, explaining that Hana was nuts and he had spent the night looking for Bridget and was so worried and she should call him right back. But there were no messages, and when she swallowed her pride and tried his phone? Straight to voice mail.

After that she'd thought about just leaving, driving Scarlett's car back into Manhattan. But it was late and she'd downed most of her champagne, and damned if she was going to let some ridiculous broken fling make her do anything stupid.

So she lay in bed with her eyes wide open until the sun came up and then she washed her face and packed her stuff and wheeled her suitcase into Scarlett's sunny kitchen.

Scarlett wasn't up yet. She never got up before ten, especially not the night after a party, but Liam Maguire was sitting at the huge, scrubbed oak kitchen table, nursing a cup of coffee and looking like a miserable, beaten and battered puppy.

For a moment Bridget almost felt sorry for him. But then she remembered, this was all his fault. If he hadn't run away with Jay's wife in the first place, Jay would have stayed married and Bridget never would have been in this stupid, broken-hearted predicament.

"Good morning," she said. She didn't smile. She didn't feel like smiling. He didn't deserve a smile, anyway.

He looked up at her and nodded.

"You mind if I join you?"

He shrugged.

She poured herself a cup of coffee. Damn, it smelled so good. She wondered what obscure, ridiculously expensive brand Scarlett was buying these days.

She sat down across from Liam and baldly examined him. He was wearing his dress shirt, which was wrinkled and stained and open at the collar, and a pair of equally rumpled tuxedo pants. His hair was a mess, and not in a casual, I-just-rolled-out-of-bed kind of way—there was nothing studied and charming about the crazy that was going on there. His skin was bleached of color, except for the black stubble on his chin and the purple bags under his eyes, and his hand shook when he lifted his coffee cup to his lips.

She took her own gulp of coffee. Bliss. "You look like hell," she said casually.

He glared across the table at her. "You don't look so hot yourself, Steele."

She shrugged and took another sip. "So did they leave together last night?"

He curled his lip. "Who?"

She sighed. "Who do you think? Jay and what's her face."

"Hana."

"Yes. Fine. Hana. Jay and Hana. Hana and Jay. Did they leave together?"

He sighed. "I have no idea."

"Well, what are you doing here? Don't you have a house in town?"

He put his coffee down. "I was too drunk to go home. Scarlett invited me to stay the night."

"You going home now? I'm going to get Scarlett's driver to take me to the jitney, but if you're driving anyway, maybe you could drop me off?"

He picked his cup back up, clenching it to his chest like he was cold. "No. I think I'm going to stay here awhile."

Bridget wrinkled her brow. "Here? Why?"

"Because Scarlett invited me, that's why. And I don't feel like going back to my house here or my loft in the city."

She finished her last gulp of coffee. "Wow. Okay. Well, enjoy. I don't know how Scarlett does with broken hearts, but she makes a hell of a frittata."

He stuck out his chin. "I don't have a broken heart."

She laughed. "Me neither."

CHAPTER 59

Jay faked it through breakfast, flipping stacks of pancakes and frying rashers of bacon to feed the hungry teens, but his mind kept flashing back to Hana, and then to Bridget, and then back to Hana again, and he couldn't bring himself to look Alli in the eye for fear she'd figure out what was going on.

As far as he could tell, she hadn't seemed to notice anything amiss. She gave him a perfunctory kiss on the cheek as the rest of the kids chorused their thanks and goodbyes and headed out the door. But it was still a huge relief to see the rearview lights of the Escalade drive out the front gate. He needed time alone with his thoughts. He needed to figure out what the hell he was going to do.

First things first. He would contact Bridget. It was total asshole behavior to leave her high and dry last night—not even bothering to check in and say sorry. She was probably furious, and rightfully so.

But what would he tell her? How could he call when he had no idea what he was going to say?

He sat at the table, amidst the piles of dirty dishes and half-eaten pancakes, and he tried to weigh his choices.

Bridget was the most thrilling thing that had happened to him for a long time. She was smart and funny and tough and sexier than any woman he'd ever known. She'd rattled his cage in the best possible way.

But when Hana had kissed him the night before, he'd felt something. There was no denying it. She was his first love, the mother of his child, and if he had made the call, she never would have left in the first place. And here she was, willing to start over, to figure it out, to knit their little family back together again.

He thought about Alli. About the fact that she was slipping farther and farther away from him, that she was starting to feel like a stranger instead of his baby girl. He couldn't take that. He couldn't stand the idea that she was beyond his grasp.

Hana was offering him another chance to be the father and husband he should have been in the first place. He didn't understand why she'd had this sudden change of heart, or even if it could be trusted, but he felt like he had to at least give things a try.

He rose from the table, stacking dishes and carrying them to the kitchen. He put the jug of maple syrup away. He piled the dishes in the sink.

For Alli's sake, he thought, he had to give things a chance with Hana. Which meant that he needed to tell Bridget.

Should he be totally honest? Did he have to tell her that he kissed Hana? Or anything about Hana at all? Should he actually break up with her? Could he even break up with her since they were never officially together? How could he explain that it was tearing him up to think about stepping away, but that, on the other hand, Alli, and therefore, Hana, had to come first?

He knew that he should have this conversation face-to-face

but he doubted his ability to walk away if she was there in the flesh. He couldn't see her and smell her and touch her and not want her. He toyed with his phone, picking it up and then putting it back down again. He knew what he had to do, but he was slammed with an undeniable feeling of loss. He was about to let something important slip out of his fingers and he couldn't pretend otherwise.

CHAPTER 60

After she got back to the city, Bridget went to pick up Dylan from Kevin's place, and when her little boy locked his arms around her neck and told her how much he missed her, she felt almost like herself again.

This, she thought, *this is what's important.* For a moment she was almost grateful for Jay's bad behavior—because it reminded her of her priorities.

They headed back to their apartment, Dylan's small hand gripping hers, a bag of take-out tacos and a jug of orange juice under her other arm, and Bridget felt like maybe she had been telling Liam the truth. Maybe her heart wasn't so very broken.

But then, when she got into the apartment and Dylan had run off to play in his room, she checked her messages and took a sharp breath when she saw Jay's name.

Hey. Sorry to have disappeared last night. Can we talk?

She quickly texted back, jabbing her thumbs at the keys.

I just got home with D. Can't really talk right now.

Well. I just wanted to say that you might not hear from me for a while. I have some stuff to figure out and I feel like it might be best if we took a break.

She bit the inside of her cheek. She'd known it was coming, but that didn't lessen the sting.

She sent him a thumbs-up emoji.

I'm really sorry. It's complicated.

This time she sent him the middle finger emoji.

Then she put down her phone, pulled out her laptop, fished his budget out of her trash and forwarded it to Ethan and Mrs. Hashemi with the message to not ask any questions, but just use it in whatever way they could, so they could get the budget over to Harrington & Kim ASAP.

CHAPTER 61

Scarlett gave Liam his own wing of her house. A massive bedroom with a king-size bed facing the French doors that opened out onto a terrace with an endless ocean view, a sitting room with walls of books and a fireplace surrounded by marble, mother of pearl and onyx tiles, a bathroom with a Japanese soaking tub, and another fireplace, and a small, eat-in kitchen, which seemed to be restocked daily by, as far as Liam could tell, an entirely invisible servant.

"I could put you in the guesthouse now that Bridget went home," Scarlett said to him as she showed him around his quarters, "but I've got a feeling that you might need a little more human company than that. No, I think I'll keep you in the house proper, so I don't end up finding you at the bottom of my pool."

Liam snorted. "Why would I drown myself when I'm sure you've got a whole cabinet's worth of Ativan somewhere in this place?"

Scarlett raised her eyebrows. "Actually, a little cocktail of

Klonopin and vodka is my drug of choice, darlin'. But you better believe me when I tell you that I do not share."

He laughed in spite of himself.

She wrinkled her nose. "Now. What are we going to do about your clothes? I don't happen to keep many manly garments just floating around my domicile. Perhaps I shall simply give you a bathrobe for now, because you do need a shower rather desperately, and then I'll send Martin out to pick up a few things. Do you have a choice of garments? Shorts? Khakis? Kilt?"

He shook his head. "This is silly. I should just go home. I literally live twenty minutes away from here."

She squinted at him. "No. I think not. I know a desperate soul when I see one, and you are most definitely him. I think our original plan is just fine. You stay here until I say you're well enough to go home. After all, I did purchase the pleasure of your company for fifty thousand rather extravagant dollars, you know."

"Fine." He had zero fight in him. And Scarlett was right—he wasn't sure he could take it if he ran into Hana. "Thank you," he added begrudgingly.

"Just don't leave me with your blood on my hands, son," said Scarlett with a smirk. "And once you've had a chance to sulk and fret all you need to, come on out and we'll play a little tennis. Exercise is good for the old black dog."

He wrinkled his brow. "Black dog?"

"Oh." She waved one hand. "That's what Winston Churchill used to call his darkest of depressions. An apt turn of phrase, don't you think?"

Liam nodded. He could see the bed from where they were standing and suddenly all he wanted was to climb on into it and pull the covers over his head.

Scarlett tracked his line of sight. "Well, that's fine," she cooed. "A little nap won't hurt, either, but Lord's sake, take that damn shower first, Maguire. Nobody likes a spoiled bed."

PART THREE

CHAPTER 62

"It's a frigging blessing in disguise, really," Bridget told Alexander Redetzke over crab toast and an Akaushi hamburger. They were having lunch at ABC Kitchen, one of Bridget's favorite restaurants. It was tucked into a hugely expensive, multilevel Aladdin's cave of a furniture store in the Flatiron District. "I mean, who needs the distraction, right? The only thing I should be thinking about right now is how we're going to crush this job."

Alexander's mustache twitched as he picked at his pretzel-dusted calamari. "Yes, well, it sounds like he did not treat you very well at all. I think you did the right thing."

"Damn right, I did. In any case, I'm so excited that you're coming aboard our team, Alexander."

Alexander inhaled sharply and then started to cough violently, turning purple. Bridget reached across the table to pound his back. "There! Are you okay?"

He nodded weakly and reached for his water.

"Well, now, um, I still haven't decided whether or not I—"

"Alexander!" Bridget's fist came crashing down onto the

table in frustration. "You told me that Liam Maguire treats you with no respect. Isn't that true?"

Alexander's eyes shifted nervously around the restaurant as if he was afraid of just who might overhear this conversation. "Yes," he whispered. "That's true."

"And you told me that he never gives you the independence to run your projects and men in the field, either. Isn't that true?"

He stuffed a tentacle-laden bite into his mouth and nodded while chewing.

"And you told me that you've been dying to leave—but you were just waiting for the right opportunity to arise. Right?"

He nodded again. He looked like a nervous rabbit waiting to be nabbed by a fox.

"Well. Here I am. The right opportunity. We are on to the next phase—our budget was comparable to the other bidders. Next step is our presentation. We need to blow them away, and I can't do it without you because you are brilliant. You've been in the industry forever, have done a lot of ground up, and you are going to help me show them something they've never seen before."

Alexander's face went pink with pleasure. "I am? I do? We are?"

"You are, you do, and we are definitely going to. So suck it up and tell Liam you quit. Or if you want, I'll tell him."

"But working without pay..." Alexander held up his hand, interrupting himself. "You know what? Never mind. I have some money saved, and it's worth it. I can't keep working for him. I'll—I'll text him. That's what I'll do. In fact—" he pulled his phone out of his pocket "—I'll do it right now."

Bridget tried not to laugh at the look of intense concentration on Alexander's face as he thumbed his way through his message. She didn't care how he quit, just that he did. She hadn't been engaging in hyperbole when she said that he was brilliant, because he truly was. And it was Liam's own fault for not seeing what he had and treating him like he should.

Alexander looked up at her, beaming. "There!" he said. "I sent it." He blinked. "Gosh. That feels like a thousand pounds off my back. I'm a new man!"

Bridget reached up and clinked his water glass with her own. "Congratulations! You won't regret it, I swear."

She took a big, happy bite of her burger and it tasted delicious. Stole the budget, underbid Jason, nabbed Alexander Redetzke right out from under Liam's nose... Bridget liked playing dirty. It got shit done.

CHAPTER 63

"Hey, Jason," said Leela, sticking her head inside his office door. Her hair was green now, he noted. "Harrington and Kim just called. They said they have some questions about our budget and wondered if you could jump on the phone?"

Jay rolled his eyes. What was there to question? It was a budget like a million they'd done before. "Fine," he sighed. "Put them on."

"Jason, how ya doing?" said Harrington's unmistakable Queens accent.

"Good, good, Mark. How are things there?"

"We're good. So I have some questions about the budget you laid out. It all looked good, really good. That is, until we got Bridget Steele's budget."

Jay's mouth went dry when he heard her name. He thought about her all the time. He forced himself not to pick up the phone and punch in her number at least ten times a day. It was torture.

"What do you mean? What's the problem?"

"Well, I just don't understand how she managed to be tighter on every single number. It puts a stick in the wheel for our usual way of doing things, you know? Makes it much harder. Now, I know you guys were playing footsie for a while. Any chance she saw your numbers?"

Jason blinked. "What? No. Not a chance. She's never even been to my office."

Suddenly, almost violently, he remembered her arched back on his desk, wet from the rain.

"Oh. Wait. Hang on. There was one time—"

"She saw your budget."

"No. I mean, I'm not sure."

"Well, judging from the way she cut your numbers, I'd say I'm sure." He dropped his voice. "You know, your father would have never let this happen."

Jay felt a swell of anger. "Yeah. Well, I'm not my dad."

"No kidding."

"I don't think Bridget would do this to me."

"Oh, yeah? Wanna bet? Did you piss her off?"

Jay swallowed, remembering the middle finger emoji she'd last sent his way. "Okay, yeah, it's possible, I guess." He frowned. "So where does this leave us?"

"Don't you worry about that. I'll step in with my partners and take care of things like we always did for your dad. Just bring us a dynamite presentation and your A team, all right? And watch your back! Bridget is hard-core."

CHAPTER 64

Liam was in Scarlett's basement. At least, he thought it was her basement. It seemed basement-like. It was definitely underground, cool, dark and damp, but instead of the water heater and boiler, there were just dozens of perfect, white-coated rounds of something in various sizes, like a series of squishy-looking hatboxes, stacked neatly on shelf upon shelf upon shelf.

He'd needed a distraction, so he'd come looking for the whiskey cellar. He'd heard about it at the gala before everything had gone south. A woman next to him, wearing an enormous diamond brooch at her neck, had breathlessly recited the specs of Scarlett's house: thirty-five thousand square feet; one thousand linear feet of direct ocean frontage. Twenty-five bathrooms, eleven bedrooms, four living rooms, three kitchens, two libraries, a full-size gym with an indoor lap pool, two elevators, a ballroom and a whiskey cellar. And that doesn't even count the guesthouse or the pool house!

But no mention of…whatever the hell this place was.

"Maguire?" Scarlett's voice came echoing down the stairs. "What in the Lord's name are you doing in my cheese cave?"

He laughed. "Ah," he said to himself as he bent closer to one of the rounds and sniffed. Smelled like warm feet, sharp and definitely cheesy.

Scarlett came halfway down the stairs carrying an armful of dog leashes.

"I was looking for your whiskey cellar," he said, "but I got lost."

Scarlett shook her head. "I do not have a whiskey cellar. Nor do I brew my own beer. Those are rumors started by a vengeful ex. I have a wine cellar—but so does every civilized person in the world."

"And a cheese cave," he pointed out. "You have that, too."

"Well," she huffed, "it happens to be very difficult to import unpasteurized cheeses from outside the US, so one must do what one must do in order to make a decent cheese plate."

He smirked. "Indeed."

"In any case, despite the fact that you are unashamedly nosing around my home, I am delighted to see you are finally out of bed. I was just coming in to see if I could lure you out into walking my dogs with me, but one of the maids said she saw you heading down here."

Scarlett rather famously had a pack of eight much doted upon rescued pit bulls, all named after various golden-age Hollywood stars. So far, Liam had managed to avoid them, but he supposed his time had come.

"Certainly," he said as he climbed up the stairs. "Listen, thank you again for everything, and since I have basically used up all my dignity and your patience, after this walk I think it's time I went home."

"Oh?" said Scarlett as they emerged into one of her three kitchens—one for everyday cooking, one in her guest wing and a full restaurant-quality one for big events and occasional filming. "I somehow feel like I got the fuzzy end of the lollipop on this. For fifty thousand dollars, I thought at least I'd have a reliable tennis partner."

Liam laughed. "I'm a lousy player. Ask anyone."

"Lousy just means I win more, and I love to win. Come on, let's go find the puppies."

Liam had been in quite a few mega-mansions and, past a certain size, they tended to have the cold feel of a hotel or museum. But Scarlett's house did not. Every room she led Liam through was so thoughtfully laid out and elegantly finished that it felt as if he was just moving from one well-loved living space to the next. The views, of ocean or garden or pool, were all perfectly framed; the colors were rich but muted and had just enough fade and wear to feel lived in; there were books in every room that actually looked as if they'd been read; the art was probably priceless, but it was displayed casually and without ostentation. The only strange part was that the place never actually seemed to come to an end. Despite the fact that Scarlett lived here entirely alone, except for the phalanx of servants and pack of mutts, of course, the house felt used in the best possible way.

"Yoo-hoo! Ava Gardner, Gene Kelly, Judy Garland!" called Scarlett in a high-pitched voice. "Now, where are my babies?"

She ushered him past the orangery, a towering glass room filled with full-size citrus trees. Even just passing, the air was thick with the sharp-sweet scent of blossoms. The room made Liam think of the huge, elegant greenhouses in the Bronx Botanical Garden, except this conservatory had a priceless ocean view.

"Liz and Dick?" she called. "Kate and Audrey Hepburn!"

They passed what Liam thought must be a game room; a billiards table, dart boards, small tables set up for bridge and cribbage…

Suddenly, a door swung open with a crash and a multicolored flood of chubby dogs came hurtling out toward them. Liam sprang out of the way while Scarlett dropped to her knees with her arms wide open. Eight overfed pit bulls all charged in to lick her face.

"Oooh," she said as she slowly bent backward under the literal puppy pile on top of her, "there are my babies! There are my babies!" She tossed Liam half of the leashes. "Would you mind helping me buckle them up?"

Liam nodded and gingerly approached the nearest dog. It was smallish and white with a black mark like a shiner surrounding its eye. He touched its collar and it immediately lifted a lip and growled at him. He snatched his hand back.

"Oh, I'm sorry," said Scarlett. "I should have warned you that Mickey Rooney has arthritis. He doesn't care for anyone to touch him except me." She quickly attached a leash to his collar. "The rest of them should be fine, though."

Nodding, Liam randomly chose another dog and clipped the leash to its collar, making his way through the squirming, wriggling mass of canine flesh until they were all on leash.

Scarlett stood back up, caught up all the leads, divided them by half and handed him four, each attached to a grinning, pulling, twisting dog. "Here. We can probably let them off once we get down to the beach. As long as my crazy neighbor isn't there."

"You mean Bono?" said Liam. "Doesn't he live next door?"

She rolled her eyes. "Yes, and he's such a terrible nag about my doggies. Threatens to call the police every time he sees them off leash. Damn his uptight Irish hide."

They walked through the garden and out the back gate down to the beach, the four dogs racing ahead and nearly pulling Liam off his feet. Scarlett carefully looked both ways once they were on the sand, and then said, "The literal coast is clear. Go ahead and let them run. They need the exercise, poor darlins."

After he unclipped all their collars, the dogs took off as one—joyfully chasing the sea birds fluttering around at the ocean's edge. Scarlett took his arm, and they followed down the beach after them.

"So," she said. "Aren't you wondering why I paid top dollar for you?"

Liam looked out at the ocean. It was a nearly perfect day, sunny, breezy, not too hot. The sea was a sparkling blue. "Pity?" he said.

Scarlett snorted. "If I wanted to rescue the pitiful, I would have bought the congressman with the unfortunate taste for penis pictures. No, even before you made such a poor showing, I was planning on bidding on you. You see, I'm rather fascinated by your story. I do believe we have some things in common."

Liam looked at her. "What could I have in common with the richest woman in the world?"

"One of the richest women in the world," corrected Scarlett. "There are others who have more in both Asia and Russia. And don't you try to cry poor to me, Maguire. I know exactly how much you're worth."

"Okay," said Liam, "I'll bite. What do we have in common?"

"Well," said Scarlett, bending to pick up a shell, "I know you come from a rather unfortunate part of Chicago—"

"Not *unfortunate*—just dirt-freaking-poor," said Liam.

She nodded. "And I happen to have been raised small-town Georgia dirt-poor. Which, trust me, is far worse than anything you've ever seen."

"Oh, yeah? I wouldn't count on that."

"Shoes, Maguire. I assume you always had at least one pair of shoes?"

He shrugged. "Sure, usually full of holes and one size too small."

Scarlett stretched out her foot and showed him the Gucci sandals on her perfectly pedicured and tanned feet. "My sister and I shared our pair—and on the days she wore them, I went barefoot and vice versa. I didn't have my own pair until I was sixteen years old, and that's only because I was the same size as the woman I cleaned house for, and I stole a pair of her ratty old gardening Keds off her back porch."

Liam cocked his head. "Okay, so you grew up poor. Lots of us did."

"No. Very few of us did, actually. Most of the people around here inherited their daddy's money and if they didn't send it all up their noses before they hit thirty, maybe they managed to hire a smart financial adviser who made their inheritance work a little harder for them. Big deal. They were born with a silver spoon shoved up their rears. But you and I, we are truly self-made. That's not so common around here."

He shrugged. "All right. What else you got?"

She squinted and smiled. "I'm guessing less than stellar parents?"

He shrugged. "Missing dad. Drunk mom."

She smiled primly. "My parents started drinking as soon as they woke in the morning and didn't stop until they fell down wherever they happened to be standing later in the day."

He nodded, impressed in spite of himself. "Why don't I know this? Seems like a *People* magazine profile waiting to happen."

She looked at him with a wry expression in her eyes. "Son, nobody wants to hear that America's tastemaker used to shove Hungry-Man TV dinners down the front of her girdle so she wouldn't starve to death."

Liam laughed.

"And the third thing we have in common—you've recently had your heart broken."

He winced. If he didn't put a name to it, the horrible feeling of walking around with his heart outside his body, raw and heaving, could almost be ignored.

"We all had a front-row seat to your particular heartbreak, of course. But mine was many, many years ago. A skinny little redhead named Lily Mae Hopkins. Preacher's daughter, but the devil himself must have taught that girl to give head. I haven't had such a talent between my thighs since." She demurely reached to pat one of her dogs who had come circling back around them. "We fell into the kind of love only a couple of in-the-closet country girls could. Of course, back then, you could hardly be open with your affections, but I somehow thought we'd figure it out. We'd get the hell out of Pine Tree, Georgia, and it would be just me and Lily Mae until death did us part." Scarlett stared off into the distance for a moment, and then sighed. "Then one day, after she gave me four orgasms in a row, she told me that she was getting married to Roddy Johnson. That she was already pregnant with his baby. And that we had to stop our sinful ways and settle down like good girls. I left Pine Tree the next week, was a fit model in New York City a month later, started my first catering business a year after that, and the rest is very well-known history.

I only saw Lily Mae once since then, when I went home for my mama's funeral. She was still wiry and red-headed but she had six squalling brats. Roddy Johnson had doubled his weight and halved his IQ sniffing glue, and for a moment I imagined that I might take Lily Mae away from it all. Just swoop her up in my private jet and fly us off to Rome or Marrakesh or Ibiza. But damned if that girl didn't give me the cut direct. Even with all my money, all my fame, all my god damned everything, she was still pretending that she'd never been a butch dyke with an insatiable tongue."

"So," said Liam. His voice cracked. "How'd you get over her?"

Scarlett laughed softly and threw the shell she'd been carrying back into the sea. "Did I say that I did?"

Liam closed his eyes. "You are not helping."

Scarlett squeezed his hand. "No, I went home and continued to work my ass off and became so successful people started saying Oprah Who? And Martha What? And I made a point of living my life so large that even those peons in Pine Tree couldn't miss it. I made myself a household name, Maguire, just to punish my ex. So what are you going to do?"

He shook his head. "Um, considering the fact that I have been holed up in your guest-room bed for almost two days straight, and only came out to find what I hoped to be a room full of whiskey, I'm not so sure I can match your achievements."

She chuckled. "Well. There are options to consider. Some people drink until they black out, and some people go and find another woman or ten to plug the hole, and some people run off to a monastery and take a vow of silence. But you hardly seem the type to pull that off."

Liam shrugged. "I dunno. Sitting in a cave in Tibet sounds pretty good right now."

"I believe that you have a business to run? Why don't you start there? Because if you don't get Hana back—and let me tell you, that woman seems undeniably fickle, so there are no guarantees that you will—you're going to need to go back to scratch and do what you do best."

He stared out at the waves. "The only reason I worked as hard as I did was for her."

Scarlett laughed. "Oh, that's a load of horse crap and you know it. The reason you work so hard is so you won't have holes in your shoes. The reason you work so hard is so you never have to go back to where you came from. Admit it, it's better being rich."

He looked at her. Her gray eyes were glittering fiercely.

"I don't think anyone around here would argue that point, Scarlett."

She shrugged. "Nor should they."

"Anyway, if I can't be a monk and you won't share your Klonopin, I suppose going back to work so I don't end up barefoot back in Chicago is the next best thing." He patted his pockets. "Man, I don't even know where my phone is. I can't remember the last time that happened."

"It's in the breast pocket of your tuxedo jacket, which has been dry-cleaned and is currently sitting in the closet of your guest room. I had your phone charged for you. I suggest that you go on home, take a couple of days to pull yourself together if you still need them and then check your messages. Because take it from me, the only thing that is going to get you through this particular situation is working until you collapse into bed every night and can barely crawl out alive the next morning." She squinted. "Oh, hellfire, there's Bono. Doggies!" she called, and the animals turned toward her en masse.

"But," she added, "before you leave, I do believe you owe me a game of tennis."

CHAPTER 65

"Just shut up and move," muttered Bridget to Christopher Lee as they inched their way down the hall and past the office the Ludley brothers shared. "As far as they know, you're just helping me with Scarlett."

"I am just helping you with Scarlett," replied Lee. "I haven't committed to anything else."

"I don't actually need your help with her," said Bridget. "I told you. I've got something much bigger on the plate. We'll talk about it once we're clear of—"

"Bridget? Christopher?" called out one of the Ludley brothers.

"Keep walking, Lee!" insisted Bridget. "Pretend you don't hear them!"

They increased their pace but halted when Larry Ludley came out into the hall and called after them. "Hey now, you two! Before you disappear for the day, come on in and have a little chat."

It was ridiculous, thought Bridget as they reversed course, that the brothers insisted on sharing one office. Their two desks were pushed together so they could gaze across at each other like Queen Victoria and Prince Albert.

Larry was still standing when they walked in, but Linus was sitting with his feet up, Italian loafers, thin nylon socks and a full inch of thick black leg hair on full view.

"So," said Larry, "we heard that Scarlett has asked Christopher to join the project." He looked at Bridget. "Is there a problem with your work, hon?"

"No, sir. But the job is just a little bit bigger than I expected so—"

"You're in over your head," finished Linus, frowning. "I knew this would happen. We should have trusted our instincts and sent Scott with you."

For a second Bridget bit her tongue. She was dying to tell him off, but then she forced herself to widen her eyes and bat her lashes and worry her lip like she was in distress. "Yes. Yes. It's true. I'm in over my head. This bedroom renovation is just too big. I can't do it alone. I need help."

She didn't know whether to laugh or spit when she saw the look of satisfaction appear on the Ludleys' faces.

Larry smirked and picked up the phone. "I'll call Scott."

"No!" cried Bridget. "I mean, Scarlett wants Lee. She—she prefers to work with gay people."

"Bridget!" protested Lee.

"Really?" said Larry.

"Well, Scott certainly isn't gay," said Linus.

"Wait," said Larry to Bridget, "are you?"

"I—I—I'm sorry, sirs, but we really have to go. Scarlett hates tardiness." She shot a look at Lee. "Right, Lee?"

"Yes," Lee intoned. "She loathes it."

"So you've already met her, Christopher?" Linus asked.

"No," Lee answered without skipping a beat, "but I read

an interview in *Vogue*. She fired her last manager because he showed up ten minutes late to a meeting."

The Ludleys nodded solemnly. "Well, by all means, then," said Larry. "But Bridget, honey, in light of these developments, we're going to need both of you to report to us with regular updates on how the job is proceeding."

"Perhaps a meeting with Ms. Hawkins herself, so we can personally apologize for the problems your incompetence caused?" suggested Linus.

Bridget swallowed. "I'll see what I can do," she said, already backing out the door.

"Tell her we'd love to take her out to dinner!" called Larry as Bridget grabbed Lee by the sleeve and pulled him out with her. "Anyplace she likes!"

"Go, go, go," said Bridget to Lee as they raced for the exit.

"This better be good, Steele," said Lee. "Harry and I just bought a one-bedroom in Tribeca. I have a big mortgage to pay."

CHAPTER 66

"But why did Redetzke quit?" yelled Liam as he waved his phone around. "I mean, Jesus, he was right here just a week ago yammering at me about some stupid drone idea he had—"

Liam's assistant, Milo Jenkins, cringed. "I'm sorry, sir, but you received the text. I don't know anything more than what you just read to me."

Liam looked at his phone again and read out loud. "'Dear Mr. Maguire, I resign. Have a good life. Signed, Alexander Redetzke, Structural Engineer and Project Manager.' I mean, what the hell did he even quit to do? Have you been able to get him on the phone yet?"

Jenkins shook his head. "Straight to voice mail."

Liam paced the office. "This is the worst possible timing. We have the Harrington and Kim presentation in two god damned days. What am I going to do without him? He knows the project inside and out and has worked on a couple of Harrington projects." He looked at the message on his phone again and then slammed it down on his desk. "God damn it!"

Jenkins winced as the phone exploded into hundreds of pieces of glass, metal and plastic. Taking no notice, Liam continued to pace and swear.

"Do you think, sir," Jenkins said meekly, "that maybe Alexander might be working for someone else?"

Liam froze. "You mean someone poached him?" His voice was hoarse.

"Well, I mean, Alexander has a wife and kids, sir. Perhaps someone gave him a better offer."

Liam looked at Jenkins sharply. "He does? How many kids?"

"Four."

"Four," Liam repeated. "Four? And why didn't I know that?"

"Well, I don't think you ever asked, sir."

Liam wheeled around and faced his assistant. "Do you have any children, Jenkins?"

Jenkins's eyes went wide. "I'm only twenty-five, Mr. Maguire."

"So? Kids or not?"

Jenkins shook his head. "None. No."

"A wife?"

He shook his head again. "I don't even have a girlfriend right now, sir."

"Good," said Liam. "But for God's sake, tell me if you get married. Now, get me Sal Delmonico on the phone. And actually—" he looked at the shards of electronics all over his desk and floor "—get me another phone, as well."

Jenkins quickly scrolled his contacts and then punched a number into the landline. "Mr. Delmonico? I have Mr. Maguire on the phone for you."

"Delmonico?" said Liam. "I need some information."

"Well, hello, Maguire." Delmonico's voice sounded even

more oily over the phone. "I heard you had quite the public humiliation at Scarlett Hawkins's party last week."

"Yeah. Thanks a lot for bringing it up. Listen—"

"You wanna know who poached your field project manager, right?"

Liam paused. "Damn, Delmonico. How do you do that?"

Delmonico laughed. "I pay attention."

"Okay, yeah, you've got an amazing gift. Now, can you tell me anything? It was Russo, wasn't it?"

Delmonico laughed again. "Well, that would be nice and neat, wouldn't it? Yeah, no, not Russo. And I'm gonna tell you who it was, but I want you to know that I'm only telling you because I want to say I freaking told you so."

"Great. Awesome. Gloat all you want. Just tell me who did it."

"Remember when I told you that Bridget Steele is an untrustworthy bitch?"

"It was Bridget? Seriously? Oh, come on."

"No doubt at all. She took him right out from under your nose."

"So direct competition for the Harrington job. Way dirty pool."

"I told you—"

"Yeah, yeah, we've already been through that part. But Jesus, how's she even paying him? She doesn't have any money. I mean, did you know that Redetzke has four kids?"

"Jenny, Jamie, John and Jack. Another one on the way, too. They're doing the gender reveal party next week. Hoping for another girl. The girls have been easier."

"Oh, for God's sake—"

"Listen, I gotta go, but just remember, sometimes it's not about the money. I know you were paying Redetzke plenty. But that didn't mean that the guy exactly liked you."

"What the hell is that supposed to mean?"

"Good luck with the presentation, Maguire. You're gonna need it."

CHAPTER 67

They had been there for hours. Jay knew he should have been running the show, but he had ceded to Leela after the first forty-five minutes. She was walking them through a PowerPoint chart for the third time.

Jay was thinking about Bridget again. He still couldn't believe that she had hacked his budget. Not that he didn't deserve it. Because he totally did. And not that she hadn't warned him, because she totally had—

"Jay... Jay?"

Jay snapped his head up only to see Leela glaring at him from across the conference table. "What?" he asked.

"I asked you if there was anything else you wanted to add about our approach to the project?"

Jay blinked, looking around at the table full of employees, all staring at him expectantly. "Oh. Yeah, no." He tried to look like he was paying attention. "But I'm very interested in everyone else's opinions."

"Nothing?" said Leela in a wheedling tone. "Not one thing

you want to change? How about the schedule? Anything we should address?"

He shook his head, avoiding her eyes. "Nope. I mean, you guys have just been so thorough—" He felt his phone vibrate in his pocket and pulled it out. It was a call from Hana. He stood up and headed for the door. "Um, excuse me for one moment."

"Hi," he said as he shut the door behind him.

"Are you busy?" she asked. "Is this a good time?"

"It's fine," he lied.

"Can I come over?" she said. "I think we should talk and I'd rather do it in person."

"Um, now?"

"Yes." Her voice got a little chilly. "Now."

He glanced back at the conference room. "You know what, why not? I'm at the office, but I can be home in twenty."

He opened the door and stuck his head back in. Leela had a new chart up. He cleared his throat and everyone turned to look at him. "Hey, guys. Sorry to interrupt, but you know, I actually think we've got this. Everyone's done a great job. I feel like we're ready. So why don't we all cut out and get some rest?"

"Wait, no!" Leela yelled as everyone started to stand up. "There are a ton of things we need to talk about before anyone goes anywhere."

Everyone sat back down. Except Jay, who stepped back into the room and started gathering up his stuff. "Okay, well, I'll let you make that call, Leela. I actually need to go home, though, but since you're going so late, why don't you go ahead and order some pizza?" He counted heads. "I think six pies will be plenty, but hey, get as many as you like. I hear that new place on Twelfth is great." He gave them a little salute as he started to back out of the room. "Good luck to everyone tomorrow. I'm sure we'll knock it out of the park like always. I'm just going to—" He didn't even bother finishing his sentence as he exited the room.

"Everyone stay here! Don't you dare move!" he heard Leela command as she followed him out. "Jay!" She chased him down the hall, tugging at his sleeve.

He turned and faced her. "What's up?"

"What are you doing?" Her eyes were bugged with fury. "You promised me. You promised that you'd pull your weight this time."

"I did," he said. "I am. But now I have something I need to do."

"You do not! And you are not!" She was shouting now. Getting up in his face.

He put his hands up and took a step back. "Hey. Whoa. I know you're a little stressed about this presentation. And I'm sorry. I really am. But I have some personal complications—"

"Sir, with all due respect, Russo needs this project, and I can't make it happen if you're not doing your job."

He stared at her for a moment and then he laughed. "Leela, you didn't know me before. Before I got divorced. Before Liam left the company. But you have to trust me when I tell you, I was a really terrible person. I mean, I was a great CEO, the company was doing just awesome, but I basically burned my life down making sure that happened."

Leela opened her mouth. "But—"

He held up his hand. "I'm sorry. I know it doesn't feel fair to you, but I can't prioritize work tonight. Because I prioritized work for fifteen years, and it ruined my marriage and messed up my relationship with my daughter, and I have a whole thing I have to deal with right now, and honestly? I just don't care enough about this Harrington job to even act like I do."

Leela's lip curled and her hand shot out and she socked him on the arm. Hard. "No!"

"Ow!" said Jay, rubbing his arm. "What the hell, Leela?"

A look of horror flashed over her face. She bent over with her head between her knees, hyperventilating. "Oh, God. Oh, God. I can't believe I just hit you. Oh, my God. And now you're going to fire me because I hit you. And I'll probably go to jail. Oh, my God. What is wrong with me?"

Jay reached out and awkwardly patted her shoulder. "Deep breaths." He could understand her frustration. He'd hired her to fill a position that, by all accounts, she wasn't remotely experienced enough for, and against all odds, she was crushing it. But if he kept her from succeeding, all the blame would fall on her, and no one would be surprised the twenty-seven-year-old COO had sunk the company.

Now her seething anger was replaced with shock. "Oh, my God. Oh, my God. Oh, my God. I'm so sorry. I can't believe I just did that."

He snorted. "I can't believe you didn't do it sooner."

She laughed, startled out of her panic attack. Then bent her head back down. "Are you really leaving?" she said. She sounded defeated.

"You know how I just told you how working too hard ruined my life?"

She looked up at him. "Yes."

"Even I never punched my boss."

She groaned.

"We're ready to present," he said. "You did a great job. Thank you. Let everyone go home and get some rest."

She looked back up at him and straightened up. "Are you sure?"

"My dad told me it was possible to overprepare, you know."

Leela shook her head. "Trust me when I tell you that we are nowhere near that happening, Jay."

CHAPTER 68

They were all crammed into Bridget's tiny living room: Ava, Ethan, Mrs. Hashemi, Danny, Redetzke and Lee. There were building plans, several open laptops, bottles of water and half-empty cartons of Chinese food scattered all over the coffee table and floor. Mrs. Hashemi and Danny, being the eldest in the group, were on the couch, but the rest of the group was sprawled wherever they could fit in the small space.

"So that's it," said Bridget, clapping her hands together. "That's everything? We're all clear?" She looked around as people nodded. "Okay, then, I think we're actually ready. I guess let's call it a night and get some decent sleep so we're fresh for tomorrow."

"Wait," said Ethan, jumping up and going into Bridget's tiny kitchen, where he pulled out a bottle of Domaines Ott that he had stashed in the fridge earlier. He expertly popped the cork, poured a couple of inches into seven plastic cups and passed out the rosé.

"I have to admit," he said, standing before everyone, "that when Bridget called me at the beginning of all this, I had my doubts. I mean, who in their right mind thinks they can go from pretty much nothing to getting a contract to build a freaking skyscraper? You gotta be crazy, right? Or delusional."

"Thanks a lot," Bridget snorted.

"But—" He smiled at her. "I've known this woman for years. I saw her rise from being the scrappiest handyman on the block, to starting her own business, to making it out of the hood, to building something huge, something that any of us could be proud of. And then I watched her lose it all and let me tell you—" he glanced at Bridget again "—that sucked." He waited a beat while everyone laughed. "And yet, here we are again, back on the brink of success. Major success. And it's all because this woman is the strongest, fiercest, most stubborn person to ever come out of the Bronx, and that—" he raised his glass and everyone followed suit "—is saying a lot. So here's to Bridget Steele, the toughest fighter I ever met." He smiled at her and clinked his cup against hers. "You make us all stronger, lady. And I thank you for that."

Everyone touched their cups together and drank. Bridget bit her lip. "You guys. Thank you. I'm not going to lie. The past few years have been really hard. And there have been more than a few moments when I wondered if I was ever going to get through them. I know that I am a lucky, lucky woman to have you all here in this room. And I am positive that we are going to do the most kick-ass, amazing job tomorrow. We are going to march in there and be undeniable. And then—" she smiled a huge, happy, teary grin "—we are going to build a god damned skyscraper."

"Yeah!" everyone cheered, tipping back their drinks.

"Now, go home!" called Bridget. "I don't want a bunch of hungover zombies at the presentation tomorrow!"

"Hey," said Ava on her way out. She dropped her voice. "Are you really all right?"

Bridget pasted on a cheerful smile. "Why wouldn't I be?"

Ava shook her head. "Well. I can think of a few good reasons. I mean, do you want to talk? I can stay."

"I'm fine," said Bridget hurriedly. "I'm great. Go on. You've been awesome. I'll see you tomorrow."

Ava looked at her for a long moment, obviously trying to decide whether she meant it. "Okay. If you say so. But I'm just a text away if you need me."

Bridget gave her a kiss on the cheek. "I know. You always have been. And I appreciate it. You're a great friend. Now, go."

Ava left, and Bridget locked the door behind her, grateful for the quiet. She moved around the living room, picking up cups and containers, straightening papers into neat piles, but then, halfway through, she sank to the couch with a sigh.

She was fine. Or, at least, she would be. She wondered if Harrington & Kim had scheduled the presentations back-to-back. She felt sick to her stomach when she imagined how it would feel to see Jay tomorrow.

She found the nearly empty bottle of rosé and brought it to her lips, tipping it back and finishing it off.

It's better this way, she scolded herself fiercely. *He made you weak. He made you stupid. None of this was a luxury you could afford. Let a man get between you and the work and it's all over. Look what happened with Kevin. You swore you'd never do that to yourself again—and yet, you were walking right into it with Jay. So what if he made you laugh? So what if he was good in bed? Men are a dime a dozen. This job is everything.*

So why was she crying?

She wiped away angry tears.

She ached, was the honest truth. Work or no work, the thought of him still made her feel shaky and weak. She missed him. And she was pissed at him. He had left her gutted.

She looked at the mess left behind by everyone who had

shown up for her tonight. She reached her foot out and shoved at a little toy truck that was sitting on the carpet.

Forget Jay, she thought. *Think about the job. Nothing else matters. Nothing else deserves your attention. Because this isn't about just me. This is so much more.*

CHAPTER 69

Hana was waiting for him in the apartment when Jay got home. He felt a small flash of annoyance when he saw her sitting there on his couch.

"I hope you don't mind me letting myself in," she said. She was wearing faded jeans and a white tank top, her hair pulled back into a long braid. Judging from the paint on her hands and smudge on her chin, he guessed she'd been working.

"I didn't know you still had a key," he said as he took off his shoes.

She shrugged. "It never occurred to me to give it back." She gave him a little smile. "Maybe it's a sign."

He raised his eyebrows in answer. "Where's Alli?"

"At Minnie's house. I guess we should call her the girlfriend now, though." She laughed. "Funny to say that, right?"

He nodded, heading for the kitchen. "I need to eat something. Can I get you anything? Hungry? Thirsty?"

"Maybe just a glass of water. I stopped at Sbarro's on the way over."

He cringed, remembering how Hana would eat just about

anything when she got hungry. "All the great pizza we have in this city and that's where you ate?"

She rolled her eyes. "Don't be such a snob. Crust, tomato sauce, cheese. A slice is a slice is a slice."

He opened his mouth to argue and then shut it again and took a deep breath as he entered the kitchen. "Okay. Never mind." He took down a glass and filled it.

She came in and sat down at the kitchen island and accepted the glass. "Thanks," she said.

He opened the refrigerator and pulled out some prosciutto, a round of goat cheese, some arugula and a jar of fig preserves. He grabbed a loaf of half-finished focaccia out of the bread box and cut off a couple of thick slices. Then he spread the jam, draped the prosciutto, added the greens and crumbled on the cheese. He left the sandwiches open-faced, side by side, in case Hana changed her mind. "You sure you don't want some?" he said, pouring a glass of cabernet.

She smiled faintly and sipped her water. "I'm good, thanks."

He didn't much like eating alone, but he was starving, so he sat down and dug in.

"So," he said, between bites, "you wanted to talk?"

"We haven't seen each other since Scarlett's," she said.

He nodded. "Well, there's been a lot going on at work."

She looked at him warily. "Is that all?"

He shook his head. "No. I needed time to think."

"What's there to think about? I thought it was all pretty clear."

He looked at her. "Seriously?" He took another bite of his sandwich, chewing slowly. "Jesus, Hana. Even before you left, when was the last time we were really happy together?"

She shrugged. "What's happy? I mean, were we any happier after we split up?"

He laughed. "Well, no, not for me, anyway. Not at first. But you and Liam seemed pretty dang good."

She stood up and paced, her braid snaking around behind her. "I told you, that was a mistake. And you know that Alli wasn't any happier after."

"What I know is that Alli was hitting adolescence and probably heading for whatever it is she's going through now, whether we were apart or together. And all the fighting we did before things ended probably didn't help that much."

She looked at him. "Jay—"

He raised his hands. "I'm not saying I didn't make mistakes, Hana. I screwed up plenty. I did exactly what my dad taught me to do. From the beginning, I never put you first, and then when Alli grew out of cute and easy, I iced her out, too. I kept telling myself that I was working hard like that for you guys— that I was providing for you. And that I was a good husband because I brought home the money and didn't screw around on you. What more could you ask for, right? But that's ridiculous. I mean, I could have quit and never worked another day in my life and we wouldn't have had to change a thing about how we lived. I could have given you both all my time, and we still would have been way more than fine financially."

Hana shook her head. "I don't need you to do that," she said. "I don't want you to do that."

He could feel his lip curl. "Wait. But wasn't that the whole reason you left? Because I wasn't there for you?"

She looked away from him and took a deep breath. "I left because I fell in love with Liam." She said it quickly, like she had to spit it out. "But that's…it's not healthy. What you and I had was healthy."

"What we had was a mess. I don't understand what you're saying."

She wrapped her arms around herself. She looked miserable. "I just… I want to be myself again, Jay. I want to do my work, and parent Alli, and not feel so much. Yes, you were never around, but in some ways, that gave me space, you know? There was quiet and solitude, and time to create. Now, it's like I'm all wrapped up—I'm never alone, and even when I am alone, I'm consumed with this need… And he—" She stopped, a scared look on her face.

Jay blinked in wonder. "So this has nothing to do with me. Or Alli, even. This is because—what? You're too obsessed with Liam? You want to get back with me because you love Liam too much? Are you freaking kidding me, Hana?"

She closed her eyes and rubbed her forehead. "That's not what I meant. That came out wrong."

Jay suddenly thought of Bridget. Of the way they sat on the beach together that night, sharing champagne, watching the moon. He felt sick.

He looked at Hana. "Go back to Liam, Hana."

She whirled on him, her braid flying. "I can't go back to Liam!"

"Then go be by yourself if that's what you want. But you don't need me. For God's sake, I don't think you even want me. Why are you playing at this?"

Her face contorted and she started to cry. "I don't know. I don't know. I just thought it would be easier, like it used to be."

He closed his eyes. "It was never really easy between us, Hana. You know that."

She stared at him, tears streaming down her face. "I'm sorry," she choked out.

He put his hand on her shoulder. "At least Alli didn't know."

"That's right," she sobbed. "No one really got hurt."

He pulled his hand away. "Well…" He shook his head. "That's definitely not true."

She looked at him for a moment. She had stopped crying,

but her cheeks were still wet with tears. "I'm going to go," she said at last.

He nodded. "You need me to call a ride?"

She shook her head. "I'll call my driver. I'm good." She reached out and tentatively put her hand on his arm. "If I… messed anything up for you, Jay, I'm sorry. I really am."

He shrugged. "I made my own choices."

"I just want you to know. I didn't want this just because I thought it would be easier, you know. I also thought…even though you weren't always around. When you were here. I think you really saw me, Jay. I think you knew me. And I always appreciated that."

He was quiet for a moment. "I'm glad," he said at last.

She dropped her hand off his arm and wiped her face, went into the living room to collect her purse. He followed her to the door. She reached up on her tiptoes and kissed him on the cheek. "Thank you. For everything."

CHAPTER 70

For Liam, the presentation was pretty much over before it began. He'd lost vital days of preparation wandering in Scarlett's house like he was stupid frigging Odysseus and Scarlett was Calypso. He still wasn't sleeping or eating much, so he was blurry and slow. And he'd never realized just how much he'd leaned on Redetzke for fresh ideas until he was in the room with a dozen guys—Harrington, Kim, the anchor tenants, all the investors, the owner's rep, the architect, the real estate brokers and the engineering firm—all staring him down, and he found himself with absolutely nothing of interest to say.

He went on automatic, woodenly reciting why South Side Construction was the best company for the job, but he could see the bored looks being thrown around the room. He knew for certain that he'd lost the whole thing when he saw Kim check his phone not once, but three times. Still, he slogged through until he had hit all his talking points and shown them all their projected schedule, the team and a lengthy approach to how they would build the project. He let each member of his team present, and then he'd wrapped it up and sent all his people out ahead of him as fast as he could, lingering just a moment longer to shake everyone's hand and thank them.

No one even made eye contact.

"See you for tennis next week, Kim?" he said just before he left, and Kim had waved his hand in the air noncommittally, as if he was embarrassed that people might think he was the reason Liam was there in the first place.

His team was waiting for him in the lobby, but Liam didn't want to face them, so at the last second, he took the stairs ten flights down and went out a back way, his heart pumping from the exertion. When he got out to the street, he texted his assistant that they'd all done a good job, and to tell everyone to take the rest of the day off. He'd see them tomorrow.

It was a warm, gorgeous late-spring day. The bodegas had dozens of plastic buckets of lilac branches stacked out front, and the purple candy scent filled the air. It was that brief, effervescent moment before summer really arrived and the city got too hot and humid. People were smiling at each other on the street, making eye contact and moving around each other like they were all partners in an elaborate vernal dance.

Liam moved through all this spring sweetness with a sour gut and the feeling that he might punch someone if they dared come too close. He had screwed it all up. No Hana. No Alli. He was living out of the N. Moore Penthouse at the Greenwich Hotel for twenty-five hundred freaking dollars a night, having ceded his loft to Hana for the time being.

So much for Scarlett's advice. Throw himself into the work? Instead, he'd wallowed and procrastinated and lost his best employee, thanks to Bridget Steele. And now he'd lost the job, too.

By now he had figured out that Scarlett's whole song and dance about keeping him around because they were two poverty-traumatized soul mates was an utter front. She had obviously been hand in hand with Bridget the entire time, inviting him to stay at her place so she could keep him distracted while Bridget put a knife in his back and finished poaching Redetzke. He almost had to laugh, he'd been played so expertly.

He'd been thinking about Hana constantly, of course, but he'd also been thinking about Jay. Everything he felt now, he suddenly realized, he had already inflicted upon his friend. The heartbreak, the jealousy, the betrayal, the sense of loss. And as much as he hated feeling it all, there was a part of him that knew he deserved it. And an even bigger part of him that wanted to make it right.

He pulled out his phone and stared at it for a moment, wondering if Jay even still had the same number. Then he shrugged and scrolled, looking for his name—he supposed he could only try.

Wanna get a drink at Locanda Verde after your presentation today?

Sure, came the answer, why not?

CHAPTER 71

Jay smiled and threw a discreet double thumbs-up at Leela as they walked out of the conference room. She returned the gesture and then let out a huge breath as if she'd been holding it for the entire two hours they'd been in the room.

The presentation had gone very well. Jay had put on the charm just like his dad had taught him. He'd warmed up the room with a little speech about how excited they were to have a chance to build for Harrington & Kim and HealthTec. He made a point of mentioning that his own father had worked for Harrington back when Harrington was a younger man, and that Jay knew his dad would be thrilled about the possibility of the relationship being carried on into the future. He talked about how many buildings Russo Construction had already built in Manhattan, and how much pride they had taken in every single one. Then there was time for the more educational portion of the presentation—Leela's flowcharts and his project manager's and field super's approach to building the monstrosity. They talked about tearing down the current buildings before they started building up the new one;

they mentioned the vendors they liked and the kind of materials they might use as alternates if lead times didn't meet the schedule. It all went perfectly—everyone covered their topics just like they'd rehearsed; no stone was left unturned as they went bullet point by bullet point through everything they would do to make this job a huge success. There was a question and answer session, then Jay tied it all up in the end—pointing out that there was no company in Manhattan with the same level of experience as his, nor an equal to Russo Construction's reputation for safety, transparency and competency. That Harrington & Kim and HeathTec knew exactly what they were getting if they contracted with Russo Construction—Harrington had grinned a giant grin when he said this, which Jay took as a sign of approval—and that he really looked forward to showing everyone in the room what they could do.

The panel applauded in a warm and polite way. Jay and his team shook hands with everyone, both Harrington and Kim themselves promised to be in touch soon, and out they all went.

As they were heading for the elevator, Harrington popped out of the conference room and called for Jay to wait up. Jay waved his team into the elevator and told them to go on ahead, they would debrief tomorrow. "Amazing job, everyone!" he enthused as the elevator door closed between them.

"Hey, Mark," said Jay. "What can I do for you? Did you have any more questions?"

"No, no. You guys were very thorough. I just wanted to say, nice work," said Harrington. "And to thank you for coming in and tell you that you really reminded me of your old man. You know, he and I had a very special relationship over the years."

"Yeah," said Jay, "I remember you guys working together quite a bit. You did all the interior work together on the first wave of Starbucks to make it into the city, right?"

Harrington laughed. "Yeah, but don't tell anyone. I don't want to be blamed for the corporate takeover of Big Coffee, you know? But yeah, we did really, really well on those projects." He darted a look around and then leaned in closer. "And you know what? I'm sure we can build a great project. Just like your dad and I used to."

"You guys already make up your mind in there?" Jay joked. "That sounds like good news for Russo Construction."

Harrington grinned a wolfish grin. "We've got a few more to see today, of course, but I can't imagine anyone coming in ahead of your team. Just like you said in there—you and your dad always knew how to get it done. By the way, once we get everything signed, I have a list of subcontractors and vendors that you might want to consider working with. They all have some connection to your father, as well."

Jay frowned. He was getting uneasy about the way Harrington seemed to be dancing around certain subjects. Of course, this business was full of grift and back-scratching and outright corruption, but Russo Construction had an impeccable reputation for honesty and transparency. People didn't bother bringing their backroom deals to Jay because they knew there was no point in even trying.

But, he reminded himself, guys like Mark Harrington were old-school, used to doing things one way and one way only. Jay might simply be reading something into this conversation that wasn't there. Maybe Harrington was just hoping to bring that kind of old-fashioned camaraderie—cigars and drinks and dirty jokes—back to the project. Maybe not Jay's favorite way to handle business, but he could certainly do it with his eyes closed and his hands tied behind his back.

"That's great," he said. "We'd be happy to take a look."

Harrington grinned even bigger and clasped his hand to

Jay's shoulder. "This is going to be beautiful," he said happily. "We're both gonna come out of this deal very happy men."

Before Jay could answer, the elevator dinged and the doors opened up, and Bridget Steele and her motley crew of a team stepped off into the hallway.

Jay froze. This was the first time he'd seen her since the Hamptons, and he felt his mind go blank.

She met his eyes but no more. Her face was a mask. She gave him nothing.

Harrington dropped his hand off Jay's shoulder and stepped forward. "Bridget!" he said with a huge smile. He leaned over and gave her the standard kiss on each cheek. "We're so excited to see your presentation today!" He put his arm around her shoulder and steered her toward the conference room. "Come this way, my dear."

She looked back over her shoulder and briefly met Jay's eyes again before being ushered behind closed doors. This time a smile played on her mouth, the tiniest of smirks, like a professional challenge.

As soon as she was out of sight, Jay slumped against the wall. He was sweating. She actually made him sweat. She'd been beautiful, in a stark black pinstriped pantsuit, cripplingly high heels, top button of her jacket unbuttoned to show the briefest flash of a lilac-colored lace and cotton camisole. Her hair was drawn back off her face, firmly secured at the base of her neck. The stern style served to make her face seem younger and softer in comparison. Under Harrington's arm, she'd looked like a rebellious teenager being escorted into the principal's office.

He could still smell her, that changeable, light, woody fragrance that she wore, that deeper, richer scent of her own skin underneath. The lingering smell and the scandalous memories that it unfurled in his mind made him want to charge into the room after her and publicly confess what a fool he'd been to let her go.

His phone buzzed. It was Liam.

Still on for a drink?

CHAPTER 72

Bridget loved giving presentations. She knew plenty of people in the industry who hated this part of the job, who felt like the work should be awarded based on numbers on the page, not some tap dance in a conference room, but Bridget knew it was where she was at her best. She loved the pressure, she loved the performance, she loved having a captive audience. She loved starting with a room full of people who doubted her, and seeing their faces change from distrust, to surprise, and then excitement by the end of her pitch. Sometimes she thought that, in another life, she would have been an actress or the lead singer for a rock band, anything that allowed her to command the stage.

No matter where she presented, some things never seemed to change. The ubiquitous mahogany paneling on the walls, the long, polished conference table with the lineup of mostly white, mostly older, men in expensive suits sitting behind it, and the look of shock on their faces when they realized that the young, pretty woman who just walked in wasn't a secretary, but actually the CEO who would be running this whole damn thing.

While Ethan set up the projected computer screen, Bridget slowly walked to the center of the room and turned to face the lineup. "I know what you all are thinking."

The men stared back at her. She noticed Harrington giving her a subtle wink, and her smile got a little bit bigger.

She looked over the assembled group of men, carefully making eye contact with each one. "You're thinking, 'Didn't Steele Construction go bankrupt? Wasn't there a big public scandal? Wasn't Bridget Steele chased out of town with pitchforks and torches? And what the hell is that woman doing up there?'"

She crossed over to the table and sat on the edge, dangling her four-inch stiletto from her right toe. "And the answers are, yes, yes, no, but I might as well have been, and I am here, we are here, because you are not going to find a better company to build your skyscraper." She jumped down from the table, giving Ethan the cue to bring up their first slide, a redesigned version of her company logo:

Steele Construction, Inc.

"Think about it," she said, pacing the room. "We all really want this project. Like, pay-the-rent, feed-our-kids really need this job. What company have you seen who will care that passionately? All these other guys, these other companies that are presenting to you—they're already set for life. What's one more skyscraper to them, right? But for me—this job will be my everything, and I am determined to get every aspect of it perfect. I will eat, sleep and dream this building until it is exactly what everyone in this room wants it to be."

Bridget knew she was taking a chance bringing up her failures; she knew that it would have been safer to just launch into her presentation and hope like hell that they focused on her strengths, but she also knew that her story, her collapse, was the nine-hundred-pound gorilla in the room, and if she didn't shoot it, skin it and then wear it as a fur coat first thing—she wouldn't stand a chance getting these guys to think about anything else.

She turned to her team, all sitting behind her, smiling at Ethan, handsome and confident in his thousand-dollar suit; Mrs. Hashemi in her little yellow sweater set; Lee, with his stylish three-piece ensemble and polka-dot bow tie; Ava, calm and collected and drop-dead gorgeous in a black vintage DVF wrap dress and cage heels; Redetzke, looking sweaty and out of place and totally freaked out by her presentation so far, but holding the keys to their success; and sweet, good Danny Schwartz, looking at her like she had hung the moon and the stars, and who had obviously pulled out his best shirt and tie and pressed them himself.

"This is my team. And yes, perhaps they may seem not exactly the type of people you are used to seeing in this business, but do not underestimate them. They are all the absolute best at what they do. You will not find a group with a greater well of knowledge about building in all of New York, and I am so excited for you to hear what they have to say."

She walked back to the center of the room. "We have been working on this presentation around the clock for weeks now. We have a vision for your building. Something big and bold and new and unforgettable." She turned to the team representing the anchor tenants. "Something that shows HealthTec cares. It will be cutting-edge and environmentally sound and you'll get as much publicity about the way we build it as you will about the final product." She shot a look at Ava, who grinned back. "We know we're going out on a limb—even bringing you a new architectural design. But we want to build something that will last for centuries. Something that will be here after we're all long gone. With

Steele Construction behind you, you can be sure that what is built will be what a skyscraper was always meant to be—a monument for the ages."

She looked over at Ethan, signaled him to dim the lights, turned back to face the table and began.

CHAPTER 73

Liam was nursing a scotch and soda at the bar when Jay finally showed up. As usual, every woman in the room followed him with her eyes as he made his way toward the bar, and, as usual, Jay took the attention for granted and didn't seem to notice a thing.

"Hey," said Jay as he slid onto the bar stool next to Liam and signaled the bartender. "So we're really doing this, huh?"

Liam gave him a little half smile. "Well, you showed, so I guess we are."

The bartender came over and Jay ordered a gin and cranberry. Liam rolled his eyes. "Still with the girly drinks?"

Jay laughed. "So how'd your presentation go?"

Liam took a drink. "We shit the bed. How about you?"

Jay shrugged. "It went all right. Decent, I guess."

Liam wondered whether that meant they had done well. Jay's blank face was not giving him much to go on. "Who's up next?" he said. "Did you cross paths with anyone going in?"

Jay nodded. "Bridget Steele," he said. "They were heading in just as I was heading out."

Liam raised his eyebrows. "Did she happen to have Alexander Redetzke with her?"

Jay laughed. "Yeah, as a matter of fact she did. How the hell did that happen?"

Liam shook his head. "Better ask your girl, man. She stabbed me right in the back while I was down-and-out."

"She's not my girl," said Jay. The waiter brought him his drink and he murmured a polite thanks.

"Oh, that's right," said Liam. "Why would you be with Bridget when you could be with Hana."

Jay took a sip of his drink and then gave him a dangerous smile. "Liam, you are really, really not in the position to complain about that particular subject," he said.

Liam knew he was right. He hadn't meant to bring it up, at least, not yet, and he certainly hadn't wanted to sound so bitter when he did. But it was out there now, so he figured he'd better just charge on.

"Have you seen her?" he said.

Jay laughed. "Who? Bridget? I told you, she was heading in as I was heading out."

"I could give a damn about Bridget. I'm talking about Hana."

"I know. I'm just messing with you."

Liam fought the urge to grab him by the collar. "Well, have you?"

Jay cocked his head. "Yeah. Last night as a matter of fact."

"Where? Why?"

"My place. Not that it's any of your business. She wanted to talk."

"About what?"

"All right, man. Slow your roll. I thought we were just gonna have a nice drink and try to pretend that we don't actually want to kill each other."

Liam felt a muscle in his jaw twitch. "I just want to know how she's doing," he said through gritted teeth.

Jay snorted. "No, you don't. You just want to know if I screwed her."

It took everything Liam had not to punch his friend right in the freaking face. Instead, he slowly picked up his glass and finished his drink in one, long gulp. His voice came out in a rasp. "Well, did you?"

Jay laughed in disbelief. "Jesus. Have you forgotten that Hana was my wife? That you slept with her while she was still married to me? Are we just skipping that part of the story now?"

Liam looked down at the bar. "You didn't deserve her," he said. "You never did."

"I—" He paused as both of their phones went off at once in loud, insistent peals of electronic music.

They looked at each other and then pulled out their cells.

"Jesus," said Jay after a moment. "Are you seeing the same thing I'm seeing?"

A blocked number had sent them both a link to a live video stream—of Bridget Steele doing her presentation for HealthTec. She was talking about how Steele Construction had reached out to cutting-edge experts all over the world in order to learn about the forefront in developing techniques that solved issues in safety, security, pollution and health. "We spoke to leading experts in India, the UK, Russia and China," she said as she paced excitedly. "We spoke to engineers and builders in Kuwait and Korea. We have the ability to build this project in an entirely new way."

Liam looked at Jay. "Someone's streaming her live. And look at the list of people this link got sent to. It's everyone in the freaking business. Do you think she knows?"

Jay shook his head. "No way. She's been keeping this as quiet as she could. She's a single mom. She's afraid of losing her job with the Ludleys if this doesn't work out."

"We'll use drones to provide progress reports and speed up construction by monitoring deliveries, and offer real-time updates on any changes that might need to be made," Bridget said. "Can you expand upon this a little, Alexander?"

The camera jerked over to Redetzke, who looked pink and sweaty, but eager to explain.

"Redetzke," growled Liam. "I should have known. This should have been my presentation."

"God," said Jay. "I thought we had this job all wrapped up, but she's actually killing it. This is kind of undeniable."

The camera pulled back and showed her entire crew. "Who's the old guy?" said Liam.

Jay squinted. "That must be Danny Schwartz. Someone she knows from her neighborhood in the Bronx."

"Wait," said Liam. "I heard about him. He's the one who pissed off the union, right? And she's still working with him?"

Jay nodded. "She's totally loyal to that guy. Brought him in on every job she's ever done." He smiled fondly at the image of Bridget on camera.

"Since your corporation is based upon health and wellness, we can offer things like designing a building with a smog-eating facade. There is a paint made from titanium dioxide that absorbs the fumes generated by traffic and converts them into harmless nitric acid and calcium nitrate before releasing them back into the air. Imagine the publicity that could generate. HealthTec not only heals their patients, they are also healing the earth."

"Damn," said Jay. "That's brilliant."

"I knew about that paint!" protested Liam. "Freaking Redetzke babbled about it for like two hours at lunch once. He wouldn't shut up."

Jay shook his head. "Yeah, but you weren't smart enough to listen to him."

"We can use 3-D printing to design shapes that have never been attempted before," continued Bridget. "Ava Martinez is our resident architectural expert and will explain the possibilities."

Liam watched Jay watching Bridget on his phone. He had a big, goofy grin on his face like a teenager with a crush.

He stuck his finger in Jay's face. "You've still got a thing for her, don't you?"

Jay looked up from the phone. "What? Who?"

"Bridget. You're screwing Hana, but you still want Bridget."

Jay sighed. "Jesus Christ, Liam. I'm not screwing my ex-wife, okay? Nothing is happening between us. There, are you happy?"

Liam blinked. "So wait, I've still got a chance?"

Jay shook his head. "You need to talk to her about that, man. Our friendship, whatever it is, definitely does not stretch this far."

Liam got up from the bar. "I gotta go. Thanks for the drink." He started to head for the door.

"Wait," Jay called after him, "so I'm paying?"

CHAPTER 74

"You killed it," whispered Ethan as they headed out the door. "Woman, you were magnificent."

Lee reached over from her other side and squeezed her arm. "The Ludleys have been wasting your talents. I had no idea you could deliver like that. We are actually going to get this crazy-ass job."

Bridget tried to tamp down what she knew must be a giddy grin on her face. They were right. She had killed it. The entire room had been in the palm of her hand from beginning to end.

"That was most well-done, my dear," said Mrs. Hashemi, patting her hand. "You really did your homework."

"Ms. Steele! Hang on!"

She turned around and saw Henry Kim heading her way. "Go on down, I'll catch up in a minute, guys," she told her crew.

"Don't be long!" said Ava. "We're going out and there will be champagne!"

"Lots of champagne!" promised Ethan.

Before he got onto the elevator, Danny Schwartz grabbed her shoulders in his hands and gave her a big kiss on the cheek.

"My girl!" he said. "Your father would have been so proud of you!"

Bridget swallowed the ache that suddenly bloomed in her throat. "Thank you, Danny," she whispered. "I'm so glad you were here."

"Ms. Steele!" Henry Kim was beaming at her. "I just had to come out and tell you that your presentation and team's expertise was top-notch. I'd heard you were good, but I had no idea. I mean, not only was it well thought out and exquisitely researched, but it was actually inspiring to watch! How often does that happen?"

Bridget smiled up at him. "It felt great," she admitted. "It felt really good to be pitching again."

He patted her shoulder. "It was a gamble bringing in a new architect, but—" he lowered his voice "—perhaps you heard that the one we hired has been struggling a bit? Anyway, HealthTec absolutely loved you. You know, we've got a couple more presentations to see, but…"

She smiled at him and then quickly craned past his shoulder, wondering why Harrington hadn't come out to congratulate her. Come to think of it, he'd been oddly quiet in the room as they said goodbye, as well…

"Whatever happens," she said, turning her attention back to Kim, "thank you for the opportunity. It was amazing to be out there again."

He grabbed her hand and pumped it up and down. "No, Ms. Steele," he said warmly, "thank you."

She rode the elevator down alone, looking at her reflection in the polished brass of the doors. She looked…happy, she thought. She was still smiling, still riding the high of the moment. Still feeling the glow of pulling it all off just like she had planned.

She wished she could call her dad and tell him all about

it. Danny had been right—he would have been proud. She laughed to herself, thinking about how he would have listened to her, thrilled, and then asked her a million questions, insisting he hear every little detail of the story, and then, after that, he would have made her repeat it all again from the very beginning.

She also had to admit that she wished she could call Jason. She wished she could call and compare notes; she wished he could have seen her in action; she wished that he wasn't such a stupid asshole who decided to go back to his stupid ex-wife. Seeing him in the hallway before she went in had given her just the shot of adrenaline she needed. She wanted him—oh, no doubt, as soon as she saw the man, she ached to touch him— but she wanted to beat him, as well. She'd heard the tail end of his conversation with Harrington. She knew he'd done a good job and that just made her determined to make sure she did better. He'd made her up her game.

The elevator dinged and the doors slid open to unveil her team, all still waiting for her, but the happy looks of triumph she had last seen them wearing were gone. They all looked sober and spooked.

Ava held up her cell phone. "Bridget, there's something you need to see."

CHAPTER 75

Liam was in a jewelry store. He had left the bar, thinking that he would go straight to the loft, needing to talk to Hana right away. But halfway there, he passed a shop window with a display of diamond rings set in the traditional black velvet-lined boxes, and then suddenly, he was in the shop.

As many times as he had asked Hana to marry him, he had never dared pick out an engagement ring. Right after she and Jay had become engaged, about a year after they all left college, she had gotten drunk at a party and confessed to Liam that she absolutely loathed the ring that Jay had given her.

It was a Russo family heirloom, a ten-carat, round, bezel-set diamond that Jay's grandmother had once worn as her own. It was platinum, flashy and ostentatious, and, Hana told Liam, she'd hated it on sight.

"It looks like some awful mob boss's pinky ring!" she giggled. "I feel like Lucky Luciano wearing it! But you can never, never, never tell Jason," she slurred as she lay her head against his shoulder. "Because Jay is a very nice guy and it's not his fault his grandmother had terrible taste in jewelry and I do not want to hurt his feelings."

Liam, who had been in a dark and desperate funk since the day Jay had confided that he was going to ask Hana to marry him, decided to take it as a sign and felt suddenly cheerful and light on his feet again. Anyone who knew Hana knew that the ring was all wrong. Obviously, it meant that she and Jay would never actually make it to the altar.

But, of course, they had. And Hana had loyally worn that ring for years. But after she and Liam started sleeping together, she kept her wedding band on, but lied and told Jay that the engagement ring was too tight and she needed to get it re-sized and then stuck it in a sock at the very back of her lingerie drawer. In all those years, she had never learned to loathe it any less. It had, she told Liam, just become more hideous to her every year.

Liam had bought a lot of jewelry for her since then. Ear-rings and necklaces and bracelets, and she had claimed to love them all. Once he'd even brought home a particularly-trashy gold ankle bracelet that turned him into a raging lump of lust whenever she indulged him by wearing it, but he'd never dared buy a ring.

That ended today, he decided, looking at a tray of diamonds. They were all wrong, of course. In fact, he was fairly certain that no diamond would do. There must be something better. He pushed the tray away and looked at the glass case beneath it—spying a glittering, dark red stone set in rose gold. "What's that?" he asked the woman behind the counter, who had been fluttering around him since he walked in the door.

"Oh, good eye," she said happily, plucking the ring up and handing it to him.

He held it up close to his face and wrinkled his nose. Suddenly, it wasn't red, it was sparkling, brilliant green.

"Alexandrite," the saleslady trilled. "It's one of the world's most precious gems. It appears red in candle or artificial light, and green in daylight."

He looked at it carefully. It was simple and strange and beautiful and he was almost certain that Hana would think so, too.

CHAPTER 76

Jay was still in the bar, rewatching the stream of Bridget kicking ass at her presentation, when the video went dark and "M. Harrington" lit up his screen. He hesitated for a moment, certain that he was going to be told that Russo Construction had lost the job.

He didn't care that much, honestly. He felt bad for his team, and especially Leela, who had worked so hard, but he knew what getting this job would mean to Bridget, and she obviously fully deserved it.

His hand hovered over the phone for another second, and then he swiped to answer, deciding it was best to be as gracious as possible about the loss.

"Jay?" said Harrington. He sounded rushed. "I suppose you've seen the video by now?"

"Bridget?" said Jay. "Yeah. I've seen it."

"She really came out of left field. I never thought she'd even make it this far."

"She was great," said Jay. "Do you know who was filming her?"

"Probably one of her people," muttered Harrington. "Having it out there makes it virtually impossible to walk away from her."

Jay blinked. "Why would you want to walk away? I haven't ever seen a presentation that good."

"Listen," said Harrington, ignoring his question. "Just hang in there. I'm going to see what I can do. She's got Kim in her pocket, and the HealthTec guys are slobbering all over her, but this isn't over yet. I want to do things the way we used to. The way your dad and I used to run the business."

"You really don't have to do that, Mark," said Jay. "Russo Construction can take the loss just fine."

"Don't worry about it. I'll find a fix, okay? And in the meantime, I'm going to have my girl send you over a list of vendors and subcontractors we like to work with. You can take this time to line them up."

"Mark, seriously—"

"I gotta go, Jay. I'll talk to you real soon. Hang in there, okay? I've got this covered."

Jay put his phone down and shook his head. Then he picked it back up and called Leela.

"Hey," she said glumly. "I saw the video. We didn't get the job, did we?"

"Well," he said, "that's why I'm calling. Nothing is actually decided yet. It's a little complicated. But I need you to do something for me. We keep all predigital copies of the records for the company in a storage locker in Midtown. I want you to go find the papers for the Starbucks deal that my father did with Mark Harrington. 1994 or '95, I think. I need your eyes on those pages."

"Okay," she answered. "Anything special I'm looking for?"

He hesitated. "You'll know it if you see it," he said at last. "And honestly, I really hope you don't see anything at all."

CHAPTER 77

"We are very disappointed in you, Bridget," said Linus Lumley.

"You, too, Christopher," said Larry. "But mainly Bridget."

The brothers were sitting at their desks, not even bothering to stand as they delivered their lecture.

"It's especially hurtful to us that you so obviously leveraged the influence you gained through working for Ludley Construction to try to steal our employees and a job that should have rightfully been ours," intoned Linus in a pious voice. "We basically picked you up from the gutter. No one else would hire you and we took you on out of the pure kindness of our hearts. And this is how you repay us?"

"And people wonder why there aren't more women working in this industry," clucked Larry.

"You exploited our sense of compassion for your own gains," said Linus. "By all rights and measures, we should fire you."

She wanted to laugh, but out of habit, Bridget held her tongue.

"However," said Linus, "we suppose we might be convinced

to look beyond this incident if you bring Ludley Construction into this job. I suppose you could still be an assistant project manager, but Larry and I would take over as the project executives and Ludley Brothers would take on the construction management role, of course."

"We have an excellent relationship with Mark Harrington," said Larry. "My daughter actually went to grade school with his eldest son. I'm sure he'd be more than pleased to see that the job was safely in more experienced hands."

This time Bridget did laugh. She darted a look at Lee, who was also obviously trying to keep a straight face, and then she couldn't hold it in anymore. She giggled. Then Lee giggled, which only made her laugh harder. Then she looked at the Ludleys, who both looked so offended that she tipped back her head and basically howled.

For a whole year she'd been forced to put up with these assholes. She'd given a pass to every condescending lecture, every patronizing pet name, every leer, every "accidental" touch, and, worst of all, their insistence on chronically underestimating her intelligence and skill. She had stood in this office and taken it all and reminded herself that she needed the job, she needed the money, that she had a child to support, and that she just had to shut up and never, ever call them out.

But, she realized with a rush of delight, that was over now. She took a deep breath and wiped her eyes.

"Screw you," she said calmly. "Screw both of you. You can't fire me because I quit. And I'm taking Lee with me."

"Yeah!" chimed in Lee. "I quit, too, and I'm going with Steele!"

"Well, now, wait," said Larry. "No need to be so hasty—"

"Oh, this is not hasty," said Bridget. "Do you know how many times I have wanted to quit this past year? Do you know that there hasn't been one day since we met that I didn't want to tell you to shove this job up your ass? I did my job and I did it well for you guys. I brought in client after client. And you guys still insisted on treating me either like a stupid child or a pair of tits you bought to decorate the office."

"Hey, now," said Linus. "Slow down, honey—"

Bridget stepped forward and slammed her hands on their desks. *"Do. Not. Call. Me. Honey."*

The brothers reared back, fear in their eyes.

Lee put a hand on her shoulder. "She's not wrong, guys," he said. "You're real assholes." He pulled on her arm. "Okay, Steele, time to go."

She took a deep breath and let him lead her out of the room, but then, at the last second she turned around and stuck her head back in the door. "Linus!" she said sharply.

Linus and Larry cringed.

"That mole on your neck? It's disgusting. Nobody wants to look at it, and I'm pretty sure it's going to kill you. For God's sake, get it checked!"

"What mole?" she heard him say as she walked away. "What is she talking about?"

CHAPTER 78

With the ring in his pocket, Liam ran the last ten blocks to the loft, hoping that Hana would be home. His conversation with Jay had sent him flying, filled with hope, though he was starting to curse the fact that he hadn't probed a little deeper before he left. Who had made the decision not to get back together, for instance? Jay or Hana? Maybe it was mutual? That suddenly seemed like something he should have taken the time to find out.

He reached his street and slowed down, giving his phone a cursory look. He knew he should probably text first, or call, but this was a conversation he wanted to have face-to-face, and he really didn't want to give Hana the chance to refuse to see him altogether.

It's my loft, anyway, he reasoned as he hit the button for the freight elevator up to his place. He had every right to return if he chose to.

He had his key out and had almost put it in the door when he stopped, suddenly afraid of what he might find. What if she's not alone? He shook his head. He was being ridiculous.

He knew she wasn't with Jay, and it wasn't like she was going to run out and find someone in the meantime. He needed to shake this off and go in, he told himself. Still, he put his keys back in his pocket and prepared to knock instead.

A voice came from behind him. "Liam? What are you doing?"

It was Alli, home from school, carrying her backpack and looking at him with wide eyes.

"Oh, hey. Hi, Alli. How are you?"

She reached past him and unlocked the door with her own key. "I'm fine. But I think the bigger question is how are you?"

"I—I was hoping your mom was home. We need to talk." He followed her in sheepishly.

"No shit," she said. "Mom!" she called. "Mom!"

"Hi! Hi! I'm upstairs," called Hana back. "I'll be down in a second!"

"Mom! Liam is here!"

There was silence. No answer.

Alli looked at him and raised her eyebrows. "So that went well."

He bit his lip. "Do you think I should go up?"

Alli turned to him, her hands on her hips and her eyes blazing. "How should I know? I have zero idea what's going on with you guys. One day you two are all over each other, the next you move out. You just ghost—not a word to me about anything. Mom gives me this whole stupid story about how you're taking time apart to figure things out. Well, guess what? Last time she said that, she and my dad got divorced." Her voice caught on a little sob and tears filled her eyes. "I mean, I know you're not technically my stepdad. I know that you don't have to be in my life if you don't want to. But I thought you at least liked me enough to talk to me one last time before you just disappeared, you know?"

He stared at her for a moment, stricken. "Oh, God, Alli. I'm sorry. I—I never meant to disappear. My plan has always been to come back and I was just trying to figure out how to make that happen. You're absolutely right, though. I should have talked to you. And listen, no matter what happens between your mom and me, I want you to know that I will always be around if you need me. I think of you as my kid, I really do. Even if I don't do a great job showing that all the time."

She sniffed. "You do?"

He stepped over and put his arms around her. "Yeah. I really do. I love you, kiddo."

She clung to him for a moment and then stepped back, wiping her eyes. "Okay. This is getting a little too extra. Go on up. Maybe she's not, like, totally crazy today."

He laughed. "Thanks for the pep talk."

She waved him up the stairs. "Mom!" she called. "Stop hiding! Liam is coming up!"

Hana was standing in the middle of their bedroom, her back toward him. He could tell from the way her shoulders were set that she was tense and miserable. All he wanted to do was cross the room and take her into his arms but he forced himself to stop and wait.

"I'm not sure I'm ready to talk to you," she said without turning around.

"I heard that you and Jay aren't happening," he blurted out.

She swiveled around, surprise on her face. "Where did you hear that?"

"Jay," he admitted.

She blinked. "So you guys are buddies again?"

"Something like that." He shrugged. "Maybe not totally just yet."

"Oh. Liam, listen, now isn't a—"

"Don't say that," he said. "You can't say that. You owe me an explanation, Hana. You know you do."

She sighed and sank down on the edge of the bed. She was wearing a sleeveless black cotton shift dress. Her hair was piled up and secured with a drawing pencil. Her feet were bare. She looked achingly beautiful. "You hate our dining room table," she said at last.

He frowned. "What?"

"Our dining room table. The one that I brought over with me when I moved in. You hate it."

"No, I don't."

"Yes. You do. But you still wanted it. You insisted that I take it with me. Why was that?"

He shrugged. "I knew you liked it. You were already giving up a lot. I wanted you to have it."

She shook her head. "I think you wanted it because you knew that Jay loved it."

He laughed. "What? What are you talking about?"

"You hate that table, Liam. You think it's tacky and cheap and that it doesn't go with anything in your place, but you wanted it, anyway. Because you want everything that he has."

He scrubbed his hand through his hair in frustration. "Okay. I see where you're going with this. And no, I don't want you because you were Jay's, Hana. I've wanted you since the moment I laid eyes on you."

"Yes. While I was on Jay's arm."

"Jesus Christ." He paced the room. "So you think I don't love you?"

"I think that you think you love me. I think that you desire me and like claiming me. I think you like to win and I'm tangible proof that you won. I think you like to take me out and show me off. I think you like to hold me, caress me like I'm some precious ornament that you acquired. But I also think that, if you had met me in any other circumstances, if I hadn't already been with Jay—you wouldn't have looked twice."

"That's insane!" he exploded. "Why are you even with me if you think that's true?"

"Because I do love you, Liam! I didn't choose you because I wanted to be with someone else. I didn't end up with you so I could win anything. I left Jay because I fell hopelessly, terribly in love with you! And it's horrible! It's horrible to love someone who doesn't really know you at all!"

He was stunned. He felt as if he'd been punched. "This is crazy," he said. "Of course I love you, Hana."

"No. You hate yourself. And you're desperately trying to be someone else. Namely, Jay. I mean, look at you. Look at the life you choose to live. You have a job that you never wanted. You live in a city that you can barely tolerate. You have a dining room table that—"

"The hell with the table!" he yelled. He grabbed the nearest thing, a glass vase full of violets on the bureau, and smashed it to the ground.

They were quiet. Both of them breathing heavily. Hana looked at the floor, refusing to meet his eyes.

Finally, she spoke. Her voice was quiet. "I hurt all the time, Liam. I love you so much and I look at you and I think, he has no idea who I really am. I can't work. I can't be a decent parent to Alli. I can't be anyone's friend. I'm constantly trying to fix things between us. I keep thinking that I can fight past this image of who you think I am and make you see me. Or even, maybe I can just actually become who you want me to be. But I can't." She slumped onto the bed again. "And I'm too exhausted to keep trying. This is not your life, Liam. I am not your love. This is all just what you think you should want. And I can't keep living with that."

She stood up. "I have something for you."

He was numb as he watched her cross the room and go to the closet. She pulled out a small parcel—wrapped in brown paper.

"I just finished this," she said, unwrapping a painting and handing it to him. "It's the first piece I've done in a year."

It was his portrait. He was naked, in a bed full of fruit and vines and flowers and insects, surrounded by fecundity and rich, blooming life. But his face... He recoiled when he saw how she'd painted his face. Oh, it looked like him, all right. Her portraits were hyperreal and she had an eerie way of taking someone's likeness and replicating it so that you felt seen on an almost uncomfortable level. But the expression on his face... It was a sexual painting. His body looked postcoital to him, relaxed and spent. But instead of the sleepy, satisfied look he thought she might create, which, really, was intimate enough already, he looked sad. And lost. It made him feel sick to see it.

She looked at him carefully. "You don't like it."

He shook his head. "No, it's beautiful. It's just that—"

She stopped him. "It's okay. I don't think I like it, either." She reached out and grazed it with her finger. "But it's true. It's what came out once I really let go. And when I finished, when I saw what I'd done—that's when I knew—" she shrugged sadly "—we're never going to work."

He gently placed the painting down against the wall. Suddenly, he was exhausted. "Actually, I have something for you, too." He fished the ring box out of his jacket pocket. "It's probably not appropriate at this point, but..."

Her eyes went wide when she opened the box. She slipped the ring onto her right hand ring finger and held it up to the light. "Alexandrite," she said, smiling. "My mother had a necklace."

He shook his head. "Of course you already know what it is."

She looked at him; her eyes were full of sadness. "It's perfect," she said.

★ ★ ★

After he left the loft, Liam stood on the street for a moment, trying to get his bearings. He was full of churning emotion; sadness and anger and a loss so deep that he felt dizzy. He was thinking of Hana, of course, seeing her face as he walked out the door, and he was thinking of Alli, wondering how he would keep his promise to her, but he was also thinking of Jay. He was thinking that if Hana was right—and he still couldn't even begin to decide whether she was right or not—then he had pulled Jay's life apart for no reason at all. Jay and Hana could still be together. Alli's family would be intact. He was a selfish asshole, and he wanted to do something to make it up to Jay.

He pulled out his phone and made a call.

"Hey, Sal. It's Liam Maguire… I'm guessing you saw that live stream of Bridget Steele going for the HealthTec build? Well, there was a part of it that I wanted to make sure you didn't miss…"

CHAPTER 79

Jay and Leela were sitting on the floor of his office and going through stacks of old, dusty files.

Leela's eyes and nose were running. "Did I mention that I'm allergic to dust?" she said as she sneezed for the fifth time in a row.

"Sorry," said Jay. "You don't have to do this with me."

"Oh," she sniffed, "I'm in it now. Might as well. But God—" she opened a new file and sneezed again "—please promise me you'll let me have these all scanned and digitized when we're done. This is positively primitive."

They were looking for records of the last ten years of Jay's father's time as CEO of Russo Construction. They had already found all the contracts with Harrington, more than Jay ever knew about, and now they needed to see similar projects that his father had done in the same time period to compare.

"Hmm," said Leela, wrinkling her nose at a file. "Here's another one that's interesting. Really close to the build-out that your dad did with Harrington about six months before. Same square footage, similar Class-A building and office finishes. And look," she said, pointing at some numbers, "nearly one half less in charges."

"Shit," said Jay, taking the paper out of her hands and squinting at it. "Some of the same people working for him, too. God damn it."

"So," said Leela, "do you want to actually talk about the fact that we're sitting here digging up proof that your dad was bid rigging with Harrington or should I just keep looking through the papers and pretending I don't know what's going on?"

Jay threw the file down with a little slap and leaned back against the wall with his eyes closed. "He was, wasn't he? Shit. My dad was totally breaking the law in like fifty different ways."

"Well," said Leela as she picked her way through the mess on the floor and leaned up against the wall next to him, "it seems like he only did it with Mark Harrington, if that makes it any better."

"Somehow that makes it worse," he said. He opened his eyes and looked at Leela. "You never met my dad but he was…difficult, in a lot of ways. He wasn't particularly warm or supportive. He worked too much and he certainly wasn't any fun. But he was moral, you know? I mean, the construction industry has a history of being corrupt, no doubt. You know how bad it can be. But back then, it was horrifying. The mob and all the politicians, the unions, everyone had their hand in the cookie jar. Except my dad. He was literally known as the last honest contractor in New York. His reputation was impeccable. And he was so proud of that. He always told me that if something couldn't be done honestly, it wasn't worth doing. And when I took over, I swore to myself that I would follow that same path. I mean, I regret a lot of ways that I ended up being like my dad—I work too much, I'm probably not much fun, but being honest was always the one connection I had with him that felt good."

"And what now? I'm assuming you won't work with Harrington."

"No," he said. "I don't want to have anything to do with him. But if I don't—"

"Someone else will."

"Exactly. And listen, I mean, bid rigging seems fairly harmless. What's the big deal? But it's actually everything that's wrong about this industry. It's why the same five families have had all the business for the past fifty years. It's why no one new can ever break in. It's why undocumented workers get hired and paid nearly nothing to do the worst work. And it's literally dangerous. It means that builders and developers are skimping on safety measures. It means people might get hurt or even die. It's wrong. And I hate that my dad was involved in it."

"So what are you going to do?"

He shook his head. "I don't know. If I make this public, it will ruin my family's reputation. I mean, I'm proud of my dad. Or, at least I used to be. It would really hurt to expose him like this."

"Not to mention what it will do to the business," said Leela. "We'll lose all sorts of work. It might shut things down permanently."

He looked at her. "You think?"

She raised her eyebrows. "Being known as the guy who snitched on his dead dad isn't exactly going to make you a hero in this industry."

"God," he groaned. "You're right." He looked at the stacks of files and shook his head. "Well, let's keep looking. Maybe we'll find something that proves my dad wasn't totally corrupt."

CHAPTER 80

So far, Bridget, Lee, Mrs. Hashemi, Ethan and Ava had all lost their jobs. The live stream had shot through the office buildings of everyone remotely connected to real estate, architecture, development or building in the city, and anyone who was in that room that day who wasn't supposed to be was called onto the carpet and immediately dismissed.

"It will be okay, it will be okay, it will be okay," promised Bridget to herself as she walked into The Polo Bar and was greeted by the kind of maître d' who looked like he would throw himself in front of anyone trying to get in with less than A-list status.

"I'm meeting Mark Harrington for dinner," said Bridget, and her magic words were immediately rewarded with a warm smile and an escort downstairs to the dining room.

Everything was perfect in The Polo Bar. The lighting, which made even the most hungover and haggard of celebrities look as if they were lit with their own personal halo capable of taking ten years off their skin; the staff, who were beautiful and knowledgeable and hovered just enough to make you feel important; the interior design, because, well, Ralph Lauren; the people dining there, because there was at least one A-list celebrity for every anonymous, super-wealthy power player hiding in plain sight; and the food, which was casual and elegant and never too challenging.

Harrington had called Bridget the day before, inviting her for dinner, and she had been delighted. She had started to get a little worried when she didn't hear back from Harrington & Kim after the first couple of days, but now she was certain that she would be landing the contract for the HealthTec job.

"Bridget," Harrington said, smiling and rising to kiss her hello. He was seated in a coveted corner table and already had a bottle of champagne on ice hovering off to the side.

Bridget smiled back as she sat down. "Did you already order for me?" she teased.

He smiled sheepishly. "Just the appetizers and the wine. I'll let you choose your own dinner."

She laughed. "You never learn, do you?"

The waiter came over to pour champagne for both of them.

"To your amazing presentation," said Harrington, lifting his glass.

She met it with a clink. "Thank you. I'm so glad you liked it." She sipped her drink and then laughed. "We're still trying to figure out who filmed it, though. That part has been a little crazy."

Harrington smiled and took a drink and then picked up his menu. "So what are you going to have? I wholeheartedly recommend the pastrami sandwich. It's Ralph's personal favorite."

Bridget looked at him carefully, noting the way he had side-stepped the subject. "What's your guess on who sent out that link, Mark?"

Harrington put down his menu. "Listen. We should just get all the work talk out of the way so we can enjoy a nice dinner and whatever else we like for the rest of the night, eh? So let's start with the headline. I'm sorry to tell you this, but we've decided to go with Russo Construction."

Inwardly, Bridget exploded in panic. She didn't have a job. Her team didn't have jobs. She was well and truly screwed and she was taking down some of her favorite people with her. *Again.*

"What?" she said, searching for words.

Harrington waved his drink in the air. "You were great, of course you were great, and I think we will certainly be happy to consider you for work in the future, but it turns out that HealthTec just can't risk hiring your firm since you are a start-up, and your track record doesn't have a history of you being union friendly with large-scale projects."

Bridget shook her head. "Wait. What are you talking about? Steele Construction will become a signatory of the union and only use union labor."

Harrington shrugged. "Well, you know, you say that, but you proved pretty clearly that it's not true. I mean, you brought Daniel Schwartz into the actual presentation, and a little birdie told me that this was the same guy who brought in the scabs for the Scarlett Hawkins job you got fired on, right?"

She shook her head. "No, that wasn't his fault and it won't happen again. Danny has worked on countless union jobs before this with no problem."

Harrington smiled and nodded. "Well, yeah, I know they know about him. Because Sal Delmonico, the head of Local 6, tipped us off to just who Daniel Schwartz was. That doesn't sound like you're very union friendly, Bridget."

"Wait, Sal? He's had it out for me for years. Ever since he got a little too handsy with me on a walk-through. I'm not even going to pull the guys from that hall this time around, I'm going with the 233."

Harrington nodded thanks at the waiter as he brought them oysters and pigs in a blanket. He pushed a plate toward Bridget. "Here, try these. They're delicious."

She ignored him. "Are you hearing me, Mark?"

He looked at her. Suddenly, his smile grew very ugly. "You know, Bridget, when you got into this industry, I think you knew what you were in for. You knew that you'd be the only woman in the room. You knew that men were going to be slobbering all over you and asking you for dates and telling you that you looked pretty. And I think you liked it. I think you liked the attention and you liked feeling in control, and I think it's probably ninety-nine percent of the reason you're even doing what you do. So when you get all 'Me, too! Me, too! I was sexually harassed!' I just find it to be really unattractive."

Bridget felt like her head was going to explode. "That's not what I was saying. I was saying—"

"You were never going to get this job, Bridget," Mark snapped. "I brought you in because the clients wanted to see some diversity. That's it. And I filmed you because I knew you were in over your head, and I was sure you'd embarrass yourself publicly, and then there'd be no question of anyone insisting you get hired just because you're a woman and they want to look progressive. And I'll admit, that backfired, because you did better than I thought you would do. But aside from the utter disrespect you showed, bringing in a new architect, how could I live with myself if I chose some outsider, some inexperienced girl, over a man with a family who's been in this business for years? It just doesn't make any sense."

Bridget closed her eyes. She felt like she was having an out-of-body experience, and yet, at the same time, she had been in this exact place so many times before. "No," she said softly. "No. I am so freaking tired of this. I can't win. No matter how hard I work, you guys will just not make room for me."

He shook his head. "Come on. You can't expect to just show up and smile pretty and be handed everything you want. You're not from around here. You don't understand how things work."

She took a deep breath, willing herself to keep her voice calm. "I can't even begin to tell you all the ways you are wrong right now. And obviously, I'm not going to change your mind, so I think I'm just going to leave."

She jumped when she felt a hand on her hand. She opened her eyes and Mark was staring at her with what he seemed to think was a sincere look on his face. "Listen, I know you worked hard, and I'm sorry it didn't pan out this time, but I could mentor you, you know. I could teach you everything I know. About the business and—" he gave her a shark-like smile and squeezed her hand "—anything else you're curious about."

Bridget snatched her drink and tossed it in Harrington's face before she could even think. He jumped up with a yell, champagne dripping from his face onto the tablecloth.

"You bitch!" he screamed as he lunged across the table. "You god damned bitch!"

It was as if her father was there in the room with her, telling her exactly what she had to do to keep safe. To win.

Put your thumb outside your fist, darling. Between your first and second knuckles. Keep your wrist straight. Now, come in at a slight angle, aiming upward at his nose. Roll your hips into it. Aim for two inches beyond that nose so you can really hit him hard. Short, hard jab, darling. Now, go!

Bridget felt Harrington's nose crunch under her fist as she hit it, saw the blood spurt as he screamed out and doubled over, his hands clutched over his face.

"Yeah," she spat at him as he stayed bent over, his back heaving, dark red blood oozing between his fingers, "you're right, Mark. I'm not from around here." He looked up at her, and she saw fear in his eyes. "And I advise that you never forget that."

CHAPTER 81

Scarlett's pit bulls had taken a liking to Liam and gave him too much attention when he was in the mansion, so Scarlett got jealous and banished him to the guesthouse.

"You'd think they'd know which side of their bread has the butter on it, wouldn't you?" she said with disgust as she watched her dogs taking turns trying to knock Liam over with their enthusiastic greeting. "It's like you're a bitch in heat."

Liam pushed off a particularly fat, silvery-gray dog and shook his head. "Why'd you bring them out here, then?"

"Oh," said Scarlett, waving them back out the door, "I told them I was going out to retrieve you for dinner, and they all insisted on coming along. Out, out, out now." She shoved the last one out and shut the door behind them. They all crowded at the door and stared at them mournfully through the glass. "Ignore them. They look tragic but really they just want to hump your leg. Now let's have a nice little chew and chat before we eat. Get me a vodka and tonic, please."

When Liam had shown up at Scarlett's door three days before, she hadn't seemed surprised at all. "Things not going so

well, Maguire?" she asked in a voice several notches kinder
than he had ever heard from her before. "Well, I don't have
anything planned for the next few days, so why don't you just
come on in?"

He didn't know he was heading for Scarlett's. He had told
himself that he was going to the Hamptons because he was
sick of the Greenwich Hotel and he had a huge house on the
beach just sitting empty. Hana had offered to move out of the
loft, but he'd told her to take her time finding something else.
He didn't want Alli to feel displaced.

But once he got to the Hamptons, he drove right by his own
driveway and straight on to Scarlett's.

First, he had convinced himself that he wanted to confront
her about making him lose Alexander Redetzke. But she just
laughed when he had started to complain about that.

"Oh, bless your heart, of course I was helping out Bridget.
At least at first. But really, the way you were treating that boy,
you were lucky he just quit and didn't poison your coffee on
the way out. He was ripe for the plucking. So I bought you at
auction and kept you around to give Bridget some time—make
sure she could close the deal, you know—but I was pleasantly
surprised to find that I actually liked you. Plus—" she gave him
a wink "—I was worried that if you went home any sooner,
you might walk in front of a bus."

Since then, he had been spending every day the same way,
having coffee by the pool in the morning, then meeting Scarlett and her pack of dogs for a long walk on the beach. His job
was to be on the lookout for Bono. Then they would lunch,
usually in the garden, then he would get on the phone and
check in to work, and pretend he cared, and then he and Scarlett would meet for dinner in the solarium. She said she liked
the trees. After dinner they would linger, nursing a nightcap
or sometimes sharing a joint.

"Hmm," said Scarlett as she settled on the couch and looked around. "I never come out here anymore. I rather think it might need a freshening up. I believe the last time I renovated was three or four years ago."

"It's perfect, Scarlett," he said. "Don't touch a thing."

He realized that he had yet to walk through and catalog the house. Something he'd never been able to avoid doing after more than twenty-four hours in any one place. He wondered what that meant.

"You know," said Scarlett, accepting the vodka and tonic, "it's really too bad that I find men's bodies about as appealing as fuzzy cheese, and I'm probably twenty years and fifty pounds outside your preferences, because I do believe that you and I just might be soul mates, Liam Maguire."

He laughed and sat down next to her. "Well, that seems kind of complicated."

"No, I think it's rather lovely. If we were to be romantically involved, I'd drop you like a stale cake in a week or two, but this—" she nestled next to him and put her head on his shoulder "—this I can see lasting."

They sat in silence for a moment.

"But you know you can't stay forever," she murmured.

"I know."

"But you can always come back if you want."

He smiled and kissed the top of her head.

CHAPTER 82

"The hell with you, Jason Russo! The hell with you and the hell with Harrington! You are a soulless piece of crap to be working with him!"

Jay blinked at the apparition standing in his office door. "Um. Hi, Bridget."

She stormed in, a whirlwind in a tight purple Gucci dress and heels, her long brown hair wavy and electric around her face. "Don't you 'hi' me," she growled. "Do you know how many people's lives you have ruined?"

"Should I call security?" said Leela.

Bridget whirled on her. "And who the hell are you?"

"This is my COO, Leela Rajan," said Jay mildly. "Leela, this is Bridget Steele."

"Oooh!" said Leela. "I knew I recognized you! Hey, really nice job on that presentation. You totally knocked it out of the park."

"Thank you," said Bridget. For a moment she was distracted. "That's very nice of you to say." Then she turned back to Jay and poked him in the chest with a pointy blue fingernail.

"You have a ton of stuff to answer for, Russo. First of all, you dumped me for your ex-wife."

"You did?" said Leela.

"It didn't work out," said Jay.

"It didn't?" said Leela.

"Then you tipped off freaking Sal Delmonico about Danny's involvement with the presentation."

"Oh, no, that wasn't me. That was Liam. And he's sorry he did it. He thought he was doing me a favor. And okay, maybe he was kind of pissed at you for poaching Redetzke. But hey, if we're playing this game, you stole my budget!"

Bridget looked sheepish for a moment, but she rallied. "Yeah, okay, but you stole my skyscraper!"

"Well," said Leela.

"And now," continued Bridget, "I have six people from my team that all need jobs and I think you should hire all of them."

Jay and Leela looked at each other and laughed.

"That might be difficult," said Leela. "Since we're not moving forward with the HealthTec project."

"What?" said Bridget. "What are you talking about?"

Jay let out a long breath and gestured to the couch. "Why don't you have a seat?"

Bridget sat down, warily keeping her eyes on him as he pulled out a folder from his desk. "Here," he said, handing her the papers, "take a look at these."

He watched Bridget's face change as she read through the papers, from puzzled to a dawning awareness of what she was looking at.

God damn, he thought as he waited, *I miss her.*

Finally, she looked up, wide-eyed. "So your dad and Harrington?"

"Yup," said Jay.

"And is he trying to rig the project with you now?"

"Yup," said Jay.

"And who are you taking these to?"

"I'm sending copies to the District Attorney and Health-Tec. I figure they're going to pull out as anchor tenants, but, doesn't matter now."

"What about Henry Kim? Do you think he's in on it?"

Jay shook his head. "I don't think so. From what I understood, he really wanted to hire you. It was only after Delmonico got involved that he backed down."

Suddenly, Bridget's face lit up. "Oh, wait, do you think Delmonico was in on any of this?"

Leela grinned. "It's looking pretty bad for him." She looked over at Jay and clapped her hands. "Hey! This is super-fun!"

Jay laughed. He looked over at Bridget, who smiled at him.

And suddenly, he felt his whole world open up again.

"Psst, Jay," said Leela, elbowing him in the ribs, "after this place falls apart, I'm going to go work for this crazy lady, okay?"

CHAPTER 83

Bridget was just about to put Dylan to bed when there was a knock on her door.

"Scarlett?" she said, opening the door and finding the world-famous celebrity standing in her tenement hallway. "What the hell are you doing here?"

"Well, hello to you, too," said Scarlett. "May I come in?"

"Mommy?" said Dylan. He was wearing his pajamas and had toothpaste on his chin.

"My, my," said Scarlett, beaming down at him. "Don't you look adorable. You probably don't remember me, but I knew you when you were a tiny little baby. My name is Ms. Scarlett."

"Hello," said Dylan. "I'm not a baby anymore, just so you know."

"Well, yes, I can see that. So how old are you now?" She looked genuinely puzzled. "I'm going to guess around, what, three?"

"No!" said Dylan, mortally offended. "I'm almost eight."

"Oh," said Scarlett, shrugging. "All children sort of look the same to me. I honestly can't guess their ages until after they're well through puberty."

"Mommy," said Dylan, looking hopefully at Bridget. "Since we have a guest, do I get to stay up?"

She laughed. "Nope. Say good-night to Ms. Scarlett." She looked over at the older woman. "You don't mind, do you? I'll just be a minute."

Scarlett grandly gestured her approval. "I'll just make myself comfortable," she said. She wrinkled her nose. "I assume there's some wine in this thing you call a kitchen?"

Bridget laughed as she scooped up Dylan. "In the fridge," she said over her shoulder as she headed down the hall.

"The rest of your home seems very nice!" called Scarlett as if she suddenly remembered her manners. "It's just your kitchen that looks like it sucks!"

"Thanks, Scarlett!" called back Bridget.

"I'm not tired," said Dylan as she tucked him into bed.

She kissed his bright little head. "Yes, you are. It's late. Now, I'm setting a timer. You can draw in bed for ten minutes, but then straight to sleep, okay? I'll read you an extra chapter of the book tomorrow."

He smiled up at her, pulling out his sketchbook. "Did you see this one, Mommy?"

She looked at it and laughed, a bit rueful.

"It's you and the skyscraper you're going to build."

She nodded and smoothed his hair, wishing she had never said anything to him about the project. "I can see that. It's really good, my love. Thank you." She gave him another kiss. "Good night, sweetie."

"Good night, Mommy."

Scarlett was standing at her kitchen counter, suspiciously reading the label on a bottle of wine. "I thought you were a Domaines Ott girl," she commented as she put the bottle down and pushed it away with a disappointed little shove of her fingers.

Bridget shrugged. "Can't afford it these days," she said. "Not until I find another job, at least."

Scarlett nodded and squared her shoulders. "And that is exactly why I am here."

Bridget looked hopeful. "Do you have a job for me?"

"Oh," said Scarlett, looking uncomfortable. "Well, no. I mean, I'm sure I could come up with something, but no, I'm here because I heard that you were rather down and out. And as I recall from a recent conversation, it is important to offer one's support for your friends when they are going through a difficult time. So here I am. All the way in the East Village, offering you my support and condolences."

Bridget laughed a surprised little laugh and then was embarrassed to find tears spring into her eyes, which she quickly dashed away. "Thank you, Scarlett. Seriously. I really mean that."

"Oh, now," said Scarlett and gave her a quick little hug. She picked up the wine again. "Maybe I'll have just a teeny-weeny little glass? I mean, how bad can it be?"

"Oh, it's bad," said Bridget, laughing. "You're totally going to hate it."

Scarlett took a tentative swig from the bottle and shrugged. "I've had worse. Go ahead, get me a jam jar or whatever ridiculous thing you serve your alcohol in."

Bridget took down two glasses and poured the wine.

"To you," said Scarlett, lifting her glass. "May all these troubles be behind you soon. And also, actually," she said smiling shyly, "to me. My company went public today and it did quite nicely."

"Oh, Scarlett!" said Bridget. "I forgot! That's great!"

Scarlett waved off her congratulations. "Yes, well, I'm not

here to talk about that. Just didn't want the night to pass without a little acknowledgment. It's a rather big moment, I suppose."

They clinked and drank.

Scarlett smacked her lips. "Not that bad at all, really. Now, back to you. I saw that cursed video, by the way. You were amazing."

Bridget raised her eyebrows. "A lot of good that did me."

"And how are you handling all this?"

Bridget laughed. "Which part? The man or the job?"

"Oooh," said Scarlett, pouring more wine. "I did not realize that a man was back in the picture."

Bridget felt her cheeks get hot. "I don't know. Maybe. We've been talking, that's all."

"All right, then, if that's all you have to report, then what about the job?"

Bridget sighed. "You know, if it was just me, it would be okay. I can hustle. I'll find work. I'll be fine. But it's all the other people I screwed over. They all lost their jobs because of me and now they're high and dry."

"But you said they were all very good at what they do."

"I mean, yes, they are, but being good doesn't always mean it all works out, right? I mean, I'm damn smart. But look—I'm not out there building a skyscraper."

Scarlett nodded. "Well, no one is now that Mark Harrington was indicted and might be going to jail." She smiled smugly. "I can't wait to see him get taken down. I never could stand that man. Once he said to me that I just needed the right cock to come to my senses." She rolled her eyes. "Can you imagine? I mean, maybe that miracle cock exists somewhere, but it is certainly not attached to a no-count man like him!" She sipped her wine. "What happens to the piece of land that was being developed, anyway? It was in a rather excellent spot downtown, if I recall."

"Oh, yeah," said Bridget. "It's prime. I think Henry Kim and the rest of the partners will be able to buy Harrington out. But anything they do is going to be kind of tainted for a while. Everyone thinks that if one partner was corrupt, all the rest of them probably are, too, you know?"

Scarlett nodded thoughtfully. "So they'll either have to hold on to it for quite a while, or they'll have to sell cheap."

Bridget shrugged. "Maybe."

"Hmm," said Scarlett, pouring out the last of the wine evenly between the two cups. "Hmm. You know what? Go ahead and lift your glass, darlin', because I have a little idea."

CHAPTER 84

"Wait, wait, wait," said Henry Kim, shaking his head, "you want to do what?"

Bridget, Scarlett and Ava all grinned at him from across the table.

"I want a skyscraper," said Scarlett. "Since I went public, I need new headquarters for Scarlett Hawkins Incorporated, and I want a whole building to myself. All designed to my personal specifications. We have talked about this, and we want to design the building based on curves. It should be organic, sexy and have hidden gardens within courtyards. It will have amazing natural light and views in every room. There will be ample space for a day care, complete with an indoor and outdoor playground for my employees' children. There will be living space for me on the top floor, as well as a rooftop garden that will be intensively farmed to provide organic, heirloom produce for the building's restaurants and commissary. We will keep bees and chickens in that garden, as well. It should be made with the latest green technology. Solar and wind everything, as far off the grid as we can make it. Recycled and environmentally friendly in every way. And since we're near the Hudson river, I want to figure out how this building can lift its skirts, so to speak, when the inevitable floods do come. Because I am intent that this will be a monument to my company long after I am gone."

Kim blinked. "Well. That sounds amazing. I'd love to be part of that vision. Should we place some calls for a design team and construction management firms?"

Scarlett laughed. "No. No, no, no. No budgets or presentations are needed. This person—" she gestured over to Ava "—is going to be my architect. And this person—" she took Bridget's hand "—is going to be my construction manager. Steele Construction will build it. And you, sir, if you are willing, are going help me develop the whole dang thing."

A huge smile crossed Kim's face as he stuck out his hand, shaking each woman's hand in turn. "Oh, count me in," he said. "Count me in."

Afterward, the three women walked out into the warm Manhattan night and stood on the street corner together for a moment.

"Well," said Scarlett, "congratulations, ladies. I believe we have accomplished what we set out to do."

"It's really happening!" said Ava. She looked giddy. "We're actually going to build a skyscraper!"

"What now?" said Scarlett. "Where shall we celebrate?"

Bridget smiled. "I have an idea."

They sat at a rickety aluminum table in Madison Square Park, Shake Shack burgers and fries in their laps, passing a bottle of champagne back and forth and gazing at the Flatiron Building.

"It was one of the first skyscrapers built in Manhattan. They called it Burnham's Folly," said Bridget, smiling at the high-rise. "Because everyone was convinced that the design was flawed and the whole thing would collapse."

"The *New York Times* called it a 'monstrosity,'" added Ava between bites of burger.

"I believe the *Tribune* referred to it as 'a stingy piece of pie,'" laughed Scarlett.

"People are going to think we're crazy, building this design," said Bridget. "They're going to laugh at us and throw up roadblocks and give us a million reasons why it won't work." She took a gulp of the champagne and passed it over to Ava. "But the hell with them."

Scarlett laughed. "That's right. The hell with them."

Ava brandished the champagne at the building. "The hell with them!" she yelled.

"Because they said that about the Flatiron Building, too. They said it was ugly, dangerous and 'unfit to be in the center of the city.'"

"They did not," said Ava.

"They did," said Bridget. "And now look at it. Here we are, a hundred years later, and it's still here."

"And it's iconic," said Scarlett with a smile.

Bridget took the bottle from Ava, stood up and raised it toward the building. "Here's to Burnham's Folly, ladies. May our building be just as unfit."

CHAPTER 85

End of summer

Bridget and Jay carried the table and chairs down to the water. Bridget set the table for ten, carefully laying out the china and silver and crystal that the Russo family had passed down. She put out big vases of hydrangeas and filled silver pitchers with iced water and lemonade.

Back in his kitchen, Jay put the final touches on his grandmother's Sunday sauce. It had been simmering since early that morning, filling the entire house with the savory smell of tomatoes and sausage, garlic and onions and basil. The kids had been sneaking in and out to dip little pieces of bread into the sauce all day. He was boiling the pasta now, the traditional spaghetti. The garlic bread was staying warm in the oven. A huge salad was waiting in a wooden bowl on the counter, along with several bottles of wine.

Ava showed up with some ice cream, and Scarlett, with her swimsuit-model date on one arm and a massive blackberry cobbler on the other, and Hana brought a bottle of brandy, and Alli's girlfriend Minnie had shown up with a bouquet of flowers for the table. Then Liam had crept in, looking a little unsure of himself, but carrying a very expensive bottle of wine. They all grabbed various bowls and dishes and trooped down to the water to feast.

It was everything Bridget ever dreamed it could be. They were practically dipping their toes in the surf as they ate the wonderful food and laughed and talked. After dinner Alli and Minnie chased Dylan in and out of the water while the adults drank more wine and watched them play. As the sun started to set and the last of the fireflies made their slow, lazy blinking drift around the table, they toasted Liam, who announced he was moving back to Chicago. Though from the way that Ava kept looking at him, and he kept looking back, Bridget wondered if there might be a little hitch in his plans.

They toasted Hana, who had just set the date for her next show. It was based on the emotional resonance of everyday furniture: beds, bureaus, tables, she'd said, darting a quick glance at Liam, who resolutely looked the other way.

They toasted to Jason's release from Russo Construction. No matter what happened with the Harrington trial, Jay had decided it was time for the company to find a new leader. It took too much from him, and now that he knew it was not as it seemed, the weight of his family's burden had been lifted. He'd left it to the board to find a new CEO, and now he talked about several new ideas that he had, including opening up a restaurant with Omar, the talented Moroccan chef from the tourist trap joint where he and Bridget had their first date. He lifted his glass and toasted his dad, forgiving him for the parts of his childhood that had never been easy, and thanking him and his mother for the memories of nights just like tonight.

And then they all lifted a glass to Scarlett, Bridget and Ava, who were due to break ground on their skyscraper next month.

Afterward, they built a bonfire, and sat close to the flames, listening to the surf hush in and out. The kids eventually grew bored and went inside to watch a movie, and one by one, the adults said good-night and thank-you and either went back to their houses or, in the case of Ava, up to her guest room.

"Wanna take a walk?" asked Jay, and he and Bridget grasped hands and ran giggling down the beach like a couple of kids, finally collapsing onto the ground, where Jay rolled over and pinned Bridget down and gave her a long, sweet, deep kiss.

She looked up into his eyes, and then up at the stars beyond. "Kiss me again," she breathed.

And he did, and they didn't even mind the sand.

EPILOGUE

Two and a half years later

The official ribbon-cutting ceremony was tomorrow morning but Bridget wanted a moment alone before then. She walked down to the riverfront on her own, not caring how late it was, confident that she could take care of herself.

It had taken longer than they expected, it had gone over budget several times, there had been the usual trouble with unions and politicians and inspectors and the press, it had created all sorts of controversy, just like they had expected it would, but Bridget had loved every moment of getting it done. From the foundation to the finishes, her heart, strength and soul had been poured into every square inch of this building.

She thought of her father as she stood across the street and gazed up at the fifty stories that she and her team had built. She didn't have to wonder what he would think, because she could practically hear his voice in her ear, praising her for the power and beauty of this building.

You did it, my darling, he whispered. *You started with nothing, bare ground and an empty space, and then you dreamed this building and brought it to life, piece by piece, just like I taught you. It will be here for centuries, long after we're all gone. It will house and shelter people, it will see the beginnings and ends of lives, it will inspire other artists, just like you, to construct more beautiful buildings like this. I'm so very proud of you, my girl.*

Bridget shivered and hugged herself, wishing it was his gentle arms around her once more.

Tomorrow there would be thousands of people, and an opening-day party like the city had never seen before. Scarlett would cut the ribbon and this building would fill with new tenants, employees on their first day on the job, customers and salespeople, and bustling building workers. It would go from being an empty shell to a hive of life, and Bridget was so excited to see it happen.

But tonight? Tonight the building was hers and no one else's. And as she stood outside it, she felt a part of herself lift and take flight, soaring over the street, towering over the other buildings, rising floor by floor and story by story until, at last, she reached the very, very top.

That place where the earth was finally allowed to kiss the sky.

★ ★ ★ ★ ★